ALSO AVAILABLE
FROM BLOOM BOOKS

CANE BROTHERS
A Not So Meet Cute
So Not Meant to Be
A Long Time Coming

BRIDESMAID FOR HIRE
Bridesmaid for Hire
Bridesmaid Undercover
Bridesmaid by Chance

How My Neighbor Stole Christmas

Till Summer Do Us Part

MEGHAN QUINN

Bloom books

Published by Bloom Books, an imprint of Sourcebooks

P.O. Box 4410, Naperville, Illinois 60567–4410
(630) 961-3900
sourcebooks.com

Cataloging-in-Publication data is on file with the Library of Congress.

Printed and bound in the United States of America.
LSC 10 9 8 7 6 5 4 3 2 1

PROLOGUE
SCOTTIE

"FUCK OFF, ASSHOLE!"

"No, you fuck off."

"Eat shit and rot!"

God, I love New York City.

There's nothing better than waiting for your breakfast burrito at the corner bodega and witnessing a fight almost break out between a taxi driver and a Postmates runner on a motorbike. Truly chef's kiss.

And it's not just the kerfuffle on the roads that has me tingling with joy. I love the palpable high blood pressure of the collective whole during the morning commute.

The summer humidity, an added obstacle that you slice through during a brisk power walk to your destination.

And the pungent smell of the human race sharing the overworked streets of Midtown.

Spectacular.

Honk.

"Watch it, you dick!"

A smile passes over my face as I take a sip of my coffee.

I'm home.

Can't beat New York in the summer.

"Scottie, your order," Vincent calls out as he places my order on the take-out corner.

"Thank you," I say and then point at him with a finger gun as if we're long-lost friends. "Same time tomorrow, my man?"

Completely ignoring me, he goes back to work, scrambling eggs and cooking bacon. It's fine. He'll get to know me soon enough. I plan on stopping by every morning and establishing a rapport, one where I walk up to his storefront, which is decked out in pictures of bagel sandwiches, and he says, "Morning, Scottie. The usual?"

And I'd say, "That would be great, Vincent. How are the kids?"

And he would say something silly, like, "Eating me out of my own house."

We'd chuckle. I'd pay and then stand off to the side, patiently waiting for my burrito while I popped my earbuds in and a classic song like "Dreams" by the Cranberries would start playing.

It would be the perfect opening scene to any New York City–based Nora Ephron romantic comedy, where love is waiting in the wings.

But instead of formulating the well-executed meet-cute where I run into a man in front of an office building, spilling my coffee all over myself only to have him dab at my bosom with his solid-blue tie, I'm going to change the story. This isn't a story about me falling in love with another human.

This is a story about me falling in love with myself.

Yup, being a twenty-nine-year-old divorcée will do that to you.

The only person I want to be in love with right now is me and me alone.

And being here in New York City, the place where I always wanted to live out my early twenties after college, walking the concrete streets, cup of coffee in hand, on my way to my—

"Watch it, bitch." An elbow slams into my cup of coffee, sending the Americano temporarily into the air, only to land smack-dab in the middle of my cream-colored silk blouse.

"Oh my God," I say, pulling my searing-hot blouse off my skin while early morning commuters spare me a wince before continuing on to their occupations.

I glance around, checking for any oncoming men ready to dab my breasts clean, but when not a single person stops to help, I realize I'm shit out of luck.

What was I saying about New York?

Oh right... I love it.

I'm going to keep repeating that to myself over and over again as I carry my burrito in one hand and fan out my shirt with the other. I'll change when I get to work. My company has more than enough polos to spare. I should know; everyone I work with wears one almost every single day.

The only sad thing about getting coffee on my shirt is that I won't be able to drink it now. But hey, it's all part of the experience, right? The New York City experience. Consider this my initiation. My rite of passage. Being a girl from upstate New York, I've always dreamed of living in the city. Not just in my dorm room but on the Upper East Side, so now that I'm here again, nothing is going to stop me from enjoying it.

Not a single thing.

Because this is my new start.

I moved to the city to be closer to my friends, got a job with Butter Putter editing their ad copy and editorials, and now I'm living the single life, trying to regain the confidence I lost when I was married to Matt.

And sure, coffee down the blouse is not the way to start building up confidence, but it's not the worst thing that could happen. It's a conversation starter. Common ground.

Something I can talk about to my new coworkers that I share nothing in common with.

Like I said, nothing, and I mean nothing, is going to stop me from enjoying this new chapter in my life.

Scottie Price is thriving.

She is single.

She's smart, she's charismatic, she's charming.

And she's living out her best Nora Ephron life, falling in love with herself.

Yup, nothing is going to take that away.

Nothing.

CHAPTER ONE
SCOTTIE

"MEETING IN TEN," DUNCAN SAYS while knocking on the casing to the door of my office.

"Well aware," I mutter as I press my fingers into my brow. I don't need the reminder.

Another freaking Thursday morning meeting where obnoxious blowhards like to hear themselves speak while absolutely nothing is accomplished.

Great.

It's been three months at this job, and it's like clockwork. We shuffle into the conference room. Brad S carries around a putter like he's King Arthur at the Round Table and talks about the eighteen holes he plans on playing this weekend while Brad F—or Finky—and Chad cheer him on from the sidelines like a bunch of fanboys, frothing at the mouth for the attention of their leader.

Yup, Brad, Brad, and Chad.

The Brads and Chad.

I stare off into the pit of the office. Rows of glass desks, all stacked right next to the other, placed on top of puttable Astroturf flooring. Bobbleheads showcasing a variety of sports heroes are perched atop said desks, jouncing while penis after penis walks by.

Yes, you read that right...penis after chino-encased penis.

To tell it to you straight, I work surrounded by a real sausage fest.

And not just any sausage fest but the worst kind.

It's what the youth are calling…the finance bros.

Shudders

Sure, they're not actually "finance bros" given they work for a golf company, but they sure as hell have the aesthetic down to a science. Every day, I'm subjected to an agglomeration of company-embroidered vests, khaki chino shorts, boat shoes, and polos, all entwining with early morning bro hugs and gentle razzing.

Why does this bother me? Well, besides the fact that they are impossibly annoying to be around, I'm the only woman at the company besides the CEO. She, however, is barely in the office, especially with the launch of a new brand of Butter Putter mini golf courses.

But what really grates on my nerves and has me breathing into my desk drawer like it's a paper bag at least once a week: they're all married.

Every last one of them.

And sure, that's not a bad thing, but if I'm honest, it's not that they're married that's the issue. I'm the issue. It's me. Because I too was once blissfully married.

And at the beginning of my marriage, there was love between me and my ex, there was excitement, there was passion. But as time went on, year by year, I could start to see my husband's interest in me slip. His passion to hold my hand, cuddle, kiss me good night—no longer there. And the love diminished until the last year of my marriage, when it came crashing down after my husband forgot my birthday, leaving me to eat a piece of cake I bought for myself alone at the dining room table while he played video games.

So being in an office building surrounded by men who are happily married…it's…it's just hard. Makes me think of Matt, makes me think of how inadequate I am, how I wasn't good enough to hold his attention.

Not to mention I have nothing in common with them, unless they want to hear about the gum that got stuck on the bottom of my shoe while on a single-lady walk through Central Park over the weekend.

Nor do they care about my Sunday night girl dinner, which consisted of two dill pickles, one single Triscuit, and a cup of applesauce that I ate alone while watching the Menendez brothers documentary on Netflix.

There is a marriage cult, and I'm on the outside, looking in. Heaven forbid they ever find out I'm divorced. I can't imagine the clutching of their embroidered vests, the horror that would wash over their freshly shaven faces.

Scottie Price, the single one, sequestered in her office, not to go near in case she's contaminated with the "divorcées," a rare condition that could spread if one comes in close contact.

"You coming?" Finky asks, nodding toward the conference room.

My nostrils flare. "Yes, on my way."

"Good, don't want to be late. Ellison is here today."

My estrogen sonar perks up.

"Ellison is here? Really?"

"Yes. And you don't want to be the last one in the conference room."

No, I don't.

I quickly grab a notepad and pen, secure my coffee, and then head out into the pit and across the office to the conference room, where the men are already gathering. As I move around the table and find a seat, I scan the room, my mind picking them out one by one in my editor brain.

Brad S: never uses an uppercase T when writing *T-shirt*, despite how many times I remind him.

Duncan: can't remember to cite his sources, ever. I'm constantly chasing after him.

Finky: funny, but if he has to describe a putter, might as well settle for *hard and gray* as his description.

Chad: oh, Chad, the resident artist. I have to go over his mock-ups with a fine-tooth comb because he'll even spell his name wrong.

Then there are Kyle, Ben, and Shawn, all righteous idiot interns who I think are here for the free swag rather than the experience in business.

And that's only to name a few.

"What are your plans this weekend?" Finky asks Chad as we wait for Ellison to show up.

"Taking Danielle out to Fire Island for a concert. She has the whole thing planned. What about you?"

"Wine tasting upstate," Finky answers. "Lindsey told me this morning that she plans on getting drunk and not remembering a thing."

"Who does?" Ellison says, coming into the conference room, looking stunning with her long blond hair tied back into a pony and her power suit tailored expertly for her frame.

Okay, it's happening; everyone stay calm. She's here.

If there's anyone in this office that I want to impress, it's her.

Finky moves aside and says, "My wife. Taking her up to the Finger Lakes this weekend for a wine tasting."

"I was just there with Sanders," she says as she takes a seat at the head of the table. God, look at her poise. Beauty and grace. Shoulders back, an air of confidence surrounding her, demanding respect. "Stayed at a really nice bed-and-breakfast. The cinnamon rolls were to die for."

"Was it the place I recommended?" Brad S asks, hope in his eyes.

"It was," Ellison says. "We did the lovers special like you said, and it was fantastic."

Freaking lovers special.

What does that entail? Petting each other with a purple rabbit's foot for luck while staring deeply into each other's eyes?

"I was thinking about taking the hubby there," Duncan chimes in, looking all kinds of squirrely, trying to get her attention. "Maybe I can take him there for his birthday."

"When is his birthday?" Ellison asks as she leans back in her chair and brings her cup of coffee with her.

"Next month," Duncan says.

"If he likes wine and cinnamon buns, then he'll love it." She then turns to Chad and asks, "How's Danielle?"

Chad's stupid face lights up. "She's great. Still trying to get pregnant. Taking her to Fire Island this weekend to help her relax. I think she's putting too much stress on herself."

"I think that's a very smart decision," Ellison says. "If you're looking for more assistance or outside-the-box thinking, I have a wonderful acupuncturist that can help."

"I'll send you an email." Chad winks.

I'm annoyed.

The winks, the suggestions, the palling around...

Of course they're all friendly with Ellison, because they're all married.

Like I said, a cult. A freaking cult, and I'm the lonely spinster on the outside. Even the interns are either married or engaged to be married. If I didn't know any better, I'd have assumed being paired up with a partner was a requirement to work at Butter Putter.

"Jenna made that recipe you sent the other day," Brad S steps in. "The buffalo wing dip in the Crock-Pot."

"How did it go?" Ellison asks.

Why wasn't I sent the recipe?

I like buffalo dip.

Brad S chuckles and shakes his head. "Let's just say she added a little too much sauce." He rubs his stomach like a forty-year-old dad wearing jean shorts and New Balance sneakers with tube socks. "I had quite the bellyache."

Ellison winces. "But I'm sure you ate it anyway, because that's the kind of husband you are."

"I sure did."

This is a living nightmare.

Surrounded by happy couples boasting about their weekend plans, talking about their partners like they worship the ground they walk on. What's that like? Couldn't tell you.

And frankly, let's call a spade a spade. It makes me jealous.

Insanely jealous.

Because, I'm going to be honest with you, the rom-com life I planned on living when I made the move to the city was not the kind of Nancy Meyers dream I was looking for. Sure, I might have the apartment aesthetic with the cozy, slipcovered furniture and herbs in the windowsill, but the falling in love with myself, not so much.

My neighbor next door to me keeps pointing out that I walk as if I have a lopsided leg. She's on the younger side of eighty and holds a broom as a cane, so I don't think she cares much about what others think of her, hence telling me I walk weird.

I also caught a reflection of myself in the Trader Joe's window a week or so ago, and guess what? I looked like a crazy bag lady who feeds pigeons because they're the only beings that will give her the time of day.

It was horrifying.

And worst of all, I woke myself up in the middle of the night precisely three days ago because I suffocated myself with morning breath. Yeah, popped those eyes right open as I gasped for air, only to realize the stench *whispers* was me.

So falling in love, not so much.

"What about you, Scarlett?"

I'm knocked out of my thoughts as I look up and all eyes are on me.

Did Ellison just call me Scarlett?

"Uh…" I drag out. "It's Scottie actually."

"Oh, my apologies," she says, pressing her hand to her chest. "I don't know why I said Scarlett. I know it's Scottie."

Bet she wouldn't call Brad Bueford. Or Chad Charles.

No, just the lopsided single pigeon lady with dragon breath.

"So, what do you plan on doing this weekend?" she asks, a smile on her lips.

I glance around the table, beards and puffy vests all staring back at me, waiting for an answer, probably expecting me to talk about the yoga class in the park that I say I'm going to but actually just watch as I eat a chocolate croissant.

They'll humor me, but none of them will ask me what class. No, they'll just move on, and after the meeting, I'll skulk back to my office and sit in front of a computer to correct all their copy for every single social media post and article.

Maybe not this time though.

Maybe, just maybe, I could fit in.

Ellison's here, this is my chance to impress her, *and maybe* she'll notice me if I actually have something to connect with her on.

Maybe she'll find me so arousing that she'll consider me for a possible promotion to, let's say, the magazine, *Golf Galaxy*. Now wouldn't that be a dream? Instead of working with all these social media munchers, I could do more print work, which could give me experience to work at other magazines, like the mecca of all glossy print, *Better Homes and Gardens*.

And then instead of just living the Nancy Meyers aesthetic, I could write about it too.

I couldn't think of anything more fulfilling than that.

Then it's settled.

We've made an executive decision.

It's time to fit in.

Smiling at my audience, I cross one leg over the other and say, "Hitting up some antique stores with the husband this weekend."

The moment the word *husband* passes over my tongue and right out of my mouth, I realize the grave mistake I've made, because the shock that registers across every single face in the room is not the kind of shock you want to see.

"Your husband?" Ellison asks. "I guess I wasn't aware that you were married."

"Well—"

"Yeah, none of us were," Chad says, crossing his arms over his chest, looking like he's ready to dive into a "gotcha" moment.

"Yeah, well, it's one of those—"

"You're not even wearing a wedding ring," Chad continues.

Then every single pair of eyes in this pressure cooker that is a conference room zeroes in on my left hand.

What's a girl to say to that?

Nervously, I smile and casually slide my ring-less hand under the table and place it on my trembling leg.

"Um, about that…"

"Scottie," Chad says, leveling with me as if he's my father catching me in a lie. "We know you're not married. If you're trying to fit in, please don't make up lies."

The audacity of this guy!

Uh, news flash, Chad, you don't know how to properly use a comma, you nitwit, so cut the investigative report on my love life.

"Is he right?" Ellison asks, her brow pulling together. "Are you really not married?"

And this, my friends, is why you don't lie.

Because you have a simp like Chad trying to play Sherlock Holmes and blow up your spot.

That being said, I have two ways I can react to such an accusation. I can nod in shame, suck in my pride, and tell the truth, letting Chad take all the fame and glory. I can confess to them that I was so desperate to fit in that I made up a fictional man to make me look like less of an old maid.

Or I can dig in deep, save face, and run with the lie while making Chad eat his words with a side of guilt and a sprinkle of embarrassment.

The first option, dignified and shows true character.

The second option, a battle cry to all women out there that the Brads and Chads of this world cannot take us down!

I think we know where I'm going with this.

Gird your loins and hoist your bras, ladies. We're digging in.

Looking Chad in the eyes, I say, "Thank you, Chad, for bringing my ring-less finger to everyone's attention." I set my shoulders back and lift my chin. "I didn't plan on sharing this with the group, but my husband and I are actually going through a rocky time at the moment, and we've taken some breaks, hence the no ring."

Ha-HA!

In your face, Chad.

Take that.

Eat it.

And gag.

Yup. Freaking gag.

The room falls silent. Only the hushed hum of computer monitors fills the office space.

I hope you're all happy, you married-loving cult. I hope you all look in the mirror and think how horrible it is that you humiliated poor, poor Scottie to the point of having to air out her marital issues in front of floor twenty-three, all because Chad just had to make his dick look big.

Well, guess what, Chad? Your hands are small, your fingers are thin, and I think we all know that that means—

"Scottie," Ellison says, grabbing my attention. "May I please speak with you in private?"

The hairs on the back of my neck stand straight up as I feel Ellison's gaze zero in on me. She, uh, she wants to see me in private?

Well, that's unsettling, because this can go two ways.

One: she can see right through my lies like the hawk that she is.

Or two: she's about to lay down an apology tour for the adolescent behavior of my coworkers.

One will terrify me. Two…now two I could get on board with.

Two could possibly lead to a long road of HR meetings for Chad, which I should probably feel bad about, but I absolutely do not. He tried to fight with fire, and he's about to get burned.

"See me out in the hallway?" I clear my throat. "Of course."

Ellison stands and gestures to the door. I stand as well, gathering my items and hoping this creates a half day for me, because I have a half tub of cookie dough in my fridge and the rest of the Menendez brothers documentary to consume, and it would be amazing if this guaranteed me some more time to rot on my couch.

As I walk past Chad, I have the distinct urge to stick my tongue out at him but realize just how immature that would be. Let's keep the childish games to Chad and lead with respect and dignity just in case this doesn't go my way.

When I exit the conference room, Ellison pulls me off to the side and presses her hand to my shoulder.

"I'm so sorry to hear about you and your husband."

Whew, bullet averted. I'm here to file all of the reports. HR, here I come.

I nod solemnly. "Thank you. It's been tough, but, you know, we're trying."

"That's commendable. It can't be easy working in an environment where everyone is happily married."

"It's had its strains," I admit, because that is the truth.

"Well, I am proud to say with confidence why everyone is so happily married here."

Huh?

I look up at her as she continues, "My husband is Sanders Martin."

Err, am I supposed to know who the hell that is?

"Word on the street is, he's the most prestigious marriage counselor in the Northeast, and he has made it his mission to work with all the people in the office who are willing and ready." She squeezes my arm and says,

"And please know, I've received consent to discuss because everyone has been so happy."

Uh-oh.

I fear that I know where this is going.

"Oh, that's really cool," I say, wanting to slowly back into a bush, maybe go watch an after-school special about lying and why it's a bad thing.

"I would really love for you to talk with him; I know he can help."

And there it is, my grave, the one I've been digging this entire time, just waiting for me to rest in it.

"And I know this is coming out of the blue, and I don't want to pressure you, but I can sense that you're trying to reconcile. Am I wrong about that? And feel free to tell me to mind my own business."

Uh, yeah, Ellison, you should mind your own business. You should be leading a company meeting right now, not trying to help me with my fake marriage woes.

But alas, it's not like I can say that to her.

"I can sense that you're not comfortable talking about it," she says.

"That's okay—"

"Oh no, I'm comfortable having this conversation." Panic surges through me because I can see the disappointment in her face. "Just, uh, wasn't expecting to have such a magnificent mind at my disposal."

Magnificent mind? Tone it down, girl.

"That's so kind of you to say. Sanders really does wonders. Let me just text him real quick."

Oh, she's just going to do that, right now? When we should be having a meeting?

She pulls out her phone from her pocket, and yup, she starts texting. "Would nine tomorrow morning work for you?"

"Tomorrow?" I nervously say. "That's, uh, well, I'm working."

Ellison waves her hand in dismissal. "You can take a break for this."

"Great." I swallow the saliva building up in my mouth.

"Oh perfect, he has an opening tomorrow morning at nine a.m."

"Ooof, nine a.m., that might be hard with the hubby's job." There we go, blame it on the husband.

"Oh, he says he can do seven thirty in the morning for you so everyone gets to work on time. You're so lucky. He rarely offers the seven thirty appointment."

7:30 a.m.? Jesus, aren't people mainlining their coffee and getting their faculties together at that hour? Not to mention, if he's the best in the Northeast, doesn't he have a waitlist? Usually takes six months and your first unborn child to make an appointment in the city, not a quick text.

"Why don't you check with your husband?" She encourages me with a head nod.

"Uh yeah, let me, uh, let me just text him."

I hold my phone, straight up so she can't see my screen, and I tap away on it, pretending to text, all the while in my head saying, *Beep, boop, bop, texting my husband, beep beep, bop, my nonexistent husband.*

"What does he say? Seven thirty or nine a.m.?" She bounces in excitement as if her happiness relies on this moment and this moment alone.

And it seems like I'm not getting out of it. No backing down, not at this point. We have dug the grave, might as well try to find a way out of it…and a way that doesn't require me to be out of the house by seven.

Smiling at Ellison, I say, "Uh, nine works."

"Wonderful. I'll let him know right now."

As she texts her husband, I glance down at my screen, where I pulled up my solitaire app rather than texting a real-life person. I can tell you right now, this is not going to end well.

"You're set for nine a.m. I'll email you the details of where to find his office. He's looking forward to working with you."

"Great." I smile, knowing damn well it's the fakest smile I've ever concocted. "Can't…can't wait."

She gestures to the conference room. "Now, let's get back to work, shall we?"

Back to work?

Does she really think I can get back to work after I just sabotaged my own world?

I'm lucky I haven't fainted from the anxiety driving through me, because I just agreed to a marriage counseling appointment with my boss's husband. With a nonexistent person who needs to materialize in, oh, about twenty-three hours' time.

What the hell is wrong with me?

"Yeah, work, yay," I say with a fist pump to the air. "Love the work."

She smiles softly. "Good, because us girls have to stick together." She offers me a wink and then walks back into the conference room.

Well, fuck. I got what I wanted. I became buddy-buddy with my boss in an instant.

But the cost will be hefty...finding a husband by tomorrow.

CHAPTER TWO
SCOTTIE

"SOMETHING STRONG," I SAY, SETTING my purse on the bar top and sliding onto a leather barstool.

"Yikes, what happened to you?" Mika, my best friend, asks as he places a napkin and a bowl of pretzels in front of me.

I lean on the counter and say, "I had the worst day of my life."

The only thing that can take this headache away is a flammable drink and a night at Stockings—the best gay bar in town with drag shows every weekend. I became addicted to coming once I found the place back in college, especially on the weekends. Not only are the drag shows fire, but I love the aesthetic of the bar. Concrete floors, black walls, and pantyhose everywhere. All shapes, all sizes, all colors. They dangle from the ceiling, they're framed on the wall, and they're the curtains for the drag show.

Looking for a good time, come to Stockings; you won't be disappointed.

Mika winces as he starts filling up a tumbler with alcohol—not even sure what kind, but I don't care. I'll take whatever I can get. "Did Chad forget multiple commas this time?"

"I wish." I toss my hands up in the air just as someone slides onto the stool next to me.

"It's time to celebrate," my other best friend, Denise, says as she slaps her hand on the counter. "Guess who just booked a big wedding for this weekend?" She points to herself. "This girl. The makeup artist booked for the Coopertart wedding got the flu, and they called me to fill in. Me! I mean, I hope the flu girl is okay, but oh my God, the luck. I'm telling you, this is going to be a game changer for me, and I plan on doing all the social media. We're talking Brie Coopertart. BRIE!" she shouts. Silence falls between us, because this is really bad timing on Denise's part, not that she'd know though. "What's going on? Why aren't you screaming for me? Mika, you love Brie."

"Yeah, it's just that Scottie came in here kind of upset."

"Oh shit, really?" Denise turns toward me. "What's wrong?"

"Nothing." I smile at her and muster all the excitement I can for my friend. "Wow, Brie Coopertart, that's amazing. Isn't that wedding the talk of the town right now? It's being held at the public library, right?"

"Yes." Denise eyes me for a second. "It's supposed to be huge, and the media is going to be all over it. I was placed as backup in case something happened to her makeup artist, and lo and behold, she got sick. And once again, not happy that she's sick, because that sucks, but also, I'm positively thrilled she got sick." Denise claps the tips of her fingers together in glee.

Being the good friend that I am, I turn toward her and give her a hug. "This is huge. I'm so happy for you."

Denise has been a makeup artist for several years now. She started doing makeup for fashion designers for their runway shows. She actually started with nails, volunteering to paint the models' nails. Then she worked her way up to makeup. She now has quite a successful online presence, has really come into herself, her brand, and I can easily see her going places with her determination. It's fun to watch her grow—even if she's wishing illness on others.

"Thank you. I met with Brie and the bridesmaids today to do a makeup trial, just to make sure I have everything they might need. I'm grateful it's just her and two of her friends. Their wedding party is small, but the extravagance. I can't wait. I'm spending all day tomorrow making a game plan, cleaning all my brushes, and making sure everything is ready for Saturday. Eeep, I'm so excited."

Mika sets my drink in front of me and whispers, "Drink slowly." Then he turns to Denise and asks, "Same as usual?"

"Please." Denise picks up a pretzel and shoves it in her mouth. "Ahhh, I'm so excited. God, is that tar and stomach acid in your tumbler? I can smell it from here."

I lift it to my nose and feel every hair in my eyebrows curl into coils. "Jesus, Mika. Is this gasoline?"

"You said you wanted something strong. That's the strongest."

Mika has been bartending at Stockings since I've known him; that's how we met actually. I stumbled into the bar, looking for a good time, and he was the one serving. I, of course, was trying to hit on him because I was drunk and his black hair and gray eyes are hard not to drool at, but sad for me, he's gay. Nonetheless, we formed a bond, and he's now my best guy.

"That should be illegal," Denise says, waving her hand in front of her nose. "Drink that and lose your esophagus."

Mika plants an Angry Orchard in front of Denise. "Don't be dramatic."

"I'm not." Denise takes a sip of her drink. "I'm scared for our friend." She pokes me in the arm. "What could be that bad that you need a drink like that?"

"Strap in, because I have a story for you…"

When I set my drink down, I look up at my friends and find utter shock splayed across their faces, both blinking, both with their mouths open.

In the distance, our favorite drag queen, Miss Guided, takes the stage and cheers erupt all around us, but it's all ignored as my friends process the day I just had.

After a few seconds, Denise says, "Why the hell would you say you have a husband?"

"I don't know," I say on a groan. "I panicked. She was in town for the first time in a long time, and I thought, why not try to impress her? But then she comes into the office, all friendly with the Brads and Chad, and I felt left out."

"That's not a way to fit in, Scottie. Ask her where her blouse is from. Don't put a nonexistent ring on your finger."

"I see that now," I say and press my hand to my head. "God, what the hell am I going to do? This is such a nightmare. And the worst part, apparently her husband is the best of the best, like a one hundred percent success rate. So am I going to be the deranged one who can't make it work with their husband?"

Denise scratches her ear. "No, you're going to be the deranged one who shows up with a blow-up doll dressed in a suit, because you have no husband."

I rub my eyebrows, my anxiety at an all-time high now. "So many bad choices were made today. So many."

Mika walks off to help another customer while I contemplate the blow-up doll situation. I mean, at least if I say things don't work out, Sanders will understand, but then again, I run the risk of him thinking I'm a nut job...

"How strict do you think the patient-therapist relationship is? Think Sanders will tell his wife that her employee brought in a blow-up doll to a therapy session?"

Denise thinks on it for a second. "You know, that's a good point. I don't think he can say anything to your boss, which means, if you're brave enough, you could take the doll and maybe make up a story about how he's afraid you might pop him and that's why the marriage is on the rocks."

I mean, there's some meat to that story. Consider me crazy, but I'm sort of considering it.

"Over my dead body will my friend pretend to be married to a plastic fuck hole," Mika says as he rejoins the conversation.

Well, tell it like it is.

"That fuck hole is her husband." Denise pounds her fist to the bar top, mirth written all over her face. "Don't talk about him that way."

"That fuck hole is not going to work."

"Fine, but the idea had merit," Denise says, sitting taller. "Hey, wait a second. Take Mika. He can pretend to be your husband."

"Ooo, that's a good idea," I say, turning to my friend, feeling an ounce of hope.

"You might not have known I'm gay," Mika says, "but your therapist sure will. The minute my mouth opens, he'll know."

"That's okay. It'll be obvious as to why it's not working out between the two of you," Denise says.

"Yeah, that's such a good idea."

We both lean on the bar counter, staring down Mika, who lets out a deep breath and says, "What time?"

I clap my hands and say, "Nine. Tomorrow morning."

"Ooo, this will be so perfect. Can I come and watch? I want to see how this plays out," Denise says.

"You have a wedding to prep for," I remind her.

"Oh right." She winces. "Jesus, one friend emergency, and I'm already forgetting my responsibilities. Yikes."

"I can't do it," Mika says, looking at his phone.

"What? Why?" I ask.

"I have an appointment with my actual therapist tomorrow morning at nine."

"Nooooo," I drag out. "I mean, good for you, happy you're making a healthy routine with your mental health, but noooooo."

Denise taps her chin. "Maybe I can wear a mustache, pretend to be the man in your life."

"That won't be obvious at all, almost as bad an idea as the inflatable love companion," I say on a groan. "Ugh, I don't want you to move your appointment, and I don't want to ask, but do you think…"

He shakes his head. "They charge me if I cancel within the twenty-four-hour period."

"Freaking capitalism," I say and pick up my margarita, which I down the rest of in one giant gulp.

Okay, decisions, decisions. Denise with a mustache or a blow-up doll?

"I know," Mika says. "Why don't you just take my brother?"

I look up from where I'm hanging my head in disappointment. "Your brother? Pretty sure he has better things to do with his life than attend a marriage counseling session with someone he doesn't know."

"He's retired."

"Retired?" I ask. "Isn't he younger than us? Or is there a secret brother I don't know about?"

"Only one brother and he's two years younger to be exact," Mika says.

"Wait, didn't he sell an app or something?" I ask.

"Yup, hence why he has time on his hands."

"Now there's an option for you. Younger brother, retired at the ripe age of twenty-seven." Denise nudges me with her elbow. "Also, beggars can't be choosers and you, my dear, are currently a beggar."

She's not wrong, but Mika's brother?

I shake my head. "He's not going to want to help me out."

Mika shrugs his shoulders. "You never know. Let me text him."

"Oh my God, Mika, do not text your brother. That's humiliating."

But Mika doesn't listen as he taps away on his phone.

"Mika, seriously, stop. I don't want to bother your brother." I lean over the bar, trying to swat at his phone, but he takes a step back, out of my reach.

"It's not like you're asking him for money or something. You're asking him for his time, and he has plenty of that," Mika says and then smiles before looking up at me. "He's in."

"What?" I nearly shout. "What did you say to him?"

"That my friend needs a fake husband for a therapy session tomorrow at nine in the morning, can you fill in? He said, 'Sounds like fun, send me the deets.'"

"Well, there you go." Denise picks up her bottle of Angry Orchard and clinks it against my empty glass. "Problem solved."

"No, not problem solved. I don't know him. This is a recipe for disaster."

"Nothing to really know," Denise says. "You go in there, knowing nothing about each other. It might help actually. You'll look like you're in so much disarray that before you know it, this Sanders character will give up. Might be perfect."

"She's right," Mika says. "Cause some chaos and leave."

"But I don't want to cause too much chaos, as this is my boss's husband after all."

"You know what? Meet up with Wilder fifteen minutes prior to get your stories straight. That should do it."

"Your brother's name is Wilder?" I ask. "How come I didn't know that?"

"Because you're not the best at paying attention," Mika says before booping my nose. "Maybe use that in your marriage counseling tomorrow. I'm giving him your contact info. Expect a text from him."

When Mika's done, he sticks his phone back in his pocket and then moves down the bar to a couple that just arrived.

I turn to Denise and whisper, "This is a bad idea."

"Just get through the session tomorrow, blame everything on Wilder to save face, and then move on, simple as that. When your boss asks why things didn't work out, you can push all blame to the husband. You look good, and then you can go and live your life."

I nod, mulling that over. "You know, that's not a terrible plan."

"Precisely, and that's why you have us as friends."

I blow out a steady breath. "Yeah, this might work." I nervously laugh. "For a second there, I thought I was going to have to FaceTime Matt into the counseling session."

Denise shakes her head. "Not an option. We don't associate with the devil anymore."

I chuckle. "No…no, we don't."

CHAPTER THREE
WILDER

"BINOCULARS, BINOCULARS, WHERE ART THOU, binoc—aha, there you are. You motherfucker, diagonal and backward, should have known."

I highlight the word *binoculars* in my word search with a green Sharpie highlighter. They have a clear window to look through while you're highlighting, making them the best on the market at the moment. I pick up my Diet Coke with lime, take a sip, and then start looking for the word *cravat*.

Tonight's word search theme—things you wear around your neck.

The night took a turn for the worse when I had to try to find *noose*. I thought it was vastly inappropriate, but this isn't my normal word search brand. It's one Mika found for me when he was visiting his friends upstate. He liked that there was a swear-word puzzle. I'm not a prude by any means—some might say I have a dirtier mouth than others—but there's a time and fucking place for it, and it's not in a word search puzzle.

I readjust my stretched-out legs, getting more comfortable, just as my phone beeps next to me. I glance at the screen, and when I see Mika's name pop up, I pick it up.

Mika: Scottie needs a fake husband for a therapy session tomorrow. You in?

Well, that's random.

But also intriguing. I set my puzzle down and text back.

Wilder: She weird?

Mika: She's my friend, what do you think?

Wilder: Slightly weird, but solid personality.

Mika: Exactly. You in?

I think on it for a second. I mean, there's not much context to his message, but then again, things have been pretty flat around here, and I could use a new experience to mix up my day-to-day.

Might give me a chance to work on my improv skills, which I've been dying to do given the classes I've been taking. Bringing my knowledge into a real-world setting, really gets the adrenaline going.

Seems like a no-brainer to me.

Wilder: Yeah, I'm in. Send me the deets.

Mika: Awesome. Here's her contact info. Meeting is tomorrow morning at nine. She's humiliated that she even had to ask. Make sure you text her.

Wilder: Got it.

Scottie's contact information comes up, and I click on it. The thumbnail picture of her shows off a beautiful girl with long, light brown hair. From what I can see, she has one of those noses that has the smallest of swoops at the end. The lightest splattering of freckles on her cheeks. And one single dimple on the right side of her face. She's hot. Why the hell does she need a fake husband?

My phone buzzes with another text from Mika, startling me from staring at her picture.

Mika: You're probably doing intel on her already, noticing how hot she is, but she's drinking right now, so you might not want to text her at the moment. She's questioning her decisions. Shoot for later.

Wilder: Understood.

Mika: Have fun.

I set my phone down and stare at the burning fireplace image on my TV that I set every night while Led Zeppelin plays in the background.

Pretend husband.

Marriage counseling.

With a girl named Scottie.

I think this is something I can run with.

Smiling to myself, I pick up my notepad and pen that I always keep close by, I tug on my lip ring with my teeth, and I start taking notes on how I can play this character.

You know, this might be the fun I need in my life right now.

———————

"Dude, why are you late?" I ask Derek as he comes striding up to me, still tying his tie.

"Sorry, man, Denise was a mess this morning." He takes a seat at the bistro table I snagged us that is right next to the window and then picks up the coffee I ordered him. "Thanks. I really need this."

"What's going on with Denise?" I ask my best friend and accountant.

"She booked a wedding this weekend, a big one. It's for an influencer named Brie Copperhead, something like that. All I know is she's freaking out, and I spent last night and this morning trying to calm her down. Didn't help that last night she came home drunk from the bar. She was saying some crazy shit."

I bite into the coffee cake I gleefully purchased this morning. It's my treat for the week. I tend to eat as healthy as I can, but every week,

I treat myself once for every meal. Breakfast this week is this coffee cake.

"What was she saying?" I turn my wrist and check my Apple Watch for the time. I have about ten minutes before I have to bolt. Luckily, I'm close to where we're meeting.

"She was going off about this Brie girl and then she started telling me about Scottie and how she's married to Mika or I don't know. She was slurring."

I smile. "I think she meant me."

"What?" Derek asks, looking all kinds of confused.

"Terrible day to be late, man. I have to leave in a few, but to make it short, Mika texted me last night that Scottie needed a fake husband, and—" I shrug. "I said sure, why the hell not."

"Wait…what?" he asks, setting his cup of coffee down. "What are you talking about?"

"All I know is that Scottie needs a husband and so—"

"Wilder, are you insane?" he asks. "Do you even know Scottie?"

"Never met her. She's Mika's friend, so I'm assuming she's at least half-way decent."

"I mean, yeah, she is, but why would you say yes to being someone's fake husband?"

I pick off a piece of my coffee cake. "Not that I'm complaining, but being retired can be pretty boring at times. Seemed like something new and fun to do."

"Don't you volunteer every day? Maybe up all the charity work you do."

"Yeah, but that's for a few hours. There's only so much I can do to keep myself busy. Plus, don't want to over commit myself."

"Okay, do more word searches. I know you love those."

"Dude, those are a sacred nighttime ritual, you know that. And why do you even care?" I say, motioning toward him. "It's not like you're the one pretending."

"No, but I'm your accountant, and I know how much stock you own in a variety of companies. You own enough stock in different places so if you do something stupid and you're caught, you can throw off investors."

"Jesus." I roll my eyes. "I'm not that important. And it's one day. It's not a big deal."

"What are you even doing with her?"

"Going to a marriage counseling class with her." I shrug again.

Derek's face falls flat, and he's forced to push his thin-framed glasses back on his nose. "You're going to go to a marriage counseling class with a woman you're not married to nor know?"

"Yeah, what's the big deal?"

"The big deal is the therapist is going to ask you questions about each other, and you don't know her last name."

"Isn't it Prince?"

"Price," Derek corrects me.

I shrug. "That's where the fun comes in and my ability to improv. Honestly, I'm kind of excited about it."

He pinches his brow. "This seems like a bad idea."

Here's the thing about Derek Hanson. I've known him since high school, and one of the things I know most about him is that he never steps out of his comfort zone. Ever. He wears the same white Fruit of the Loom undershirt under all his dress shirts. He listens to the same three albums over and over again: the *Harry Potter* soundtrack, the *Star Wars* soundtrack, and *The Best of Dolly Parton*. He knows numbers; he liked them growing up, therefore, he became an accountant. Anything that steps outside what he knows, what he finds to be comfortable, he doesn't dare touch.

So understanding my intentions behind helping Scottie out? They're beyond him.

He also doesn't quite understand what it's like to feel bored.

He likes a routine. He has said time and time again, he wishes his life were just as regimented as mine, whereas I wish that I had more spontaneity.

And sure, I have the money to be spontaneous, but I don't want to use my money like that. I want more life experiences…and convincing and lying through my teeth is one of them.

"There's nothing bad about it. Seems like fun to me."

Derek shakes his head. "If Denise wasn't so crazy stressed right now, I'd ask her what the hell she was thinking by allowing this to happen, but I'm sure she'll bite my head off if I do."

"Yeah, I'd stay away." I shove a big piece of cake in my mouth.

Derek watches me chew for a few seconds and then says, "Breakfast cheat?"

I swallow and then nod. "Yeah, been eyeing it all week."

"Good?"

"Slightly dry."

"That sucks."

"Eh, you live and you learn." I pop another piece in my mouth and then stand up. "I should get going. I don't want to be late for my wife."

Derek rolls his eyes and then stands as well. "Dude, please."

I chuckle. "Don't roll your eyes at me. I'm getting into character."

"I knew you taking improv classes was going to be idiotic."

"Idiotic?" I scoff and adjust my beanie on my head. "Derek, I'm saving lives out here with my improv skills."

"Yeah, really saving lives." He lifts his coffee in my direction. "Thanks for the drink. Sorry I was late. Same time next week?"

"Yup." I pick up the rest of my coffee cake to eat on my short walk and then head toward the door.

We offer our goodbyes, and then I take off toward Third Avenue, where I'm supposed to meet Scottie. I texted her late last night, introduced myself, and sent her a picture so she knew what to look for. She responded that I looked like a bulkier version of Mika. I took that as a drunk confession, because I doubt she'd say something like that to someone she didn't know. And then we agreed to meet in front of the Anthropologie on Third. She stated it was appropriate because there were wedding dresses in the window display.

But that's about all I know.

I thought about asking Mika for more information, but since he works late, I knew he wouldn't have time to answer me, and also, I kind of want this to be a mystery. I've known Denise for years, but I've yet to meet Scottie. I think Mika said she'd only recently moved to NYC a few months ago.

I finish my coffee cake, throw my garbage in a bin, and then cross the street to the Anthropologie, where I find a woman standing in front of the window display, arms crossed, glancing around as if she's looking for someone.

From the uneasiness in her stature to her wandering eyes, there's no doubt that it's her, so I pause for a moment to take her in.

Standing at what I'm going to assume is five six with heels, she comes off as professional in a black pencil skirt with a tucked-in white blouse, the sleeves rolled up to her elbows. Her legs are bare, and her feet are fit into simple heels. Her hair is tucked behind her ears, curled at the ends, and she doesn't have one strand out of place. She seems poised, ready to take on the world, but the knit in her brow and the worry on her lip lend me to believe as an onlooker that something's troubling her.

I can only imagine what that is…

With my hands in my pockets, I cross the street, and just as I hit the sidewalk, her eyes connect with mine.

She stands a bit taller, adjusts her purse strap on her shoulder. "Wilder?"

"That would be me," I answer as I watch her eyes not so coyly take in my black worn jeans, forest-green T-shirt with a hole in the collar, and my loose-fitting beanie.

"You're…you're not what I expected," she says, giving me one more once-over.

"Yeah? What were you expecting?"

"Well, I mean, someone with…" She gestures toward me but doesn't follow it up with a definition.

"Might have to catch me up on what you're trying to say, because it's not making much sense."

She clears her throat. "Sorry, I just thought given your position in life, that you might look more…professional."

"Ah." I nod and then glance down at my clothes. "Not much of a clothes guy. Don't bother spending my money on something that in the grand scheme of things doesn't matter."

"Some might argue that appearance matters."

"Others might argue that you should never judge a book by its cover," I counter with a smirk.

She studies me for a moment while I nervously tug on my lip ring. I was not expecting such a lukewarm welcome. I thought that I'd show up, she'd express her gratitude for my help, and then we'd go have some fun in marriage counseling. But this cold, standoffish exterior is quite chilling.

Clearing her throat, she says, "Well, I guess this will have to do."

She guesses I will do?

Well, glad I could accommodate.

She then holds her hand out and says, "Hi, I'm Scottie."

Knowing I really have nothing better to do today, I take her hand in mine and give it a shake. "I'm Wilder. Nice to meet you."

She presses her hand to her skirt, fidgeting with the fabric as she avoids eye contact. "Yes, well, I'm sorry that we had to meet for the first time under these circumstances."

"I'm not," I say with a smile, causing her eyes to meet mine, confusion evident.

"Excuse me?"

I shrug. "Breaks up the normal routine, and it allows me an opportunity to practice my improv—"

"Um...improv?"

"Yeah, Mika didn't tell you? It's a hobby of mine, so kind of frothing to test myself in real life. Not to mention, really enjoying the whole angle of this. Thinking I should start a business to pretend to be fake husbands all around the city."

Her mouth parts open in surprise as she adjusts her purse strap again. "I'll have you know there is nothing exciting or enjoyable about this 'angle' for me. I woke up this morning on the verge of losing all contents of my stomach—"

"From nerves or from drinking last night?"

She lifts her chin, showing me that this woman has a lot of pride and she plans on displaying it often. "Nerves. I had two drinks last night."

"If they were made by Mika, two drinks are more like six."

"Doesn't matter," she says, swiping her hand at me. "What matters is that there's nothing I want more than for all this to be over. I hate that I got myself into this mess, and now that I have to dig myself out, I'd appreciate it if you didn't find joy in my demise."

"Demise?" I say as I rock on my heels. "Babe, a demise would imply there'll be death at the end of all this. From where I'm standing, you're looking pretty healthy."

"First of all"—she holds up one finger—"do not call me babe. Second of all, if I screw this up, I might as well throw myself off a cliff, because there's no way I'll be able to step foot in my office building ever again."

"Wow, seems like high stakes."

"Yes, it is. And I'd appreciate it if you'd go along with my plan, and in return, I'll do anything you'd like—within reason. I'm not into sexual favors."

The corner of my lip tilts up. "Good to know, but I need nothing from you. I have everything I need."

"There has to be something in this for you."

I shrug. "Nah, just something to do on a Friday morning."

"That makes no sense. There must be something you want."

I shake my head and rock on my heels. "Nothing." I then take a look at my watch and say, "Also, if you don't want to be late, you better set the scene for me. Are we talking about a grounded act? I'm assuming it will be in the sauce."

Her nose scrunches up. "What the hell are you talking about?"

"Different types of improv."

"Oh my God, this is not... This is not a classroom skit. This is real life."

"So in the sauce. Got it."

She presses her hand to her forehead, looks around for a second as if she's calming herself down and counting to ten. After a few seconds, she says, "Look, we've been married for five years. We met at the bar. We had a whirlwind of a romance, got married too young, and now we both want different things."

"What do I want?"

"I don't know," she says.

"Well, don't you think that's a question this guy is going to ask?"

"I don't know. Maybe I want children, and you don't."

"Technically, I think children are pretty awesome. Wouldn't mind a few."

"Okay, but this isn't about what you personally want," she says. "This is just a character. So the Wilder that goes in there, he doesn't want kids."

"Sure. I mean, I don't like it, but I can go with it. If anything, I'm adjustable."

"Great. Let's go."

"What do I do for a living?" I ask, not moving as she starts to walk away. She turns around to face me. "Uh, I don't know... Sell pharmaceuticals."

"I know nothing about the pharmaceutical industry."

"Can't you make it up?"

"That's tougher."

"Okay, then what do you know?"

"Word searches. I know how to solve a Rubik's Cube in seconds. I know the difference between Coke, Diet Coke, Coke Zero, and the pure shit that is Pepsi."

"Dear God," she mutters and looks away.

"I also know a lot about green roofs," I continue, sidestepping her clear irritation.

"What are green roofs?"

"It's a partially covered or fully covered roof of vegetation. They're great for cities because they help reduce the heat island effect by reducing sunlight, and they help cool the buildings surrounding them. Not to mention they reduce energy consumption and water runoff, and they have psychological benefits."

"Okay, sure, you do green roofs."

"I can see someone cares about the planet," I say offhandedly.

"Please, Wilder." She takes a deep breath. "I'm just trying to make it through this hour. Once this is done, we can go on our merry ways and never see each other again."

"I wouldn't say never. Your best friend is my brother. If he ever gets married, we'll definitely see each other, unless there's a falling-out between the two of you."

"You know what I mean. This, us, we won't have to play these parts again. Okay?"

"What if I need you to return the favor in a fake marriage scheme?"

"Then obviously, we'd see each other again, but that's only because I would feel the need to do so."

"Good to know."

"Now, are you ready? Or do you have any other questions?"

"Nah, let's do this." I rub my hands together and then follow my fake wife up the street to our first marriage counseling session.

Let the games begin.

CHAPTER FOUR
SCOTTIE

THIS WAS A TERRIBLE IDEA.

Probably one of the worst I've ever had.

I should have just told Ellison the truth yesterday, that I spoke out of turn, forgot that I got divorced, and that I won't make that mistake again. Instead, here I am riding up an elevator with a man I don't even know to share a marriage counseling session.

And what the hell is wrong with Mika?

Why didn't he ever tell me that his brother is a hipster version of Prince Eric? I wasn't expecting such a...such an attractive man to show up. The gene pool in that family is incredibly impressive. Black hair peeks out from his knitted beanie, a square jawline dusted in black scruff, and the lightest gray eyes I've ever seen. I had to look away a few times because they were so unique. Mika's are gray, but they're not this light.

When Mika offered up his brother as Tribute, I was thinking that a squid of a man who sells apps with gelled-back hair was going to show up in a suit, ready to play pretend, but this...this I was not expecting.

He's tall, probably six feet, maybe six two. His shoulders and biceps pull against the threadbare cotton of his about-to-fall-apart shirt that probably costs three hundred dollars. His waist is narrow, causing his pants to sag ever so slightly off his hips, and his black Converse have seen better days. And then there's his tattoo. Inked on his right forearm just below his elbow are three solid black rings that wrap around his arm like bracelets.

But that's not the worst of it.

Nope, it's the lip ring.

On the right corner of his mouth is a small black ring that wraps around his lip. I zeroed in on it the moment he started tugging on it with his teeth. The movement made me feel embarrassingly weak in the knees.

It's a lip ring, yet here I am, panting and bouncing my leg up and down.

These are all things Mika should have conveyed when suggesting his brother.

I could have handled the bored, uninterested brother.

I could have worked with the hipster vibe.

But the lip ring? What the hell am I supposed to do with that?

The elevator dings as the doors part, opening up to a serene office space: white walls, white furniture, calming music, and plants everywhere. It feels like we're walking into a couples massage rather than couples counseling.

"You must be Scottie," the receptionist says as she stands from her desk. "We're ready for you."

"Oh, uh, great," I say as I move forward.

"Can I get you anything to drink before you enter your session?"

"Water would be great," I say.

"Do you have any Coke Zero?" Wilder asks.

"We do."

"I would love one. Thank you."

"Of course. Let me show you into Sanders's office, and then I'll bring you your drinks."

"Thank you," I say as we follow her down to the end of a hallway.

She knocks on the door three times and then pushes it open, revealing...

What the hell is this?

"Please take a seat on the leather couch. Sanders will be right in."

We both shuffle past stacks and stacks of boxes, across a brown rug, right to a brown leather couch that is worn and torn in every manner. Tears in the seat. Tears in the couch arms. Even in the back cushions. Above the couch is a framed Knicks jersey, signed by who knows, as well as a Mets pin-striped jersey.

Mets, really?

You live in New York City, and you're going to be a Mets fan when the Yankees are the clear option? Not sure Sanders can be trusted.

The rest of the office is filled with boxes, some opened, some sealed shut. Some are in pristine condition; some have seen the inner depths of postal hell. There is a desk tucked back in the corner that is covered in files and a computer and keyboard that has not been stroked since at least 1995. Chipped and stained floating shelves hang unevenly around the room and are decked out in sports memorabilia ranging from signed and encased basketballs to what I can only assume is a size twenty-two basketball shoe to a few hockey sticks and even some Jets footballs.

Okay, now I really know he can't be trusted.

"Jets," I mumble to Wilder. "Out of all the football teams to choose from, and he chooses the Jets?"

"Shows resilience," Wilder says. "Because who would really be able to survive that kind of suffering without a heavy dose of enduring tenacity?"

I mean, he has a point. No one can be tortured for that long without building at least an ounce of resilience.

"This, um, arsenal of athletic archives was not what I was expecting when I was told Sanders is the cream of the crop of marriage counselors. Especially given the design aesthetic of the front of the office."

Wilder scratches his jaw. "Think he's going to pass around a hockey stick that must be held in order to talk? Because I'd be down with that."

Seems like Wilder would be down for anything.

Before I can answer him, a door off to the left opens, and an average-size man in navy blue basketball shorts and a hot pink Hawaiian shirt walks into the office. His beard is peppered with gray, laugh lines define his face, and the sideways baseball hat he's wearing is giving more *Fresh Prince of Bel Air* rather than esteemed marriage counselor of the Northeast.

This is Ellison's husband?

Not to be rude, but he's giving Adam Sandler impersonator taking a walk on the streets of New York City.

In a run-down pair of Birkenstocks, he struts toward us with a smile plastered across his face and a football spinning in the palm of his hand.

"Hey, man," he says as he reaches his arm out to Wilder. "Nice to meet you." Sanders then turns to me and shakes my hand as well. "And you must be Scottie." He chuckles lightly. "Never met a female Scottie before."

"Neither did I," Wilder says, surprising me. "Fell for her name though, because of—" and to my despair, they both say, "Scottie Pippen" at the same time.

"Yes," Sanders says as he lets go of my hand and then takes a seat. "Back in the nineties, I was obsessed with the Bulls, despite being a Knicks fan. It was hard not to follow the phenomenon."

"My dad was obsessed with the Bulls as well," Wilder says, jumping right into conversation. "He had memorabilia and newspaper clippings hung all around his office. After school, I'd go into his office, and he'd put in a VCR tape of a game he recorded, and I'd watch while doing my homework. Scottie was my man."

"Did you watch the documentary, *The Last Dance*?" Sanders asks with a wince.

"I did." Wilder sighs heavily as I sit back, watching a bromance unfold. What...what is happening right now? "I try to block out the fact that he ended up being a prick."

Sanders tosses his football in the air and catches it. "Made your taint shrivel up, didn't it?"

Uh, did my marriage counselor just say "taint" and allude to it shriv-eling up? What the hell kind of professional setting is this?

"To fucking dust," Wilder says and then leans back on the couch and drapes his arm over it.

Sanders chuckles. "A man after my own heart. What's your name by the way?"

"Wilder. And you met my wife, Scottie, or Pips as I call her."

Pips? Where the hell did that come from?

"For Scottie Pippen, obviously," Sanders says.

Wilder raises his hand in a charming yet annoying way. "Guilty."

"Well, it's nice to meet you two. Ellison was telling me that you work for her, but she didn't say much other than that." Sanders directs his atten-tion to me.

"Um, yes. I work as her copy editor."

He nods. "You play golf?"

"Not exactly," I drag out.

"She's good though." Wilder whistles, stepping in. "Girl has game when she wants to. Beats me every time we hit up the turf, although I don't excel at handling a club, so maybe I'm not that great of a judge."

Okay, what is he doing?

What kind of angle is he pulling?

He's not supposed to come in here and be all buddy-buddy with the therapist. Because now, when we talk about our problems, who do we think Sanders is going to empathize with more?

The copy editor with moist palms? Yeah, they're moist. I'm nervous.

Or the gray-eyed comrade with loose lips and an impressionable smile?

I'll give you one guess.

"Ellison and I like to play mini golf. We have an ongoing score, and right now, she's leading me by a few points, but with the new Butter Putter line coming out, I think I have a solid chance at gaining on her."

Is this how all marriage counselor sessions go? Because if so, how are more people not divorced? This feels like a chat over a coffee, not a "help me, my marriage is falling apart" situation.

"Do you two ever play games together?"

"We used to," Wilder answers. "Not so much anymore."

"What did you used to play?" Sanders asks as he spins the football in his hand. That's not distracting at all.

"Everything," Wilder says. "Isn't that right, Pips?"

It takes everything within me not to flare my nostrils as I turn toward him and say, "Yup."

"Like what?" Sanders asks.

"Go on, tell him," Wilder encourages me, but for the life of me, nothing is coming to mind.

Absolutely nothing.

I'm drawing a blank.

All my mind can focus on is the stacks and stacks of boxes crowding the space of this office and the way Sanders keeps fidgeting with the football.

"No, you can tell him," I finally say. Wilder likes improv; he can figure it out.

Smiling, Wilder turns toward Sanders and says, "Lots of games in the bedroom, if you know what I mean?"

No.

No, no, no, no.

I take it back. Ask me.

Now multiple games are flooding my brain.

Monopoly. Yahtzee. Kings in the corner. Bowling. Freaking slapjack!

Choose any one of those.

Not bedroom games.

"Interesting," Sanders says. "I'm glad you're comfortable talking about that."

Uh, we're not actually.

We are not comfortable at all.

I would like to have him ask the question again. I'm prepared with answers. Thanks.

"Would you say you're adventurous in bed?"

That would be a no.

"Very," Wilder answers. "We've done it all. Name the position, check. Name the angle, done it. Name the body part, licked it."

Dear God in heaven.

I can feel my cheeks flame with embarrassment as a smidge of sweat starts to drip down my back.

"And would you say those games have died down?"

Wilder hangs his head and gently nods it. "Yes, they have." He looks over at me. "Right, Pips?"

Can we just pause for a moment and take a step back, because this therapy session went from zero to sixty in what feels like five seconds. We're discussing our sex life already? Whatever happened to gentle pleasantries?

I guess there are none when you're paying by the hour.

I clear my throat and try to put on a neutral expression. "Yes, the passion has died."

"Do you know why?" Sanders asks.

Wilder looks at me, waiting for me to answer as I nervously wet my lips and try to think of an answer. "Um…"

"She doesn't want kids," Wilder says.

What?

No!

You were the one who was supposed to not want kids, not me.

"I think she's afraid that we might get pregnant."

"That's, uh, that's not true," I say.

"Babe." Wilder levels with me, turning in my direction. "A few months ago, when you wanted me to pull out—that was you telling me you didn't want kids."

Christ.

What happened to sticking to the plan?

"Was that the case?" Sanders asks as he tosses the football in the air now. Someone needs to revoke his credentials, because this is…this is childish behavior. No wonder all the Brads and Chad like him, because he's just like them. Makes me sick!

"No, I…I want kids."

"You do?" Sanders asks. "Then why does Wilder think otherwise?"

Both sets of eyes are on me, waiting for an answer. One that I don't have, because this is not how this session was supposed to go.

"Pips, you told me that you weren't ready."

Attempting to keep a smile on my face despite the raging inferno building inside me, I say, "Uh, that's because we're still young and trying to work on our careers. Just because I said I wasn't ready doesn't mean I don't want them."

"She has a point," Sanders says, finally joining my side. "But did you communicate that specifically with him?"

Oh, never mind.

"Not to throw her under the bus, but she didn't," Wilder says, rubbing his palms on the tops of his thighs.

"Is this when the passion started to fizzle?" Sanders asks.

"Yeah, that and after the trip to Montauk," Wilder says.

What on God's green earth is he doing?

Montauk?

I've never been there in my life.

Pretty sure if you handed me a map and told me to point to Montauk, I would have no idea where to begin.

"What happened in Montauk?" Sanders asks.

Wilder gestures to me. "Do you want to tell him, or do you want me to?"

I think he knows the freaking answer to that question.

Through clenched teeth, I say, "By all means, you lead the way."

He pats my leg and then says, "It was my twenty-seventh birthday trip."

God, I forgot he was two years younger. Shouldn't really be that big of a difference, but I'm starting to see the contrast between the two of us.

"She surprised me with a trip because she knows how much I like lighthouses."

Oddly, I could see him liking lighthouses in real life.

"Very thoughtful," Sanders says.

Finally, some praise. I nod in agreement. See, I'm not the bad guy in this situation.

I take my husband to see the lighthouses he loves so dearly.

"Everything started off fine. We were holding hands. We were joking around. There were smiles for days." Wow, quite the cheesy picture he paints. "She booked us a room in a beautiful yet quaint bed-and-breakfast near the coast. One of those places you see in a Hallmark film. White picket fence. Flowers decorating window boxes. The older couple at registration, willing and ready to welcome you in."

"I know just the kind of place you speak of," Sanders says, leaning into the storytelling.

"We were set up for a successful weekend of lovemaking and lighthouse watching until we tried to check in. To our dismay, they didn't have us on the reservation list. Naturally, Scottie showed them the confirmation number, only for the couple to point out that she booked the stay for a different date." He pauses for dramatic effect and then says on a whisper, "She booked it under her ex's birthday."

Oh no. He. Did. Not.

Nope.

Not happening.

"Ex-friend," I say, jumping in quickly. "Just want to clarify, ex-friend.

We used to, uh, we used to go to Montauk, and I think I just had her on the brain." I glance at Wilder to try to telepathically blow his head up into a million little pieces.

Wilder pats my leg and then turns to Sanders. "They had a really strong bond," Wilder continues. "Met when they were in elementary school, but then Petunia, that's her name, started dating a man Pips didn't approve of, and well, their relationship soured from there."

"He was a rampant cheater," I say, wanting to get in on a little of this action so Wilder doesn't think he can run away with the story.

"Rampant cheater at games." Wilder nods. "Scottie couldn't take it. Pictionary, charades, even Wordle, you name it, he cheated."

Oh, so now he can remember games. Where were these a few moments ago when he was talking about our bedroom antics?

"Yeah." I clear my throat. "Only appreciate people with integrity."

How ironic. I say that as I'm pretending to be married to the man next to me who I only met about fifteen minutes ago.

"A great value to have," Sanders says.

"One of the reasons I love her," Wilder says as he reaches over and picks up a piece of my hair, twirling it around his finger. He stares at me for a couple of seconds, and I want to reach out and pop both of his eyes with my fingers, because those eyes, they're too much. "Anyway, they didn't have a room for us at the bed-and-breakfast, they were all booked, but they did have a cabin out back that didn't have electricity or any running water. It was just a cabin. Since it was late and we spent all day under the shadow of the Montauk Point Lighthouse, we were tired and just needed a place to sleep. So we took it. But it was a mistake," Wilder says. "Because the moment we got in there, we noticed that there wasn't a bed, just sleeping bags. Right, Pips?"

"Uh, yeah. And you hate sleeping on the ground."

"Only because I sleep naked, and I'm pretty wild when I sleep. Can't seem to stay still."

"Same," Sanders says. "Sometimes I end up on the bottom of the bed, teetering, only for Ellison to save me from plummeting to the ground."

"Same with Pips. She's good at saving me, but not this time."

Oh Jesus, what now?

"Weren't you on the ground though?" Sanders asks, seemingly invested but also confused.

"We were. But it wasn't the height of the bed that she needed to save me from," he says. He sighs and then presses his hand to his chest. "Sorry, this is tough to talk about. Pips, do you want to take it?"

Uh...no.

Because I have no idea what you would need to be saved from while sleeping in a sleeping bag.

"You know, it's all still fuzzy to me," I say, circling my hand over my head.

"Not me." Wilder shakes his head. "I remember it like it was yesterday." He stares off into the distance as he lies out of his ass, telling a story that I'm sure will end up incriminating me. "I was naked, ready to have some birthday fun with my wife, who had just given me the best day frolicking under my favorite lighthouse. She was naked as well and looking so fucking fine."

I mean, thank you, but please stop talking about me naked.

"Can I be explicit when talking to you?" Wilder asks.

Please, God, no.

"No judgment here," Sanders says, setting the football down and instead picking up a baseball that he starts tossing in the air.

"Thank you. Well, I was hard as a fucking rock, we're talking full mast, ready to go. Pips had me turn away from her because she wanted to try something new. All for it, I turned, and she wrapped her arm around me to start stroking me. It was heaven. Then she saw that I didn't zip the sleeping bag all the way up, so she leaned forward, pulled it toward her, and, in one tug, zipped up the sleeping bag and my frenulum along with it."

Oh my GOD!

Also, who says *frenulum*?

"Shit," Sanders says in a whisper and a wince while he slowly closes his legs together. "We're talking your penis skin, right?"

"Sadly, we are."

Horrified, because how loose is the skin down there if a "full mast" penis can be zipped up, and needing to desperately defend myself, I say, "I...I didn't know his penis was there."

"She always underestimates the size of my dick. The only time she remembers is when I bottom out inside her and she can practically taste me in her throat."

I seriously think I might faint, because the wheels have fallen off.

"Anyway, that night, she became the Serial Zipper."

Serial Zipper? How on earth did he come up with that nickname that quickly?

"A name that I don't like," I say. "Because it was an accident."

"We had to get the zipper surgically removed," Wilder says. "I was wheeled into the emergency room, wrapped up in the sleeping bag, praying to the penis gods that everything would stay intact. The surgery took two hours and a heavy dose of anesthesia, but I left with light scarring and some pride still intact."

"Wow." Sanders shakes his head. "And I'm assuming there was animosity from her zipping up your penis."

"No." Wilder shakes his head. "None."

"Then how did your Montauk trip kick off your problems?" Sanders's brows pull together in confusion.

Funny.

I have the same question.

"I'm glad you asked," Wilder says. "Pips, tell him." Wilder gestures toward Sanders.

I hate him.

I truly do.

I've never in my life hated a person this fast in my entire life, not Finky, Brad, Chad, or even Duncan. Took them at least a whole day. Wilder is setting an all-time record.

Wanting to settle the score, I say, "He gave me a present the day after. It was a shirt made for me that said Serial Zipper. I didn't think it was funny. He did." Then I shrug. "He can be an ass like that."

There, threw the first punch. Maybe we can stop all this lovey-dovey bullshit and start actually fighting in front of this man so he believes there's absolutely no hope for us.

"I was trying to make light of a tough situation." Wilder thumbs toward me. "She's always been uptight, can't take a joke."

"I can take a joke when it's funny," I say. "You think I wanted to zip my husband's penis inside a sleeping bag?"

"You once wished I zipped my dick in my pants when I forgot to unload the dishwasher."

Ohhh no, you don't. You're not throwing me under the bus.

Gearing up for a battle of wits, I turn toward him, gloves on, ready to fight.

"That's because you never unload it. You think I like coming home after working a hard day to find that you didn't do the one thing I asked you to do?"

"Says the girl who never cleans up her hair off the shower wall."

"Or the guy who doesn't know what it means to shave his face over the sink."

He laughs. "Real rich, coming from the girl who doesn't understand what a recycling bin is. If it's paper, it gets recycled."

"Don't play the saint. You miss recycling things all the time."

He gasps in shock and then narrows his eyes. "I never do, and you fucking know that. But speaking of missing things, how about all the times I've asked you to wait to watch our shows together, but instead you just watch them yourself while I'm at the gym?"

Motioning to him, I shout back, "You spend hours at the gym, and your muscles aren't ever bigger."

His face falls in shock. "Yeah, well, all those food blogs you read are useless, because your chicken tastes like cardboard."

"That's a family recipe!" I yell, unsure of where that came from.

"Okay, okay," Sanders says as he lifts a hockey stick and puts it between us, backing us up against either side of the couch. "This was exactly what I was waiting for. I could see it in your body language, I could see you wanting to get it out, and now that you have, we can really start working."

"There's no use," I say, waving off Sanders. "This is a joke. I think we both know where this is going. No point in continuing."

"You see. This is what I'm dealing with," Wilder says, gesturing toward me. "She doesn't want to try. She doesn't want to give me the benefit of the doubt. She's ready to walk away." He shakes his head and are those...oh my God, are those actual tears forming in his eyes? "I'm not ready to let go."

Sanders nods slowly. "Yes, I see that." He stands from his chair and then moves to the coffee table, where he takes a seat right in front of us. "I've seen many couples with this same sort of attitude. Some pettiness and built-up animosity cloud their vision on how to work on their marriage. I'm here to tell you, this is never over. Ever. Even if you think it is, you're not even close to being over."

Not the thing I want to hear.

But then there's Wilder, nodding and taking my hand in his as if to say, "Yes, Sanders, we might still have a chance to repair this."

No, you moron, we're supposed to be mad at each other.

Hating each other.

Not holding hands in hope.

"Now that we've gotten here and found the point of contention, here is what I suggest—"

"Can we just pause for a second?" I say, not wanting there to be a solution but really wanting to end this farce once we leave this office. "I'll be honest, walking in here, I told Wilder to make it seem like we're okay, because I wanted to save face. You're my boss's husband after all, but to be truthful, we're both unhappy. And we've been unhappy for a while. And I don't want to fool you into thinking that there is a chance we can change things."

"She's right." Wilder nods, surprising me. "We can't seem to get past the bitterness we hold in our hearts."

Oh, give me a break.

"So I appreciate this session," I say with finality, "but I think it's best if we just move on."

Sanders's eyes go wide, and he sits back, looking between the two of us. His dark, beady eyes study our faces, our body language, and as he sizes us up, he must see something that I don't see, because he slowly starts shaking his head. "No, this is not over. I can feel your energy."

Feel our energy? Coming from the guy tossing a football around during our session?

"It's charged. There's still a spark, and if you'll allow me, I'll help you turn that spark into a full-blown inferno."

Yeah, not interested. Thanks though.

I'm about to tell him that we'll discuss this when Wilder and I get home, but before I can even put on an expression of gratefulness, Wilder jumps in and ruins everything. "How?"

Nooooo.

Visions of shoving my shoe into his mouth cloud my brain as I hold back the feral cry of anger bubbling up inside me.

Dude, we were good.

We were on our way out.

Stop making bad choices.

"I'm glad you asked," Sanders says with a touch of perkiness in his voice as he stands from the coffee table and moves over to his desk. He sifts through a mound of papers and then pulls out a brochure.

What the hell is that?

"Starting Monday, I'm putting on an eight-day marriage camp up in the Catskills. I only invite a select few couples. We spend eight days talking over our feelings and rediscovering the original spark of connection. I have couples on the verge of divorce like yourselves and couples who come to rejuvenate their marriage."

A marriage camp?

He's got to be joking.

"Like a summer camp for adults?" Wilder asks, looking far too interested for my liking.

He reaches for the brochure, but I snag it from Sanders before Wilder can even lay a finger on it.

Oh no, you don't, mister. Don't even freaking think about it.

"Precisely. Like a summer camp for adults," Sanders answers. "We focus on bonding techniques, open conversations, and finding the true reason why we fell in love in the first place. It's activity focused, so if you think we're going to be sitting on a couch all day, that's not the case at all."

"Oh good, because I'm not good at sitting still," Wilder says.

What do you mean, oh good? No, we don't show interest in adult marriage camps. We don't show interest in any sort of resolution.

I need to nip this before it gets out of control, before I end up spending eight days up in the Catskills with a man I don't know, trying to work out our nonexistent marriage. But I need to tread carefully, because I don't want to look like the bitch who doesn't want to work on her relationship.

Clearing my throat, I peruse the brochure and nod slightly. "This all looks so nice, but I don't have enough vacation days to make this work—"

"Oh, that's nothing you need to worry about. Ellison always gives time off to attend my camps."

Of course she does.

Sanders looks between us, a smile stretching across his face. "So what do you think? Want to give it a shot?"

"This is so nice," I say again, "but—"

"We'd love to," Wilder says, taking my hand in his as he lovingly looks in my direction. "I'm self-employed, so I don't need to worry about vacation time from work."

Did he just say what I thought he said?

Did he just agree to a marriage camp for eight days?

"Fantastic," Sanders says and then picks up his football and tosses it over to Wilder. To my horror, Wilder catches it, gets off the couch, and starts charging toward Sanders, jukes him out, and then spikes the ball to the office floor before raising his hands in the air.

"Touchdown."

Yup, he's getting my shoe. The heel right to the esophagus.

CHAPTER FIVE
WILDER

"THAT WENT REALLY WELL," I say as we make it out on the sidewalk, where I turn to find a very pissed-off Scottie.

Through clenched teeth, she says, "That went well? You think that went well?"

"Yeah, he said he thinks our marriage still has potential."

"You *idiot*!" she shouts, clenching her fists at her sides. "I don't want our marriage to have potential. I wanted it to die dead on the floor of that office. I wanted us hemorrhaging up there. I wanted there to be no ability to resuscitate."

I gesture toward the office. "After the potential he saw in us?"

"Potential?"

"Yes, he said we could still make it."

She stands taller, blinking. "Oh my God." She takes a step back. "You're crazy. You're actually crazy. Does your brother know this?"

"I'm not crazy."

"Yes, you are. That's the only explanation I can fathom for why you're carrying on this farce. You...you come dressed like you just left a My Chemical Romance concert, you have total disregard for anything you said in there, you talked about penis skin and then held my hand on the way out. It's not real, Wilder. We are not real." She gestures between us.

"I understand that."

"Do you though?" She tucks her hair behind her ear. "Because you just paid for eight days in marriage camp at reception."

I shrug. "I know, because that seemed fun."

She rubs her temples. "Seemed fun? Wilder, don't you hear what you're saying? I can't afford a marriage retreat, even if I was married."

"Don't worry about it," I say nonchalantly. "My treat."

"Okay, besides the fact that you can just throw down fifteen grand as a 'treat,' I don't have the luxury of picking up and going to the Catskills for eight days. I actually have a job, a life."

"He said Ellison would give you time off. I didn't think it would be a big deal, and from what I experienced in that office, it seems like you might be a touch uptight and need to loosen up. This camp might do that."

"I was uptight because you were not following instructions."

"What instructions?" I ask. "I assumed we were playing it by ear up there, which, by the way, the family recipe thing was gold. Took everything in me not to bust out in laughter. Seriously, you should take improv classes. You were really good on your feet."

"I...I can't take you right now." She blinks a few more times and then charges down the sidewalk away from me.

I chase after her and match her stride when I catch up. "Don't you think we have some things to talk about? To hammer out?"

She shakes her head. "No. There's nothing to talk about. This was all a huge mistake. I'm just going to have to go talk to Ellison and tell her the truth. Tell her that I lied to fit in. Sure, it'll be a great way to get fired probably, and my hopes of moving on to bigger and better things will crumble at my feet, causing me to have to start all over again. But who doesn't like a second-chance, rock-bottom storyline?"

"Stop," I say, tugging on her hand. "You're not going to get fired."

"You don't know that," she says. "You don't know my company. Being happily married is apparently a cult there. They find out I lied, not only will the Brads and Chad point and laugh in their stupid embroidered vests, but they will gleefully watch me walk out of the office building with a boxful of my supplies." She stops and looks out dizzily toward the street. "I don't think I can stomach the thought of it."

Fearing she's on the verge of a mental breakdown, I spot a juice bar across the street, so I guide her by the small of her back and say, "Follow me." Thankfully, she doesn't put up a fight and allows me to guide her. I open the door, usher her in and straight to the back, where there's seating and no one around. I sit her down, and she leans against her side of the booth, looking like she's in a daze.

Yeah, I think I might have broken her.

Should I have not paid for the eight-day adult summer camp? Maybe, but I really couldn't see another option. *And Scottie looked like she needed the break.* Also, it didn't seem like Sanders was going to let up on the idea. Not sure Scottie even had a choice in the matter. The minute he saw us starting to fight, he had it in his head that we were meant to attend his camp. Either way, I thought we'd be going.

I snap my fingers in front of her face, knocking her out of her daze.

"We need to talk."

"What is there to talk about?" She tosses her arms in the air. "I'm going to be the laughingstock of the office. I'm never going to be able to show my face again. I'm going to have to move back in with my parents." She shivers. "My mom is going to want to wear matching pajamas every night, and my dad will suffocate me with questions. God, it'll be the absolute pits."

I hold back my chuckle, because who says "the absolute pits"?

"What if it doesn't have to be that way?"

She tosses her hand in defeat. "What are you going to do? Ask for your money back?"

"No. I'm thinking, what if we went?"

"Oh my God, there you go again with the delusions." She presses her fingers into the table between us and says, "Earth to Wilder, we are not married."

"I know we're not married."

"Then why in hell would you want to go with me to a summer camp where all the activities are centered around married couples?"

"I'm just spitballing here, but tell me if I'm wrong. You don't want to look bad in front of your boss and coworkers, who seem to all be obsessed with being married. Is that right?"

"Correct. Marriage is very important to them."

"Do you like your job?"

"It's fine. I don't like golf, but that's unfortunately what I have to read about right now."

"And you want to find a new job, but this current job is a step in the right direction."

"Yes…" She leans back in the booth. "Do you have a point to all this?"

"What if…what if we go—"

"Oh my God," she says with a roll of her eyes.

"Wait, hear me out." I hold up my hands. When she gives me the chance to continue, I say, "We get to the summer camp, we act snarly toward each other at first and then pretend as we move along the activities that we're slowly falling back in love."

"What is it with you? Do you find me attractive or something? Why are you clinging on to me? We're supposed to be splitting up, Wilder. Not getting back together."

"For the record, you're an attractive woman, but that's not why I'm suggesting this." Her cheeks blush from the compliment. She's more than just attractive. She's stunning with her light blue eyes and sultry body. And call me crazy, but I like the ornery side of her. It makes her that much more interesting. But she's also been an amazing friend to Mika, especially through his darker moments, when he wasn't opening up to his family, so I'll do whatever she needs. "I'm saying that you prove to

Sanders that his camp worked so he feels good about himself, you can report back to your boss that her husband is a miracle worker and that you and your husband are better than ever, and then in a few months, when you're ready, you can move on to a new job. In the meantime, if there's an event or something you need from me to prove that we're still a married couple, I have no problem filling in."

"What do you mean, filling in?" she says, looking skeptical but also interested in my idea.

"I mean if, let's say, you have a company Christmas party and spouses are invited, I'll go with you."

"Why…why would you do that?"

"Because you're Mika's best friend, and I'd do anything for him." And because she's right. I didn't really follow the script with Sanders. She *did not* want to go to a marriage camp. "And, well, because I feel like I sort of failed you today even though I thought we excelled on the spot."

"What if you fall in love in that time?"

"I won't," I say on a chuckle.

"How do you know?"

"Because I'm not interested in love at the moment."

"What if you are three months down the road?"

I level with her and say, "It's not easy dating when people find out who I am."

"What do you mean? Who are you?" Scottie asks skeptically.

"I mean, it's just not something you need to worry about. Okay?"

Her lips quirk to the side as she mulls over my idea. After a few seconds of silence, she asks, "What if they ask about you at work and inquire why you never come to pick me up at the office?"

"Is that a thing?"

She slowly nods, her eyes wide. "You don't know these people. They're obsessed with their spouses. This is a commitment. This isn't just something you haphazardly do. If you're going to pretend to be my husband, then you're going to have to go all in."

I tug on my lip ring, a little unsure about what I just offered. "How long do you think it would take you to find a new job?"

"In today's job market? I think I need at least six months to gain more experience with the company and then try to find somewhere else to work."

I tug on my lip ring again, looking out toward the empty New York street. "I can commit six months to you. Anything after that though, you'll have to figure it out on your own."

"You're serious?" she says.

"Yeah, I'm serious. In the grand scheme of things, six months is nothing."

"Six months is half a year, Wilder. You're okay with dedicating half a year to randomly going to couple events with me?"

"I honestly have nothing better to do, so yeah. Plus, I'll get to keep practicing my improv."

"What…what are you?" She gives me a quick once-over. "Some wannabe actor, trying to get into Groundlings?"

I smirk. "Something like that. What do you say?"

She studies me carefully. After a few seconds, she finally says, "I say no to any more of that improv stuff. For all I know, you're going to tell everyone I'm pregnant, and what the hell would we do with that?"

"Get you pregnant."

Her expression falls. "No."

"I'm just kidding. I wouldn't ever commit to something like that."

"No, you'll just commit to an eight-day marriage camp."

"How long are you going to hold that against me?"

"For-ev-ver," she drags out. "Forever, Wilder. As long as you're alive, I will always remind you of that grave mistake. When Mika gets married one day, I will remind you. When we run into each other at Stockings, it's the first thing I'll say, and when I spot you randomly in Central Park, because the universe will constantly make us run into each other now, I will say, 'Remember that time you signed us up for an eight-day marriage camp when you were supposed to help me make our marriage look like it's in shambles?'"

"To be fair, we did make it look like it was in shambles, hence the invitation to the marriage camp. So if you ask me, mission accomplished."

She's unamused.

Not even a smirk.

So I clear my throat and say, "Anyway, do we have a deal?"

She crosses her arms at her chest. "Honestly, though, what's in it for you?"

"An experience," I answer.

She shakes her head in disbelief. "I mean, if you think this is what you need in order to bring joy to your life, then to each their own."

I can sense the judgment in her tone, but I'm not going to let it bother me, because yeah, maybe this is what I need to bring me some joy. To get me out of this rut I'm living in. To live the life I know my dad would have wanted me to live.

"So then it's a deal?"

She shrugs. "I guess so."

"Great. Then I guess I'll see you Monday...Pips."

She rolls her eyes, grabs her purse, and scoots out of the bench. "See you Monday," she mutters and then heads out of the juice bar and down the street.

Well, this was productive. Now to do some research on this camp. I need to know what to expect.

CHAPTER SIX
SCOTTIE

Scottie: What the actual fuck, Mika? Ooo, take my brother, he can do it, he can be your knight in shining armor. Uh, here's a not-so-low-key update, he just made this situation a whole lot more complicated.

"KNOCK, KNOCK," I HEAR ELLISON say as she walks into my office, looking extremely giddy, like she has a secret she wants to divulge. I quickly stash my phone to the side and smile back at her.

"Hey, Ellison."

"Now, I don't want to pry, because it's none of my business, but… how did it go?"

None of her business, but then she goes and asks how it went. Make that make sense.

"It was great," I say, plastering on a happy smile. "Sanders was just what we needed."

Ellison fist-pumps the air. "I knew he would be. I'm telling you, he's amazing. Not what you're expecting when it comes to a marriage counselor, but I think that's what makes his approach so unique."

You can say that again. Talking to him felt like I was signing up for a team sport at the local YMCA. Makes me highly question the validity of his degree.

"Yes, very unique," I say. "But it worked. Actually, I need to talk to you about something. Sanders was saying there's a marriage summer camp—"

"Did you sign up for it?" She's practically bouncing.

"Uh, yeah, we did. I hope that's okay."

Ellison claps her hands. "Oh, that's wonderful."

"Yeah, but, uh, Sanders says you don't use vacation time for it. Is that true?"

She nods. "As you must know, we truly value the relationships our employees have, so we allow any time off to build and mend those relationships. So yes, you can have the time off."

"Wow, okay. That's very generous of you. Is it okay that I didn't give much notice?"

"Yes, most of the guys in the office will be going as well, so there won't be much going on here."

Uh…what?

"The, uh, the office is going?" I ask, tugging on the end of my hair.

"Yup, they do every year, and it's tradition at this point. Great time for rejuvenation. I'll be there as well. We caravan up to the Catskills, if that's something you're interested in, but I'm not going to pressure you, given how sensitive your relationship is at the moment."

Is that the nice way of putting it? Sensitive?

If using that term allows me to avoid any sort of direct, unnecessary interaction with the Brads and Chad, then by all means, let's eat up the term.

"Thanks, yeah, I think Wilder and I will probably just drive up by ourselves."

"Wilder." She hugs her hands to her chest. "That's his name?"

I will seriously never get over this marriage obsession of hers. It's so weird.

"Yes, that's his name," I say with a curt smile.

"How did you two meet?"

What happened to not prying?

"At a bar. His brother is actually the bartender, and we just happened to bump into each other, and we hit it off."

"Meant to be." She sighs. "Well, I won't hold you up. You probably have a lot of things you want to get done before you take time off for the next eight days."

My phone buzzes with a text on my desk, but I ignore it and center all my attention on my boss.

"Yes, I have a lot of editing I need to get done to make some deadlines." Lies. I have about three articles that won't take me very long, because Brad and Chad are basic bitches when it comes to their writing.

"Wonderful. Well, I'll leave you to it. Can't wait till Monday," she says with a whole lot of gratuitous joy.

"Can't wait." I try to match her enthusiasm with a simple thumbs-up.

When she's out of sight, I reach for my phone, hoping for a possible reprieve from this nightmare I created for myself, only to find a text from Wilder.

I sigh and lean back in my chair to read it.

Wilder: Been doing some research on this camp. I'm going to make a trip to Target and pick up some necessities. Anything you need?

Necessities? What could we possibly need?

Scottie: What kind of necessities?

Wilder: Bug spray for one. I need some sandals because I don't ever wear them. I also need some swim trunks. Some new socks. Toothpaste. Probably a new toothbrush. Some word searches. A deck of cards. And it says not to bring any food, but I'm a dick if I don't have a sweet at night when on "vacation." Nerds Clusters are my jam.

Why do I find it so amusing that this emo, beanie-wearing wannabe actor is going to just go grab some socks from the local Target? He does not give off those kinds of vibes.

He's very different from what I pictured in my head, and I refuse to think that's a good thing.

Also, he likes Nerds Clusters?

We unfortunately have that in common.

> **Scottie:** I'm good, I'll probably head out this weekend and get some things for myself. But if you're stocking up on Nerds Clusters, get me a pack too.

I almost don't send it, because I don't want him thinking we can bond over Nerds Clusters, but I also don't want to be trapped in a cabin with him chewing on his own bag that I'll have to share. The text was a risk I was willing to take.

> **Wilder:** You like Nerds Clusters too? 😵

God, I knew he'd be excited about that. Why do I feel like I know him already? I need to ask Mika about his brother, because they're nothing alike. Mika is more jaded, rough around the edges, can be flamboyant at times but not so much that it's blatantly obvious. He tends to look at the glass as half-empty most of the time and rarely has a positive outlook on life.

Whereas Wilder, he seems to have his rose-colored glasses on at all times.

> **Scottie:** I do, and please don't make this a thing between us. The only reason I said something is because I can search those out like a hound dog, and I'd rather not have one of my

cabinmates see me hunched over on my bed, shoving cluster
after cluster into my mouth.

Wilder: Cabinmates? Pips, you have one cabinmate, and it's me.

I pause, reading his text. Uh, is he sure about that?

Scottie: What do you mean it's you? I'm not sharing a cabin with
the other wives? You know, like in a real summer camp?

Wilder: No. Didn't you look at the brochure?

Scottie: Uh no, I just snatched one, hoping you wouldn't grow
attached to the idea of going. Boy, was I wrong.

Wilder: You should have looked at it. Of course it has the adult
summer camp vibes, but each couple gets their own cabin...
We're going to have to share a bed.

I stare at the words, over and over again.

Share a bed.

With a stranger?

With a man I know nothing about?

I mean, what if...what if he snores? What if he, oh God, what if he's
one of those guys that gets wet dreams all the time?

Gasp, what if he sleeps naked?

Scottie: PAJAMAS! Get yourself pajamas! I refuse to sleep with
a naked man. Actually, while you're at Target, get an air mattress and extra blankets, because one of us is sleeping on it.

Wilder: You nervous to sleep with me?

Scottie: Uh, yeah!

Wilder: Why?

Why?

Seriously, has this man ever been in the likeness of society? He seems so oblivious to the most obvious things.

Scottie: Uh hello, I don't know you. I don't know if you're going to roll over at one point and breathe your hot breath on me.

Wilder: Who's to say I have hot breath?

Scottie: Everyone has hot breath in the morning. Also…are you a wet dream guy?

Wilder: I mean, I was when I was younger, can't help that shit, but not anymore.

Scottie: Thank God for small miracles.

Wilder: It'll be fine. I promise. I don't snore. I keep to my side. Not to mention I brush my teeth, floss, and use mouthwash twice a day. Good dental hygiene over here.

Scottie: How do you know you don't snore?

Wilder: The clinic down the street from me was doing sleep studies and needed some bodies to fill in; it was just one of those experiences I took advantage of. They told me I was an excellent sleeper, very unlike some of the people they study. Felt bad because I was boring to watch.

Scottie: Are you always doing random things? Is this a money thing?

Wilder: I don't need the money. Seriously though, no need to worry on the sleeping thing, and I'll be sure to give you plenty of privacy whenever you need it. The camp backs up to a forest, so I plan on going on a lot of walks. I have a bird book I'm going to bring with me so I can do some bird-watching in our off hours. I'm also excited to bust out my binoculars. It's one of the very few things that I've spent good money on.

Curious, I type back a question, because why is he making it seem like money is not a thing to him?

> **Scottie:** What other things did you spend money on?
> **Wilder:** My house—a brownstone in Brooklyn. My binoculars. My computer—because that's a necessity. A charcoal set for drawing. And a first-edition signed copy of *Misery* by Stephen King.

A brownstone? Did I read that right? Uhhh, have I completely misread this man? Not that money matters to me, but my brain starts to connect the dots. Is he…is he wealthy? Is that why he has all this time on his hands? I have questions for Mika.

> **Scottie:** That's all really random stuff.
> **Wilder:** They're all things that matter the most to me.
> **Scottie:** Interesting. I feel like you can learn a lot about a person with such eclectic taste.
> **Wilder:** And what did you learn?
> **Scottie:** That if we met at a bar, we probably never would have hooked up.
> **Wilder:** Ouch. LOL. But good to know. Well, I'm off. If you need anything, just let me know.

I don't bother writing back; instead, I set my phone down and stare out at the pit in front of me.

Misery… Should I be worried?

"Is your brother a psychopath?" I ask as I take a seat at the bar.

Mika smirks and sets a napkin down. "He is not."

"Then why are you smiling?" I point at his curved lips.

"Because I find it funny that you asked the moment you saw me. Knowing Wilder, you probably had quite the experience today."

"Uh yeah, you could say that." I reach over the bar and snag a bowl of pretzels before he can offer them to me. "You owe me a drink. Your best margarita."

Mika pulls out a tumbler and starts pouring liquid in it as he asks, "What happened?"

"Oh, I don't know. You just set me up with someone who didn't read the instructions."

Mika winces. "Did he go off script?"

"That's one way to put it." I pop a pretzel in my mouth and lay it out for him. "It was simple. Pretend to be my husband, fight with me, show that we're not compatible, leave. But noooooo, that was too easy. Wilder needed to complicate things. He went in there, speaking praises of me, which of course had me needing to do the same so I didn't come off as the ornery wench."

"Did you?"

"Who knows." I toss my hands in the air. "He played the 'she doesn't want kids' card, which is a dirty hand to play. Oh, and speaking of hands, he held mine during the session and then after when we walked away." I connect both of my hands in front of my face and shake them. "Held it."

Mika starts shaking the tumbler on his right side. "So he made it seem like you two were happy and in love?"

"At first, but then we started fighting, and for a moment there, I thought, this is what I'm talking about. The insults, the blaming. I never felt more alive in my life than during that thirty-second spat, but then it was all squashed when Sanders, the therapist, said that we would be perfect for the marriage summer camp he's putting on up in the Catskills."

Mika is midpour of my drink when he pauses and looks up at me. "No, tell me you're not going."

I pop another pretzel in my mouth and say, "Oh, we're going."

"Fuck, seriously?"

"Uh-huh, paid for and everything. Which, by the way"—I sit taller—"not that it matters to me, but does he have money or something? Because he paid for that camp outright, called it a treat."

A smirk crosses his lips, a very familiar one that I experienced today. "Scottie, he sold an app for a significant amount of money. He's rich, hence the whole retirement, has-a-lot-of-time-on-his-hands kind of thing."

"What?" I ask, shocked. "I thought he was an out-of-work actor."

Laughing, Mika slides my drink onto the bar counter and then wipes his hand on a towel before flipping it over his shoulder. "Yeah, I don't talk much about him or my family for that matter, other than some of the things you know. Should have informed you, especially about his current thirst for experiencing life. He heard the word 'camp' and you were instantly fucked."

"Yeah, a minor detail, Mika. Jesus. You told me he was into improv, not some, I'm assuming, millionaire who is into using humans as real-life chess pieces." I take a sip of my drink. "He picked up bug spray today. Freaking bug spray. Oh, and sandals, because apparently, he's never worn those before."

Mika thinks on it for a second. "You know, I don't think I've ever seen him in sandals."

"I'll take a picture for you," I say, my voice dripping with sarcasm. "I know this is my fault. I understand that. I'm not blind to my shortcomings, but by God, how hard is it to follow instructions?"

"Did you give him instructions though?" Mika asks.

"Yes," I shout and then think on it, because Wilder questioned the same thing. "I mean, I told him what differences we had."

Mika lifts his brow.

"And I asked him what his pretend job would be."

"Did you tell him that you were in there to break up?"

I tap my chin, trying to recount the moments before we went into the office for our first therapy session. It all seems like a blur now. "Uh..."

"I'm going to take that as a no." Mika leans over and boops me on the nose with his finger. "Seems like you didn't set the scene for him."

I groan and rest my head on the bar counter. "I didn't set the scene," I mumble into the wood.

"So he was probably just going for it, feeding off the situation, and now you're stuck going to an eight-day summer camp with him."

I groan even louder. "Why am I like this?"

"Because you are," Mika says. "But I love you anyway."

I sit up and take a large gulp of my margarita. After a few seconds of silence, I say, "He likes Nerds Clusters."

"He does."

"I like Nerds Clusters."

"You do."

I look into Mika's eyes. "He's buying some for our trip."

"Because that's the kind of guy he is. He's the most humble rich fuck you will ever meet." Mika winks and takes off down the bar to help another customer.

CHAPTER SEVEN
WILDER

"LET ME GRAB THAT FOR you," I say as Scottie makes her way down her apartment steps and to the sidewalk.

"Thanks," she says as she hands me her suitcase.

I open the gate to my Jeep and slip her bag in the back. "Do you want your backpack back here as well?"

"Sure," she says, looking uncomfortable.

Don't blame her. She's about to spend eight days with a guy she doesn't know in a cabin in the Catskills. Screams horror movie. Like everyone in the theater is telling her "No, don't do it," but she's not listening and instead is taking every wrong step down the path of being murdered.

Lucky for her though, I'm not a murderer.

"What about your, uh, your purse thing?"

She glances down at what I can only describe as a cross-body fanny pack. "No, I can keep this up front."

"Sounds good." I shut the back of the Jeep, and I'm about to get in on my side when I notice she's not moving.

"I thought you said there are only certain things you spend your money on." She motions to my vehicle.

I glance at it and then back at her. "Well, everyone needs a vehicle," I say. "And I would hardly say a lime-green Jeep Wrangler is forking out the big bucks. Now, if I had something fancier, like...I don't know, a useless

Ferrari, then sure, but this is an everyday utility vehicle." I study her. "Is this mode of transportation going to be okay?"

"Yeah, and I guess you're right, other than the fact that not everyone needs a car when you live in the city."

"True, but my family is from New Rochelle, and when I visit, I like to control my own transportation. I'd rather just drive, because then that gives me freedom, and I'm not held down by train times."

She nods. "That checks."

I chuckle. "Are you testing me before you get in my car?"

"And if I was?" She crosses her arms.

"Then I approve." I move around to her side and lean against the car.

"I wasn't looking for your approval."

"How dare I even hand it out then. Shame on me."

The smallest of twitches tugs on the corner of her lip, but she hides it well.

"Listen," I say. "I understand this situation is weird, and going to a camp with a stranger might be a little more adventurous than what you're used to, so if there is anything I can do to make you feel more comfortable, let me know." When she doesn't say anything, just stands there and stares, looking very unsure, I continue, "Do you have questions? Concerns? Do you want me to grab you an AirTag to keep on your person and have Mika hook up to it so he knows where you are at all times?"

Her brows raise up to the sky. "Am I going to need an AirTag?"

"No, I'm just trying to figure out how to make you more comfortable."

"None of this is comfortable," she says on a sigh and leans to one side. "But...maybe you can answer a few questions."

"Okay, have at it."

She purses her lips for a moment and then asks, "Where did you go to college?"

"NYU."

"What did you study?"

"Art," I answer.

"Really?" Her nose scrunches. "Oh wait…the expensive charcoal set. Is that the medium you like to work with?"

"Yeah, charcoal is my favorite. I'm pretty good at watercolor, but it's not as messy. I like getting my fingers dirty." I almost wiggle my eyebrows but then realize I don't have that kind of relationship with her…at least not yet.

"What do you draw mainly?"

"Birds," I answer with a shrug. "I like bird-watching. I take pictures and then I draw them."

"That's…not what I was expecting you to say."

"No?" I ask with a smirk. "What did you think I drew?"

"Honestly, not sure, but birds weren't on my radar."

"Here to surprise you," I reply.

"Yeah, maybe a little too many surprises."

That makes me chuckle.

"Um, what did you think you were going to be when you were going through school?"

"Wasn't really sure." I shrug. "Was kind of just trying to figure things out. Didn't quite have a clear direction."

"Then how did you come up with your app thingy?"

"Soda Tracker," I correct her.

"Wait." She shifts on her feet. "You came up with Soda Tracker? That's like…Yelp for Soda. That's…that's a huge app."

I scratch my neck. "Uh, yeah."

"How did you come up with *that*?"

"It was my freshman year, and I was tired as shit most of the time from staying up too late and waking up early for class. I wasn't a big coffee drinker but loved any type of Coke. Diet Coke, regular, Coke Zero. But I found out pretty quickly that not all Cokes are the same, especially around the city. I'd get irritated when I thought I'd be getting a crispy

Coke straight from the fountain, only to find out that it was flat. So one late night, I was bouncing ideas around in my head and came up with Soda Tracker. It allows users to see who serves what brand of soda—which is important—and then it also allows the user to rate the soda, therefore not having to deal with disappointment. It started small, but now it has millions of users constantly rating, offering suggestions."

"I can't believe Mika never said anything."

"He doesn't say much about me in that aspect. Tend to keep it private."

She thinks on it and then says, "That's why you said you don't date much, because if people find out who you are."

I nod. "Yeah, people tend to get weird when they find out you have money."

"I mean, when you casually drop fifteen thousand for a life experience, I can see why."

"But a fun life experience." I point at her, making her smile ever so slightly.

She nods at me, arms still crossed. "Why did you sell it?"

"Got bigger than I could handle. I hold stock in it though, and I go to investment meetings often. Now they're introducing paid services for companies who want to offer the users a unique drinking experience. Influencers are getting on board, and a recipe section is being updated as we speak. Kind of cool seeing a small idea turn into something so large."

"That is pretty nice." She shifts on her feet. "So then when you sold it, you retired, right?"

I nod.

"Why did you retire if you're so bored?"

She's really going for it on these questions. I kind of like it. "Thought it was what I wanted at the time. But it got old pretty quick, so it's why I volunteer a lot."

"Where do you volunteer?"

"Well, mostly for Green Roofs in the City. Also, on Tuesdays and

Thursdays, I volunteer at a few different animal shelters. I'll take dogs for walks, sit with the cats, clean out a lot of shit. Just started learning how to administer medicine. And then the other days, I split my time between Green Roofs, helping with maintenance and awareness, and then I sometimes volunteer with a few out-of-school STEM programs."

"That's...that's a lot of volunteering."

"Yeah, but I like it."

"Have you had any serious relationships?"

Switching gears, okay.

"Not really. Nothing earth-shattering. I had a girlfriend in high school, but she broke up with me our senior year because she was going to school in California, and she didn't want to try to make it work. I mean, I don't blame her. She's actually married and has a kid on the way now. Then there were some girls in college, but nothing that's worth talking about."

She nods, her lips twisting to the side. "What do you think about someone who is twenty-nine and lies about being married to gain favoritism in her job?"

"I think if you were able to realize that putting yourself in such a position would help push your career forward, then you're pretty damn smart."

That seems to encourage her, because she stands a little taller.

"Music of choice?"

"Anything but hard metal and screaming."

"Do you listen to audiobooks?"

"Love them."

"Well then"—she drops her arms—"unless you have any questions for me, I think we can be on our way."

Huh, it was easier to win her over than I expected. Her standards must not be very high.

"Two questions. Is the money thing going to be weird for you? And what are the instructions for these next eight days?"

A smile tugs on the corner of her lip. "Absolutely not. Kind of find it funny. You don't give off rich snob vibes...especially when going to Target for socks."

I chuckle. "Not who I am," I say with a shrug. "And what about the instructions?"

"Let's discuss in the car."

"Great." I move over to her side and open the door for her. Her eyes travel up my body to my face. She says, "What are you doing?"

"Being a gentleman."

"You don't need to do that."

"I know I don't need to." I keep the door open and nod toward the opening. "Come on. Get in."

Tentatively and skeptically, she maneuvers into the car. When she's settled, she glances back at me. I smile, and she nervously nods. As I shut her door, it makes me wonder who made her so jaded.

From the quick rundown Mika gave me, I know he met her at Stockings, she moved back to the city recently to begin a new chapter in her life, and she's not a fan of her current job. Given all those factors, I'm wondering what made her run away from the life she was living.

Not something I need to find out right now though.

Once she's in, I shut the door and then round the front of the Jeep and get in on my side. Once the address is plugged in, we head off.

"I've never been in a Jeep Wrangler before," she says, looking around. "Very utilitarian. Nothing fancy about it."

"That's why I like it. It has everything I need without a lot of the fluff."

"Do you ever take it off-roading?"

"Sometimes," I say.

"Do you ever scale rocky cliffs like it shows in the Jeep commercials?"

"No," I answer as I stop at a stop sign and wait for a lady pushing a stroller to walk by. "But I did drive over a trash can once. It was small, but I felt cool doing it."

"Wow, really living on the edge over there. My fake husband is a genuine thrill seeker."

I chuckle. "I am. I like doing things like bungee jumping and skydiving."

"Really?" she asks, surprised.

"Yeah. Why so shocked?"

"Because you're telling me that you're bored, hence this current situation. Why don't you skydive or do more bungee jumping, things like that?"

"That's something I do for special occasions. It's not an everyday thing. And it's not that I'm bored. It's that I just want new experiences is all."

"Yeah, but with your money, you could go off to Africa and help build schools. There's experience there. Why are you staying here, in New York, when you could literally go anywhere in the world?"

I grip the steering wheel tighter and say, "I can't leave here for long."

"Why not?" she asks.

"Because of Mika," I answer as I stop at a light.

"Oh," she says, and I can see her working through the information. She knows what I'm talking about. She's stayed by his side through the mental health struggles he's dealt with over the years.

"I'm not comfortable leaving him," I continue. "Not when I know there are times in his life when he looks to me, when he needs me. I could do whatever I want, but being here, close to him, that's what matters to me the most."

"I never really thought about that," she replies. "Makes me think that the chance of you murdering me is now at an all-time low."

That makes me laugh out loud. "Why do you say that?"

"Because you're not just a robot in a pair of jeans and a beanie. There's a heart in there."

"Yeah, there's a heart," I say. "Beating and everything."

"Fascinating. What's that like?"

"Thrilling," I answer.

"Okay, what's the plan?" I ask now that we're out of the congested city and driving on the Taconic State Parkway. "What do you need me to do and most importantly not do? I want to make sure I get this right for you."

"I'm glad you asked. I was talking to Mika, and he was telling me about your improv classes. I really know nothing about improv, so I'm a bit clueless there, but he told me the first rule to improv is you always say 'yes, and…'"

"That's correct," I say.

"Well, I need you to drop that rule."

I glance at her quickly. Has she lost her mind? "That goes against the very tenets of improv."

"I understand that," she replies. "And I'm sorry to impose such a harsh rule, but I can't have you out in the wild saying yes to everything."

"What could I possibly be saying yes to? All the camp activities are nonnegotiable. We have to do them. It's not like you can pick and choose. Trust me, I was looking for an à la carte option when I was researching."

"It's not really the activities. It's more about who is going to be there."

"What do you mean?"

"Well, I was speaking to Ellison on Friday and telling her how we're headed up to the camp, and she happily informed me that we weren't the only couple from the office."

"Oh, is she going to be there?"

"She and the Brads and Chad of the office that I can't stand."

"Oh shit, really?"

"Yeah, and Chad in particular, as he's the reason I'm in this whole mess." She pauses and then adds, "I mean, sure, it was my big mouth that got me into this situation in the first place, but he was the one who questioned me."

"Tell me what happened," I say, curious about the timeline of events.

She sighs heavily. "To keep it short and sweet, everyone was bragging about doing something with their significant other this past weekend, and I felt left out, so when it was my turn, I talked about me and my husband. Well, Chad pointed out I wasn't wearing a ring. I told him we were going through marriage troubles, and that's when Ellison pulled me to the side. So yeah, he called me out in front of the company. He's a dick."

"Sounds like a giant one at that."

"Yeah," she sighs. "So he'll be there along with his nimrod friends. Which makes things more difficult, because I'm going to have to navigate all of them. Not that anyone talks to me in the office, but there were rumblings that Chad was pulled into Ellison's office for calling me out. Either way, I wouldn't put it past him to try to sniff out the fraud between you and me."

"Sounds like a weasel thing to do."

"I agree. So we need to be on our A game."

"I'm in. Just tell me what I have to do."

"First of all, we should never be split up. As much as we can handle it at least. If they separate us, we can't stand as a united front, and that's what these next eight days are about: being a united front."

"Got it. I'm stuck to you for eight days. Good thing for you I have excellent hygiene."

I can practically hear her roll her eyes.

"Second, we need to be affectionate but not overly affectionate. We're a couple on the rocks, but there's still love between us, potential for us to reconcile. So let's keep it to hand-holding and pelvis-to-pelvis hugs. Side hugs are for strangers, and kissing is for couples who are not having issues. We're looking for a healthy middle."

"Got it. Hand-holding, no kissing, definitely no public tongue action, and crotch-to-crotch hugs."

"I said pelvis-to-pelvis."

"Isn't that the same thing?" I ask.

"Yes, but 'pelvis' sounds less vile rolling off the tongue."

"Don't hate on 'crotch,'" I say with a smirk that she doesn't find amusing. Oh-kay. "What else?"

"We need to figure out what the hell we're fighting about. What our downfall is. The story we came up with during the therapy session was…a little out there."

"That's what happens when you're flying by the seat of your pants. You never know what might be said."

"No," she says sternly. "We had a plan, you veered away from the plan, and then we were stuck with me zipping your dick in a sleeping bag."

I chuckle. "Honestly, that would have killed at my improv class."

She looks unamused as she says, "Yes, but we're not at improv class, so no more dick zippering. We need to find simple differences that don't make us look bad."

"Okay," I say. The weekend gave me more time to consider this, and I knew Scottie would want to hash this out, so I came up with something that should track with our personalities well. "Uh, well, since I'm into green roofs, maybe the bigger issue that we haven't gotten into yet is that I've been pressuring you to travel with me to other countries to educate them on green roofs, while you want to work your way up the corporate ladder. Gives you the freedom and independence of wanting to make something of yourself and makes me look a little dickish assuming my job is more important than yours."

"Oh," she says in a gleeful surprise. "That…that could work."

"And maybe all the other things we've been fighting about are just nuggets compared to the larger, overall picture. Like when you're mad about something, but all the little things drive you to the boiling point."

"Yes, that's a good idea." I see her fully turn toward me from the corner of my eye. "That's very astute for a twenty-seven-year-old."

"Just because the number is young doesn't mean the brain is young. Uh…wait…"

"Nice try." She chuckles. "Okay, so then we'll run with that, because I'm assuming there are going to be some therapy sessions we have to go through?"

"Yes," I say. "They're not always on the couch like Sanders said, but there are some one-on-ones."

"Okay, so then midway, I say we bring up that issue, we're truthful with ourselves, we let him believe he's working his magic, and then slowly we start acting like we're falling in love all over again."

"That works for me."

"Great. Okay, this could work." She clasps her hands together and then gasps. "Wait, another rule. You're not allowed to be friends with the Brads and Chad. I can't stomach the thought of you high-fiving them. They're not our friends; they're mere pawns in the game we're playing. Got it?"

Pawns, not sure why I find that so funny...and charming.

"Got it. We're not friends with them. Anything else?"

"Well, of course the respectful rules of sharing a cabin together."

"Right, no looking, no touching, no snooping."

"Snooping? I didn't even think about that. Is that something you normally do?"

I shrug. "I mean, on the occasion. Depends on who it is and where I'm at."

"Wilder, that's an invasion of privacy."

"Well aware, never stopped me. I'm fascinated by people. I like to see what they're doing, what they're going through, what kind of deodorant they're using and if it has lead in it." I glance at her. "Does yours?"

She shakes her head. "I use Native."

"Hey, so do I." I point to my chest. "And here you were worried, but we're already bonding. Nerds Clusters and lead-free deodorant. Like two peas in a pod."

CHAPTER EIGHT
SCOTTIE

"WHY IS THIS EXACTLY WHAT I pictured in my head?" I say to Wilder as he puts the Jeep in park.

I stare out the window at the sight before me: a combination of vintage cabins, dirt paths framed by rocks, and tall oak trees that stretch up toward the sky, providing a canopy of shade with their pointed lobed leaves.

It's as if the movie *The Parent Trap* has come to life and sucked me into a vortex.

The main building is a log A-frame with a flagpole right outside the office, the camp logo of a simple *H* freely flying in the air. A lake runs along the backside of the camp, stacked with canoes and rowboats ready to be tossed into the water. Toward the middle, there's a large firepit with Adirondack chairs circling around it and piles of logs stacked high, ready to be burned. Off to the right, back into the woods, are the quaint log cabins where I'm assuming the camp attendees stay. Cutely, they are all adorned with porches and seating areas in the front, each with a decent width between.

This is it.

Camp Haven.

"I was reading up on Camp Haven before coming here," Wilder says. "Apparently Sanders's grandparents started it as a sports camp for children, a place to escape to during the summer. But over the years, it lost its luster, and only recently has Sanders revived it into a marriage camp. He does quite a few retreats every year."

"Yeah, and at fifteen thousand a pop, he's probably sitting pretty." I chuckle.

"Probably, but seems peaceful," Wilder says as he opens his door.

"For now," I mutter as I get out of the car as well. Despite the picturesque scene in front of me, I know for a fact that I don't want to be here. The drive up wasn't terrible. There were long moments of silence when we didn't say anything; he just drove and I stared out the window, soaking up all the greenery I miss at times while living in the city. And when we did talk, it wasn't really anything of substance. Things like have you ever hit a deer while driving? This was asked because we saw several carcasses on the side of the road while making our way up to the Catskills. For the record, neither of us have experienced such a horrific event.

But yeah, it was just…awkward, and now that we're here, I feel even more awkward because it's game time now.

This is it.

No going back.

Wilder is my pretend husband, I'm his pretend wife, and we're here to fix our marriage.

A squeaky screen door opens and then slams shut against the wood of the doorframe, startling me. I look up to find Sanders standing just outside the main building with a large smile on his face, waving his hand. "You're here. How was the drive?"

"Beautiful," Wilder says as he walks up to Sanders and offers him a handshake.

One thing I've observed about Wilder is that he's a social guy. Outgoing. He's not shaking Sanders's hand because he's playing a part; he's shaking his hand because that's the kind of guy he seems to be. I need to remember that if he starts shaking the hands of all the Brads and Chad.

"What about our passenger princess?" Sanders says as he smiles at me. This man has zero fashion sense. On camp day one, he's wearing a pair of swim trunks accompanied by a bright blue bowling shirt. His hair hasn't seen a comb in what I'm assuming is a week, and caressing his feet are a sturdy pair of ankle rain boots.

I mean, I guess it must be nice though, not having to think about putting an outfit together. He probably just sticks his hand in his dresser and pulls out the first pair of bottoms and shirt he sees with not a care in the world if they work together.

He's a stark contrast to Ellison, who's always so put together.

"It was a very nice drive," I say.

Together, we move to the back of the car, where Wilder starts pulling out our bags and setting them on the ground.

"Run into any weather?" Sanders asks me.

Putting on a gentle smile, I nod. "Ran into a sprinkling of rain, but other than that, just a nice drive upstate. Always nice to get out of the city on occasion."

"That's what I say," Sanders says, and then from his pocket, he pulls out a white golf ball and says, "Think fast." He tosses the ball at me, and somehow out of sheer panic and surprise, I'm able to catch it.

"What's this?" I ask.

"That is what they call a golf ball," he says. "Don't you write about those?"

Very funny, Sanders—said with absolutely no sarcasm.

Trying to hold back from nailing him in the head with said golf ball, I say, "Why, yes, but I was just wondering why you were handing me one."

"It's for our first activity of the day. We like to jump right into things. We'll have a proper welcome a little bit later, but we find it's a good ice-breaker for all the couples to start with an activity. Leave your bags here, Wilder. Our staff will bring them to your cabin. For now, you two need to follow me."

Okay, so we're just doing this, huh? No easing in? No tour? Just right into an activity. God, I don't think I'm mentally prepared just yet.

Wilder comes up next to me, and then together, we follow behind Sanders, who brings us around the main building and to a much bigger building that I didn't even notice behind the A-frame. Half of it is inside, the other half outside seating covered by a portico.

The covered area is decorated with couches, wingback chairs, coffee tables, ornate rugs, gold-framed pictures… It almost reminds me of Central Perk from *Friends*, coffee bar and all.

"There they are," Chad says as he lifts his hand with a wave. "Nice that you could make it."

He says it in a gentle tone, but I know it's a barb at us for being what looks to be the last couple to show up. Not a way to start things off, Chad.

Next to him sits his wife, who is intensely coloring a golf ball with Sharpies. I want to say her name is Danielle. That or Diana. I'm having a mental block. I've seen her quite a few times in the office. I remember her specifically because she likes to sit on Chad's lap and make out with him in the middle of the day, in the middle of the office. Massively inappropriate, but apparently since we are a marriage-positive workspace, make-out sessions are approved.

"Hello," Wilder says with a friendly wave. "I'm Wilder. Really excited about being here."

Wilder, what did we just talk about in the car? We're not making friends with these people.

Then he loops his arm around me and says, "You all know my wife, Pips."

Pips.

Why do I hate that name so much?

"Pips? I might have to use that in the office," Chad says with a smirk.

Oh no, you don't.

"I'd rather you not," I say. "That's Wilder's special name for me."

"We can chitchat later," Sanders says, standing in front of us and blocking off the view from the rest of the crowd. "First things first, please take out your phones."

Wilder and I exchange glances but then pull our phones out and hold them in our palms.

"Great. Now turn them off," Sanders says. "This is an electronics-free area."

"But what if we need to make a call?" I ask.

"Did you not send the information to your loved ones?" Sanders asks, a pinch to his brow.

What information?

"Uh, I did," Wilder says. "I think I forgot to tell Scottie."

"Ah, well, Scottie, send a quick text to your loved ones about where you are for the next eight days in case they need to get in contact with you. We have a pay phone that is available for emergency calls, but it's monitored, so you're not allowed to spend an exorbitant amount of time in there."

A pay phone? Did we just road-trip back to the nineties?

"Okay," I say, feeling like I'm losing a limb. I type out a text to everyone and then remember what Wilder said to me in the car. "Does Mika know how to get in contact with you?"

Wilder nods. "I talked to him this morning about it. He has all the information he needs if he has to get in touch with me. Thanks," he says softly.

Feeling better about that, I send out a quick text, and then both of us turn our phones off, only to hand them to Sanders, who pockets them.

"Wonderful." He clasps his hands together. "You will get these when we're done with camp. Now, head on over to your coloring station by the far end of the dining area. You'll have about twenty minutes to color your golf ball. We want to see you color it in a way that represents the love you share for each other."

Okay...

"Sure thing," Wilder says like a doof as he places his hand on my back, and then together, we head over to two wingback chairs that are placed side by side with a small coffee table in front of them. We are far enough away from the other couples that I feel comfortable whispering to him with no one lending an ear to listen in.

"Color our love? How does one do that?" I ask.

"Well, there are many possibilities," he replies while he takes the ball from me. "For instance, we could interpret the assignment as a love time-line displayed in color."

Interpret the assignment? Why do I feel like he's way more into this than me?

"We can use a color for each line, telling a story of how we've moved about over the last few years, ranging from hot to cold. Love to anger."

Huh, that's actually a pretty good idea.

"Right, I forgot that you're an art major."

"Or we can use symbols, but that might be more labor intensive as we attempt to find symbols that could represent a marriage despite not knowing much about our marriage. A story timeline using color symbolization could really tell the story Sanders is looking for. But if you're into the symbols, we can do those too."

"Uh, I think the color timeline thing would be best."

"My thoughts exactly."

"Okay, um, what colors do we need?" I ask as I glance down at all the colors available for us to use.

He lifts the can of Sharpies. "Well, we can start with black, which could represent the time right before we met, because our lives were dark and colorless."

I mean, that tracks for the beginning of a beautiful love story.

"Then," he says, getting more excited, "maybe yellow for happiness, because that's when we met. Then glow it up from there, going from yellow to orange to green."

"Why green? Why not red?"

"Because red I think screams anger and hurt."

"Oh, I assumed red because we were...you know...red-hot."

He raises his brow. "Red-hot, huh? You saying we have a steamy sex life?"

I feel my cheeks heat. "Well, you did say you found me attractive, so I just assumed. And also, you mentioned it the other day during our therapy session."

He nods. "Well, you assumed right, but that's why I think green would be best for that period in our marriage, because green represents wealth, and that doesn't need to be wealth in a money sense but a surplus of wealth in the mental capacity. Wealth in love. Wealth in marriage. Wealth in joy and happiness."

Okay, did he take a crash course on marriage counseling before he came here? He's so profound, something I did not expect in the least.

"Yeah, I guess I can understand that."

"Then I think we switch back to yellow and start mixing up yellow, orange, red, and green until we get to brown, which is where we are now."

"Huh," I say, thinking about it. "That's actually a really good representation."

"Thank you," he says and then hands me back the ball. "Do you want to do the honors? I can hand you the markers."

"Sure, that works," I reply.

Getting to work, he hands me a black marker, and I start coloring in a circle at the very top.

"So who was that guy who said hi to you when we got here? Is that Chad?"

"It is," I answer, focusing on making the ball look nice. "How could you tell?"

"He has weasel written all over him."

"Right? See, I told you."

"You did. I'll be sure to avoid friendship with him at all costs."

"Such a good husband."

"Hey, according to the rules, we're not saying nice things like that to each other just yet. Remember, we're in a cold phase right now. We're not frozen, just in our cold era."

"Right, sorry." I straighten out my lips, attempting not to smile, but it's hard.

When I catch him glancing at me, he says, "Stop. You're not supposed to be smiling."

"I'm sorry." I let out a low chuckle. "This is all just so…stupid."

"Yes, but remember, you're the one who got us into this, so don't be the one who screws it up. You can't blow up our spot."

"Please, if anyone is going to screw it up, it's you."

"Want to bet?"

"Sure," I say. "First one to misstep has to hand over five of their Nerds Clusters."

"Only five?" he asks. "Scared you might mess it up?"

"No, scared you might mess it up several times. This is so you don't lose them all."

"We'll see about that." Then he reaches out his hand and says, "Deal."

I take it and give it a shake.

Game on.

Easy win ahead for me.

Which is good, because I'll need all the candy I can get to see me through the next eight days.

"This is stupid," I say as I stand with my back to Wilder's chest. Our ankles and our hands are tied to each other, plastering us together and making it nearly impossible to move. "If we fall, we have to roll, or else I'm taking the earth right to my nose."

"We're not going to fall," Wilder says, his lips so close to my ear that his breath tickles me, sending a shiver all the way up my spine and causing goose bumps to spread over my skin. "We just need to communicate when we move. See, like them." He nods toward Finky and his wife, Lindsey, who are moving through the mini golf course with ease.

There are five holes to play, and said holes are pretty simple, flat, nothing too dramatic when it comes to slope and obstacles. We were told before we started that the best score wins a prize at the end. No one knows what the prize is, but you can bet with a camp full of embroidered vest–loving freaks, they're gunning for it. And yes, because I don't want to feel like the loser of the bunch, we're going for it as well.

"It looks like he's whispering in her ear as they move along." Then he points to Duncan and his husband. "Let's not be like them."

"Is that dirt in his nose?"

I feel Wilder lean closer to get a better look. "Shit, it is," he says. "Okay, if we end up falling, tuck and roll and I'll take the hit. But for the record, I don't plan on falling. I'm sturdy as an ox. All we need to do is take our time, concentrate, and work together. This isn't a race. This is about communication."

"Understood." I lightly nod. "But given our situation, don't you think we should bicker a little? You know, to show everyone that we're here for a reason? But then surprise them when we end up pulling out the win? Like classic chaos on the outside, but when push comes to shove, we excel at everything we do."

"Yeah, I like that." He pauses for a moment and then says, "Chaos I can do." He clears his throat and speaks slightly louder so the couples around us can hear. "Can you not do that?"

Brad S and his wife, in front of us, glance in our direction from the sound of Wilder's voice. A look of surprise and understanding falls over their expressions. Almost like they're trying to say been there, done that.

Well then, I guess it's time to put on a show.

Squaring my shoulders and wanting to match his energy, I say, "Do what? Tell you exactly what to do so we can win?" I derisively snort. "Remember, I'm the one who works for a putting company, not you."

"Yeah, you edit content written by others," he shoots back. "Strike me if I'm wrong, but you're not out on the greens, teaching Tiger Woods how to zone in his putting. You have no idea what you're doing when you have a stick in your hand. Trust me."

Hey!

I glance back at him, murder in my eyes.

I know exactly what to do with a…ahem…stick in my hand.

"Don't look at me like that." He lifts his chin. "Tell me I'm wrong."

I make a mental note to talk to Wilder about insults that we can toss at each other while not going below the belt, if you know what I mean.

"Not what you were saying two weekends ago when you were panting and squealing from my…hands."

"Squealing, really?" he asks with a gigantic eye roll that I'm pretty sure could have been spotted from space.

"Yeah, squealing. People thought a farm walked into the apartment building from the amount of hee-hawing coming from your lips." I nearly let out my own impression of the donkey braying sound that's on repeat in my head, but Sanders clears his throat in front of us, bringing our attention back to the golf course and the competition. "Sorry," I whisper with an apologetic smile.

"Apologies," Wilder replies, but then after a few seconds, he clears his throat, and in a very sarcastic voice, he says, "Wife, you're so good at this. I can't wait to see how you eat up all these men, just like you swallowed all those men in college."

Jesus, Wilder.

He pokes me in the back, encouraging me to shoot back. So I turn to look at him and say, "Pretty sure you were the one eating in college."

"You've never had a problem with my munching."

Ugh, why does he have to be so quick?

"And you, uh, you've never had a problem with my, uh, swallowing," I shoot back, proud of myself, but that pride quickly vanishes as Sanders walks right up to us this time, blocking us out from the rest of the couples.

"Hello," he says, pressing his hands together.

"Hi," Wilder and I say at the same time.

"Now, I understand there might be some growing tension between the two of you, and maybe you aren't entirely comfortable with not only being here but being tied up together and put to task within a half hour of arriving. But please, for the sake of peace at the camp, save the snarky commentary for our lash-out sessions. While we're together as a group, we need to keep the harmony."

My cheeks flame with embarrassment, because I'm usually one to follow directions and listen to the rules.

"Sorry about that," Wilder says and then lets out a heavy breath. "Tension is high."

"Yes, sorry," I say again. "Long, tense road trip, and now we're tied up together without taking a breather. Not sure I can remember the last time we spent this much time together consecutively."

Understanding crosses Sanders's face, thankfully. "I get it, but please don't disturb the peace of others."

"Sure," Wilder says. "Apologies again. We'll do better."

"Thank you." Sanders nods and walks away.

When we're left alone, I turn away from everyone and whisper, "Well, we made people believe we hate each other. Good job."

"Yeah, I think people are thinking they might have issues in their marriage, but at least they're not as bad off as us."

"Precisely."

"By the way, I didn't do a lot of munching in college."

"Nor did I do a lot of swallowing," I reply, feeling so ridiculous saying that.

"But that doesn't mean I'm not good at it," he adds. "Not about quantity, it's about quality."

"Same, Wilder. Same."

"Deep breath," Wilder says into my ear as we line up our last hole. "We got this."

It's been a pretty intense game. We've scored two holes in one and two pars while arguing the entire time. There has been staring from the others. Whispering. And even the occasional wince when I've accidentally elbowed Wilder in the ribs. And through all that, we are miraculously tied with Chad and his wife.

You can imagine their displeasure.

But despite all that, we have a solid chance at winning if we can get this hole in one. The course is basic, has smooth greens and very few obstacles, and just needs precise accuracy and communication with your partner to get a hole in one. Seems easy, but it's not. Especially when you're tied to each other.

"You lead," I say.

"I know what I'm doing," Wilder snaps, startling me. "You don't have to lady-nag all the time."

A collective gasp sounds throughout the women of the group. And when I glance up to catch the reactions of our fellow golfers, I can see just how uncomfortable everyone is.

Well, we wanted to sell how much our marriage is failing. I guess we're doing a great job at it.

To really add the final nail to the coffin, I say, "Maybe if you were actually intelligent enough to read simple putting lines by yourself, I wouldn't have to nag you."

"Just get in position," he says, moving me easily around.

Satisfied with our squabble, I allow him to line us both up, and then together, we bring our club back, and with our arms stiff, we swing through, propelling the ball forward. It sails up the small hill in the middle of the course, then down, and straight toward the hole. I hold my breath as it bypasses the hole. Wilder squeezes me, both of us on edge as the ball hits the stone behind the hole, giving it a good bounce, and we watch as the ball, as if in slow motion, inches closer and closer to the hole until…

Plunk.

It falls in.

"Fuck yeah!" Wilder yells and throws his hands in the air, taking my hands with him. *God, he's tall.* "And that's how it's done."

Chad tosses his club to the side and grunts in frustration, which naturally causes his wife to chastise him for the outburst.

Other couples offer their congratulations, even though they don't want to, because losing to the Bickersons is flat-out embarrassing. Let's call a spade a spade: no one wants to lose to the dysfunctional couple, yet here we are, taking the W.

While everyone begrudgingly tells us good job, Sanders, with his arm around Ellison, studies us.

"We did it," Wilder says, now dancing behind me, causing me to move around as well.

"Hey, don't do that," I say as I feel myself start to lose my balance.

"Why aren't you excited? We beat the Brads and Chad," he shouts, using my nickname for my coworkers that I've never said out loud. "And didn't I tell you? I said, listen to me, and we will win. Maybe you should listen to me more often."

"Maybe you should stop moving around so much so we don't tip over."

"Is that all you're really worried about?" He huffs behind me and then gestures his hand out, making my hand move as well. "You can never celebrate the small things."

"Hey, whoa, I'm going to fall," I say. "Stop moving."

"Always have to complain. Always have to be angry about something," he says, gesturing again.

"Wilder, seriously, stop,"

"Stop what?" he asks, leaning forward.

His weight presses into my back.

My legs shake beneath me.

And because I'm already off-balance from his erratic cheering, I can't take on the minimal amount of pressure from him, and before I can adjust our feet, I start to tip forward.

And because I tip forward, he tips forward.

And before I know what's happening, the ground seems to be moving closer and closer...

And closer...

Roll.

"Roll," I screech.

"Fuck, what?" Wilder says as we head straight to the ground... face-first.

"For the love of God, roll." It's the last thing I shout right as I attempt to overthrow the giant man behind me, but there's no use, as the pounds of muscle on him are too heavy. Watch out, ground. We're coming in hot.

I brace for impact, closing my eyes and holding my breath just as I plow face-first into the ground, my eye connecting with what I can only assume is a rock, sending a jolt of sharp pain through my skull.

And from there, everything goes black as I hear Wilder mumble, "Oh...roll."

CHAPTER NINE
WILDER

I CAN'T REMEMBER A TIME in my life when I've ever felt this guilty.

There was that time that I was mad at Mika back in middle school when his friends were over, and I grabbed his superhero underwear that he still wore and paraded it around like the asshole little brother that I was, telling his friends that Mika wore baby underwear.

But this…this beats it.

"There, that should do it," the nurse says as she finishes putting a butterfly strip over Scottie's swollen eyebrow.

I don't know what came over me, but when we won the golf challenge, a challenge that a real couple should have been good at, I felt a sense of pride, energy, invigoration that I haven't felt in a long time. I lost control, forgot that I was strapped to Scottie, and before I could calm myself down, we were tipping over and going straight to the ground.

I forgot about rolling.

I forgot about putting my hands out. And fuck, her cry when she hit the ground…

Once we were untied and I rolled her over, the blood already coming from her upper eye freaked me out. *So. Much. Blood.*

Horrified, I carried her in my arms to the nurse's station, where they tended to her head.

Thankfully, it was not that big of a cut—just a small butterfly taping and she's good.

"Do I have a black eye?" Scottie asks, looking up at me.

"Uh, I mean...a little."

She nods and then whispers, "Cool."

Cool?

And here I thought she was steaming with anger.

"Cool?" I ask her. "Are we going to have to check your head again?"

"No. I'm fine."

The nurse cleans up while I say, "Can you explain to me why it's cool to have a black eye?"

"I've always wanted one," she says in a dreamlike state.

Okay, I do think we need to check her again. Because I've spent maybe a few hours of my life with this lady, and I can tell you right now that there is no way that the woman who wanted to murder me after our first therapy session would find a black eye at a company marriage retreat dreamy.

Continuing, she says, "I've been hit in the head many times, but never a black eye. Always such a letdown. I thought my eyes were incapable of blacking out. But looks like it only took a rock and a two-hundred-plus-pound man behind me, pushing me into said rock, to make it happen."

"Uh, what do you mean you've been hit in the head many times?" I ask. "And who the fuck hit you?"

She looks up at me and tilts her head to the side. Cupping my cheek, she says, "Aww, look at you caring about me."

"Who hit you, Scottie?" I say, a hard edge to my voice.

"No one." She shakes her head. "But you know, like a ball or a can of beans, something like that."

"Did you get hit in the head with a can of beans?"

"I'm not a very good catch."

The nurse leans in and says, "She might be a bit off for a little while. I arranged a golf cart to take you to your cabin, and I believe Sanders is waiting out front. Would you like me to help you carry her out?"

"No, I can do it," I say as I stand and then go to pick Scottie up, but she whacks me away.

"I can stand and walk myself. I can't possibly be carried out of here. Humiliating. I need to look tough. Scare people with my bloody, black eye."

"I think it would be best if I carry you," I suggest.

"I think it would be best if you listen to my request," she counters. And there's determination in that swollen black eye, telling me she's going to get her way no matter how hard I try.

So not wanting to get into another fight, I nod but then wrap my arm around her so she doesn't wobble and walk her carefully out to the front, where Sanders is waiting in a decked-out golf cart. Christmas lights wrap around the poles and roof, fuzzy pink seat covers jacket all the seats, and a pair of plush diamond rings hang from the rearview mirror.

And then there's Sanders, in his same outfit from earlier, but this time, he's added moose antlers to his head and a neck pillow around his neck.

I mean, to each their own, right?

"You got her okay?" Sanders asks.

"Yes," I answer as I help Scottie into the back seat with me.

"Glad you're okay. That was quite the fall."

"Yeah, I kind of forgot we were tied together when I was celebrating," I say, guilt still consuming me.

"I could see that," Sanders says as he pulls out and starts driving toward the cabins. "Something we tend to forget when married, that we're tied together in all aspects. What one partner might do affects the other. Whether good or bad. One move tugs on the other and vice versa. That's why when we're making our way through life, we need to be aware that our every move is tied to our loved one. We need to be conscious of that."

Huh.

I mean, what a great analogy.

"It's a good lesson to learn, especially when you're in a situation like the one you're both in," Sanders continues. "When we get caught up in ourselves and become complacent with our everyday life, we tend to forget how our choices can affect our partner."

"Something I tend to struggle with," I say, really wanting to take the blame for this because I feel terrible. Getting Scottie hurt within the first few hours of being at camp is not really setting the tone in the right direction.

"Me too," Scottie says.

"I'm glad you can both admit to that." He pulls up to a cabin with a red circle and the number eight on the door. "This is where you'll be staying." He puts the cart in park and then pulls a key from the dashboard. "Right this way."

I help Scottie out of the cart and then gently help her up the ramp that leads to our cabin.

When we're all inside, Sanders flips the light switch on, and it takes everything in me not to bust out in laughter, because holy shit.

I will say this: when looking at the website and pamphlet for the camp, they didn't show much about the accommodations. There was one picture showing a regular bed but nothing else too specific.

I can see why now, because this…this is not what I was expecting in the least.

Let me paint a picture.

The focal point is a king-size four-poster bed…*with* handcuffs and chains hanging from every wooden post. The floor is covered in a giant, white, fluffy rug, the walls are decorated with pictures of body parts, zoomed in, all in black-and-white. Nipples, tips of penises, stomachs… butt cracks. The bedding and the curtains are also a heavenly white color, while accents of red pop up in the pillows and erotic decorations. But the centerpiece of the room, the eye-catcher some might say, is the white dresser with black knobs covered in products. We're talking lubes, sex toys, lingerie…and lots and lots of condoms.

Is this a cabin or a sex dungeon?

"Oh...wow," Scottie says, her voice cracking. "This is, um, this is different."

Sanders chuckles. "That's the same response we get from all our couples when they first see this cabin. But we're very intentional with our rooms. Ellison..."

Ellison appears from the doorway that I assume leads to the bathroom. Jesus Christ.

How long has she been waiting there...in the dark?

No longer in the Bermuda shorts and polo she was wearing, she's now strutting toward us in a bikini and open silk robe.

What the hell is going on?

If this is a swinger-type camp, I'm out. I know I gave my word to Scottie, telling her I'd help her, but there's no way I'm taking my clothes off in front of the Brads and Chad and Sanders, who is wearing moose antlers and a neck pillow. Not fucking happening.

"Welcome to your sanctuary," Ellison says, gesturing her arm to the space. "This is where you'll be able to escape and have some of your most important conversations while also reconnecting with each other."

"It's where our couples find the most success and the most renewal in their relationships," Sanders says. "We believe here at Camp Haven that a marriage is not only a team effort but requires a deep emotional connection that needs to be solidified between partners. And that starts here in the bedroom. Therefore, we provide every aspect of what it means to have a thriving physical connection. Now, you don't have to take part in everything we offer in this room, but we want to give our couples the option to explore. To have fun. To possibly test things out they might have been nervous to ask for back at home."

Ellison places her hand on Sanders's stomach, which is on display because in addition to the antlers and neck pillow, his shirt appears to be a crop top, and she says, "We've found so much joy here at Camp Haven, so we encourage you to explore, to be adventurous, and to always use a safe word. Start with consent"—she presses her hand to her chest—"and lead with your heart."

Jesus. What the hell is this?

"Very well said, darling." Sanders turns her head toward his and then kisses her, using tongue. Straight-up tongue. In front of others.

So much tongue.

Yikes.

When he pulls away, Sanders licks his lips aggressively, and it takes everything in me not to dry heave into my sleeve. "We have our camp welcoming and dinner at six. Please feel free to come however you're comfortable, but don't be late. And if you need anything for your head, please let us know."

"Thank you," I say as I stick my hands in my pockets, unsure of what to do in this room.

"Oh, and your bags are over there in the corner," Sanders says. "Let us know if you need anything." Then they take off, and when the door clicks shut, I turn toward Scottie.

"Am I dreaming?" she asks, dizzily looking around. "Because right now, it seems like I'm in some sort of X-rated room made for erotic torture."

I slowly nod, taking in the space. "Yeah, you're not dreaming, unless we were both knocked out and this is us simultaneously dreaming together. Although that seems less likely."

"Less likely than a camp cabin set up for erotica?"

"Good point." I walk up to the bed and tug on one of the handcuffs. "That's taut." I drag my hand over the plush comforter. "Surprisingly full." I then turn toward Scottie and say, "This is really fucking weird."

"Yeah, there's no way I'm sleeping here," she says with a shake of her head. "It's a sex dungeon."

"I think dungeon is a strong word, because there's a window with curtains. Maybe consider…sex palace. The comforter has palace-like qualities."

"Wilder."

"Hmm?"

"We're not sleeping here."

"Okay, want to grab a tent? Because I think that's our only other option, unless you want me to see if the Brads and Chad don't mind us crashing with them. Then again, Sanders made it seem like all the other rooms had the same design style."

"I'm being serious, Wilder."

"So am I. This is it. I don't think there are other styles of accommodations."

She glances around, hugging her arms tightly around her. "I don't want to touch anything. How much sex do you think has been had in this room?"

"I mean…" I look around. "If these walls could talk, they probably would moan from the amount of sex they've seen."

"Gross." Scottie shivers. "Call me a prude, but I don't want to sleep on the same mattress where people get tied up and stare off at zoomed-in nipples on the wall."

"To be fair, it looks like there are handcuffs, not ties. A bit of a difference there."

"Why are you making light of this?" she asks, looking very annoyed.

"Because," I say, "if I don't make light of it, then I think both of us would spiral, and we can't both be spiraling."

"We need to spiral. We need to find a different place for slumber, because sex palace isn't it."

"I'm right there with you on the sex palace thing, but I honestly don't think there is another option, and listen, I read online that they have a pretty intense cleaning service."

"Ew, why is that something they need to state?"

"Probably for this precise reason." I gesture around the room. "So couples like us come into the sex palace and feel comfortable having fun."

Still looking really uncomfortable, she walks over to the dresser and takes a look at the "offerings" just as there's a knock at the door, startling the both of us.

"Come in," I shout.

Sanders pops in, holding a basket. "Almost forgot, here's your prize for winning the golf tournament." He winks. "Have fun."

I take the basket, and then he leaves, his heavy footsteps heading down the ramp. I glance down at the basket, and my eyes nearly pop out of their sockets.

"What is it?" Scottie asks.

I turn it toward her, showing off more condoms, dildos, lube, blindfolds, and, in the center of it all, a book on sex and positions.

"Oh my God," she whispers as she comes up to me. "What the hell is going on?" Without touching anything, she scans the contents. "Why would they give us more? Do they not know there is a plethora of items on the dresser over there?"

"I mean, they really want us having sex." I take the basket to the dresser to set it down with its friends when I notice a menu on the dresser. I pick it up and start looking over the contents, everything coming into place. "Holy shit."

"What?" Scottie asks.

I set the basket down on the floor and turn toward her. "Do not touch a damn thing on this dresser unless you want to pay a surcharge for pleasure."

"What are you talking about?" she asks, walking up to me.

"This dresser is a minibar for sex."

"What?" she snaps and then pulls the menu from my hand. She scans it over and then gasps. "Fifteen dollars for a three-pack of condoms? That's outrageous!" She turns to me and whispers, "That's outrageous, right? I haven't bought some in a while."

"Yes, it's outrageous," I whisper back.

"Outrageous," she shouts again. "That's five dollars per possible orgasm. Given the user, there isn't even a solid chance of orgasm. What a rip-off."

"To be fair, there'd be a solid chance with me."

She rolls her eyes in my direction. "Really, Wilder? You don't seem like the kind of guy who needs to brag about his ability to make their partner experience pure pleasure."

"Yeah." I pull on the back of my neck. "I'm really not that guy. Not sure where that came from." I gasp, and my eyes widen. "Shit, are the Brads and Chad already wearing off on me? Am I…am I turning into a douche?"

"I don't know. How do you feel about boat shoes?"

"Unfavorably," I answer. "But that doesn't mean that I'll still feel the same way about them if I continue to be around them."

"Dear God." She shakes her head. "I refuse for you to become a douche. Refuse. We must get rid of all the things." She reaches for the dildos lined up in the back, and I quickly swat her hand away.

"Don't touch anything."

"Why?" she asks, staring down at the cluster of copulation.

"Because what if the dresser has a weighted sensor like the minibars you find in hotels? You pick it up, and the hotel automatically charges you."

"Do you think that's a thing?"

"I don't know." I shrug and then open one of the drawers to explore. I move around the dresser, running my fingers along the wood, examining every facet of it, even the back wall to see if it's plugged in. When I detect no feel of a sensor, I blow out a heavy breath. "No sensor. We should be good."

"Thank God." Scottie opens a drawer and then scoops everything inside, leaving one single dildo poking out from the top as she closes the drawer just enough for the head of the fake penis to be peeking out.

"Why are you leaving the dick out like that?"

"Because if there's no sensor, that means they come in here and count everything to see what we've used, and I don't want them charging us. You might be rich, but to hell if we're getting charged"—she stares down at the menu—"twenty-seven dollars for a three-ounce bottle of lube. If we leave the dildo poking out, they'll know we just shielded our eyes from the sex minibar."

"Smart."

"Thank you." She then takes a look around the room. "Any chance we can take off the handcuffs?"

"I can work on it." I head over to the bed and start assessing as Scottie looks at the erotic pictures on the wall.

Gesturing to one of just a single breast with a very erect nipple and a water droplet hanging off the tip, she asks, "How do we feel about the nipple?"

"It's a great nipple," I answer honestly.

She then moves to the picture right next to it of a scrotum and motions to it. "And this nut sack?"

"I mean, it's a well-manicured set of balls."

Her head tilts to the side as she studies it. "Looks kind of old."

"Scrotums are supposed to have wrinkles, Scottie."

She purses her lips, unamused as she glances in my direction. "I know they're supposed to have wrinkles, this set just seems... Oh God."

"What?"

She clasps her hand over her mouth. "Do you think this scrotum belongs to Sanders and that nipple belongs to Ellison?"

Well, there's an unnerving thought. I turn toward the pictures, giving them a better look, focusing more on the scrotum than anything. "Ehh, I don't think Sanders would be that well landscaped. I mean, the man was walking around with a goddamn neck pillow hanging around his throat like a necklace. No way do his nuts look that good."

I catch the swallow in her throat as she glances at the pictures. "Maybe you're right, but just to keep the visual out of my head, do you mind if I take them down?"

"Nope. Please do." I chuckle as I pluck the handcuffs off one by one and then set them in the drawer along with the rest of the lovemaking loot.

Scottie places the pictures in the corner and then scans the room, her watchful eyes taking in every nook and cranny. "There, I think that's better. All we needed to do was take the sex out of this marriage."

"Couldn't be prouder," I say and then go for our bags. I place them on the bed so we can unpack. "No wonder everyone was gunning to win the mini golf competition. They probably knew they were going to get a free basket of sex toys and condoms."

"Yeah, I didn't think about that," she says. "Makes sense."

I flip open my suitcase, and I'm met with a paper on the top from Camp Haven.

"What's this?" I ask, holding it up.

"I have no idea," she says, walking up to me. "What does it say?"

"'Dear Camper, your suitcase has been examined by the camp staff, and we've found the following contraband in your bag.'" There's a list of different contraband items, and at the bottom, food/drink is circled. "Holy shit, I think they took the Nerds Clusters."

"Nooooo," Scottie says next to me. "Check."

"I don't need to. They were right here, on top. They're gone." *What the fuck is this? They just go through our bags without our consent?*

"The hell? What else is on that list?" She takes it from me and scans it for a few seconds before looking up. "Condoms, sex toys, lube, edibles, it's all on here. What a scam! They want you buying their costly condoms."

"And here I thought Sanders was an upstanding man." I shake my head. "I'll tell you this, my opinion of him has severely dropped with this blatant display of capitalism."

"Took the Nerds Clusters. Wow, first a blow to the head, and now a blow to the heart." She drops the piece of paper and walks over to the bathroom.

I start pulling my clothes out when I hear her yelp.

"What's wrong?"

"Wilder, come here."

Curious, I set my clothes down and head over to the bathroom, where Scottie is standing, staring straight ahead.

I follow her line of sight, straight to the steam shower, where a large dildo is stuck to the wall.

"Dear God," I whisper. "Whatever you do, don't drop the soap, Scottie. For the love of God, don't drop the soap."

CHAPTER TEN
SCOTTIE

"HOW DO YOU FEEL?" WILDER asks as I slip on my shoes.

We're about to head out for the welcome dinner, and frankly, after being in this cabin, I'm now terrified as to what to expect. Is this an orgy thing? I don't think I can handle it if it is. I can't afford to quit my job, but the image of Finky walking up to me wearing *only* an embroidered vest, looking to see if I'm ready to have a good time? I'd have no other choice but to quit.

Is that why they like coming here so much, because it's their one time a year to let loose and have fun?

I really hope not.

"Okay," I answer as I stand.

"Just okay? Do you have a headache?" Wilder asks, looking really concerned.

I have to hand it to him: he might have forgotten to roll when we fell, but he sure knows how to make up for it. He's a really caring guy, has looked out for me consistently, and has made sure I'm taken care of.

Matt was never like that.

I'm pretty sure if I was attending this camp with Matt, he would have laughed at me, probably pointed, and made fun of me later for smashing my head on a rock.

There would be no apology.

Most likely, he would have blamed me for making us fall rather than taking responsibility.

Wilder—not that I'm comparing them, because Wilder and I aren't actually together—you can see the remorse in his face. Makes me think, if I ever decide to put myself out there in the dating world again, this is an attribute that I would be looking for.

Doesn't laugh when girlfriend gets her face smashed by a rock.

"No headache," I say. "Pretty excited by the bruising though."

He chuckles and presses his hands into his pockets. "I'm happy for you. I hope it looks even worse tomorrow morning."

I press my hand to my chest. "That's so sweet. Thank you."

"You're welcome." He nods toward the door. "Ready to go? We don't want to be late. Sanders was adamant about that."

"Yeah, I'm ready. Let's go."

Wilder opens the cabin door for us and then locks up. He turns toward me and says, "Can't have the other campers sneaking into our room, knowing the kind of free goods we have in there."

"Oh, smart. You know, I wonder if it's something we could trade."

"What do you mean?" Wilder asks as we walk down the ramp together.

"Well, you know how they trade in jail, like a cinnamon bun for a cigarette? What if we can use our prized condoms and dildo for trading fodder? Who knows what the other prizes are going to be? We have to be smart about this. There could be an opportunity for us to trade up."

Wilder pauses and turns toward me. "Is it weird that your suggestion just made my nipples hard?"

"Yes."

"Fair." He nods, making me laugh. He points at me and says, "Hey, no laughing. We're supposed to not like each other at the moment."

"That's not that hard to fake," I say. "Given that you didn't roll when we started falling." I lift a brow at him.

"I apologized. I asked you how I can help. I have offered you all the things, like meds, an ice pack, and a drink. What else do you want from me?" he replies in a teasing tone.

"To live with the regret that you nearly cracked your fake wife's head open on a rock."

"Listen, I gave you an amazing gift. Without me, you might never have experienced your first-ever black eye. And now that I'm saying that out loud, it doesn't sound great."

"Not really, but I know what you mean. So what you're saying is that I should feel honored to be in your presence."

"Exactly," he says as we walk down the path toward the food hall. "Anything I need to be aware of when we get in there?"

"Not really," I say.

"What if people ask us if we liked our prize for the mini golf? What do you want me to say?"

"Um, I don't know. What would a couple who is on the rocks right now say to that?"

"Hmm, maybe that we found it interesting."

"Interesting…that could work. Doesn't give commitment either way whether we like it."

"Yeah, a solid answer that keeps our private life private."

"Very diplomatic of you."

"See." He bumps his shoulder with mine. "I'm not that bad."

"I never said you were bad, just…a loose cannon. I don't know what you're going to say or do."

"That's the fun of improv," he says. "It's all fly by the seat of your pants."

"Yeah, well, less pantsing please and more plotting."

When we reach the dining hall, Wilder opens the door for me and leads me in with his hand on my lower back. The spacious hall is set up with individual tables, each decorated with a fake, flickering candle in the middle and a rosebud in a milk glass vase. The tables are draped in red-and-white checkered tablecloths, and the lights are dimmed to create an intimate experience.

"Why did I think we'd be sitting at picnic tables with the rest of the couples?" he whispers.

"Because that's what summer camp is."

"Right," he says.

"Scottie, how is your eye?" Sanders says, coming out of nowhere. He's now changed into a pair of black basketball shorts, a white button-up shirt with a bow tie, and a suit jacket but with the sleeves cut off.

Nothing but class, class, class.

"Um, a little sore, but it's doing okay."

"Ooo," he says, examining me. "That black eye is coming in good."

I lightly dab my fingers around the affected area, trying not to show how pleased I am about the black eye. "Yeah, so I've been told."

"Well, we'll be sure to keep you safe moving forward, no more tying up…at least on our end." He wiggles his brows, and I feel my insides turn.

When we signed up for this, I wasn't aware there was going to be such a large emphasis on sex. Nor did I think there was going to be a minibar of lovemaking. The entire situation is granting me a new perspective on all my coworkers.

Sanders leads us through the dining hall, and as I pass each and every one of them, my mind drifts to different scenarios.

Does Chad tie up his wife? Or use toys on her? He seemed really adamant about winning the basket.

What about Duncan? He's such a klutz, I couldn't imagine him being able to locate any of his husband's erogenous zones.

And Finky, he's so involved with his fantasy sports teams that I'm not sure he's even aware what sex is.

Not to mention Brad. He's such a weasel, there's no way he's hitting up the minibar, thinking, *What can we do tonight?* Or heaven forbid… gulp…drop the soap.

I can't imagine any of them engaging in this kind of camp. Then again, here they are, willing and ready to keep the spark alive in their relationships.

Wonder what that's like—to have two equal parties invested in a relationship.

God, I sound like such a bitter divorcée.

"Here we are," Sanders says, gesturing to a table. "We have you sitting right up front."

I pull out of my reverie and find our table smack-dab in the front of the stage. A table so centered, so singled out, that it almost seems like it's going to be a dinner and show for one.

"This will be your permanent table for the remainder of the camp. We like to create a sense of comfort by offering our attendees routine. The menu is on the table, my staff will be by shortly to collect your order, and then we'll get started with the welcome."

"Great," Wilder says in that cheery voice of his. "Thank you."

Sanders nods and then takes off.

I'm about to take a seat when, to my surprise, Wilder pulls out my chair for me.

"What are you doing?" I whisper through clenched teeth. "This is a nice gesture. We don't do nice gestures for each other."

"Oh shit," he whispers back. "Sorry, uh, just habit."

Not wanting to make a scene, I take a seat, but I let his words settle in. Pulling out a chair for someone is habit for him? Pulling out a woman's chair? Well, that's a really nice habit to have.

It's sweet.

Thoughtful.

Not necessary but thoughtful, something you don't see too often anymore.

Once he sits down, he picks up his cloth napkin and spreads it on his lap. Talking softly, he says, "I mean, I don't think it's that big a deal that I pulled out your chair. We might not be getting along, but I don't have to be an asshole and not pull out my wife's chair for her."

"True," I say and then pick up my menu. "For a twenty-seven-year-old though, that habit surprises me."

"Are twenty-seven-year-olds supposed to be assholes?" he asks.

I shrug. "I don't know, but with my experience, I'd say they're more self-absorbed than anything."

"Your experience, huh?" he asks. "Care to elaborate?"

"Not really," I say, taking in the three Italian options for dinner. Chicken parmesan, eggplant parmesan, and lasagna. "But seriously, when did you start pulling out chairs, opening doors, things like that?"

"Ever since I was young," he answers and sets his menu down. "My mom was adamant about me and Mika being gentlemen. We took turns opening doors for her and pulling out her chair. She said she didn't want to be the reason her sons didn't treat their partners well later in life."

"You have a good mom."

"I do," he says softly.

I know a little bit about Wilder's family situation to know what that look on his face means.

Mika and Wilder's mom is an absolute rock. She worked as a paralegal, took care of the boys, made sure to get them to all their events, and took care of their dad, who was in a terrible car accident when they were teenagers. It left him a quadriplegic, which led to some darker moments in the family. And then when Mika was in college, their dad passed away. It was tough on all of them, including their mom.

Clearing his throat, Wilder asks, "What, uh, what do you think you're going to get?"

Seeing he wants to change the subject, I study my menu again, even though I know the three choices already.

"I think maybe the eggplant parm."

"That's what I was thinking as well." He smiles up at me. "Look at us twinning."

"Dear God," I say with a shake of my head, causing him to chuckle. "Hey, stop that. No laughing. You need to look irritated around me."

"Then don't make me laugh."

"Don't say dumb things, like 'twinning.'"

"That's not dumb," he replies. "That's stating the facts."

Just then, our waitress steps up to our table and says, "Welcome to Camp Haven. My name is Meghan, and I'll be your personal server during the duration of your stay. Can I interest you in some sparkling water?"

"Do you have wine?" I ask.

Meghan, with the long ponytail and freckles dotting her nose, shakes her head. "No, this is an alcohol-free camp. Sanders only allows alcohol two nights during your stay, and tonight is not one of them."

Should have figured since the minibar was replaced with condoms and lube.

Although, some of the toys they're upcharging for, I'd suspect I'd need some alcohol to even think about using. Especially the one in the shower. The girth on that thing is terrifying.

"Sparkling water will be fine," I say, disappointed that I can't lean on my good friend merlot to get me through the next eight days.

"And for you?" she asks Wilder.

"Sparkling water as well. The wife and I are twinning."

Dear God in heaven.

"We'd also like the eggplant parm." He sniffs the air. "And is that garlic bread I smell?"

"It is," Meghan says with a smile. "I'll bring you out a basket in a few."

"That would be great, thank you," Wilder says.

"Certainly. Is there anything else I can get you?"

"We're good," I say.

"Wonderful." Then she reaches into her apron pocket and pulls out a sheet of paper. "Here are your questions for tonight."

"Questions?" I ask. "What are these for?"

"Every evening, you'll be given a set of questions that you must ask each other. Sanders requires it. If you need anything else, just flag me down."

"Thank you," Wilder says while taking the questions from Meghan.

She takes off, and I lean forward, trying to take a gander at what's on the piece of paper.

"What kind of questions are we talking about over there?" I ask. "Because if it's 'Will I pay fifteen dollars for a pack of three condoms,' the answer is no."

He shakes his head. "No, they're regular, thought-provoking questions."

"Really?" I ask. "Like what?"

"Well, they're listed out by the questions I need to ask you and the questions you need to ask me."

"Do you think we have to do them?" I ask.

Wilder looks up and glances around the food hall. "I mean, it seems like everyone is doing them. It would be odd if we didn't."

I look around as well and notice how deep in conversation each couple is. Hell, okay, maybe we do have to do the questions.

"Okay, do you want to go first?"

"Sure, we can go back and forth," he answers. He studies the first question and then looks up at me. "Why are superheroes portrayed as heroes who wear their underwear outside their pants?"

"What?" I ask. "That's the question?"

He nods. "Yup."

Leaning more forward, I whisper, "This place is weird. Between the cabin sex-a-thons, the owner with the moose antlers, and the superhero question, like what are we really doing here? I mean, it's weird, right?"

"It could be perceived that way," Wilder says. "But that's not an answer to the question."

"My answer to the question is it's a weird question."

"Everything okay over here?" Sanders asks as he walks up, straightening his bow tie.

"Yup," I nearly shout because he startled me. "Everything is great." I offer him a thumbs-up.

"Any problems with the questions?"

"Nope." I shake my head. "They're great. Very thought-provoking."

"Wonderful. Let us know if you need anything, and we'll take care of it." And then he takes off.

When he's out of earshot, I ask, "Does he just come out of nowhere all the time?"

"Nah, I saw him walking up." Wilder smirks.

"And you didn't bother to give me a warning?"

Wilder shrugs. "We never talked about a warning sign. Is that something you're interested in?"

"If he's going to keep popping up like that, then yes."

"What do you want the warning sign to be?" he asks, still holding the list of questions.

"Maybe bulge your eyes out."

He presses his hand to his chest and asks, "I'm sorry, were you under the impression that I'm a cartoon character with eye-bulging capabilities?"

"I mean, like widen them and shift them side to side." I offer him an example of what I'm talking about, and he snorts. "What?" I ask.

"Pips, going to tell you right now, that's not going to work. There's nothing discreet about that expression."

"Fine." I cross my arms at my chest. "Then what is your solution?"

"I can say 'colonel.'"

"Colonel?" I ask. "Why on earth would you say that?"

"Because," Wilder says simply with a light shrug of his shoulder. "Colonel Sanders."

Huh.

That is actually pretty good.

"You like it, don't you?" he asks, knocking his foot against my leg under the table. "Admit it. Admit that I'm clever."

"You're annoying," I reply as Meghan sets down our drinks and a basket of bread. When she's gone, I add, "And for the record, I think the underwear is worn on the outside of the superhero costume because it's an extra layer of protection from the greedy eyes of people trying to catch a glimpse of the bulge and all the defined parts that go along with it."

Wilder nearly spits out his sparkling water, clearly not ready for my answer.

He dries his mouth with his napkin and then says, "Jesus. I think you might be right."

"I know I am."

CHAPTER ELEVEN
WILDER

WHAT I KNOW ABOUT SCOTTIE, my brother's best friend, is very limited to what I learned in the car and what Mika has told me.

I know that she moved back to the city and Mika was really excited about it.

I know that she likes Mika's heavy-handed drinks at the bar.

I know that her other best friend is Denise, who is my best friend's girlfriend.

I know that she's obsessed with Nerds Clusters, like me.

And I know that she doesn't care for what she edits, but she likes editing.

That's the extent of it.

So listening to her is fascinating, because the way she speaks is different from the way she presents herself. She's slightly jaded, a little rough around the edges, has a good sense of humor, but doesn't show it often. She's a bit grumpy most of the time but also lighthearted when she's excited about something...like a black eye.

She's observant, constantly watching the people around us, processing their body language. She's serious but also comical. She can let loose but also holds herself together almost all the time.

She's captivating, full of depth, and someone I want to ask a ton of questions to, because I want to get inside her brain. Unfortunately for me, I'm stuck answering dumb questions that mean nothing.

"What are your thoughts on rocky road ice cream? Too much, too little? If you had to add one more ingredient, what would it be?" I ask. What a fucking stupid question.

She shakes her head and cuts another piece of her eggplant parm. "These questions really are ridiculous. Like the Cheetos one. If they weren't orange, what color would you want them to be?"

"I still think my answer was a good one," I say.

"Black was not a good answer. Do you know how much food dye would go into those? Your innards would turn black."

"My thoughts exactly," I say. "Seems like a fun science experiment."

She plops another bite of eggplant in her mouth while I reach for a piece of garlic bread. I've almost devoured the entire basket. Not sure what recipe they used, but the ratio of butter to garlic and the broil time in the oven is absolute perfection. Crispy, buttery, so much goodness.

"Now come on, answer the question. Sanders is going to be starting soon, and these are our last two."

"Fine," she says on a sigh. "Um, I've never been a huge fan of rocky road ice cream, so I would say there is too much going on, but if I had to add something…probably graham cracker. Make it a bit like a s'mores treat."

"Solid addition. I was thinking another nut."

She shakes her head. "That's too much chewing. Ice cream should be sucked on, not chewed."

"Reasoning you could use on other things you put in your mouth," I say, causing her eyes to widen, which makes me smile.

Did I mention she's a bit of a prude?

And I don't know why I like that.

When she was taking in every last dildo and cock ring in the cabin, I could see her clutching her proverbial pearls. And when her eyes landed on that shower dick, I thought she was going to faint. Honestly, I can't wait to give it a solid poke when I take my shower later.

"Oh my God, Wilder, don't be a pervert."

"That's not being a pervert. That's called making a joke." I nod toward her. "Lighten up, Pips."

She dabs at her mouth and sits back in her chair. "Hand me the paper."

I hand it over to her, knowing exactly what the last question is. Holding back my smile, I wait for her to read it, only for her to peek up at me, her head cast down, offering me her pretty irises.

"I'm not asking this."

"You have to," I say. "And if you notice, there is a *B* next to the number, meaning it's a question we both have to answer."

She sets the paper down. "I'm not asking."

I pick it up and smirk while I say, "Fine, I'll ask, and then we can both answer." Clearing my throat, I ask, "What's the best oral your partner has ever given you?"

She picks up her water and takes a sip, clearly avoiding the answer, so I step in.

"It was our fourth date."

She snorts. "God, you wish." She then leans forward and whispers, "I'd never give oral on a fourth date."

"Really?"

"Would you?"

I grin. "Given it on the first." *And that was one of my finest dates, I might add.* Not that there were *too* many first dates during college.

Her mouth falls open, and then she quickly closes it. "That's... that's—"

"You can unclench, darling. It's going to be okay," I say. "Now, back to our fourth date. It was when we went out to the pumpkin farm."

She sits back, looking far too annoyed, but I keep going.

"You were high off apple cider doughnuts and fresh country air. You just got off the hayride, so your hair was tousled, and your cheeks were bright pink. You were irresistible."

"Oh my God," she mutters.

"You pulled me in close and whispered in my ear that you wanted to get lost in the corn maze. Then you gave me that little wiggle of your eyebrow that told me you wanted to play with my corn on the cob."

"For the love of God."

I smirk. "So hand in hand, we went into the depths of the corn maze, and when we found a spot that no one was going to traipse through, you dropped to your knees, pulled my jeans down, and went to town. I don't know if it was because your mouth felt like a fall festival, all cinnamon and cidery, but I don't think I've ever come that hard while being blown."

She runs her tongue over her teeth and says, "First of all, your dick doesn't have taste buds; there's no way you'd have been able to know that my mouth was a fall festival. Second of all, I'd never do anything like that in public."

My brow shoots up. "Wait, you've never had sex in public?"

"Uh, do I look like a heathen?"

"I mean…the black eye is giving you a certain vibe."

She rolls her eyes, and I push her with my foot under the table.

"Your turn," I say. "When was your favorite time I went down on you?"

"Never."

"Ouch," I say, clutching my chest. "Pips, now that's hurtful. I've spent five years on the assumption that I've been licking you the right way. Is that why we're really here? Because I haven't been pleasuring you correctly?"

"You realize there's something seriously wrong with you, right?" she says, leaning forward on a whisper.

"Babe, just tell me. Is it my tongue? Is that what the problem is? Because I can get it pierced again."

Her expression morphs into interest. "You had your tongue pierced?"

"Yeah, for a while, but when I was trying to sell off Soda Tracker, my advisors thought it would be best if I got rid of it."

"Did you have your lip piercing then as well?"

"No, got that after I sold Soda Tracker."

"Why not the tongue again?"

"Why so interested?" I ask with a large smile.

Flustered, she says, "I'm not... I'm just... Seems like the typical thing to do would be to get the piercing again that you had to get rid of."

"I'm not the typical kind of guy," I say.

"Clearly." She wets her lips casually and asks, "Do you have any other piercings?"

"Does it look like I have any others?" I ask.

She looks around my ears and then shakes her head. "No, I guess not."

Wiggling my eyebrows, I say, "Didn't look hard enough, Pips."

She offers me a confused look, but I don't get to elaborate, because Sanders gets on stage with a mic, and the room falls silent as they start clapping for him. I join in because you have to hand it to the man. If he's going to stand up there in front of a room of people while sporting a cutoff suit jacket, then he deserves some praise.

"Thank you," he says, offering the room a quick wave. "I hope everyone enjoyed their dinner. We're going to have plates cleared off soon, and then some gelato will be brought around, but in the meantime, let's give a warm welcome to you and the staff."

We all clap, and honestly, this whole thing is so fascinating to me. Clearly, I've never been married before, but what I can tell you from being here so far and from watching my parents' marriage is that people work at it. Coming to this camp, this is work, and look at them, they're excited about it. Makes you wonder how many people are like this out in the world.

The consensus I hear about a troubled marriage is that it ends in divorce. There isn't enough light shed on couples actually working through their troubles and rifts.

This situation might be weird with the moose antlers and lit-up golf cart, but at least there's a healthy commitment to connecting with your spouse.

"To those of you who have been here before, welcome back. And to our new couples, we welcome you with high fives and butt slaps."

The crowd laughs, and I find far too much joy in this, as opposed to Scottie, who, I see with one glance in her direction, is clearly trying her hardest to put on a smile and be happy about the fact that she's stuck in a room with a bunch of married couples. Makes me wonder, is there something she hasn't filled me in on? Is there a reason why being around all these married couples makes her stiff and uncomfortable?

"As we speak, staff are placing itineraries in your mailboxes that are just outside your cabins. You will receive one of these every day, the night before. Sometimes, they will just be a letter. Other times, they'll be a package with a challenge. It's our responsibility as your guides to give you the best experience with your spouse and to cater to the level of your commitment and comfort with each other. Some of you are coming back for a recharge. Some of you are here to have fun, generate a spark you might be missing. And some of you might be going through a more troubling time. Whatever brought you to Camp Haven, we want you to know we hope you find what you're looking for."

Inspiring.

If I was truly here to fix my marriage, I'd be ready to tackle the hard stuff.

Pumped.

Frothing to take charge and make up with my girl.

Possibly test out those cock rings…

"Your itinerary must be followed. I understand that you might feel like you want to be pulled in different directions while being here, but we have crafted these itineraries specifically to your situation. There isn't any wiggle room. We have a process. Please join us in that process so we can give you the best experience. And I hate to bring negativity into this welcome speech, but it must be announced that failure to follow the itinerary will result in a consequence."

Consequence, huh? Wonder what that could be. Maybe a spanking from our spouse? If that's the case, catch me being naughty on day one.

"As for your luggage, we did find some contraband in your bags. You received a note if something was taken. At the end of camp, you may receive your contraband back, but at a cost."

Seriously? Jesus.

Talk about a money grab.

Although Sanders must be doing something right, because all these couples are back here. Maybe they don't mind being price gouged. Personally, I feel slightly violated that my luggage was pawed through and my Nerds Clusters were confiscated.

Sigh. RIP, Nerds Clusters. RIP.

"Okay, enough with housekeeping, on to our welcome. As tradition, we like to welcome our couples to the stage to introduce themselves. I'll start with myself and my wife, Ellison. Sweetie, can you please come to the stage?"

The lights dim, and a faint sound of music plays in the background.

What is happening?

I glance over at Scottie, who looks positively horrified, her eyes searching for what's going to happen next.

The music grows louder and louder until I recognize it as the Bulls intro song, "Sirius." A smile parts my lips, and I lean back in my chair, ready for whatever they have planned, because this is good.

Fingers crossed. *Please let it be a choreographed dance.*

Lights flash onstage while two staffers walk up to Sanders, who is holding his arms out, and then at the same time, they tug on his clothes, pulling his outfit apart and revealing a black Bulls jersey. And then from the ground, a basketball appears, and he starts dribbling while a voice-over plays over the music.

"There is no *I* in team."

Scottie covers her mouth on a snort.

"There is no Michael without his Scottie."

I don't think I've ever smiled this large before.

"And there's no dynasty without teamwork."

The lights flash on, and out of nowhere, Ellison appears at Sanders's side, wearing a pair of black booty shorts and a cropped Bulls tank top. Both of them are wearing Air Jordans, both of them decked out in sweatbands. Honestly, this has got to be one of the best things I've ever seen.

I couldn't be happier about saying yes to this experience, because this is what I'm talking about. This is the kind of life I want to see with my own eyes—a couple dressed up as the '90s Bulls, acting like they're part of one of the greatest dynasties in sports history.

Someone tosses Sanders a mic. He catches it and then spins a basketball on his finger with the other hand while Ellison squats down and holds on to his leg.

"We are the Martins. Well into our fifties, married for thirty years, and still very much sexually thriving."

Yikes.

He hands Ellison the mic while he continues to spin his basketball.

"If our marriage has taught us one thing," she says, "it's that without effective communication or a game plan, we're not going to win the trophy."

Terrible sports analogy, but I'll let it pass because the lights and fog machines are doing it for me. Hell, when they first came out to the music, I got goose bumps.

"And without a trophy," she continues as she stands and butts her back up against Sanders's back, "how can we be the dynasty you look up to?"

Then at the same time, they both shoot their fists up to the sky and bow their heads, and the music and lights shut off.

Cheers erupt from the other couples as the lights start to illuminate the stage again. That's when I notice everyone standing, cheering them on.

Really, an ovation for that? I mean, it's not a Meryl Streep performance, but sure, why not stand? I rise with the rest of them and clap, causing Scottie to nearly fall out of her chair as she stands as well.

And I swear to you, as we stand there, clapping and clapping and fucking clapping, I realize one thing: this is seriously going to be the most interesting eight days of my entire life.

The sound of our shoes crunching against the dirt path is the only noise between the two of us as we make our way back to our cabin.

We left the dining hall in a state of shock. Can you blame us though? My mind is still reeling from the performance, and after they were done with the intro, they made us introduce ourselves—which made Scottie nearly dissolve onstage. Then they slid in a giant whiteboard, and like Phil Jackson in the early nineties, they mapped out the keys to a successful marriage.

It was entertaining.

Confusing.

Slightly inappropriate when Sanders made the *X* keep humping the *O* over and over again.

And then at the end, they made us all stand, put our hands in, and then shout "Camp Haven" together as a dismissal.

Now that we're walking back to our cabin, only the pathway lights illuminating the way, I can't quite get a gauge on how Scottie feels.

When we reach our cabin, I ask, "Should we check the mailbox?"

"Oh right, I almost forgot about that," she says, looking like she's in a daze. "Yeah, go ahead."

I open the mailbox and find a red envelope. Intrigued, I pull it out and study the front.

"Mr. and Mrs. Price." I smile at her. "I took your last name."

She rolls her eyes and snags the envelope from me. "Just open the cabin door."

Chuckling, I unlock the door, switch on the light, and walk in, only to come to a complete stop.

Scottie runs right into me, and I feel her bounce back as she says, "What are you doing?"

"Uh, someone's been in our room."

"What do you mean?"

I move to the side, and she steps in as well. I watch her take it in, eyes wide, mouth slightly ajar.

This is not how we left it.

The dresser is once again stocked full of lube, dildos, and cock rings. The erotic pictures that we took down are again hanging on the wall, and the handcuffs on the bed have been put back in place.

Holy shit.

I start laughing while Scottie scours the room with a look of disgust. "They can't be serious with this."

I shut the door behind me and take off my shoes.

"I mean, do they really think this is a relaxing aesthetic?" She gestures to a vibrator on the dresser. "This is intimidating."

"You say that as if you've never played around with toys."

She purses her lips and turns away.

"Wait," I say, walking up to her. "Is that true? Have you never played around with toys?"

"You know, it's getting late. I think we need to get to bed if we have any chance of being on top of our game tomorrow."

"Oh no, you don't," I say, tugging on her arm to turn her toward me. "You can't change the subject like that."

"I'm not changing the subject. I'm stating facts. We've had a long, confusing day full of erotic toys, face-planting, basketball analogies, and unnecessary twerking. I think it's best that we get some sleep so we're refreshed for the morning."

I run my hand over my jaw. "The twerking was weird."

"All of it was weird, Wilder," she says. "Every last bit of this is weird." She gestures around the room. "This room is weird. The people are weird. The theme of this entire camp is weird. It feels like we've dipped into a seventh circle of couples' hell on the verge of a basketball-themed orgy, and I'm just trying to keep my head afloat."

"Why?" I ask as I wiggle my eyebrows. "You don't want to become one of them?"

"I don't even know what that means, but no, I don't."

"Shame, as it seems like they have fun," I say as I pick up a vibrator, still in its packaging. "These are a real good time."

She lifts her chin. "Well, good for them." She clears her throat. "I'm going to take a shower, and then I plan on sleeping on the right side of the bed if that's okay with you."

"That's fine," I say. "Want me to put up a wall of pillows, you know, for your own personal space?"

She nods. "That would be appreciated."

Then she grabs some clothes and heads into the bathroom, shutting the door behind her.

I grin to myself while I grab some clothes of my own. I wish I had my phone, because I would be texting Derek all kinds of things right now. Instead, I sit down on the bed, lean back on my hands, and stare at the nipple picture on the wall.

It's a great nipple.

"Are you comfortable?" I ask Scottie as she shifts on the bed, tugging on the blankets.

"Yes, sorry. I think... I think the pillow barricade is a little much?"

I lift up so I can look over the stack of three pillows. "Really? I thought it was fortress-like. Would take a lot for one of us to cross the moat."

"Yes, very well built," she says. "But it's pulling on the blankets, and I don't want to be cold at night."

"Yeah, that makes sense. So do you want me to take down the pillows?"

"I think so, unless you want to keep them up."

"I'm chill. Whatever you want."

"I say we get rid of them."

"Okay." I start tearing down the wall until there is one left, a soft one that could easily be rolled over, but I keep it there so she at least feels safe. After all, she's sharing a bed with a stranger. I can't imagine that being comfortable for her. "That better?"

"I think so, as long as you're comfortable."

"I'm fine," I say and then lift up the red envelope that was in our mailbox. "Shall we read it?"

"God, I completely forgot about that. I was so distracted by the flesh poker in the shower that I bypassed the thought of us having a task tomorrow."

"The flesh poker?" I ask. "Is that what the youths are calling it?"

"Uh, you are the youth, so you tell me."

"So are you," I counter. "You're still under thirty."

"Yeah, but it doesn't feel like it," she says on a sigh. "Either way, I tried removing the flesh poker, because I couldn't stand it being so close to me when I was showering, but all I ended up doing was sliding my hands over the shaft, and, well...I swear it got harder."

I let out a whopper of a laugh, because I was not expecting her to say that at all.

"Stop it," she says, poking my arm. "It's not funny. I think it's real."

Tears come to my eyes as I keep laughing.

"Wilder, I'm serious."

I wipe at my eyes and shake my head. Once my laughter is under control, I say, "It's not real."

"How do you know? Did you touch it?"

"I mean, I swatted at it to see what kind of material they made it from, but if it was real, it wouldn't have enjoyed the swat. Also, it's not coming out of a wall. It's suction-cupped to tile. There's a difference."

"You say this as if you have experience."

I roll my eyes. "If it was real, it would be coming out of a hole, and someone would be standing on the other side. There was nothing real about it."

"It felt real, and to my dying day, I will swear that it grew in my hands."

"How long did you hold on to it?"

"Not that long."

"Seems like a decent amount of time. I mean, your shower was longer than expected."

"Stop that," she says while snagging the envelope from me. "You know I want nothing to do with all the erotica in here."

"Shame. You could have a lot of fun."

"We are not here for fun, Wilder. We are here to get a job done." She tears open the envelope and then pulls out the letter. Clearing her throat, she starts reading out loud. "'Mr. and Mrs. Price, you are expected in cabin ten, green square, tomorrow morning at eight. Breakfast will be provided to you via room service at seven thirty, so do not be late.'"

"That's it?" I ask.

She flips the paper over and confirms with a nod. "That's it."

"Hmm, I wonder what it's going to be."

Her lips twist to the side while she starts to think. It's kind of cute, the way that she gets lost deep in thought, as if no one else is around.

"Oh God." Her eyes widen.

"What?"

She turns toward me. "What if...what if all this sex stuff is a prelude to the activities we have to do? What if we have to perform our sex live?"

Expressionless, I say, "Do you really think that would happen?"

"I don't know, Wilder. Did you expect Sanders and Ellison to come out onstage and do what I can only describe as a terrible rendition of one of the choreographed songs from *High School Musical*?"

I snap my finger at her. "That's why it felt familiar. You know, I couldn't quite place it, but yes, it had a Vanessa Hudgens, Zac Efron spark to it."

"Seriously though, what if we have to have sex?"

"One, that's not going to happen. Two, it's illegal. Three, consent is a real thing. They can't force us to do anything."

"You don't know that," she says, looking panicked now, her eyes going wild. "We could have joined a commune and not realized it. I just signed the papers to attend. I didn't read the fine print. Did you read the fine print?"

"I had my lawyers read the fine print," I say as I toss the pillow that's between us and scoot closer so I can comfort her. I place my hand on the top of hers and rub her knuckles with my thumb. "I never sign anything without them looking at it. You have nothing to worry about."

"It didn't say anything about sex in there? Like...live sex or sex shows?"

"No." I chuckle. "There was nothing in there about sex."

"Okay." She blows out a heavy breath. "And you're sure? You're so sure that you would bet your life on it?"

"Yes," I answer. "Trust me when I say there are no sex shows at this—"

Ding.

"What was that?" she asks.

"I don't know," I say, glancing around.

Whispering, she says, "Do you think it's a camera? Maybe they have this place miked up. I don't think mics can pick up a lower register in the voice." She starts talking in a deep, husky tone. "We need to come up with our own language to bypass the spying."

"For the love of God," I say, getting out of bed. "They do not have the cabin miked up."

"You don't know that," she says, still in a deep voice. "This could be how they choose what we do every day. It could be how they knew we'd taken all the erotica merch down too. Quick, come over here, and act like we're doing it. Maybe they'll release us from this hellhole early because all our problems are solved." She slaps the wall but then shakes her hand and says, "Ouch."

"What are you doing?"

She picks up a Kama Sutra book that is on her nightstand and starts tapping it against the wall. "Oh...oh, Wilder," she says in a girly voice. "You big, big man. Look at that...at that slayer of yours. Enormous." She continues to tap the wall, replicating the sound of a steady headboard hitting the wall. "You're so...full of girth and ready to explode."

A cringe takes over my expression. "Jesus Christ, is that how you talk while having sex?"

She doesn't listen to me though. She keeps pounding. "Oh yes, right there. You're hitting the spot made by the gods."

"What does that even mean?"

"Look at my nipples. They're hard for your penis."

"That's a first."

"And oh wow, yeah, shimmy again for me."

I point at her. "I don't shimmy during sex. Only when I'm singing 'Luck Be a Lady.'"

"Yes, you wear those nipple tassels. Shake them, baby."

Okay, that's enough. I walk up to her, take the Kama Sutra, and toss it to the side. "Stop that. They don't have mics in here."

"Then what was that sound?" she asks. "We don't have cellular devices. They took them from us. There are electronics in here, and we need to sniff them out."

She flies out of bed and starts sniffing the air.

I rub my hand over my forehead and say, "What the fuck are you sniffing for?"

"Warmth."

Okay, seriously, Mika did not warn me about this. I know I said life experiences wanted, but having to calm down a paranoid woman because she's sniffing for "warmth" while looking for electronics—that's not what I had in mind.

Ding.

The sound fills the room, causing Scottie to stand upright in her matching pink pajama set. "Did you hear that?" She walks up to me and shows her arm. "Look, goose bumps. Someone is in here." She hurries over to the dresser, picks up the longest dildo from the minibar, and wields it like a sword before walking up behind me and gripping my shirt, using me as a human shield.

And then, in the creepiest voice I think I've ever heard, a voice that will haunt me in my dreams until the day I die, she says, "Come out, come out wherever you are. We're ready to play with you."

"What the fuck is wrong with you?" I shout and then shake her off me. "Jesus Christ, Scottie, it's probably just a smoke detector needing a new battery."

She lets that process for a second and then stands taller. "Huh, you know, I never thought about that."

"No, instead, you go right to trying to beat someone with a ten-pound dildo."

She crosses her arms at her chest and juts her hip out. "You know, must be nice walking around as a man, not a worry or care that something bad is going to happen to you." She jostles the dildo at me as she speaks. "We women have to be on guard at all times, so excuse me for covering all bases."

"You're not covering bases. You're going straight to insanity."

Ding.

She stiffens and then crouches around me again, holding out the dildo. Whispering in her lower register, she says, "That is not a smoke detector. That is an electronic device. I can sense it."

"Yeah, and I can sense that you're losing it."

"Can we please just look around?"

"Fine," I say, exasperated. Then together, we walk the perimeter of the cabin, her hiding behind me, holding the dildo out. What is she going to do? Penetrate someone to death with that thing?

We check under the bed, inside the closet, in the bathroom even though we already both took showers. She sneers at the flesh poker, and then we arrive back at the bed just as another ding goes off. This time, I hear it come from her nightstand.

"I think it's in your nightstand," I say.

"Really?" she asks, clawing at my shirt. "Well, go...go look."

I'm about to reach for the handle to pull it open, but she stops me.

"Wait, use this," she says, holding the dildo out to me.

"No."

"I'm serious," she says, stopping me from opening the drawer. "You might need to bludgeon something to death, whatever it is."

"I'm not going to bludgeon whatever is inside. Jesus."

I lean forward, grip the drawer pull, and feel her tense behind me as her free hand claws at my shirt. When I pull the drawer open, whatever is inside dings one more time.

Scottie screams bloody murder, scaring the ever-loving shit out of me while she tosses the dildo into the drawer and then takes off into the bathroom, where the door shuts and the lock clicks.

"You're on your own," she yells through the crack.

Wow.

What a wife.

Taking a calming breath in an effort to get my shit together, I look inside the drawer, where I find a tablet, plugged into an outlet in the drawer.

Jesus.

"Wh-what is it? Are you still alive? Did it eat you? Have you been stung? Do you need antivenom? If it's a snake, I'm crawling out of this small bathroom window, and I'm using the emergency phone to call Denise to rescue me." She pauses for a moment as I pull the tablet out. "Hello? You dead?"

The door clicks open, and I glance over my shoulder to see her peek her head out.

"Why aren't you answering me?"

"Because you're acting like a numbskull," I say. "It was a tablet beeping. It's a message to the both of us."

"A message?" She comes out of the bathroom and walks up next to me. "What is it?"

"I don't know." I tap on the button that says *Read message*. It blacks out for a moment, and then a screen pops up of a naked woman straddling a man on a bed.

"Dear God in heaven," she shouts and covers her eyes. "Is that porn?"

"Yeah, looks like it." I read the top of the screen. "Welcome to Camp Haven. Your Nightly Show is waiting for you."

She peeks from between her fingers. "You have to be kidding me. They send everyone porn at night?"

"Yup."

"Why on earth would they do that?"

"I don't know. Probably to upsell the minibar," I say while slipping the tablet back in the nightstand.

"What do you mean?"

"Well, if they are running their business the way I think they're running it, they probably send a video to couples every night, couples are curious and watch, the video probably has one of the toys or products on the dresser, the couple gets more curious, and before you know it, they're reenacting what they saw in the video. Great way to sell the lovemaking minibar."

"Wow." She shakes her head. "Is there not any decency in this world?

Whatever happened to helping couples find love again? Now it's all about product consumption. And the couples are falling for it. Just fools."

"Yeah, real fools. Pretty sure they're not the ones wielding a dildo out of fear that a beeping snake might attack them when they open their nightstand."

She stares at me, running her tongue over her teeth. "You know, your sarcasm is tiresome."

"Already?" I ask. "This is day one. We have a long way to go, Pips. Better get used to it." I flip the cover down on the bed and climb back in. "Now, hop in. We have a video to watch."

She scoffs. "If you think we're watching that together, you are sadly mistaken."

"Okay, if you want to watch it first, I can go hang out in the bathroom, and then we can rotate."

Her nostrils flare, and she turns away from me. "Good night, Wilder."

Smirking, I turn off the light and say, "Night, Pips."

CHAPTER TWELVE
SCOTTIE

I DID NOT SLEEP WELL; I kept worrying about keeping to my side of the bed. I wish I'd worn socks; I was freezing. And while I heard Wilder quietly sleeping, all I could think about was how many of the cabins' inhabitants were getting it on.

My guess was all of them besides ours.

No wonder the Brads and Chad like to revisit the camp often. It's like a kinky sex club in the woods. And here I thought it was going to be about bonding and therapy and trying to patch up my broken, nonexistent relationship.

Sure, I'm judging the camp based off one day and a cabin full of paraphernalia. We'll see what today brings, but if I had known, I would have cancelled and come up with a different solution, because this makes me embarrassingly uncomfortable.

And what makes it even more uncomfortable is that it seems to me that Wilder is loving every second of this.

With the video, he didn't even scoff. I think if I said we were going to watch it, he'd be all about it. He laughs about the fleshy poker in the shower. I've seen him perusing the overpriced lovemaking minibar. I even caught him staring at the nipple picture, as if he was trying to come up with a backstory for it.

Which leads me to believe that he's very confident in his sexuality—something I wish I was.

I found out quickly with Matt that I was not comfortable in my own skin.

And I know it wasn't his responsibility to boost my ego, but I wish he would've at least once looked at me like he wanted to devour me. I wish he had given me a touch of confidence in the bedroom when I took my clothes off with just one hungry look or nod of approval.

But there was nothing.

He was more interested in his own pleasure than mine.

And once he found completion, that was about it. It got to the point where I wasn't really trying anymore. I was just doing what I needed to do, and then I could get on with my night. I know it was one of the reasons why we disconnected. I tried talking to him about it once, even suggested trying something new, like toys, and he scoffed at the idea. I felt so humiliated, as if it was wrong to ask for more sexually. It drove home this insecurity that my sexual needs simply don't matter and at the core of it all, I just wasn't good enough. And that's a hard perception to shut down.

So being immersed in a situation where sensuality and sexuality— which I have no experience with—are at the forefront of conversation makes my skin itch, especially since my fake husband seems to be very well versed in the matter.

"Ready?" Wilder says, knocking me out of my thoughts.

"Yeah," I say as I down the rest of my orange juice and then dab my mouth with my napkin. Breakfast was delivered right on time, an assortment of pastries, coffee, tea, and yogurt parfaits. For a summer camp, it was pretty fancy. I was expecting pancakes and a vat of scrambled eggs to be cooked on a flat-top grill, only to be divvied out by the scoopful. But our tray was beautifully decorated with cloth napkins and a daisy in a vase and set in cotillion style.

Fancy.

"That apple Danish was really good," he says as he opens the door to our cabin for us, the humid summer air already penetrating my skin.

"Yeah, I liked the cheese one. Kind of hope that's something we get every day."

"Hey, I was thinking the same thing." He bumps my shoulder with his. "Look at us being friends."

"Friends? I think that's pushing it."

"We shared a bed last night, Scottie. I think that makes us at least friends."

"No, I think that makes you lucky."

He gasps. "Holy shit, did you just make a joke?" He tugs on his ear. "Did I hear that right?"

"Can you not, please?" I try to hold back my smirk.

"I'm sorry, you just caught me off guard. I wasn't expecting you to come out like that, acting all funny after a long night of you clinging to the edge of your bed, trying to stay as far away from me as possible."

"I was not clinging to the side."

"Scottie"—he gives me a look that says he knows better—"if you had levitation capabilities, I'm pretty sure you would have levitated next to the bed instead."

"Well, excuse me for wanting to give you space."

"You could have slept in my armpit, and I wouldn't have cared," he says.

"Oh, is that right? Well, I guess I'll consider that for tonight."

He chuckles. "Glad to hear it. Just don't move a lot. I'm ticklish."

As we approach the cabin, I say, "Okay, time to focus. Remember where we are at in our relationship at the moment."

"Dramatically trying to find our way back to each other," he answers.

"I don't know why you used the term 'dramatically,' but yes, we're not happy with each other. This is our low point, and from here, we climb."

"Right." He rubs his hands together. "This is what I've been waiting for."

We reach the cabin, and I stop him. "What are you talking about? Do not go off script."

"There is no script," he counters.

"I mean, stick to what we know. Don't start rambling on about things that you just decide to make up."

"But that's what improv is all about."

I grip his shoulders and look him in the eyes. "Stay focused, Wilder. Please, for the love of God, stay focused."

"I'm focused, dear."

"Promise me." I point at him.

"Promise," he says with a smirk just as the cabin door opens and I spot Sanders.

Showtime.

Smiling, I turn toward him and say, "Morning."

Standing in a pair of flannel pajama pants and a Jets shirt, he says, "Morning. Everything okay?"

"Yes," I answer in a cheery voice, probably overplaying it a bit too much. "Just checking to make sure I don't have anything in my teeth. Breakfast was delicious, by the way." I turn to Wilder. "Everything, uh, good?" I flash him my teeth.

He squats down, playing the part, and takes a gander. But then to my horror, he tilts my head back farther, peels my lip up, and really gives them a good examination.

When he's done, he sets me up straight and then says, "Clean, babe."

I straighten out my shirt and try to telepathically warn him that such nonsense is not necessary.

"Well, if we're all set, shall we?" Sanders gestures to the inside of the cabin.

In a cheery, nonplussed voice, Wilder says, "I think we shall." And then we walk up toward the door, and as we pass Sanders, Wilder offers him a fist bump. "That Danish was fire."

"What flavor did you have?"

"Apple," Wilder answers.

"Wait until tomorrow when they bring out the cherry. Your life will be changed."

Wilder rubs his stomach. "I look forward to it."

Ignoring them, I make my way inside the cabin and then take a look around to get familiar with my surroundings. All I can say is... wow.

I'm stunned.

After seeing Sanders's office in New York and the basketball presentation last night, I half expected to bear witness to an agglomeration of sports memorabilia with a roomful of trophies, basketball hoops as seats, and bleachers as a couch.

But this cabin...it's...it's normal.

There's a comfortable-looking couch off to the left, a wingback chair to the right with an oak coffee table in between. A blue area rug breaks up all the wood and coincides with the blue checkered curtains that hang over the window. A small fridge is near the door, and a balcony in the back offers a view of the lake.

Very, very normal.

It almost makes me feel uneasy.

"Welcome to the office."

"This is your office?" Wilder asks, taking it in as well. "I wouldn't have guessed that."

"Well, it's not as fun to be in as my other one in the city, but I tend to not want to have distractions when we're in this room. The conversations we share in here are more intimate, tougher. Couples need a space to be our honest selves, and I find with minimal decorating, we can have those honest conversations."

"Makes sense," Wilder says.

"Please, take a seat on the couch."

Wilder and I both take a seat and get comfortable. Wilder drapes his arm over the back of the couch, while I cross one of my legs over the other.

When we're situated, Sanders sits himself in the chair across from us and then leans forward.

"How are you feeling so far?"

Well, here we go, a true and honest therapy session.

"Great," I say with a smile. "Really great. It's been a fun experience so far, and the cabin—"

"Why are you lying?" Wilder asks, surprising me.

"Wh-what?" I ask, talking through my smile as I turn to face him. I attempt to speak through my eyes, saying, *What the hell are you doing right now? Remember what we talked about?*

"Why are you lying to him right now?" Wilder gestures toward Sanders. "Everything is not great."

"I was just—"

"No, enough with the lies," Wilder says in a frustrated tone, jumping right into conflict. I'm…I'm not prepared. "We're here to fix things, so let's be honest with ourselves and with Sanders."

"Thank you," Sanders says while clapping. Oh brother. "I know that must have been hard on you, Wilder, but I appreciate the honesty."

No, not this again.

Not this bromance in a therapy session all over again.

I don't think I could take it.

"Well, if we're going to do this, then we need to do it right," Wilder says, a challenge in his eyes.

And I can see it, that spark, that intrigue. For him, this is fun. This is what he's looking for in his life. And if that's what he wants, then fine… I can play this game too. I don't have to sit back and be embarrassed. If he wants to have a life experience, then by all means, Wilder, let's play.

"He's right." I lean back on the couch and relax my body, shaking my limbs out. "I'm sorry. I was trying to put on a good face, but he's very, very right. I'm lying. Nothing is great about being here, other than the cheese Danish I had this morning."

"And why is it not great?" Sanders asks, not a ball in sight, no hockey stick to be seen. And apart from the pajama pants, *this* feels like we're seeing the true therapist, which seems odd. Don't you think you'd want to show this side of yourself on the first therapy appointment? Or is that just me?

Then again, nothing about his practice is conventional, so not surprised that he's switching tactics.

"Well, you know, we're in a rough patch right now, and staying in the cabin that we're staying in is just a reminder of everything we're not… participating in."

Sanders nods knowingly. "I see. You're in the red square cabin, correct?"

"Yes," I answer.

"That's the one you chose."

Um, what?

"Chose?" I ask.

"Yes," Sanders says, looking confused. "It was the one chosen in your application."

Wilder filled out the application.

"Are there different cabins?" I ask.

"Oh yes, they're all themed to the couples' preferences. On the application, when asked about your sex life, you marked 'thriving' and 'adventurous,' so the staff thought it was appropriate to put you in the red square cabin."

I shoot a look at Wilder, who has a guilty expression. Smiling, I say, "Um, Sanders. Would I be able to have one moment alone with my husband?"

He looks between us and says, "Normally, I'd say whatever you need to say to each other should be said in front of me, but I can see that maybe something needs to be discussed here without a witness, and because of the fragility of your marriage, I think I'm going to give you a quick five." He walks out on the balcony and shuts the sliding glass door.

I turn to Wilder, and in a scary whisper, I say, "You said our sex life was thriving and adventurous?"

He starts chuckling, his smile stretching across his cheeks. "Holy shit, is that why they put us in that bedroom?"

"Uh, duh, you idiot! The reason handcuffs kept rattling against the bedpost last night was because of you."

"You know, that's really funny actually. Makes me wonder what the other cabins are like."

"Probably normal. They probably don't have a giant flesh dildo attached to the tile of their shower." I press my hand to my forehead. "Oh God, what my coworkers must think of me. They must have noticed we were in that cabin and said—"

"Scottie must have such an active sex life."

"Noooo," I drag out. "They probably thought I was a sex fiend and that's why our marriage wasn't working, because I wanted to be surrounded by plastic, jiggly prosthetics rather than the jiggly shaft in my husband's pants."

He chuckles some more. "I mean, that looks worse for me than you."

"This is not funny, Wilder. This is exactly what I'm talking about. We need to keep it tight. We can't just be flailing about, thinking there are no consequences to what we say and do."

"In my defense, when I filled out the application, I wasn't aware that there were themed cabins. This just happens to be a unique coincidence. And I did mention in that first meeting with Sanders that we were pretty kinky."

"Yeah, a unique one I want nothing to do with." I catch Sanders turning toward the door and offering me a thumbs-up, looking to see if we're ready. I hold out a finger, asking for one more minute. "Remember what we talked about, okay? Be cool. This is no time to go off the rails with your improv. I saw that look in your eye."

"What look?" he asks.

"The one that said 'we're about to have fun with this.'"

"Yeah, I don't think that's a look I have," he counters.

"Oh, you do. I saw it. Clear as day."

"I think you're making things up in your head."

"I am not," I shoot back.

"You are."

"Wilder." I sit taller, growing frustrated with him. "I am—"

"I see that you're arguing," Sanders says, coming into the room. "And I know you asked for privacy, but I think that it's important I'm a part of these conversations. So"—he takes a seat in his chair—"please, tell me what you're arguing about."

I glance over at Wilder, panic filling me, but of course, he apparently has no sense of anxiety, because he crosses one leg over the other and casually says, "She hates our cabin, and she's mad at me for filling out the application incorrectly."

Okay, well, that's a truthful answer.

"I see," Sanders says and then reaches into his seat cushion and pulls out a baseball.

Ahh, there we are.

He tosses it in his hand and says, "Why did you lie on the application?"

"Simple," Wilder says flippantly. "I filled it out to inspire us, to remind us of the couple we used to be."

How this man can just lie so casually is fascinating and scary at the same time. It makes me wonder why I'm trusting him to go through this journey with me.

Yet here I am, going along with it.

Sanders turns to me and says, "What does he mean by that?"

Christ.

Swallowing the saliva that has built up in my mouth, I say, "Uh, we used to be, uh, hot and heavy, in the bedroom."

"I see," Sanders says and then tilts his head to the side. "Does that make you uncomfortable, saying that?"

This entire situation makes me uncomfortable.

Everything about it.

From the camp.

To the lies.

To the fleshy sword in the shower.

"Yes," I answer. "I'm not proud of the fact that our love life isn't what it used to be."

"And what did it used to be?" Sanders asks.

I'm about to answer when Wilder steps in. "Wild. Out of control. Couldn't get her off me even if I wanted to. Addicted to my penis."

My cheeks flush, and I grind my teeth together, attempting to remain calm.

A simple "active" would have sufficed.

"Addicted to your penis seems a little much," I say, clearing my throat to avoid showing how much I want to shove my foot in Wilder's mouth.

"Says the girl who made a mold of my penis so she could have it when I was gone on work trips."

My lips purse, and my jaw tenses.

He turns to Sanders and says, "She uses it when I'm gone. Used to send me pics of her using it."

This motherfucker!

"Yeah, well, I got the idea from him, as he needed a mold of my breasts because he wanted to make a pillow to sleep on when he was away."

Sanders looks over at Wilder, who raises his hand and says, "Guilty. She has great tits."

God, does nothing faze him?

"Were you offended by the breast pillow?" Sanders asks me as he tosses the ball in his hand back and forth.

"I was offended when he pierced it," I say, folding my arms across my chest. "He's been begging me to get my nipples pierced, and it's just not for me, so when he pierced the breast pillow, it was like a slap to the face."

Ha, take that, you fuck.

Wilder turns toward me and says in a reserved tone, "You said on our honeymoon that you'd get them pierced after I got my dick pierced for you." He wets his lips. "So you can just use my dick piercing for your personal pleasure, but I can't even get one goddamn nipple?"

The challenge in his eyes spurs something inside me, and before I can stop myself, I yell, "I told you my nipples are too small for it, yet you consistently make me feel bad over and over again about not piercing them."

"The guy at the shop said he could do smaller barbells." Wilder's voice raises.

"At a higher expense," I shout back.

Wilder's face contorts into pure anger. "And I told you, I don't care about the expense. There's no price I wouldn't pay for you to have that experience."

Sanders holds up his hand. "Okay, we're going to pause right here." He lets out a deep breath. "I see there's a lot of deep-seated animosity between the two of you, and that's what today is about. Today's about getting it all out there, not holding back anything that might be sitting on your chest. So I'd like you to get comfortable, because we're about to get down to the nitty-gritty."

I glance over at Wilder, facing off. Seems like he has no intention of keeping this tight and pulled together. So I slip my shoes off my feet, turn toward him completely, and sit cross-legged.

Let the games begin.

———

"It started when he stepped on Velcro," I say.

"They were brand-new, expensive socks," Wilder snaps. "The Velcro was going to tear them apart, and then what, I'm just going to flush fifteen dollars down the drain?"

"Maybe don't buy the expensive socks," I counter.

"Says the girl who has caveman feet. You know my feet are sensitive. You know if my socks touch me in a weird way, I can't walk properly. That's how I ended up with that lopsided gait."

"You ended up with that lopsided gait because there was a rock in your shoe."

"There was not a rock in my shoe. Stop saying that. You make me sound like a crazy man."

"Because you are," I shout. "You're crazy. You ruined an entire day at the pumpkin farm because you stepped on Velcro. Velcro, Wilder! Who ruins a day over Velcro?"

"The people whose socks get destroyed from it!"

"You should have seen her," Wilder says as he walks back and forth in front of the sliding glass window, tossing Sanders's baseball. "The look of utter satisfaction on her face as I rummaged and rummaged and rummaged, looking for the lid. Sitting there, on her high perch, looking down at me as if I was her Tupperware peasant, and the entire time, she knew there was no matching lid. Fucking knew the whole time."

I shrug my shoulders. "I told him he needed to organize the drawers. He needed to learn a lesson."

"You got rid of it on purpose." He points at me. "Vindictive, that's what you are."

"Lazy." I point back at him. "Utterly lazy. You can't do one thing when asked."

"Oh really?" he says, stepping up. "So when you asked me to pick you up pads with wings, did I not deliver?"

My face falls flat. "You came back with pads...and buffalo wings."

"That's what you said, pads with wings." He turns to Sanders, whose eyes are bouncing back and forth between the two of us. "She said pads with wings! What the hell am I supposed to assume?"

"If you knew me, like you claim you do, you'd have known that I was talking about the type of pads that have wings attached to them."

"How am I supposed to know that when you won't even talk to me about your period? I don't know what you've got going on down there. And it's not from a lack of effort on my end. I've asked to help."

"You've asked to insert my tampon," I deadpan.

He throws his hands up in the air. "I was curious. It was for science!"

"Don't you dare say it," Wilder says, shaking his head. "Don't you fucking dare."

I run my tongue over my teeth and very slowly and deliberately say, "Bologna."

His nostrils flare.

His chest heaves.

And in a very maniacal voice, his eyes boring holes into me, he says, "You son of a bitch."

"I think we should all take a moment to remember the breathing exercises we learned a few seconds ago," Sanders says.

But Wilder holds his hand out to him. "You stay out of this." Then he gets close to me and whispers, "Say it again. I dare you."

Wetting my lips, I lean even closer and whisper, "Bologna."

"You...strumpet."

"Bologna, bologna, bologna."

"No!" he screeches, holding his hands to his ears. "Don't you dare Beetlejuice me. Don't you fucking dare." He glances over his back, checking around the room. "Is it here? Is he here?"

I point off to the window and yell, "There he is."

Wilder lets out an ear-splitting scream and then falls to the ground and shimmies under the coffee table. "You devil woman."

"Is that a hint of horseradish I'm detecting?" Wilder asks as we chow down on our lunch.

"A homemade sauce," Sanders says with a nod.

"Really brings out the roast beef flavor, don't you think, Pips?"

"Delightful." I lift my bag of chips to Wilder. "Barbecue?"

"Yeah, thanks, babe."

———————

"Do you see what I'm dealing with?" I say as I walk around the room, a hockey stick up against my shoulder like a bayonet while Wilder lies across the couch, tossing the baseball up and down.

"So I have to take interest in her love of cacti, but she can't bother to learn the correct Pokémon names?" He sits up. "It's Jigglypuff. For fuck's sake, it's Jigglypuff!"

"No...one...cares."

"Everyone cares," he shouts, his voice cracking.

———————

"You should see it," I say. "He stands there, tilting his head back, gargling and gargling and gargling, only to throw his head forward and spit the mouthwash all over the mirror. It's absurd. Where's the accuracy?"

"I asked you to help me," Wilder counters. "Since you're so good at spitting, I thought I would get help from a professional..."

"Is that a jab at me?"

"What do you think? Wouldn't hurt you to swallow once in a while."

"Swallow your mouthwash, and I'll swallow you," I say.

"Gladly. I'll gladly swallow my mouthwash if that means you'll accept my seed."

"Don't call it that," I yell. "You wonder why our sex life is the way that it is. You're over there wielding your willy around, asking me to swallow your seed."

"Wielding my pierced willy. Don't forget that."

"You…mother…fucker," I say, standing. "You're really going to bring it back to that?"

He stands as well. "Just get them pierced like you said you would. Just…get…them…pierced."

I move in close, going nose to nose with him. "Over my dead body."

Spinning away, he screams, "Outrageous," and then falls to his knees and buries his head in his hands.

"Well," Sanders says, his hands clasped in front of him, his hair pulled in all different directions. He clears his throat. "That was…productive."

Wilder and I are sitting on opposite ends of the couch with our arms crossed, both breathing heavily.

"You know"—Sanders scratches the side of his head—"I think I'm going to need a second to process this. So why don't you, uh, why don't you two head back to your cabin and maybe just…relax for a moment?" He lets out a heavy breath. "I'll, uh, I'll be in touch."

"Thank you," Wilder says while he stands. "We appreciate you listening to us."

"Yes, that's, uh, that's my job." Sanders blinks a few times and stares down at the floor. "Feel free to see yourselves out."

With Wilder behind me, we head out of the cabin, shutting the door behind us. Without a word, we walk toward our cabin as anger thrums through me.

Once we reach the cabin, Wilder unlocks the door and opens it wide for me. The door shuts behind Wilder, and I spin on him.

"That was incredible," he shouts, a huge smile on his face. "I've never felt more alive."

Staring him down, I ask, "Have you lost your goddamn mind?"

"What?" he asks, looking genuinely surprised. "Lost my mind?

Scottie, that was…that was unmatched. I've never in my life sparred like that. You just kept going with it, over and over again."

"Because you were forcing me to act like a lunatic!" I shout. "Oh my God, Wilder. We broke him. We actually broke Sanders. I said to keep it tight."

"We did. We didn't balk once. And the way we fucking ended it, tying it back into the pierced nipples…you realize it takes comedians years to learn how to do that in their stand-up shows, to bring everything full circle to the initial joke. That's a special talent, and we did it, on the fly, without even communicating with each other. Fuck." He holds his arm out to me. "Look, goose bumps."

Goose bumps?

He has goose bumps.

Is he really that dense?

"Wilder," I snap. "That was not how it was supposed to go."

"No, it went even better." He takes his shoes off and then flops back on the bed, the shake of the mattress causing the handcuffs to clatter against the poles. "I've never felt so alive."

"Are you really not going to acknowledge how badly you incriminated me back there? The basis of our marriage problems revolves around pierced nipples, Wilder. Pierced nipples!"

"A problem he's probably never heard before."

"Because it's a problem that doesn't break up a marriage," I shout and start pacing. "God, I never should have gone through with this. I never should have thought this was a good idea. Now my boss's husband thinks I'm a prude with small nipples and that my husband is a Velcro-hating, pierced sex fiend with a fetish."

"I mean, the pierced thing is accurate."

I pause my pacing and glance over at him, only to catch him wiggle his brows.

"Are you…are you really pierced?"

"You tell me."

I shake my head. "We're getting off topic. This was bad. This was really bad."

"This was good, Pips," he says and sits up. "I was really impressed with you. The number of things that you kept coming up with, things that bothered you... I was seriously frothing at the mouth, waiting for your next complaint. I loved it. You exceeded my expectations. It's almost like you've done this before."

That causes me to pause, because...I have done this before.

I've been through this.

I've experienced this anger.

The yelling.

The wedge placed in the middle of the marriage, constantly being hammered in with every little, pesky fight.

Did I just spend the entire day airing out my grievances from my previous marriage?

I try to think back to what I said, but it all feels like a distant memory now.

"Hey," Wilder says, his voice growing concerned. "Everything okay?"

But I ignore him as I take a seat in the chair in the corner, slowly beginning to consider my time with Matt.

How he never did anything I asked him to do.

How he complained about buying my feminine products because he believed it was embarrassing.

He never attempted to show interest in what I thought was fascinating.

He never took the blame, never participated in our marriage, and never helped out around the house.

"God, Scottie. Everything is always about you. Nothing is ever good enough for you, no matter what I do, say, or think. I have no idea why I ever wanted to marry you."

Everything I complained about during that session with Sanders, every little thing, pertained to Matt. *God. Will I ever be free of the pain that man caused?*

"Scottie?" Wilder asks, concern heavy in his voice.

"I...I need to go."

Before he can stop me, I leave the cabin and go for a walk.

CHAPTER THIRTEEN
WILDER

"HEY," I SAY TO ONE of the staff in the main building. "Uh, could I possibly use the pay phone? I want to check on my brother."

"What's your name?" the staff member asks.

"Wilder Price," I say, using my wife's name.

She checks her books and then nods while reaching into a container full of quarters. "You have ten minutes."

I take the quarter from her, thank her, and then head into the UK-style pay phone that's off in the corner. I shut the door behind me, pick up the receiver, drop in the change, and then dial Mika's phone number.

I turn toward the main building so I can see if anyone walks up behind me and wait as the phone rings.

I'm hoping that Mika answers; he shouldn't be at the bar just yet.

After a few rings, the phone picks up, and I hear, "Hello?"

"Mika, it's me."

"Oh, hey. I'm glad you told me about the weird phone number that might call, because normally I wouldn't answer."

"Yeah, they took our phones. How are you? Feeling good?"

"Feeling good," he answers, a hint of something in his voice.

"You sure?" I ask. "You sound a little off."

"Yeah, nothing like what you're thinking."

"What's going on?" I know I have ten minutes, but my brother will always come first before what I'm going through.

"Do you really want to know?" he asks.

"You know I always want to know."

"Digestive issues."

"Oh." Relief washes through me. "Uh, sorry to hear that."

"Yeah, me too."

"Other than that, everything else good?"

"Yeah, man. Thank you for checking on me. How is everything over there?"

I tug on my hair as I say, "Well, I thought it was going okay. We had a session with the therapist today, and what I thought was really good banter back and forth actually turned into so much more."

"What do you mean, so much more? Like...did you guys kiss or something?"

"What? No." I let out a sigh. "Listen, I have to make this quick, because I only have ten minutes, but after our session, we went back to our cabin. I thought we'd nailed it, you know, convincing the therapist that we had a lot of issues, and when I started talking to Scottie about it, she withdrew, which made it seem like she'd experienced the things we were complaining about. I know you probably want to keep your relationship with her confidential, but...did she go through a bad breakup or something? That was the kind of impression I got."

He's silent for a moment. "She didn't tell you?"

"Didn't tell me what?" I ask.

He sighs and then says, "She's divorced, man."

"Wait, what?" I stand taller. "Divorced?"

"Yeah. That's what brought her back to New York City. She met him in college, got married young, and then a few months ago, the divorce was final. She was in Ohio but came back here to make something of herself, to start a new chapter."

"Fuck, really?" I drag my hand over my face, guilt consuming me, because here I thought we were just having fun. I had no idea that she was pulling from experience. "I–I had no idea."

"I'm surprised she didn't tell you. She didn't mention it at all?"

"No, this is the first I'm hearing of it. Why didn't you tell me?"

"I thought she would have told you when you first met. But yeah, if you guys were going at it today, she probably had flashbacks. She and Matt, they weren't...well, they weren't connected in the end. A lot of fighting. A lot of distrust. A lot of anger."

"What happened?" I ask.

"That's not my story to tell," Mika answers. "But I will say this. She might act like she's tough, but I know deep down, she's still hurting. Being at this camp, around married couples, acting like her marriage is failing, it can't be easy on her."

"Shit," I say, rubbing my palm over my eye. "Okay, I, uh, I need to go find her."

"Hey, Wilder," Mika says before I can hang up.

"Yeah?"

"Be careful with her, okay? She needs a good guy on her side."

"You don't have to say it twice," I answer. "Love you, Mika."

"Love you, Wilder."

I hang up the phone and head out of the booth with one thing on my mind: finding Scottie.

The day has gotten away from me. After hours upon hours in a therapy session, we are now closing in on dinner time as I walk around camp looking for Scottie, trying to act casual, like I'm just walking off the intense session I had with my wife, even though deep down inside, I'm desperate to find Scottie.

I feel like such a jackass. I was simply trying to play along with her energy, but she was hurting, projecting, and now she's struggling with whatever is going on in her head.

It's why I need to find her. I don't want her alone right now.

"Looking for the wife?" I turn to the right to find—I want to say Chad—sitting on a bench eating an ice cream sandwich that looks fucking delicious. One of those Chipwich things.

"Yeah, have you seen her?"

"Surprised you don't know where she is."

What is this guy's problem?

"We decided to take a break from an intense therapy session," I answer.

He slowly nods, almost as if he doesn't believe me. "Intense, huh?"

Eyeing him, I answer, "Yeah. Intense."

"Well." He takes a bite of his ice cream sandwich. "Good luck with finding her." Then he leans back on the bench and crosses one leg over the other.

Fucking weirdo.

Ignoring him, I scour the camp for Scottie, searching until I spot her sitting on a bench under a large oak tree, looking out toward the lake that borders the property. Her legs are tucked into her chest, and her arms are wrapped around her shins, squeezing them in tight.

I approach slowly, not wanting to scare her away or cause a scene.

When I step on a branch, she turns her head, and that's when I see her tear-soaked face. She quickly wipes at it, but it's too late. I've already seen it.

Fuck, I made her cry.

My stomach twists in knots as I close the distance between us. When I reach her, I ask, "Can I sit down with you?"

She shrugs, trying to be nonchalant. "Do whatever you want."

I'll take that as an invitation to join her.

I move around the bench and take a seat next to her, keeping a few inches between us. Leaning forward, my forearms on my thighs, I stare out at the lake as well.

After a few seconds of silence, I say, "I talked to Mika." I glance over at her, but she doesn't say anything, so I keep going. "Was calling to check on him. He's doing well, but, uh, he told me something about you—"

"We don't need to talk about this," she says.

"Scottie," I say softly, turning toward her. "Why didn't you tell me you were divorced?"

She shakes her head. "Please, Wilder. It doesn't matter."

But it does.

It clearly does.

I can see it in her defeated shoulders.

I can hear it in her heartbroken voice.

But I don't want to push her. She's already been pushed enough today, so instead, I'm just going to be here for her. I drape my arm along the back of the bench and scoot an inch or so closer to her, letting her know that I'm here for her.

And then we sit and stare out at the lake together, letting the sound of nature fill the silence between us.

The lake ripples at the shore while a bird sounds off in the distance, and the sun slowly starts descending behind the tall pine and oak trees, still providing a lot of sunlight. Off to the left, some of the couples are moving toward the dining hall, their laughter in the far distance, but Scottie just keeps her head forward, her chin now resting on her knees.

Taking a chance, I scoot closer and place my hand on her back. When she doesn't shake me off, I give her a gentle rub.

From the corner of my eye, I catch her lip start to tremble, and then after a few more seconds, a tear falls down her cheek.

I can't let her just sit there and cry in silence, so I say, "Scottie, come here."

Ready for her to push me away, I brace for her response, but when she leans into me instead, I wrap my arm around her shoulder and let her lean on my chest.

She shakes under my grasp as she cries into my shoulder.

And I don't bother saying anything, because what is there really to say? Instead, I hold her. I hold her as the sun dips behind the trees.

And I hold her while the lights around the camp begin to turn on.

I hold her until there are no more tears left for her to shed. I hate that I misunderstood her today. I hate that she's experienced so much pain that she needed all this time to vent and feel. *I hate that she's hurting.*

Mika said she needs a nice guy. Well, I'm going to make sure I'm that guy for her.

Scottie walks out of the bathroom in a matching green spandex short and shirt set, her hair wrapped up in a towel and her lotion in hand.

When she spots me sitting in the chair under the nipple picture, she offers me a soft smile.

"I grabbed a quick snack for you and a water," I say, pointing to the table. "I thought you might want to eat something in case dinner comes with a sideshow again."

"Thank you," she says softly as she moves to the seat next to mine. She sets her lotion on the table and then turns toward me.

When she looks up, her walls seem lowered, like she's allowing herself to be vulnerable—it's the first time I've seen that—and she's exposed rather than guarded.

"Um, I just want to, uh, I want to apologize about earlier."

"Apologize for what?" I ask her.

Her eyes meet mine, her blue to my gray, and she says, "About, um, about crying by the lake."

"Why the hell are you apologizing for that?"

"Because," she says, raising her chin. "This is…this is a mutual relationship where we are trying to—"

"I'm sorry, Scottie, but I'm going to cut off whatever you're about to say, because I'm telling you right now, I'm not going to agree with it." I turn toward her and say, "You don't need to put on a brave face for me. You don't need to act like everything is okay. You don't need to act like you don't have feelings or emotions. Hell, you don't need to cry by yourself. I'm here for you. Do you understand that? For you, Scottie. No one else. I'm at this camp, in this cabin, for you. I'm here for no other reason. So you can try to act like this is all business, but I refuse to let you go through what's clouding your mind by yourself."

She shakes her head. "Wilder, you don't have to do that. I'm Mika's friend—"

"Which means, by extension, you're my friend."

She exhales, and I can see her wanting to push me away, but I'm not going to let her. "Please, I don't want you thinking you need to treat me differently."

"Treat you differently. How the hell would I treat you differently?"

Her eyes meet mine. "Pity, Wilder. I don't want your pity."

"Good, because I'm not offering pity. But I am offering understanding. I'm offering a shoulder to cry on when you need it. I'm offering a listening ear. I'm offering you an opportunity for escapism. I'm offering a reliable friendship."

Her lips tilt to the side, and she looks away, not saying a damn thing until she sucks in a deep breath and then mouths, "Damn it," as she starts to cry again.

She dabs at her eyes with the back of her hand, clearly not wanting me to see her cry. But I don't give a shit. I take her hand in mine, tugging her closer to me, and wrap my arm around her shoulders, bringing her into my side.

And we stay like that for I don't know how long, her quietly crying and me holding on to her, making sure she knows she's not alone.

I've never been through a hard breakup, or a divorce for that matter, but I've seen the toll it takes on a human when they see their loved one slowly slip away. I watched my mom go through it with my dad. Sure, it wasn't a divorce, but as my dad became weaker, I saw the light dim in my mom's eyes. I saw her come to the realization that the man she once loved, the man she married, was no longer the same person. And just like I was there for my mom, I'll be there for Scottie.

"You okay?" I ask after a few minutes.

"No," she says, answering honestly, giving me hope that she's going to open up.

"Want to talk about it?"

"Not really," she says.

"I understand." I clear my throat. "But I do want to apologize about today. I thought I was feeding off your energy, trying to show Sanders that we're a couple in trouble. If I'd known about the divorce, I wouldn't have—"

"Please don't apologize," she says, shaking her head. "You didn't know. There's nothing to apologize about. We actually did a good job convincing him. Maybe too good of a job." She lets out a breath and then lifts her head up. "I think the piercings really threw him for a loop." She chuckles, which gives me hope.

"I'm pretty sure it's the first time he's ever seen a couple fight about that."

"There's no doubt in my mind," she replies.

"And I know I said it before, but I really want to reiterate—us bringing it full circle at the end with the piercings, that was poetic."

She shakes her head in mirth. "I've found that I don't want to play into your ridiculousness, but I'll admit, that was a nice touch at the end."

I chuckle. "See! Isn't improv fun?"

"No. It's stressful, and I don't want to be a part of it anymore."

"Well, it seems like we have a hole we have to dig ourselves out of for the next seven days."

"Yeah. Any ideas on how to do that?"

"No clue."

She nods. "Perfect. Glad we're being smart about this."

———————

"Ready for dinner?" I ask Scottie, who just slipped her shoes on.

"Yeah." She stands and presses down her shirt. "Can you tell I've been crying?"

I shake my head. "Not even a little."

"You sure?"

"I wouldn't lie to you," I say. "About anything." I look her in the eyes, but she quickly diverts her gaze as if she can't stand to make eye contact with me. Not wanting her to brush off my comment, because I need her to know this about me, I close the space between us and then press my finger under her chin, lifting her gaze to meet mine. "I'm serious, Scottie. I won't lie to you. Okay?"

"O-okay," she says.

I release her and then stick my hands in my pockets. "And, you know, if you want to tell your husband that you don't plan on lying to him either, it would be appreciated," I say, lightheartedly.

She rolls her eyes. "I don't plan on lying to you."

"The way you said that, with such promise and conviction." I press my hand to my heart. "I truly felt it all the way in my bones."

"God, you're annoying," she says, moving past me. "Do you have the key to our sex palace?"

"Yup," I say, and then together we head out of the cabin, only to be stopped at the door by Sanders.

"Hello, you two," he says while holding a football.

"Oh, hello," Scottie says, taking a step back and running into my chest.

I decide to hold her hips, keeping her in place.

"I'm glad I caught you before you headed over to dinner. I've given our day some thought, and I wanted to deliver this to you." He pulls out an envelope. "It's your task for tomorrow. I'm also having dinner being delivered to you so you can eat in your room and spend some time thinking about the session we went through."

Scottie takes the envelope and thanks him.

"There seems to be a lot of tension between you, more than I expected, and I think it would be good for you to think about if you want to continue with the camp or maybe...go home."

"Go home?" Scottie asks.

"Yes." Sanders twirls the ball on the palm of his hand. "I'd recommend weekly, maybe biweekly sessions with me to work through some of these issues. I don't know if we'll be able to handle it during camp though, and I don't want to put you two in a tough spot. So the decision is up to you. If you'd like to stay, then we'll see you bright and early in the morning, but if you'd like to go home, we can discharge you around ten. Just stay in your cabin, and staff will come and get you."

"Oh, okay," Scottie says.

Sanders looks between the two of us, determination in his eyes. "I see the love you two have for each other. It's clearly there, but the animosity is clouding it. Without working through that animosity, you're never going to find the love again." He grips the ball tightly. "Have a good evening."

Both Scottie and I step back into the cabin and shut the door behind us. I slip off my shoes and place them over by the dresser before lying on the bed. Scottie takes a seat in one of the chairs at the table and looks up at me.

"Was not expecting that."

"Yeah, and he wasn't expecting us to fight over petty things like... bologna. I think we all surprised each other today."

"I guess so." Then she glances at me. "Do you really have a problem with bologna?"

I shrug. "I mean, I don't hate it but I don't love it."

"I think you might be the first millionaire to ever say that."

"I'm down-to-earth, babe. What can I say?"

"I thought I told you not to call me that."

I wink. "It's got a good ring to it." She rolls her eyes and sighs, so I take that moment to change the subject and nod toward the envelope. "What do you want to do? It's up to you. We can call it quits now, maybe even say that we couldn't make it work. Thank Sanders and then move on with our lives."

"I guess we could do that," she says, staring down at the envelope.

From the droop in her shoulders and the defeat in her voice, I can tell that's not what she wants to do. But why?

"You don't want to leave, do you?" I ask her.

"I...I don't know."

"Hey," I say, causing her to look up at me. "Come here. Come talk to me."

She walks over to the bed, sitting down and leaning against the headboard.

"What's going on in that head?"

She tosses the envelope from Sanders to the side and drags both of her hands over her face. "God, I'm so sorry I roped you into all this. I know this is not what you were expecting. You probably thought you were going to have a little fun, role-play, and be on your way. You didn't know you were bunking up with a girl who has a truckload of baggage."

"You act as if that's a bad thing," I say.

Her eyes meet mine. "Isn't it though?"

"Who doesn't have baggage?" I ask. "There isn't one person on this earth who hasn't opened a metaphorical suitcase and dumped in it. No life is perfect, no journey unmarred. Everyone's carrying around something. So there's absolutely no need to apologize."

Her head tilts to the side as she studies me.

"What?" I ask after a few seconds.

"Nothing." She shakes her head.

"Uh, no, you're not going to get away with that. What were you just thinking?"

She drags her finger over the comforter beneath us, avoiding eye contact. "Just that, you know, you're pretty mature."

"Jesus, Scottie. I'm two years younger than you, which is not that big of a difference."

"I know, I know. I'm just not used to such maturity in a man your age is all. I mean, even Mika isn't as mature as you."

I chuckle. "Mika's on his own path."

"That he is." She pushes her foot against my leg. "Seriously though, you know how to say the right thing."

"I'm not saying it just to say it." I look her in the eyes. "I mean it."

She nods. "I know."

I turn toward her and ask, "So do you want to go home, or do you want to stay? I'm good either way."

She looks toward the window, and I can see her wavering on what to do, so I decide to help her.

"Please tell me if I'm overstepping here, but it almost seems like after today's session, you're considering staying because you might think it could be helpful. I don't know what happened in your divorce, and I won't ask because I know that's personal to you, but if it seems like being here could help weed out some of the negative feelings you're experiencing or the animosity or anxiety, then maybe it might be good to stay. If anything, staying might break the patterns of behavior for you. I know I can get into them sometimes, and breaking a routine helps break through some of the baggage we hold on to."

She stares up at the ceiling as she leans back on her hands. "Yeah. I was thinking that, but I don't want to keep you. The option to leave is there, and I feel like you should be able to get back to your regular life."

"But do you really think I want to do that?" I ask. "Why do you think I'm here in the first place? Because my regular life is boring me."

Her eyes meet mine. "You'd really stay an extra seven days with me, knowing that we could leave tomorrow?"

"Gives me an extra seven days to shower with the fleshy poker. I call that a good fucking time."

That makes her smile. "I'm being serious, Wilder."

"So am I."

And I realize that I honestly want to stay here. It's not just about experiencing something fun to relieve my boredom now. It's for Scottie. It could be because she's such a good friend to Mika that makes her okay in my book. But I think it's just her too. I like her. I'm enjoying spending time with her. And if this helps her unpack her marriage and heal? Then I'm in.

"I say we do it," I continue. "Stay. Enjoy the ride. Have fun basking in the knowledge of throwing off Sanders, because he's probably never met a couple like us before. Enjoy watching the other couples scramble while we win challenge after challenge while bickering the whole time. I say we stay, paint each other's faces, canoe out in the lake, go on hikes, and just be adults at an adult summer camp."

Her smile grows ever so slightly. "I mean, when you put it like that, it does sound kind of fun."

"Exactly. And I say you just let loose. Shake off the insecurities, don't worry about what your coworkers might think, and just do this for you. Experience everything for you. Because you and I both know you won't be working with the Brads and Chad forever, so might as well give them a show."

"It does sound entertaining, but I've never done that."

"Done what?"

"Dropped the insecurities," she says. "I've always tried to save face, put myself out there in a positive light. Make it seem like I'm living a good life."

"Are you though?" I ask. "In all seriousness, looking back, are you living a good life?"

She pauses, giving her answer some thought. From what I can tell, I'd say she's living life, but she's not living it to its fullest. I think she believes she's making the right moves, but she's not really making the moves that help her find joy.

Finally, she says, "I don't think I am."

"Then maybe it's time you stop trying to save face and start living without a care. Throw caution to the wind. Do things you may never have done before...like attend a marriage camp with someone you only met a few days ago."

"Yeah, I think you're right." Her beautiful eyes, a soft shade of blue with a unique ring of brown around her pupil, meet mine again. "Will you help me?"

A smile tugs at my lips. "Pips, you've come to the right place."

CHAPTER FOURTEEN
SCOTTIE

"GOOD MORNING," I SAY TO Ellison and Sanders, who are holding hands and standing by the dock.

The sun is barely peeking over the trees, and a mist is lifting off the lake, where blow-up obstacle courses are stationed. Brad and his wife, Jenna, are off to the right, having an intimate conversation. Chad and his wife, Danielle, are quietly arguing about some fantasy league he is in. Finky and Lindsey are passing a cup of coffee back and forth. And Duncan and his husband are doing jumping jacks off to the side, looking like they're gearing up for a takedown.

There are a few other couples who I haven't met yet, but maybe in time, we will.

Sanders offers me a nod. He lifts a megaphone to his mouth and says, "Are we ready to test your agility? Your comfort level with each other? Your athletic prowess?"

The Chads and Brads all lift their fists in the air while Wilder leans in and whispers, "Douche canoes."

I chuckle but then remind myself that we're still supposed to be angry with each other.

Over dinner last night, we laid out a game plan. Wilder took the lead and wrote in his journal how we're going to become the best couple to have ever walked the grounds of this camp. His evil cackle had me laughing, and he had me smiling while he pointed out ways for us to start slowly, showing Sanders how his tactics are working. And when he made a game day plan with X's and O's like Sanders did, showing our way to the end zone of best couple of the year, he had me doubled over in a fit of giggles.

And when I went to sleep last night, feeling lighter, like a weight had been lifted, I realized that this was exactly what I needed. Maybe Wilder was right; in order to break away from the dark cloud hanging over my head, I needed to break the routine.

Funny thing is, I didn't know that dark cloud was there until yesterday. It appeared out of nowhere, shocking me to my very core. I went into yesterday's session with the idea that we'd simply battle it out and then leave, but bringing up past grievances I had with my husband shook me.

I had no idea I would be airing out my frustrations, the hurt I felt from his indifference. From his lack of love. And after realizing that, crying through the grief, mourning those thoughts and feelings, it was cathartic to release the pain.

More than I expected.

I've been sitting on those feelings, repressing them out of fear of having to relive it all, and sure, in the moment, it didn't feel great, but God, today, I feel lighter. I feel better. I feel like a new me is starting to blossom, and I'm ready to have fun.

I'm ready to experience life, as Wilder says. And if I'm honest, I can attribute a lot of that transformation to Wilder. He's pushed me—*even if unintentionally*—and I'm a stronger person for it.

"As you can see, we have wet suits lined up along the shore," Sanders says into the megaphone. "It is up to you whether you want to put them on or not. Wearing your bathing suit is just fine, but the lake is cold in the morning. So you make the choice. Once everyone's ready, we'll line up. First couple to complete the obstacle course wins. Time will be added to your overall score if you fall into the water, so try to avoid that as much as possible. There are questions at every station. Those questions will be answered carefully with a staff member, and you will only be allowed to proceed if you answer correctly. Time is of the essence, so be truthful with each other."

I'm unsure what these questions might entail, but by the looks of the way the other couples are huddled up, I can only imagine what the prize is going to be. This is going to be a bloodbath.

Wilder turns to me, places his hands on my shoulders, and says, "We need to win this."

"I'm sensing that."

"Do you see everyone around us? They have their game faces on."

"They do."

"We need to have our game faces on."

"I don't know what a game face is. Tell me how to morph myself, and I will."

He holds back a smile and says, "Are you finally ready to enjoy some improv with me?"

God, he must have been waiting for this moment. It's all he's been wanting to do, engage in his silly improv and loop me into it. Well, after the convo last night and my newfound goal of trying to let go, the time has come.

I wet my lips and nod. "I think I am."

The smile he was holding back turns into a full-fledged smirk. He tugs on his lip ring and moves even closer, our foreheads nearly touching. "Good. Let me set the scene." He nods behind him. "See those fucks over there?"

I glance over his shoulder at my coworkers and their significant others and then back at him. "I see them."

"They're enemy number two."

"Who is enemy number one?" I ask.

"Us," he says. "I am enemy number one, and to me, you are enemy number one."

"Right, because we're mad at each other."

"Precisely. We need to seem chaotic but still work well together. We need to surprise everyone. They need to think we're without a doubt going to lose, only to pull out the win and take home the condom basket."

"Do you think it's going to be another condom basket?"

"No idea," he says. "But whatever it is, we need it. We can't let these douche canoes have access to lube and cock rings or, better yet, Nerds Clusters."

I gasp and clutch his shirt. "Do you think they'd do that?"

In a low, menacing tone, he says, "I have no fucking idea, but I'll be damned if they gain access to them. So are you ready to annihilate?"

"Ready," I say, grateful that I have Wilder at my side for this.

"Then let's get suited up."

Once we're given our wet suits, we kick off our sandals. I'm wearing a one-piece bathing suit because I had no intention of wearing a two-piece in front of my coworkers. Wilder's dressed in a pair of black swim trunks—not surprised by the color choice—and a black T-shirt.

And today is the first time I'm seeing him with his hair somewhat styled, which I think is funny, since we're going to get it wet anyway. But he put some pomade in it, making the longer strands go in all different kinds of directions. Very messy, very, dare I say, hot?

Let's not go there; that's only asking for trouble.

"Are you going to need help with your wet suit?" he asks as he pulls his shirt up and over his head, revealing his carved upper torso.

Um…excuse me?

No, this can't be right.

I ordered a fake husband who was into improv, not the moody GQ model with the ripped chest and stacked abs.

Forgive my wandering eyes, but does this man live in the gym?

I guess he really does have time to do whatever he wants, because I don't think I've ever seen anyone this fit in person. Broad chest with rounded shoulders that meet well-toned arms. His pecs are flat but still pop off his chest like a swimmer's. The muscles along his rib cage ripple under the early morning light, and his stomach is stacked with individually carved abs, one right on top of the other. There's a small patch of hair that's under his belly button, leading down to his waistline, and the tattooed rings on his arms are the only ink—from what I can tell—on his body.

"Scottie?"

"Huh? What?" I ask, snapping my eyes up to his, where I find him smiling at me.

"You're staring."

My cheeks flush, and I look away. "Was I? Uh, sorry. I've just, um, I haven't noticed, I mean, I've never seen…" I let out a breath and then look up at him, feeling defeated. "You have nice muscles."

His lips quiver, his eyes sparkle, and I can see him wanting to laugh, but he holds back, staying in character as much as he can. "Thanks, Pips. You have great legs."

I look down at my legs and then back up at him. "They're short and my knees are weird."

"Are you really going to insult yourself in front of me?"

"That's what Matt used to say about them." The moment the words leave my lips, I know it's a mistake, because Wilder's semijovial expression morphs into pure anger.

"Please tell me you're kidding."

"You know, I don't know why I brought that up. Just forget I said it."

"No," he says, taking a step forward. "Did he really say that to you?"

"Sometimes," I answer reluctantly. "But it was in a joking way."

"Yeah, well, that 'joke' seems to have tarnished your opinion about yourself, and that's unacceptable." He tips my chin up with his thumb. "You hear me? Unacceptable. Do not take other people's flawed opinions about you and turn them into your own. There is nothing wrong with your legs. Personally, I think they're hot. The moment I saw you in that skirt standing outside Anthropologie, I thought to myself, she has hot legs. Nothing weird about them."

Once again, I can feel my cheeks heat up as I quietly say, "Thank you."

"You're welcome. Now, take off that cover-up so I can assess the rest of your body."

"What?" I ask, snapping my attention to him, causing him to smirk.

"Just kidding, Pips. But seriously, suit up. We have a challenge to win."

Wilder has his hand on my hip, his chest pressed against my back, as he leans over and points to a square-shaped blow-up obstacle in the middle of the lake. We're both suited up, but instead of him all the way in his wet suit, he has the top half hanging at his hips, keeping his chest and arms exposed. He claims the sun is starting to make him hot, so he doesn't want to burn up and overheat before it's our turn, but a part of me wonders if he's doing it to show off to the other guys. There's no doubt Wilder has the best body out of all the husbands.

Not that it's a competition, but I did see Chad and Duncan pointing at Wilder before they took on the challenge. Luckily, we didn't have to go first, so we can watch where people are messing up and readjust our method.

"Right there, that's where everyone falls in, and it's because the woman is jumping first, and when the guy jumps on, he sends the woman into the water. We need to switch up there."

"Yeah, I see. But should we argue about it when we get to that point?"

He squeezes my hip. "That's my girl. Take all that built-up anger you have, and let me have it."

"I think I can do that."

"Prices," Sanders calls out. "You're up."

Getting into character, I push Wilder to the side and say, "For the love of God, stop showing everyone your body and zip yourself up."

The smallest of smiles pulls at his lips before Wilder says, "Well, at least someone was looking at my body."

I roll my eyes and walk up to Sanders, arms crossed, looking none too pleased to be here.

"You guys ready?" Sanders asks.

"Let's just get this over with," I say.

"Odd, I think I said that to you last night when you got in bed," Wilder says, causing me to gasp.

"Says the guy who took forever to—"

"Okay," Sanders cuts in. "Let's leave the arguing to a minimum. Remember, this is a team event, so you must work together as a team."

"We know," Wilder says as he finishes zipping up.

Sanders steps aside and says, "On your marks, get set, go!"

Wilder pushes me to the side and takes off like a bat out of hell, making me chuckle as I follow behind him.

"Hurry up, wench."

"Don't call me that!" I yell.

"Put those short legs to good use."

I chuckle again and hate him for it, because he's not supposed to be getting me out of character.

When we reach the first obstacle, Wilder waits for me. It's a small zigzag with palm trees at every turn. The inflatables are incredibly unsteady as they float on the water, and there's a solid chance we'll fall into the water just like every other couple that has started this race.

Pulling me in close, Wilder whispers, "You go first. I'll rock it too much with my weight, causing you to be off-balance. Remember, the palm trees are just air. You can't hang on them."

"Got it," I say and then shout, "Stop freaking mansplaining everything," and pretend to whack his hand away.

The first two zigs are easy, but then the float starts to become pretty rocky, so I stay light on my feet and tackle the next two. When I feel myself start to go off-balance, I leap to the end of the zigzags and land on all fours on the inflatable, causing it to rock. I look over my shoulder just in time to see Wilder tiptoe his way across with ease, the rockiness of it not bothering him once.

"What are you doing? Get up," he yells.

When I make it up, we go to our first staff member who's holding a card.

Looking between us, they ask, "Do you feel you two spend enough quality time together?"

Without blinking an eye, Wilder says, "No. I'm too absorbed in my phone, and I miss a lot of things she says to me."

Wow, okay, that feels all too real.

I answer, "No. I stopped planning fun activities because he always ruined them when something didn't go his way."

The staff member steps aside and says, "You may proceed."

Next is an archway of swinging balls.

"You have to run fast. If you see one headed for you, dive and stick yourself to the floor. They will knock you off. We saw that with Duncan."

"Got it," I say.

I wait for the first one to move by, and then with all the speed I can muster, I fly down the center of the archway, missing all the balls but one. The last one hits me and throws me off-balance, and I'm about to fly off. Luckily, Wilder is right behind me and grabs me by the waist, pulling me to the ground.

Together, we stand in front of the next staff member, and they ask, "How do you really feel about your sex life?"

This time, I answer first. "Used to be thriving and adventurous, but now I'm too tired and come up with excuses why I don't want to have sex with him. I have a lot of built-up animosity toward him and don't have any need to please a man who can't understand me for the woman I am."

Wilder looks me in the eyes, seeing the truth right then and there, but thankfully, he doesn't say anything. "She's right. We used to be hot and heavy, and now I don't think she even knows how to undo my zipper."

"Oh my God," I yell. "I know how to undo your zipper. Maybe if you looked up from your video games for a moment, I wouldn't feel so irritated by you, and I would want to please you."

"Maybe if you didn't nag me over and over and over again, I wouldn't want to get lost in my video games."

"I don't nag you."

"Yes, you do," he yells. "I can never do anything right. Ever. It's always your way or no way. You would think that there's compromise in a marriage. Well, not in this one."

"Because you don't help around the house!"

"Because I don't want to help a dictator," he yells back, only for the staff member to step aside and allow us to enter the next obstacle.

Bingo.

"You okay?" Wilder whispers as he moves in behind me.

"I am."

"Promise?"

"Promise," I whisper back.

"Good. You're doing great, Pips." He gives me a gentle squeeze on my hip, and pride surges through me. "Okay, this is the one that I'm going to go first on. I'm going to jump, and then I want you jumping after me. I'll steady the square, and then we can jump to the next one."

"Got it."

A single floating square is about three feet away, and this is the one that everyone has been tripping up on. I appreciated Wilder's insight, if I'm honest. He's determined to do well and was watching carefully, but he was gentle when he explained his game plan. *He must know how much I loathe a mansplainer.*

Wilder leaps easily onto the square and then holds his hand out to me with a nod. I get a running start, leap, and then land right in Wilder's arms as he steadies the square with his legs. Once it stops shaking, he says, "Squat down while I jump off it."

I squat down on the square. He takes off, sending the square rattling, but I hold on, and then he reaches his arms out, waiting for me on the other side. I get as close to the edge as I can and then jump, my foot nearly missing the target, but because Wilder's waiting, he's able to grab hold of me. Then he leans back, sending us both to the ground but staying out of the water.

Playfully, he pats my hip and then helps me up so we're now facing another staff member.

"Have you ever felt tempted to cheat on each other?"

Wow. Can't imagine being confronted with this if we were really married. I can't help wondering what Matt's answer would be to that one too.

Wilder turns to me, looks me dead in the eyes, and says, "Never. I might get frustrated with you, but I'd never cheat. Ever."

The sincerity in his voice, the conviction, hits me harder in the heart than I expected, and I attempt to not apply that answer to reality. "Same. I made vows to you, and I'd never do that."

"Thank you," Wilder says, his voice almost…shaky. And it stuns me for a moment, because there's a part of me that believes that wasn't part of the act. That his answer had meaning behind it. Personal meaning.

I don't have time to think about it though, because the staff member moves to the side, allowing us to reach the bridge. It's a rock-climbing wall that leads up to a thin bridge and down a slide for one more question. Once we pass this obstacle, we jump into the lake and swim for shore, and then our time is stopped.

"Get going," Wilder yells, startling me. "Shit, sorry," he whispers. "Didn't mean to scare you."

I chuckle, turning my face away from everyone as I say, "It's fine. Great timing."

I start up the rock wall, and I'm about to step on one of the pegs when one of his hands connects with my foot and he says, "Push off me."

He's right behind me, so I push off his hand, and he sends me right to the top. He scours the rest like a freaking spider, then picks me up, draping me over his shoulder, and runs across the bridge. It's hard for me to keep it together, because this is so ridiculous, and if we're doing this for another basket of condoms and dildos, then our hard work will go unrewarded.

But to add to the fanfare, I yell, "Put me down! You never let me do anything."

"Because you have the coordination of a geriatric wildebeest," he yells back and then tosses me down the slide.

I roll down and almost off into the water but thankfully hang on.

"You almost threw me off."

"It would be the first time you were wet in years," he yells back.

"Doesn't say much about you."

He joins me, and we stand in front of Ellison. When did she get here?

With pursed lips, she looks us in the eyes and asks, "Do you feel truly happy in your marriage?"

"No," Wilder says. "But I know we could be."

"No," I answer. "And I like to think there's potential, but I just don't know. He's too selfish."

"She's too focused on work."

"He thinks because he's helping save the environment with his green roofs that my work isn't important enough."

"Because you could be writing about something other than putters." He leans toward Ellison and whispers, "No offense."

"We don't see eye to eye, and I'm not sure we ever will."

Ellison looks between the two of us and then says, "Say something nice about each other."

I look at Wilder, my chest heaving as I try to catch my breath.

My mind draws a blank, and isn't that incriminating?

Thankfully, Wilder steps in and says, "Even when she's mad at me, she kisses me good night. Every night. I think it's her way of saying that we

might have a lot of animosity, but there's still love there. She…she gives me hope, and that's why I'm here."

I wet my lips and look Wilder in the eyes. "He reminds me to not be so serious all the time, that there is more to life than just the day-to-day. That it's okay to break routine. To let loose. To be the person that maybe I hold back from being."

And isn't that the most honest thing I've said through this entire obstacle course?

Smiling, Ellison moves to the side, and Wilder shouts, "Let's go, Pips!"

We both leap into the water and swim to the shore. Wilder's clearly faster than I am, to the point that he comes back and pulls me up by the waist, dragging me across the finish line, where we both sprawl across the grass, gasping for air.

"Impressive," Sanders says as he stands over us. "Very impressive."

"Thank…you," I say, still trying to catch my breath.

"And for the amount of arguing I heard, incredibly impressive."

"Fueled the fire," Wilder says as he stands and offers me a hand. He helps me to my feet and then tugs me into his chest. He smacks me on the ass, surprising me. "Good job, Pips."

When he pulls away, he undoes his wet suit, letting the sleeves and torso fall to his waist and allowing his chest to be on display once again.

Yum.

Okay, just…yum.

And I know I shouldn't care. I shouldn't even be looking, but I'm sorry. Mika's younger brother is hot. There, I said it. It's out in the open. He's hot.

Hard not to notice. *And if we were married, I would notice, so this is okay, as far as I'm concerned.* Just playing the part…

"Are we sure they answered all the questions correctly?" Chad asks as he walks up to us. "It seems like they were granted access to the next obstacle rather quickly."

Wilder snaps around to look at Chad in his zipped-up wet suit, all the way to the top of his chin.

"Excuse me? Are you claiming we cheated?"

Chad takes a step back but then gestures toward the obstacle course. "Just seems convenient that you flew through that despite arguing the entire time. Seems like you got some help along the way."

"Yeah, and it seems like you're jealous. If anything, we might have been arguing, but we were truthful at every stop. Maybe you need to point that finger at yourself and ask why it took you so damn long. Maybe you were the one not being truthful."

"We were being truthful," Chad says, almost stomping his foot at the same time.

Sanders steps in and says, "I can assure you, our staff has been prepped very well to understand the differences between our couples' truths and lies. I have no doubt that they all were accurately allowing couples through based on their answers. Now, we have one couple left. Let's watch them before we start fighting."

"Yeah, let's do that," Wilder says before draping his arm around my shoulder and pulling me off to the side to a log. We both take a seat, and he looks off toward Chad, who is now bitching to Finky. "Looks like we got under his skin," he says. "How does it feel?"

"I'd be lying if I said it didn't feel good. After him calling me out in the conference room for not wearing a wedding ring, it feels really good seeing him upset over our obvious success. We killed that course."

"We did."

"Carrying me like a potato sack wasn't necessary though."

"Eh, I thought it was a nice touch. If anything, it looked cool."

"Cool for you maybe, but I was the one flailing around."

"Flailing in a cool way." He bumps my shoulder.

"There is no such thing."

As the last couple finishes up and the time is being tallied, we remain on the log while everyone gathers around us. Sanders and Ellison speak, nod, and then walk up to the group.

"Well, what a great way to start off the day. I hope everyone feels refreshed, maybe a touch more exposed? Because if we're not uncomfortable, then we're not moving together as a team, right?" Sanders fist-pumps the air.

Seriously, was he a coach in a prior life? Because he has all the makings of one.

"As always, we hope you had fun and learned something about each other. We'll be taking individual meetings today to go over your answers to the questions recorded."

Great. Looking forward to that.

"But I know what you're all wondering: who won, and what is your prize?"

Ellison starts a drumroll on her clipboard, and Sanders, into his megaphone unnecessarily, says, "Mr. and Mrs. Price."

That's us!

"Told you we'd win," Wilder says as he stands. "All you had to do was listen to me."

Seeing where he's going with this, I stand as well. "It's rare when listening to you actually pays off."

"You listened pretty well when we were in the Hamptons, and I'm pretty sure that paid off really well for you." His voice is dark, deep.

I lean in and say, "I was faking it."

"Bull*shit*!" he yells.

"Okay," Sanders cuts in. "Okay…save it for your session." He lets out a deep breath and then slaps on a smile and starts clapping. "Let's give it up for our fastest couple."

There's grumbling irritation behind us but some slow claps, celebrating our victory.

"As winners, you'll receive a basket brought to your cabin later. For now, let's get washed up and head on over to the dining hall, where you'll be given your session assignments, and you can make marriage bracelets together."

Wow, this really is like camp.

Wilder and I start heading in the direction of the dining hall when Sanders stops us.

"Whoa, whoa, whoa. You two." He points at us. "You're up first. Go change, and meet me in the therapy cabin in half an hour. We have some work to do."

CHAPTER FIFTEEN
WILDER

"THAT SEEMED PRETTY SERIOUS," I say as we make our way back to the cabin.

"I know. Did he seem mad?"

"I was getting more of an irritated vibe."

"Think we're in trouble?"

"For what?" I ask. "We did everything right. You need to stop worrying so much."

"I was born into this world worrying," she says. "I don't know any other way of living."

"You need to hang out with me more often," I say. "I can teach you not to worry or sweat the small things." We reach our cabin and head up the stairs, where we find a box with a bow on top waiting for us. I pause and whisper, "The prize?"

"What do you think it is?" she asks, examining the box.

I shake my head. "No idea. But it's concealed. That could be a good thing or a bad thing."

"How could it be a bad thing?" she asks as we both stare down at the package.

"What if it's...really dirty, like something they don't want people seeing? Like...like a sex swing."

She toes the box with her foot. "Doesn't seem like a big enough box for that."

"Do you have experience in box sizes for sex swings?"

"Absolutely not," she says. "This is just an assumption. I don't even know what a sex swing looks like. Do you?"

"Do you really want to know the answer to that?"

She rolls her eyes. "Maybe not. Should we pick it up?"

"I don't know. Should we?"

"I think we should." She nudges me with her shoulder. "You pick it up."

"You know, it's not a bomb."

"Could be. We don't know." She nudges me again. "Go ahead. Pick it up."

Rolling my eyes, I snag the box and then open our cabin. She follows in behind me, keeping what I'm sure she believes is a safe distance from "the bomb." News flash: if this is a bomb, she's still going to be blown up.

"Is it heavy? Does it rattle? Does it feel like a sex swing?"

I lift it up and bring it close to my face, where I give it a quick sniff. "You know what…it does have the faint scent of a sex swing."

She grips my arm. "Really?"

"No." I set it down on the bed and then take off the top. Together, we lean over to look inside, and then at the same time, we both gasp. I'm the first to reach into the box as I pull out two big bags of Nerds Clusters. I raise them to the sky and say, "The angels have spoken!"

"Dear God in heaven," she whispers as she pulls out another bag from the box. "We are rich!"

We tear into our respective bags immediately, putting a fistful in our mouths.

Chewing, she says, "Now this is the kind of prize I'm talking about. Screw the dildos, give me the Clusters."

I pause as I'm about to put another fistful in my mouth. "You heard what you just said, right? Screw the dildos? Sorry to let you know, Pips, but that's what you're supposed to do."

"Please don't ruin this moment for me." She pops another Nerds Cluster in her mouth.

Smiling, I do the same.

"How did we feel about our answers during the competition this morning?" Sanders asks as he scoots a ball around on the floor with a hockey stick.

He went and changed as well, now wearing a pair of Grinch pajama pants and a bright pink shirt with Camp Haven on the front. He's paired the outfit with a Goofy baseball hat. You know, the one with the ears and teeth hanging down from the bill.

Normally, his attire doesn't distract me, but today I'm having a hard time paying attention. I mean, at least pick a theme, man, and stick with it.

"I felt pretty good about the answers," I say. "I felt they were honest, even if some of the answers hurt to hear."

He flicks the ball against the wall, startling Scottie next to me. "What about you, Scottie? How did you feel about them?"

"Same," she says as she scoots closer to me on the couch, probably out of the hope that I'll block any ball that might come her way. "Hard to hear but necessary."

"And how did you feel about the win?"

"Personally," I say, "it makes me realize that when push comes to shove and we're faced with something tough, we still have the ability to work together and get the task done."

"Do you think that's important in a marriage?" he asks as he starts bouncing the ball off the edge of the hockey stick.

"The ability to work together?" I ask. "Uh, yeah, because a marriage is like working with a team, right?"

He pauses and looks up at me, a smile on his face. "Precisely, Wilder." He tosses the stick to the side and takes a seat across from us. "You both

were asked if you were happy in your marriage, and both of you said no."
He looks between us. "Did you hear that? You both said no."

I nod my head, keeping my lips locked, because I don't really know what to say to that. From the corner of my eye, I catch Scottie bowing her head, and I can't help but wonder what's playing through her mind right now. It can't be easy, going through these courses after a failed marriage. Does she wonder if things might have worked out if she had attended this camp with her ex?

"Not to mention you made it through the entire course arguing. Did you hear anyone else argue the way you were?"

"No," I answer for the both of us.

"Precisely, which brings me to my point. We need to work on communication. That's the biggest challenge in your relationship. If you paused for a moment to listen and communicate with each other, I don't think you'd be in the position that you are now."

"Probably," I say.

"Which is why we're going to practice listening and communicating today. I'm going to need you to turn toward each other and hold each other's hands."

Unsure of where this is going but excited, I turn toward Scottie and then take her hands in mine.

"No, this is not the position I want." Sanders stands. "Wilder, lean back against the couch, and Scottie, I want you straddling his lap."

"Wh-what?" she asks, her head snapping up to Sanders. "You want me to straddle him?"

"Yes."

"Isn't that...inappropriate?"

"He's your husband," Sanders says, pointing to me, looking confused. "There's nothing inappropriate about it. I think the closeness will help you."

Noticing how uneasy she is about the whole thing, I try to soothe her.

"It's fine, Pips. Not like he's going to make us dry hump or anything." I glance over at Sanders. "Are you?"

Sanders shakes his head. "No, but being intimate with each other is important, and I think you need to start to grow comfortable with showing each other affection. That starts with your body language when together."

"If it makes you more comfortable," I say to Scottie, "you can sit on the couch, and I can straddle your lap."

Her expression falls, and I lightly chuckle, because I would really be up for anything.

"We're not doing that," she grumbles.

"Or you can sit on my face." I wiggle my brows, really trying to lighten the mood. "Haven't tested that seat out in a while. You always used to find it comfortable."

She side-eyes me, and it takes everything within me not to burst out in laughter.

"Your lap will do," she mumbles as she moves over my lap and takes a seat.

"Comfortable?" I ask with a grin.

"Hardly," she answers.

I don't know. I'm pretty damn comfortable.

"You know, this reminds me of the time we were in Vegas…"

"Don't even start," she says, eyeing me.

"But it's such a good story."

"This is a good jumping-off point actually," Sanders says as he stands and picks up a basketball. I swear, there weren't any balls or sticks in the first session. Dribbling it and making the entire floor rattle, he continues, "For this lesson, I want you two to look each other in the eyes and mirror what you say to each other. So, Wilder, recount your time in Vegas and, Scottie, I want you to repeat it. Make them short sentences so she can really listen and repeat."

Great fucking activity.

Smiling up at her, I say, "It was our anniversary. You were wearing that short pink dress that rode dangerously high, showing off those delicious legs."

She bites the side of her cheek and says, "We were in Vegas. I was wearing a pink dress."

"Nope, that's not what he said," Sanders says, cutting in and tossing the basketball in the air. "He gave you a compliment, and you didn't acknowledge it. And from what I've learned about Wilder, compliments are his love language."

I mean, I'm not going to tell him he's wrong. Then again, I think any man would enjoy a compliment, especially from someone as stunning as Scottie.

Scottie turns toward me and asks, "I didn't notice a compliment. What did you say?"

"I said your dress was dangerously high, showing off your delicious legs." And then I rub my hands over the sides of her quads. She tenses above me, and it makes me wonder how much this tool of an ex of hers actually paid attention to her. Gave her affection. Said something nice. Because a simple stroke of the leg shouldn't make her this tense.

"Oh, um…thank you?"

"Tell me what you like about her legs," Sanders says. "Scottie, I want you to mirror what he says by starting your sentence with 'what I heard you say was' and then end it with 'tell me more.' Think you can do that?"

"Yes," she says and then turns toward me.

Wanting to have some fun and make this woman feel good about herself, I say, "I love how your legs aren't stick thin. I love that they give me something to grip on to. I love the way they look in heels. Your calves are fire. And your ass is unbelievable."

I tug on my lip ring, challenging her, wanting to see if she's going to repeat what I said.

"Umm, what I heard you say is you love how my legs aren't stick thin and that they look good in heels, and you have something to grip on to and, uh—"

"Calves," I help her.

"Oh, right, my calves are fire, and my ass is unbelievable." She clears her throat. "Tell me more."

"Don't mind if I do." I slide my hands up to her waist. "I know you don't need to know just how smart and clever you are, because you know that through and through, but I can get lost in your eyes for days. They're such a unique shade of blue with a brown ring around the pupil that causes me to stare at them just a touch longer than I should."

She glances over my shoulder to avoid eye contact, but I don't let her. "Look at me, Scottie."

"Good," Sanders says, now taking a seat and spinning the ball on his finger. "Scottie, repeat what he said."

She clears her throat and says, "What I heard you say was that you think I'm smart and clever. But you know I already know that. What you like are my eyes and the brown ring around the pupil. You can get lost in my eyes for a long time." She swallows. "Tell me more."

A wave of goose bumps spreads over her arms as I creep my hands farther up her waist, holding on to her tightly.

"Back to that night in Vegas, when you were in that dress. We were at that strip club, per your choice, but then you wouldn't let one single woman near me. That night, you gave me my own personal lap dance, right then and there, in front of everyone. It was one of the hottest things I've ever experienced. I like that you claimed me as yours."

She nods and blows out a heavy breath. "What I heard you say was simple...you like it when I claim you as mine."

"Good, Scottie. Good. Ask him why." Sanders is leaning toward us, immersed.

"Why do you like it when I claim you as mine?"

"Because it makes me feel needed."

"Tell me more," she says, sinking onto my lap, her hands falling to my chest.

"I like knowing I can be of value to you. You're so independent, so strong, that there are times where I feel like you might not need me."

She twists her lips to the side. "What I heard you say is that in order to feel love from me, you need to feel like you're needed."

"Wonderful, Scottie. That's great listening," Sanders interjects.

I nod, feeling this conversation heavier in my heart than other sessions we've had with Sanders, because shit...I think what I just said was actually true. I like knowing I can be of value to someone, more than just a bank account. I like knowing that I can offer my humor, my touch, my mind...my soul. I like knowing that I'm helpful, that I can bring joy. That's very much my love language.

"And do you need him?" Sanders asks.

Scottie's eyes meet mine as she tilts her head, studying me. "Yeah, I do."

"And how does that make you feel, Wilder?"

I wet my lips, pride surging through my chest. "Fucking amazing."

"Good. Now, Scottie, tell him what your love language is."

She lets out a sigh and plays with the collar of my shirt, the subtle movement of her finger near my neck causing my stomach to dance in playful knots.

Jesus, man, pull it together.

A girl sits on your lap, and all of a sudden, you have butterflies in your stomach?

Tighten up.

"Attention," she says quietly, and from the droop in her shoulders and the lack of eye contact, I know she's speaking from experience. She's speaking her truth.

"What I heard you say is that you need more attention from me. Tell me more," I say.

She draws a circle over my chest. "I want to feel like I'm the most important thing in your life. I want to come home from work to find you excited to see me. I want you to want to kiss me. Hug me. Touch me other than when it's for sex." Her eyes lift to mine. "I want to know that if I were to walk out that door, walk away from this relationship, that you would know it was the biggest mistake of your life."

"Pips, I already know that. That's why I'm here."

"Repeat what she said," Sanders says as he takes a seat on the arm of the couch, moving in on us.

"What I heard you say is that you want to know that you're the most important thing in my life. You are. That you want me to want to kiss you, hug you, touch you. I fucking do, Pips." I run my hands up and down her sides. "And if you walked out that door, ending us, I would be devastated. Tell me more."

Her hands slide to my neck as she says, "I don't want you to hide. I want to know everything about you. The good and the bad."

"What I heard you say is that you want to know everything about me, the good and the bad. And I want to tell you, Pips. I really fucking do."

My mouth goes dry as those words hit me harder than I expected, because fuck, I've been shouldering so much ever since my father passed away. I've been holding my mom's secrets close to my chest. I've been taking care of Mika, making sure he stays mentally healthy. I've been making sure that as a family unit, we don't fall apart. And...and it's tiring.

"Great," Sanders says, bouncing the ball and startling the both of us out of the trance we were just in. "This was exceptional. Wilder, you want to be needed. Scottie, you want to feel special. Have you told each other this before?"

I shake my head. "No, we haven't told each other that."

"Then this is what we call a minor breakthrough." He tosses the ball across the room and then moves back over to his chair. "The key to a successful, championship-winning team is understanding each other.

Understanding what you can offer and understanding what you need the most. We explored that today. Now, I want you to take what you spoke about and go see Ellison, as she has an activity ready for you two to participate in. I expect for you to continue down this path of honesty. And before you start yelling at each other, please remember the communication we experienced today in this room. And if you need a reset, remember this position you're in. Return to it. Speak to each other like we did. Practice. Because if we're not practicing, we're never going to win."

Eh, the last part could have used some adjustments, but then again, there's only so much you can do when it comes to comparing a marriage to a sports team.

"You can find Ellison over by the dining hall. I'll let her know that you're looking for her." He shoos us. "Now get out of here."

"When we signed up for this camp, I never thought we'd be stringing beads," Scottie says as her feet dangle over the dock, the lake right below us.

"Neither did I," I answer. "Nor did I think I'd enjoy it."

"Same," she says as she holds up her bracelet. "What do you think?"

I take in her pink, purple, and white alternating beads and her name in the middle of it all. "Love it," I say. "You need to add more beads though."

"My wrist isn't that big," she says.

"Who says that's for your wrist?"

She stares down at the name and then back up at me. "It has my name on it."

"Yeah, and are you forgetting who is supposed to be claiming you?" I point to my chest. "That would be me."

"Are you telling me you're going to wear this friendship bracelet?"

"Isn't that why you're making it? For me?"

"Uh, I was making it for me."

"Well." I shake my head. "Don't I feel like a fool." I hold up my bracelet, showing her the black beads and the letters in the middle that spell out "Wilder's Girl."

"Wait, did you make that for me?"

"Yeah, Pips. That's the whole point of this activity. To make something for each other."

"Where the hell did you get that idea?"

I reach to the side and lift up the activity paper that Ellison gave us. "The directions."

She takes the paper from me and looks over it for a few seconds and then says, "Huh, it does say that."

"Yeah, it does. Then again, you've been in a fog since we got here, not saying much."

She starts stacking on more pink, purple, and white beads and says, "Yeah, I know. Sorry about that."

"Want to talk about it?"

"I don't know," she sighs.

"Maybe you should. Because isn't that what we're here for? For you to shed the burden of your ex that you've been carrying around?"

She slowly nods. "Yeah, I guess so."

"Let me ask you this," I say, helping her out with the conversation. "Did your ex not give you the attention you deserved? It seems to be a recurring theme with everything we've talked about in these sessions."

She sighs. "Because toward the end, he just stopped caring. Didn't say hi when I got home from work. Didn't care to kiss me good night. Didn't even think it was important to have dinner with me at times. He just... just didn't consider me important enough to grant me his time."

"I'm sorry," I say. "Seems like his loss though, because I've enjoyed spending time with you immensely."

"You don't have to say that to make me feel better," she says.

I tie off her bracelet and then take her hand in mine. I slide it over her wrist and say, "There's one thing I can guarantee you—I won't say shit just to make you feel better. I say what I mean." I look her in the eyes. "I enjoy spending time with you, Scottie. You're fucking cool."

Her cheeks blush as she stares down at her bracelet.

"Thank you."

"And this is where you say I'm pretty cool too."

She chuckles and then ties up her bracelet as well. She slips it onto my wrist and says, "You're pretty cool too, Wilder."

CHAPTER SIXTEEN
SCOTTIE

"THAT BAKED POTATO WAS FUCKING phenomenal," Wilder says while patting his mouth with his napkin.

Something I've noticed about Wilder is that he's the glass-half-full kind of guy. Anything and everything has some sort of positive spin on it. He's a millionaire at a marriage summer camp, claiming a baked potato—that I believe was slightly dry—was fucking phenomenal. Making bracelets was a "sick" activity. Running an obstacle course this morning was the most fun he's had in a while. It's the simple things that are making him happy, and I find that fascinating.

He has a thirst for life.

The need to explore.

To engage.

To experience the journey beyond a screen. He wants to capture moments on this earth, and I find it so refreshing.

"Wasn't that good?" he asks as he downs the rest of his drink.

"Yeah, it was good," I say, even though it could have used a little more sour cream in my opinion.

"The bacon was extra crispy too, and it turned into dust when I bit down on it. That's what bacon should be. Dust in my mouth."

"I'm not sure everyone would agree with you."

"Would you?" he asks.

I shrug. "I like bacon in any form. It's bacon. Just put it in my mouth."

His lips cutely turn up in a smile. "Put it in your mouth, huh?"

I give him the side-eye. "Your lack of maturity is showing."

"Is it? Or am I just clarifying?"

"It's lacking."

He clutches his chest. "Ooof, a man never wants to hear that."

I'm about to tell him he's being ridiculous when a pair of chino shorts steps in front of us.

Who could this be?

My eyes slowly travel up until Finky's face comes into view. "Are you joining the group for some s'mores?"

S'mores with the Brads and Chad? Yeah, I think I'm good.

"We are," Wilder says before I can stop him.

What? Nooooo.

"Great. We're all headed out to the firepit now."

"So are we. Catch you over there," Wilder says jovially.

Finky nods and takes off.

Trying to keep my expression neutral and not spit fire at my pretend husband, I say, "What the hell are you doing?"

"What?" he asks.

"I don't want to go have s'mores with them."

"Why not?" he asks. "S'mores are good. Have you ever had one?"

"Of course I've had one. My God, Wilder."

"Sorry. It's just surprising you don't want one."

"This is not about the s'mores. This is about not wanting to spend time with my coworkers."

"Oh, well, we don't have to talk to them. We can construct our s'mores and then peace out." Leaning in close, he says, "One thing you need to know about me: I have a sweet tooth, and my night is not complete without a little something sweet."

"We have Nerds Clusters in the cabin. We could have had those."

He shakes his head as if he's really thought about this. "Those are not an after-dinner treat. Those are in-between-scheduled-event treats. We must savor and hold on to those as much as we can. If something like s'mores is offered to us, we must take it and hoard the Nerds Clusters for a day when no treats are offered."

"Why are you this way?" I ask, hand on my hip.

"I wish I had an answer for you." He loops his arm over my shoulder. "Come on. Let's roast some marshmallows and melt some chocolate."

"Okay, but we're not staying, and we're not getting friendly with them. We're taking care of business, and then we're leaving. Understood?"

"Got it," he says, and then we head out of the dining hall and toward the firepit, where everyone is circled around the flames in chairs. There's Brad, Duncan, Chad, and Finky and their respective partners—my living nightmare. Sort of surprised Ellison didn't join the group. Then again, she seems to wander off with Sanders after dinner is served and they've done their theater production for the night. By the way, it was a reenactment of *Space Jam* tonight. The acting was so terrible that I almost lost my appetite.

Wilder, on the other hand, clapped louder than anyone in the room when they were done. Wasn't sure if he was clapping because the torture was over or if it was because he truly enjoyed the show. I wouldn't put it past him if he found the whole skit utterly entertaining.

"There they are," Chad says and then motions to an Adirondack chair next to him. "I saved you two a seat to share."

Of course he did. I can already tell you right now, I want to leave. I haven't even sat down yet, and I want nothing more than to go back to the cabin and wash the day away.

Wilder though…

"Thanks, my man," Wilder says as he takes a seat first and pulls me down on his lap. His hand finds my hip, and he tugs me in tight.

With a smirk that could actually make skin crawl, Chad hands us a stick with a marshmallow already attached to it. "Here you go."

"Thanks." Wilder wastes no time and hovers the marshmallow over the flame as Chad's wife hands us a plate with the makings of two s'mores.

"Now that everyone is here," Finky says, "let's get the game going."

Pardon? I didn't sign up for a game.

"Game?" I ask, looking around.

"Yeah," Chad says with a grin. "We're going to play Never Have I Ever."

What are we, in high school? We are grown adults; we don't play games like this anymore. Of course this is what the frat bros want to play. Then again, we are missing one key factor.

"Uh, don't you need drinks for that?" I ask, because if I'm forced to play this game with my coworkers, I'm really going to need a drink.

"This is the virgin version," Chad says.

I'm going to tell you right now, if I had a boner, that shit would go flaccid immediately from that one sentence.

"We play every year and just raise our hands if we've done it."

Wow, even more fun.

Please note that was said with sarcasm.

"You know, we're actually getting pretty—"

"Never have I ever had sex on the roof of a car at a scenic overlook in Connecticut," Wilder shouts, causing everyone to quiet down. What the hell is he doing? When no one raises their hands, he takes my arm and shoots it straight up to the sky. "Come on, Pips. Be proud. That was an unforgettable night."

Excuse me? Sex on top of a car roof? Has he lost his mind?

Chad glances at me, his eyebrows shooting straight to his hairline. "On top of a roof?" he asks.

"Yup," Wilder says casually while spinning the marshmallow carefully. "Had a dent in the roof for years, but I didn't care. Worth it."

"Wow, okay." Chad turns to Finky. "Keep it going for us."

Or we can end it now and all go to our respective cabins, because I have a feeling that this is not going to end well for me.

Finky taps his finger to his chin and then says, "Never have I ever used something from the minibars in the cabin."

Everyone raises their hands, including Wilder, who also raises my hand. "The condoms are trash," Wilder says. "Can't even get 'ribbed for her pleasure'? What the hell is that?"

"Right," Brad commiserates. "And fifteen dollars for three? My woman likes how I meet her needs, but five dollars per orgasm—outrageous."

Not, uh, not something I want to know about Brad. Meeting his "woman's needs" just made me gag.

"Wait, so do you all have lovemaking minibars too?" Wilder asks. "Because I thought we were the only ones with the kinky cabin?"

"You are the only one," Chad says, almost irritated. "It's the coveted cabin."

Ew.

Coveted?

That's not something you want to hear.

"It's rare when they let a couple stay in it," Duncan adds from the side.

Well, at least that's reassuring. Can't imagine what it would look like if you took a black light to the place. Probably startling.

"We've only had it once," Brad says, making bile rise in my throat. Brad has been in there? That's very unappealing to me. Good luck sleeping tonight. "And it was the best eight days of my life."

His wife elbows him, but he doesn't seem to care.

Guess what? I do. I care. I don't need the image of Brad in our cabin while I try to go to sleep tonight.

"I can see that," Wilder says.

And, Wilder, for the love of God, stop engaging.

"Are the handcuffs still there?" Brad asks.

"They are," Wilder lazily answers as he stares off to the sky, almost like he's reminiscing about using them.

"The lining on them is nice, right?"

"Really nice," Wilder says with a nod. "Top tier if you ask me, and we've seen our fair share of handcuffs."

Jesus, Wilder, please stop talking. I don't need everyone knowing about my sex life, well…my nonexistent sex life. I mean, well, I don't need them assuming what my sex life is like. There.

And then, to my chagrin, Wilder keeps talking. "Never have I ever been handcuffed to a bed." He looks around the firepit, and then without breaking to pause, he raises his hand high toward the sky.

Why is everyone allowing him to control this game? Wasn't this someone else's idea? Why aren't they the ones asking the questions?

But then, of course, the handcuff brigade starts chiming in. Brad's wife raises her hand, Duncan raises his hand, and, boy oh boy, am I seeing him in a new light.

"What about you?" Chad asks me while Wilder pulls the marshmallow from the fire.

"Nah, she handcuffs me," Wilder answers and then plops the marshmallow on the plate while my cheeks heat with embarrassment. "If you're not letting your partner do the tying up, then you aren't doing it right." He sticks another marshmallow on a stick and then casually places it over the flames.

Chad doesn't seem to care for that answer, and I have no reason why, but I can feel him look us up and down, ready to pounce. "You know, you two seem to be very comfortable with each other," Chad says, a squint to his eye.

"I would hope so," Wilder says, "We're married."

"But only this morning, you were arguing. Now you're snuggling next to a fire? Make that make sense."

"Chad, don't," Brad says.

Wait, hold on. Don't what?

"It's a simple question," Chad says, pressing.

"No, a simple question would be asking what kind of handcuffs we use in the bedroom," Wilder says. "Your question is loaded with doubt and unnecessary curiosity."

"It just seems convenient is all."

"What is so convenient?" Wilder asks, now sitting taller. I can feel him tense beneath me, no longer focused on the marshmallow but on the man next to us.

And this is a different side to him, a protective side. This is what Mika must see when Wilder is making sure he's okay.

"Hey, how about we continue the game?" Duncan says. "Uh, never have I ever—"

"Stop acting like we're not all thinking or talking about it," Chad says as he sets his s'mores plate to the side. "You're faking it."

Oh my God, what?

"Excuse me?" Wilder asks as my body goes numb from the thought of them finding out about us.

Call me a fool, but I thought we were doing a good job, that we were successfully presenting ourselves as a married couple. Sure, we're not wearing wedding rings, nor do we seem like a happily married couple like the rest of them, but they knew that ahead of time, since we're a marriage in crisis.

"Seriously, Chad," Brad says. "Don't."

"No, something has to be said, because they're playing the system." He turns to us and says, "We take this camp seriously. This is a time for us to recharge our marriage, and you're making a mockery of it, faking your issues so you can get more attention."

My skin prickles.

My nerves jump in fear.

And I think it's time we leave.

The tension from the group.

Wilder's budding anger.

This can explode and not in a good way, especially since we have no leg to stand on when it comes to being here.

Wanting to step in before things get out of hand, I say, "Maybe we should—"

"You think we're faking our issues?" Wilder says, sitting up now and completely ignoring me.

"I think you're not being genuine."

"Is that why you brought us over here?" he asks. "To confront us?"

"No," Brad says from the side, his wife looking like she wants nothing to do with this. "We were playing a game, like we always do."

"Brad, don't lie," Chad says. "Just this afternoon, you were complaining about them."

They were talking about us? All of them? What exactly were they saying? Were they judging me?

"I was not," Brad says. "I was...I was complaining about the cabin they got." Brad's poor wife. "Everyone was."

Confused, I ask, "Do you not have good cabins?"

"They're not your cabin," Chad says.

Lucky them. What I wouldn't give to be in a normal cabin where I don't wake up to the sight of a scrotum staring me down.

"Is this really what this is about?" Wilder asks. "You're jealous we got a sex cabin?"

As if they would answer that...

The guys all look around and then lightly nod their heads.

Okay, maybe I was wrong.

Either way, I wish this conversation would end. Is that marshmallow burnt yet?

"Let me get this straight. You're jealous we have a sex cabin, so that means you can gang up on us and make us feel bad about it? Call us out on supposed lies that are simply not true? Jesus." Wilder lifts me up off his lap, tosses his stick into the firepit, and then says, "You're all pathetic."

Oh boy.

The anger has peaked.

"That cabin is reserved for the most problematic couple," Chad says. "We know what you're doing. Sanders's philosophy is all about having an intimate and thriving sex life while combatting communication roadblocks. It all seems too convenient. You two are not communicating and don't even touch each other, therefore, he's going to make sure he works on you the hardest. They're going to get the tent."

What the hell is the tent?

"You don't know that," Brad says.

"Oh, I do. They're going to get it. Just watch." He shakes his head. "Mark my words, this is all a fucking farce."

Umm, can we get clarification on the tent?

"I don't know what the hell you're talking about," Wilder says. "But it seems like you're projecting. If you came here for some sex-a-thon with your partner, where cabins and tents matter to you, then maybe you're in the wrong place." He loops his arm around my waist. "We've been through a lot, the both of us, and we're trying to figure things out. If you can't handle that, if you can't believe it, then that's your own fucking problem, not ours."

The looks on everyone's faces. Shock.

Consider me shocked as well, because I don't think I've ever had someone stick up for me like this before. *How does he seem to suddenly comprehend my triggers now?* And why do I feel so exposed and on edge?

Before anyone can make a comeback, he directs us away from the firepit, me still holding the plate with the s'mores, and we head to our cabin.

The walk back is in complete silence as we're shrouded in the dark, only the pathway lights leading the way while crickets chirp in the distance and fireflies dance among the trees.

I'm not sure what to say honestly, because this whole situation was weird. Wilder upset—angry actually—that's unsettling. He's always happy-go-lucky, ready for anything, but I can feel the irritation coming off him. Did Chad strike a nerve?

And then there are my coworkers, talking about us behind our backs, jealous over a cabin. It's all, like I said, weird. And that weirdness makes me feel incredibly insecure.

When we arrive at the cabin, Wilder unlocks it and lets me in first before he shuts the door and locks it.

Once again, silence falls between us while I stand awkwardly in the middle of the room with a plate of s'mores. Unsure of what exactly to do and slightly out of sorts about Wilder's steaming attitude, I ask, "Are you okay?"

"Am I okay?" he asks, pointing to his chest while he slips his shoes off. "Why are you asking if I'm okay? The real question is are you okay?"

"I mean, I think so. You just seem very agitated."

"I am agitated," he replies. "Why aren't you agitated?"

"I guess I don't know how I feel," I answer honestly. "For a second, I thought they were saying we were faking the marriage, and that got scary for a moment, because I didn't want to get caught in that lie, and maybe they do have an inkling about us faking it all, but it just seems like you're really angry."

"I mean, yeah, I fucking am. Where does that douche come off, attacking you like that? He has no right. And over what? A fucking cabin? You know what..." He looks around the room. "I've got an idea."

Oh God, he has a crazed look in his eyes.

"What are you thinking?" I ask.

He slips his shoes back on and then goes over to the basket of dildos and condoms and the Kama Sutra book. "Let's spread the wealth."

Uh, I don't like that idea.

Not even a little.

"I think maybe we should just stay here," I say.

He shakes his head and walks over to the nipple picture and snags it off the wall, only to toss it on the bed. Then he grabs the handcuffs from the bed, detaches them, and tosses them in the basket.

"Wilder, what are you doing?"

"Teaching these fucks a lesson." He tucks the picture under his arm, grabs the basket, and says, "Come on."

"Wait. Maybe we should think this through."

"I've thought it through. If they're so desperate for all these things, then we are going to give them the items they crave. Come on, Pips."

There's no stopping him, so out of desperation to make sure he doesn't say anything insane, I follow him. As we approach the firepit, I hear Brad shush everyone just as Wilder sets the basket and picture on the empty Adirondack chair.

The circle stares at him, waiting for his next move, as an acute sweat breaks out on the back of my neck. What is he going to do?

"Since you all seem to be so jealous of the things in our cabin, we thought we would spread the wealth. Chad." Wilder turns toward him. "Here's a picture of a nipple. You seem to want to rev up your sex life. Maybe treat it as a genie lamp, rub it, and ask for your sex dreams to come true." He tosses the picture at Chad.

Oh my God.

He then turns to Duncan and picks up a dildo and some lube. "For you and your husband. Probably the most useful thing I can offer you in this basket besides the handcuffs, but I think we all know who desperately wants those." Wilder picks up the handcuffs and tosses them at Brad as my stomach churns with embarrassment. "I did not include a key—not even sure if they're needed—but if you're tied up for the rest of the days we're here, it would be a gift for us all."

"Hey, I was defending you."

Wilder points at him. "You were bitching about the cabin."

He then hands Finky a bunch of condoms and a vibrator and leaves it at that.

"Mind your own goddamn business, and keep your noses out of mine and my wife's." He starts to walk away but then says one more thing. "I have no idea what this tent is that you speak of, but if I have anything to say about it, none of you are going to get it."

Then he takes my hand, and he charges us back to our emptied sex cabin.

It's so weird not having my phone with me. Normally at night, I'd lie in bed, scroll through social media, maybe play a game on my phone, but without my device, I feel…weird, lost. Like I don't know what to do with my hands while Wilder is in the bathroom, getting ready for bed.

I don't know how to feel about what happened tonight. It was kind of comical, kind of insane, slightly embarrassing. Just a bunch of chaos—probably the best way to put it.

The bathroom door opens, and Wilder walks out in his typical sleep shorts, but this time, instead of wearing a T-shirt to bed like he has been the last few nights, he's shirtless, and once again, my eyes wander all over his chest, as if I've never seen a man before.

"I'm still fucking fuming," he says as he turns off the bathroom light, casting him in a shadow from the light on my nightstand. "I mean, who the fuck do they think they are? Trying to make you feel bad because they have an issue with us having the sex cabin? Jesus Christ, grow up."

He flips the covers down and then gets in the bed.

Not used to seeing him this worked up, I say, "Do you think that Chad will rub the nipple tonight and ask for three wishes?"

"Knowing him, he'll try it." Wilder lies down and places one of his arms under his head. From the corner of my eye, I shamelessly watch his chest move up and down as he breathes. His pecs look much larger from this angle, and the divots in his stomach look sharper, more defined.

I shouldn't be looking, but here I am, drooling over my best friend's brother.

Has it really been that long for me? I think back to the last time Matt and I were intimate. Yeah, it's been a long time. A really long time. Because even the last time we were together, he didn't deliver.

I bet Wilder delivers every single time.

"Did you hear me?"

"Huh?" I ask, my brain snapping back into the present.

"I asked if you were okay."

"Oh, uh, I mean, sort of. It was kind of a crazy night, you know? Chaotic."

"Yeah." He drags his hand over his face. "I'm sorry if I lost it there. I just…I don't like it when I see people get picked on, and I felt like that was what was happening. Those dicks ganged up on you, and I don't fucking appreciate it."

Well, this is new.

Not sure I've ever had anyone stand up for me like this before. I'm not sure I know how to handle myself.

"It's fine—"

"It's not fine," Wilder says as he turns toward me. "You should never settle for that type of behavior from anyone."

"I mean, they were just upset about the sex cabin. At least that's all they were upset about."

Wilder's eyes widen. "Are you really sticking up for their behavior right now? Please tell me that's not the case, Scottie."

I pause before answering, because am I? Am I sticking up for their behavior?

"Is that what you used to do for your ex?" he asks.

Uh, pardon me? Why did he go there?

"No," I say, feeling offended.

"Are you sure?" he asks, pressing.

"Yes," I say. "And it's rude that you're even asking."

"I'm sorry," he says, "But, Scottie, this is the kind of behavior that should not be tolerated, and you're letting it slide."

"I'm not letting it slide." I sit up now. "If anything, your behavior was out of line."

"What?" he asks, eyes widening. "You're kidding me, right?"

"No, I'm not."

"You're saying that I was out of line because I was standing up for you back there? Tell me how that makes sense."

"You made a bigger deal out of everything than you should have."

"Me?" he asks, pointing to his chest again. "You're saying I'm the one who made a big deal out of that conversation? Scottie, they were bitching about a fucking sex cabin. They were calling us out on being fake—"

"We are being fake!" I shout. "Everything about this is fake, Wilder. We could have just shrugged it off, but you didn't. You kept pushing."

"I was pushing to protect you."

"No, you were protecting something else...maybe your pride."

"You think this has to do with pride?" He shakes his head. "There is one thing I can guarantee you, babe. My pride will never be a thing you need to worry about getting in the way. Never. I'm not a prideful man. I don't walk around, puffing my chest, needing to be the top dog."

"Well, you did tonight."

"You're wrong," he says matter-of-factly.

"Excuse me?"

"I said, you're wrong. I'm not that man."

"Well, you sure acted like it tonight."

"I don't understand why you're mad at me. I stuck up for you—"

"You embarrassed me," I yell, causing him to pull back. "What you did was unnecessary. Okay? It was just not needed. I take that stuff from them all the time. It's why they're the Brads and Chad. And this might be all fun and games and improv for you, but this is my real life. I have to go back to work with them, and they're going to see me, knowing that I'm the girl with the husband who was handing out pictures of nipples and dildos to my coworkers. That was…embarrassing."

He twists his lips to the side, and after a few seconds, he says, "I'm sorry you see it that way. I see it differently."

And then with that, he turns away from me and tucks his hands under his pillow, signaling that this conversation is over.

His back's toward me, and there's silence. It all feels so real, so familiar that as I turn away from him as well and turn out my light on my nightstand, my stomach churns with insecurity. It feels like we had our first genuine fight.

CHAPTER SEVENTEEN
WILDER

"DOES ANYONE CARE TO EXPLAIN to me what happened?" Sanders asks as he sits on the top of his chair with a tennis racket and tennis ball, bouncing it annoyingly.

I'm not in the fucking mood to watch this man toss a ball around and ask us about our feelings.

Nope, I had the worst night's sleep I've had in a while.

I haven't spoken but two words to Scottie all morning.

And even when we were on a morning reflection hike with the group, we kept our distance. And everyone felt it. Even Chad, who tried to strike up a conversation with me, but I ignored him and moved toward the front of the group, nearly leading the hike on my own.

I embarrassed her.

Me.

I was the one sticking up for her. I noticed the mob mentality, and I was not putting up with it. Yet I'm the one who got in trouble.

Unbelievable.

"So is no one going to speak?"

Scottie has her arms crossed, sitting on the very edge of the couch, not even attempting to look at me.

Jesus, she wasn't this mad after the s'mores incident. I'm simply lost as to how it went so downhill after I asked my question about defending her coworkers. But I'm not sorry for what I did, and I'd do it over again. I'd make sure that no one even considers attacking her.

"Okay, I see how this is going to go." Sanders walks over to a hockey stick positioned against a poster of LeBron James. When was that hung up? I swear with each day that we're here, this becomes more and more like a man cave.

He brings the hockey stick over to us and says, "Whoever is holding this stick must speak. You can't transfer it to the next person without speaking. So, Scottie, since you're practically crawling out of here with every inch you've made toward the door, let's start with you." He hands her the stick and says, "Why are you mad?"

She takes the stick and answers, "I'm not mad. I just don't want to be around him."

Then she tosses the stick in my direction, and I luckily catch it before it nails me in the head. "I don't want to be around her either."

I send the hockey stick right back to her, and it hits her in the leg.

"Ouch." She rubs her thigh.

"Sorry," I mutter, because I'm not a dick.

Sanders takes the stick and looks between the two of us. "This is not productive. Remember what we talked about? Communication. Do we need to have you sit on Wilder's lap again?"

Scottie leans forward, snatches the stick from Sanders, and says, "I will tell you right now: I will die before I sit on his lap again. And if you try to make me, I will scream bloody murder. Not happening."

I take the hockey stick from her and look Sanders in the eyes. "That's one thing we can agree on. I refuse to have her sit on my lap. Absolutely refuse. No way in hell is she coming near me."

She snatches the stick from me and looks me in the eyes. "I never want to sit on your lap ever again actually. I even took a poll with myself, and the results are in: your lap is an abomination. Contaminated. An absolute disgust."

I snatch the hockey stick right back. "Well, I took a poll with myself too, and those results are in as well. Although you have a nice ass, my legs have come to the realization that they don't want to support ungrateful women."

"Ungrateful. Why is she ungrateful?" Sanders asks.

"Ask her." I stick the hockey stick between us and cross my arms over my chest.

She doesn't reach for the stick this time though. She turns away, causing Sanders to exhale.

"Listen, if we can't be civil and have a mature conversation, then there will be consequences."

"Whatever the consequence is, it can't be worse than this," Scottie says.

"I wouldn't say that if I were you," Sanders says.

"Trust me." Scottie puts her hand up in dismissal. "Nothing is worse than this."

"What are we doing?" Scottie asks as Sanders finishes paddling the rowboat to the middle of the lake.

"Isn't it obvious?" I say, arms crossed. "He's going to leave us stranded in the middle of the lake with no other option than to work together to get back."

"That's idiotic. He wouldn't do that."

Just then, a Jet Ski comes out of nowhere and pulls up next to us. Sanders hands the driver the paddles to the boat and then climbs out of it and onto the back of the Jet Ski.

"Wait, what are you doing?" Scottie asks, panic in her voice.

Sanders, with his chin lifted high, says, "We spoke about communication and it being the problem in your relationship. Well, here is where you can learn to communicate."

"You're just going to leave us here, in the middle of the lake with no paddles?" Scottie asks.

"Good job stating the obvious," I mutter, only to cause her to snap her attention in my direction.

"You know, I could do without the snarky comments."

"I could do without the snide glares," I snap right back.

"I've barely looked at you. How could I give you snide glares?"

"You might not realize you're doing it, but every time you look at me, there's side-eye." And in a guttural voice, I say, "I fucking hate side-eye. Just look at me with regular eyes."

"You're delusional," she says and then offers me the greatest side-eye ever to be achieved by a human being.

"You...wench," I whisper.

"Enough," Sanders shouts. "Just...enough. This is not productive."

"None of this is productive," Scottie says, tossing her hands in the air. "Do you really think leaving us out here in the lake is going to do anything?"

"It will force you to work together and find a way back to the shore."

"Yeah." I cross my arms over my chest. "It's called swimming, and I tend to be excellent at that, so the minute you leave, I'm jumping overboard."

"You would just leave me stuck in a boat by myself?"

"After that side-eye you just gave me, uh, yeah, I would."

"That's a dick move," she says.

"Listen, last time I attempted to be your knight in shining armor, I was chastised and punished for it, so beg your pardon if I don't feel very knightly at the moment. Actually, I'm feeling more like the villain."

And then without giving it another thought, I toss my body overboard and start swimming for the shore.

Tires peel out and kick up dust as Sanders drives away on his four-wheeler, leaving me and Scottie alone in the middle of the woods with a tent and a cooler.

After I made it to the shore, I headed back to the cabin, took a shower, got changed, and then was met at the door by Sanders, who dragged me onto his four-wheeler.

"Great job," I say to her. "You just had to test him, didn't you?"

"You think this is my fault?" she asks. "Uh, you weren't talking either. And you were the one who stranded me in a boat."

"Yeah, but you were the one who was like 'It can't get worse, nothing is worse than this.'" I gesture to the tent and pile of supplies. "This is worse, Scottie. This is way worse."

"Do you really think they're just going to leave us out here?"

"Uh, yeah. They were going to leave us in a boat. What makes you think this is any different? It's why he took off. Do you think he forgot something and is coming back?"

She folds her arms across her chest. "You know, you don't have to be so sarcastic."

"Well, you don't have to ask ridiculous questions. Of course they left us out here. They...they parent-trapped us."

"What are you talking about?"

"Have you ever seen the movie?"

"Of course I have. I'm just surprised you have."

"Don't be sexist," I say.

Her eyes narrow. "I wasn't being sexist. I was surprised you've seen it given the emo vibe you give off."

"This is not an emo vibe. This is me being me."

"It's emo."

"Stop," I say and then take a deep breath. "They parent-trapped us. This is what they did to Lindsay Lohan. They sequestered her away from camp until they got along again. That's what they're doing to us."

"That's not parent-trapped. Parent-trapped is when you trick your divorced parents into being close together."

"Jesus fuck, the technicalities don't matter. Can't you see what they're doing?"

"Yes, but I think it's good to have it on record that I know the proper term for parent-trapped."

"You're...impossible," I say in a seething tone and then walk over to the packed-up tent to start unzipping it.

"What are you doing?"

"What does it look like I'm doing?" I ask. "I'm setting up the tent."

"You don't actually believe that we have to sleep here..." Her voice trails off. "Oh my God, do you think this is the tent they were talking about last night?"

"If they were, not sure why they wanted this form of torture. Couldn't think of anything worse than having to share a tent with you tonight."

"Aren't you pleasant?" she asks as she sits down on a log.

"What the hell do you think you're doing?" I ask.

"Uh, sitting."

"Do you plan on sleeping in this tent tonight?"

"Yes," she says.

"Then I suggest you come over here and help me set it up."

"Well, I see chivalry is dead." She stands from the log and walks over to me.

"This isn't a chivalrous thing to do. This is team bonding, and isn't that what we're supposed to be doing? Team bonding?"

"We're supposed to be in our sex cabin, getting ready for dinner. That's what we're supposed to be doing."

"Yeah, well, your refusal to talk and incessant repetition that this couldn't get any worse wound us up here."

"Please, you weren't talking either. You can't blame this on me."

"Oh, I can," I say as I shake out the tent poles. "This is all on you. This was your idea."

"My idea? You were the one who paid for the camp up front."

"You're the one who brought us together because you were trying to look like you belong."

"You're the one who said yes to the idea."

"Because I was bored," I shout, raising my arms to the sky. "Because I was being helpful. Sorry for lending a hand."

"Apology not accepted."

"You are…insufferable."

"Say that into a mirror," she shouts.

———

"I swear to my left fucking nut, Scottie, if you don't hold still, I'm going to feed myself to the bears."

"Well, in that case," she says, moving the pole I'm trying to connect.

Speaking through a clenched jaw, I say, "I have zero problem sleeping under the stars tonight. You're the one who requires a tent. Not me."

"I don't require a tent," she says, lifting her chin, as if she's trying to call my bluff.

Well, guess what? I'm not bluffing. I drop the poles, dust off my hands, and walk over to the cooler, where I pull out a Diet Coke. I pop open the can while taking a seat on the log. "Looking forward to my slumber."

"As if you'd really sleep without a tent."

"I would. Try me."

I challenge her with a stare off, and after a few seconds, she grumbles, "Just come help me."

———

"Pole six connects to pole seven," I yell. "It says it in the instructions."

"What instructions?"

"The instructions next to your foot. Just find pole six!"

"I did. It's right here," she yells back as she holds it up to the sky.

"Then insert it."

Nostrils widening, anger searing, she says, "And like I said before, it doesn't freaking fit."

"It's supposed to fit. It says so in the instructions."

"This one doesn't fit. Maybe it belongs to another set."

"Let me see that," I say as I snag the pole from her and take in the number. My expression falls as I look back at Scottie. "This is pole nine."

"No, it's six," she says.

"It's fucking nine," I shout back. "See this line under the foot of the number? That indicates it's a nine."

"What line?" She takes the pole from me and examines it. "Huh, I didn't see that. Well, consider me wrong."

"Jesus Christ."

"What are the odds of that happening?"

"I don't know, fifty-fifty?"

"You can be so smug at times, you know that?"

"Scottie, just find the fucking six pole!"

"Do you see it right there?"

"Where?" Scottie asks as I point toward a branch on a tree.

"See that big branch that looks like a camel's back? Three branches up, that spot of red. That's it."

She follows my direction and says, "That's it?"

"Yup, that's it. A scarlet tanager. Beautiful, right?"

"Stunning."

"It's a male."

"How do you know?"

"The brightly colored ones are male. Females have olive backs and brown wings."

She shakes her head. "Even Mother Nature represses women. How depressing."

———————

"Scottie, the pole. Hand me the fucking pole."

"This is not the right pole."

"It is. Just hand it to me."

"It's not going to work."

I breathe out a heavy breath, count to five, and then say, "Just… hand…me…the…pole."

She hands me the pole, and I attempt to insert it into another pole that's supposed to hold up the tent. When it doesn't fit, I scream bloody murder and chuck the pole like a javelin straight into the woods.

———————

"You know, that wasn't as hard as I thought it was going to be," Scottie says as she places her hands on her hips and stares at the erected tent in front of us.

"I think once we found the right poles, it all worked out from there," I say, feeling the delusion myself.

"And it doesn't matter that we didn't fully listen to the instructions, because they weren't making sense anyway."

"None of it made sense, yet look. It's standing."

"It is," she agrees and tilts her head to the side. "It's standing…standing slightly crooked."

"I know."

"One gust of wind might send it falling down."

"Yup, we might die of asphyxiation tonight."

"As long as you're aware."

"Well aware, Scottie. Well aware."

CHAPTER EIGHTEEN
SCOTTIE

"THANKS," I SAY, TAKING A rolled-up cob of corn in foil from Wilder.

"Sure," he says as he sits back against a rock, since there was only one chair provided in the bin. And even though I'm irritated with him, he's still a gentleman and let me have the chair.

After we set up the tent, Wilder took a walk in the woods, sticking somewhat close to camp while I tried to adjust the tent and make it less crooked. Unfortunately for me, I knocked it down just as Wilder came back.

So we spent another half hour straightening it and making sure it wouldn't tip over in the middle of the night. You'd think that the tent would be something that could easily pop up, but no, this is a tent from the seventies with rust and broken ties. I swear they provided this tent on purpose so couples have to work together to erect it. Well, job well done. Only problem is I think it made things worse.

After a few seconds of silence, I say, "How long do you think they're going to leave us here? Like do you think they're coming back tonight?"

"No." He shakes his head and bites away at his corn. "We are here for the night."

"They can do that?"

"I mean, if we really wanted to, we could try to hike back to camp, but I'm not really into the whole hiking-at-night thing."

"Me either." I sigh. "Does this mean we have to talk about our problems?"

"No," he says. "You can do whatever the hell you want."

I don't like this side of him. And sure, I've only known him for a few days now, but I've gotten to know him well enough to see that when he's free-spirited and having fun, he's really great to be around. I feed off his energy, and he actually makes me feel better about everything. Not so uptight.

But this side of him. This indifferent side? It's not fun. It's not pleasant. And it's very cold.

And I don't think I can last another however many more days we have here together, so I decide to do something about it.

"About last night—"

"We don't need to talk about it."

"I think I need to," I say softly, which of course pulls his attention. I'm learning that even though he might be irritated with the entire situation, he's still a good guy at heart. He's a guy who will sit and listen if he hears that someone needs that kind of attention.

"Okay." He turns toward me. "Do you want to start?"

"Yeah." I set my corn on the cob down on my foil. "I have a whole bunch of feelings from last night."

"Start with the first one you felt."

This is what I'm talking about. He's a good guy. Instead of getting defensive and wanting to be the one who is right all the time—something Matt would do—he intently listens, asks me to speak my feelings. It's so...healthy.

"I was confused at first, because...well, I've never really had anyone stand up for me like you did. It was different, and I didn't know how to react really."

"That's understandable."

"And then when I did figure out how to react, that reaction turned into embarrassment. I was embarrassed that they were talking about us. I was embarrassed that you were handing out dildos, and then, when we were in the cabin, I was embarrassed that you thought I was making excuses for them."

He slowly nods. "Okay. What else?"

Taking a deep breath, I make eye contact with him and say, "And I didn't like it when you asked if I made excuses for my ex."

He wipes his fingers on a napkin. "Yeah, that was really shitty of me, Scottie. I'm sorry. You deserve better than to be questioned like that. I fucked up and should not have said that."

Wow.

Just…wow.

I don't think I've ever in my entire life had someone apologize to me like that, taking full ownership and not even coming up with an excuse. Just a straight-up apology. It nearly throws me off.

"Th-thank you," I say, stunned.

"Did you have any other feelings?"

"I think those were the main ones."

"Okay, well, I'm sorry that I embarrassed you. That was not my intention. I was frustrated with how they were treating you, how they were treating us, and I lost control. I don't like it when people are picked on. I've had to deal with that nearly my whole life—"

"You were picked on?" I ask.

He shakes his head. "No, Mika was."

"Oh," I say softly, completely understanding.

"He was always different, and the people around us made sure he knew." He stares off toward the forest, probably thinking about the past. "There have been many times in my life when I've stood up to kids bigger than me because Mika wouldn't stand up for himself. I've taken fist after fist to the face for Mika, but I regret nothing."

My hearts aches as I think about Wilder taking hits for his brother. He's such a good guy. Guilt consumes me about how we've been fighting, how we've been ignoring each other. Sure, what he did was embarrassing, but in the long run, he was trying to stick up for me in the best way that he could, and maybe that's something I need to start recognizing. That maybe, in this situation, I'm not entirely alone. Maybe I need to start trusting people again.

"I'm sorry you had to deal with that, but Mika is really lucky to have you as a brother."

"Thank you," he says softly.

"And I'm sorry that I got angry with you. I should have seen that you were just trying to protect me. I guess I'm just not used to such selfless behavior, so I didn't know how to react."

He slowly nods. "Well, let this be the standard," he says. "You should accept nothing less from here on out from the people you surround yourself with."

"You're right." I stand from the chair. "Can I give you a hug?"

He nods and sets his food down too. He closes the space between us and wraps his arms around me in a tight, comforting hug.

"I'm sorry," I say to him as I press my face to his chest.

"I'm sorry too, Pips." His cheek leans on the top of my head as he holds me tight. "I didn't mean to embarrass you."

"I know," I answer.

And then we stand there, holding each other for longer than I expected to be holding him. Yet it doesn't feel strange. I don't feel the need to pull away from him. I don't feel awkward. I actually feel like...like this all seems right. And that realization seems stranger than him actually holding me.

When he pulls away, he tilts my chin up and asks, "You good?"

"Yeah, I'm good. Are you?"

He nods. "Better now." He lets out a breath and asks, "Did you see if they had any sweets in the food bin?"

I let out a laugh. "I don't know. Let me check."

"God, it's so quiet out here," I say, looking around at the dark woods surrounding us. "Like, eerily quiet. Makes me feel uneasy."

"Same," he says as he leans against my legs while he sits on the ground in front of me. I offered him the chair, but he told me to keep it. He didn't have a problem sitting on the ground; he just needed something to lean against. That turned into my legs, and oddly, I like it. "Look at us city folk surviving the outdoors."

"Surely you've gone camping before though."

"Yeah," he answers. "Many times actually. I've done a few trips here and there on my own. Nothing too far from home, but this isn't new to me."

"Uh-huh, so then why was it so difficult to erect the tent?"

"Because that thing was made in the seventies and shouldn't be around anymore. Tents are easier now. Some of them you just blow with air and it's up."

"Blow it with air and it's up. You heard that, right?"

He turns to look at me. "I think sleeping in that cabin is making you perverted. Good thing you're getting some fresh air tonight."

"Good thing," she says. "Who knows what I might have said if I stayed in there another night."

"For real, you might start asking where the titty tassels are so you can perform."

"Is that actually attractive? Like, do people really like that? Swinging tassels from a breast?"

"I mean, they have to be somewhat popular if they're still something. For me personally, I'd prefer to just have nipples in my face. They don't need to be covered up."

"Just pierced...right?" I tease.

He chuckles. "Listen, I was with a girl once who had pierced nipples, and they were just as much of a treat for me as they were for her."

"Really?"

He nods and stokes the fire in front of him with a stick. "She loved them, and she loved when I played with them. We're talking feral behavior. And hell, they were nice. She had great tits too, so they worked well on her."

I don't know why I feel a little awkward with him talking about someone else's boobs, but I do.

"Is that, uh, something you look for in a woman? Piercings?"

"Nah, that's a superficial requirement. If she has piercings, that's just a pleasant surprise. I wouldn't fuck someone just because of that."

"Oh, you, uh, you wouldn't?"

He shakes his head. "Now, I'm not saying that I haven't made a mistake here or there, but for the most part, before I fuck someone, I have to have a connection with them, you know? Can't really go after the empty vase. The woman needs some substance to her."

"You don't find a man who says that every often."

He shrugs. "I'm not like every other man."

That's for certain. I've come to find that out very quickly. In fact, their parents did a great job raising their boys. It stands to reason that Wilder would be as good a man as his brother.

"What about you?"

"Oh, um, I've only ever been with my ex, Matt."

He turns. "Wait, really?"

I nod. "Yup. Just him. We met in college. That's when I lost my virginity, and yup, I've only ever known sex with him."

"That's...kind of sweet in a way."

"Would have been if we didn't end up getting a divorce. Now I'm a twenty-nine-year-old who has only ever slept with one man. I mean... what if I do it wrong?"

"Probably not the case."

"*Could* be the case, as things definitely petered out toward the end of the marriage."

"That doesn't mean you were doing it wrong," he says. "That just means that you two weren't compatible anymore. Having compatibility with your partner is really important. Without compatibility, there's no urgency to want to fuck each other."

"Yeah, there was no urgency at all. He barely even looked at me in the final months of our marriage. He was more invested in his online gaming than in me."

"Sad," he says. "Because you're far more fascinating than any online game." My cheeks heat up as he turns to look at me. When those light gray eyes connect with mine, he says, "His fucking loss, another man's gain." Then he stands from the ground and stretches out before dusting his butt off. "Okay, I think it's time for bed."

"Yeah, sure," I say, unsure what to do with myself after that comment.

"I think I saw a toiletry bag in the bin." He rifles around and then pulls out a bag. "Yup. Here's a toothbrush and some toothpaste. Oh, and some biodegradable toilet paper and hand sanitizer. I can get the sleeping bags set up while you take care of business."

"Thanks," I say.

He points to a large tree and says, "That might be a good spot. Take a bottle of water with you."

Not comfortable with this at all, I walk over to the tree, and before I can even consider starting to get ready, he jogs after me with a flashlight.

"Hold on. Let me check and see if there is any poison ivy. Squatting over that would not be fun." He checks around the tree and then nods. "You're good. Do you want to keep this flashlight so you can see better?"

"Yeah, that would be great. Thanks."

"Holler if you need anything."

He jogs off, and for a second, I watch him. Never would I have imagined that the man I met on the street that one Friday morning would turn out to be so kind...thoughtful...caring. The way he uses his words makes me feel important, validated. His attitude toward the whole camp, so positive compared to what I was living with for so long. Matt was always negative, always complaining about something. It…it took a toll on me. So being around Wilder feels like a breath of fresh air.

Awkwardly, I take care of business, hating every second of it. I'm so not an outdoorsy girl. And because I was so scared of peeing all over my only pair of clothes, I took my underwear and pants off, peed, and then slipped everything else back on. I will dehydrate myself before I have to do that again. Mark my words.

I brush my teeth next and then head back to camp, where Wilder is standing in front of the tent with a worried look on his face.

"What?" I ask. "Oh God, did you see me with my pants off back there?"

"No." He shakes his head. "Uh, I was just setting up the tent, and it seems like there's only one large sleeping bag…for two."

I gulp, because I think we all know what that means.

"Are you sure?" I ask.

"Yeah, I scoured the bin. And there's only one pillow. I think that was their intention."

"You could say that," I say as I rub my arm, the chill of the night setting in as the fire goes out and the only light provided is by the lantern and the moon peeking through the tall trees. "Well, um, I guess I could take the pillow and you could—"

"I'm going to stop you right there. That's not happening."

"We can take turns sleeping."

"Scottie." He levels with me. "We're both adults. We've been sharing a bed ever since we got here. We can make this happen. I just need to know that you're going to be okay with…snuggling."

With you?

Absolutely.

I'd be lying if I said I haven't thought about what it might feel like to have him snuggle in close. His broad chest and welcoming arms are just asking to be snuggled into, but that's also a line that we haven't crossed yet. A line that I'm sure I probably shouldn't cross given how fragile I am at the moment. One good night of snuggling might do me in.

Then again, do I really have any other option? If I offer to be the one who doesn't take the sleeping bag, he's not going to allow that to happen. He'd go without a sleeping bag and pillow, and I don't want that to be the case. It's already kind of chilly, and we're both in shorts and T-shirts.

So I guess…we're doing this.

"Snuggling is fine," I say.

"You sure?" he asks.

"Positive," I answer with a smile.

"Um, do you want to get in first or do you want me to?" I ask as I kneel in the tent, probably making this way more awkward than it has to be.

"You go first, get comfortable, and then I'll slide in."

"Sure." I clear my throat and then slip into the plush sleeping bag that is definitely made for two but not a roomy two. Like there is no chance that we won't be touching all night.

Once I'm comfortable, Wilder asks, "You good?"

"Yeah, I'm good."

"Okay." He reaches behind his head and pulls his shirt off, surprising me. He must see it in my face, because he says, "I'll burn up if I go in there with you and my shirt on."

"Yeah, it's no problem," I answer as I swallow another bout of nerves.

He slips his socks off as well and then slides into the sleeping bag, taking up every last inch of room we might have had.

"Shit, this is really tight."

"Are you talking about the sleeping bag…or something else?" I say before I can stop myself.

He pauses and then sits up to look at me. "Did you just make a sexual joke?"

"I think…I think I've been hanging around the Brads and Chad too much."

He chuckles. "Yeah, you have. But also, good one. I was talking about the sleeping bag."

"Yeah, it is kind of tight."

"You seriously okay with this?"

"Yes. I don't want either of us to be cold."

"Okay," he says and then lies down and slides his hand over my stomach, causing me to jolt. "Shit, sorry, should have warned you. Uh, do you want to be the big spoon or the little spoon?"

"I think I would feel awkward as the big because you are much broader than me."

"I don't know. It could work. Want to try it?"

"Not so much."

He chuckles and then slides his hand over my stomach again and pulls me into his chest. The heat of his skin sears through my shirt. My nipples go hard and press against the cups of my bra, reminding me that I still have it on.

"Crap," I say.

"What? Am I doing something wrong?"

"No," I answer. "I forgot to take my bra off, and I know it will be an issue if I keep it on all night. Do you mind if I take it off?"

"Have at it. I'll cover my eyes."

I scoot out of the sleeping bag. "I can take it off under my shirt."

"Oh, you hold the power of the 'bra under the shirt removal' magic trick."

"Is that the official title for it?" I tease.

"I think they're still trademarking it. Other names could be in the works."

I laugh and then remove my bra and shove it off to the side. Then I slide back down into the sleeping bag and up against his body. I wiggle in close to get comfortable and feel his hand on my hip, stopping me.

"Whoa, uh, easy there, Pips. Not too much wiggling, okay?"

"Am I too close?" I ask.

"No, but you keep moving that cute ass of yours up against my dick, and you're going to realize just how close you are."

My cheeks flame from the compliment. "Oh, sorry."

"No problem. Just going to state for the record, if things in the morning are…happy to see you, I'm sorry in advance. I'm sharing a sleeping bag with a hot-as-hell girl who's no longer wearing a bra. I did the best that I could."

Oh, umm, was that just a compliment?

Hot as hell?

Does he really mean that?

Does it really matter?

Shouldn't matter to me. I should just let it roll off my shoulders, but then again, I can't remember the last time I was complimented in such a way.

"Um, don't worry about it if it does happen. I'll take it as a compliment."

He chuckles, his chest rumbling behind me. "Please remember that in the morning."

His hand shifts over my stomach as he finds his comfortable spot, and butterflies erupt in my chest from the caress. God, it's really been that long for me. Hard to imagine that a small touch like that can erupt so many feelings inside me.

"Can't remember the last time I was held like this," I say, not wanting to hold that thought in.

"Really?" he asks, sounding surprised.

"Matt wasn't much of a touchy-feely guy. And as distance started to crawl into our relationship, it drove him further and further away."

"Shit, I'm sorry," Wilder says, sounding truly sympathetic. "And one of your love languages is touch, right?"

"I mean…yeah, I like to be touched. I like to be complimented. I don't need someone telling me how beautiful I am every second of every day, but if I dress up, it's nice to know that someone notices me."

"That's just human decency," he says softly. "For what it's worth, when you wear shorts and a T-shirt, you're beautiful. When you wear a pencil skirt and a tucked-in shirt…equally beautiful."

"You don't have to say that." The minute the words leave my mouth, I know I shouldn't have muttered them. It just feels reactionary, to not accept a compliment but rather put myself down.

And Wilder calls me out on it.

He lifts up and pushes me to my back. Even in the dark, I can see the crinkle in his brow. "We've talked about this. I don't say shit just to say it. When I say you're beautiful, I fucking mean it. Got it, Scottie?"

I nod my head, feeling ashamed that I allow myself to think such negative thoughts about myself. "I'm sorry. I know we talked about it. I'm just…I'm struggling to believe what's true and what's…what's you just being nice to me."

"What do you mean?" he asks.

"Well, you're my best friend's brother, and I know you're on a mission to help me. And when people are trying to help others, they sometimes… embellish to build confidence, you know? And I'm trying to figure out what is true and what is embellishing."

He slowly nods but keeps his eyes on me. They feel like they're boring a hole straight into my soul as he says, "I wouldn't fucking embellish on that shit. Do you want me to give it to you straight? Because I will."

"That's not necess—"

"You're beautiful," he says. "Stunning actually. I get lost in your eyes when I shouldn't because they're so unique and I want to know more about the brown ring around your pupil and why it fades into this ocean blue that I can't quite figure out. I've caught myself catching glimpses of your lips, wondering why they look so soft when I never see you put lip balm on. When you speak, there is hurt in your voice, like someone took a piece of your soul and hasn't returned it, yet it makes you who you are—makes you that much more interesting. There have been times when I've wanted to touch your hair, push it behind your ear, just feel it because it's so silky. You're unlike any woman I've ever met before—complex yet simple. Insecure but also very confident. And I'd be lying if I said that I wasn't attracted to you. And I'm not saying this to hit on you. I'm not saying this to try to get you to tear your shirt off. I'm saying this because you deserve to hear it. You deserve the truth. You are beautiful, Scottie."

My heart is hammering against my rib cage.

My mouth is dry, but my palms are sweaty.

And for a girl who has a hard time taking a compliment even though she wants them...I felt that one all the way to my soul.

I wet my lips. "Th-thank you."

"You're welcome."

And then we stare at each other for a few seconds, his hand still on my stomach, his frame nearly hovering over mine, the proximity of our bodies so close. I have this overwhelming sensation to trail my hand down his chest. To ask him to lift my shirt and caress his warm palm over my skin. To wrap my hand around the back of his neck and bring him in even closer.

"You know," he says, breaking the tension building between us, "it wouldn't hurt you to compliment me."

A sense of ease works its way through me as I chuckle. "Fishing?"

"Maybe a little. Go ahead." He nods. "Say something nice. Boost my ego for me."

I sigh but continue to look him in the eyes. Honestly? There are many things I could compliment Wilder with. He's a faithful, kindhearted brother, someone who defends people he feels are being wronged. No matter the consequences. He's funny. He's super sexy with those nearly colorless eyes and ripped muscles. *But the need to tease him is overwhelming.* "You're not normally my type."

"Wow." He laughs. It's hearty and from the gut. "Jesus, please, stop. Don't say more. I don't think my ego will be able to fit in this tent if you keep up with the compliments."

"You didn't let me finish." I laugh.

"Oh, by all means, please continue to regale me with your compliments. I think you were saying how I'm normally not your type. Continue."

I roll my eyes. "What I was trying to say is that I wouldn't normally go for a guy like you—"

"Uh-huh, you said it differently, but it still feels the same."

"Stop." I laugh as I gently pat at his chest. "What I'm trying to say is that I would normally go for someone different, but the moment I saw you in front of Anthropologie, I thought to myself, how on earth did Mika not tell me about you?"

"Oh?" He raises an eyebrow. "Interested, were you?"

"And this is why I do not compliment you."

He laughs and lies back down, wrapping his arm around me and holding me close to his chest. "It's okay. You can say it. You have a crush on me."

"You're annoying."

"Annoyingly attractive."

Yup, exactly why I didn't want to say anything.

"It's the lip ring, isn't it?"

Yes.

"Or my eyes—I've heard they're mesmerizing."

Also those.

"Or my strapping body that I spend countless hours training in the gym?"

That doesn't hurt.

"Or is it the fact that you're questioning whether I'm pierced anywhere else?"

Also, dying to know such things.

"Nope," I say. "It's your chin. It's well structured."

"My chin?" he asks in such a comical way that it almost makes me laugh.

"Yes, your chin. So...great job growing it. Okay, going to bed now."

"I don't believe you."

"That's your choice," I say and snuggle against the pillow. "Night, Wilder."

He's silent for a second, and then his hand moves slightly under the hem of my shirt, inching over my heated skin. Immediately, a dull throb erupts between my legs as his palm connects with my stomach. And then he leans in, and, in a sultry, deep voice, he asks, "Are you sure it's just my chin?"

Dear God.

No, it's not.

It's the whole package.

It's how kind you are to me.

How you make me feel special.

The way you look at me with those eyes, like I matter. Like I'm of importance.

It's the way you walk, the way you talk, the way you have no problem sticking up for me.

It's everything. On first glance, I wouldn't have thought he was my type. And actually, given how good he is, I still wouldn't have thought he was my type. But I'm starting to learn what I deserve in a man, and Wilder somehow ticks all those boxes.

Wetting my lips, I nod as his thumb strokes my skin. God, I might burn up right here on the spot. "Yeah, your chin," I say, barely getting the words out.

"Hmm, shame, I thought it was so much more." And then he lies back down but keeps his hand under my shirt. I swear it's a test. Like he's waiting for me to tell him to remove himself. Like he's seeing where my head is at.

And the thing is, I don't want him to move. I want him to hold me like this. I want to feel his skin against mine, because it's been so long. Because it's comforting. Because deep down inside, I'm starting to figure out that I wouldn't mind just a little more from him.

"Well, we all learn something new every day."

"I guess we do," he says softly, his thumb still stroking my stomach. "Just like I'm learning that you don't mind having my hand under your shirt."

I would actually prefer it a little higher, thanks.

"Um, well, I wouldn't, uh, I wouldn't want your hand to get cold."

He chuckles, the sound so addicting. "You're so considerate," he says as his hand moves farther north. "I wouldn't want my hand to get cold either."

I bite my bottom lip. "Cold hands are no fun."

"Not even a little," he says, his thumb stroking the spot just below my breast.

Mother of God.

Within minutes, this man has not only reinvigorated my confidence, but he has turned me on faster than my ex ever had with just the lightest stroke of his thumb.

"G-glad we can establish that," I say, really unsure what I'm saying at all.

"You know, you sound nervous, Scottie. Is there a reason why you're nervous?"

Yeah, because all I can think about is how I want you to touch me more than you are. And I shouldn't be thinking that. I shouldn't be thinking about him in any sort of sexual way. But my God, I'm panting. Begging. Needing.

"Not nervous," I say.

"You sure?" he asks in a teasing tone.

"Positive," I say.

"Because if you want, we can change positions. You can lie on my chest if you want, and you can place your hand on my stomach."

That would be a very bad idea.

Incredibly bad.

Because whereas he has some semblance of self-control, I know I'd have none. Nope, the minute I had a chance, I'd be running my finger over every ab, circling his nipples, slipping my hand under the waistband of his shorts...

It would not be good.

"Um, that's okay. This works. Unless you're uncomfortable."

"Nah, I'm quite comfortable," he says, splaying his hand across my stomach, one of his fingers just grazing the underside of my breast.

"Yup." I gulp. "Me too."

"Good." He sighs and then says, "Well, good night, Pips."

I wet my lips and try to even out my breathing. "Night, Wilder."

CHAPTER NINETEEN
WILDER

I SHOULD NOT LIKE THIS as much as I do.

Holding a woman…waking up next to her in the morning…her hair brushing against my face as she quietly sleeps.

Yeah, I should not be so caught up by this feeling, but I am.

I like it.

I like that she let me sleep with my hand under her shirt.

I like that she didn't move an inch last night.

And I like that she smells like fucking flowers and pine.

Last night, when we solved our differences, all I could think about was how easy that was. How simply honest conversation resolved animosity. There was no holding grudges. We just…continued on. It was so healthy that I almost didn't know what to do with it. I appreciated it.

And I know she did too. Because the rest of the night was spent enjoying each other, which definitely decided how we slept last night.

When I saw that there was one sleeping bag, I chuckled, because typical Sanders, right? Pushing two people together, moving past comfort levels and forcing them to make that connection. I appreciated it. I looked forward to it.

Because even though I know I shouldn't be touching Scottie like I did last night, I fucking loved every second of it. Craved it actually.

And when I accidentally grazed her breast, fuck, it took everything in me to not move my hand up farther and play with her.

Because I wanted to. I really wanted to.

She shifts next to me, stirring awake, her ass rubbing up against my cock for what feels like the hundredth time. I try to back away, but she presses closer, causing me to smirk.

"Mmmm," she moans softly, circling her ass against me again.

Jesus.

One more of those and she's going to feel something unexpected.

"Touch me," she mumbles.

Yeah, I know a sleeping voice compared to an awake one, and there is no way she's awake at the moment. Meaning I need to not listen to her.

Her hand falls to mine, and she grips it. Then to my surprise, she drags it up her body, right to her breast.

Her soft, full breast.

Fuck...me.

"Yes," she mumbles again and then swirls her ass against me, making me go hard.

Yup, told you. Just one more, and I was a goner.

"More, Wilder," she mumbles. "More."

She's having a sex dream about me. Consider me flattered, but I'd hate for her to wake up and find me groping her with a boner, because telling her she did it to me in her sleep isn't really the kind of excuse people accept.

I need to find an exit before things escalate, so I remove my hand, her hard nipple scraping against my palm—my mind whirling with what could have been—and then I move to my back so I can climb out of the sleeping bag, but to my dismay, she rolls with me and presses her face to my chest, her hand falling to my stomach.

I still and look down, unable to see anything but the sleeping bag, but I'm sure as hell feeling a bunch of things.

"Mmm, yes," she says, her hand sliding down my stomach and right to the waistband of my shorts.

Fuck.

Fuck.

Fuck!

Sweat breaks out on my skin as her fingers play with my lower abs, circling, scraping, teasing my waist to the point that I'm now hard as stone, my cock aching.

I need to shimmy out of here.

I reach to the side of the sleeping bag, looking for the zipper, but I'm having a hard time locating it while her hand inches closer and closer until…

"Fuck," I hiss as her hand slides over my erection.

I turn away, find the zipper, and then roll right out of the sleeping bag, startling her awake from the jostling.

"Everything…everything okay?" she asks.

"Bathroom!" I shout as I crawl toward the exit of the tent. "I have to go to the bathroom."

I make quick work of the door, take off out of the tent, and run behind one of the large trees, where I lean against it and breathe heavily, glancing down at my fucking dick poking against my shorts.

I drag my hand over my face and blow out a heavy breath.

Okay, that was…that was not supposed to happen.

And yet it did.

And for the brief moment that it did happen, I fucking liked it.

Yup, I liked it. And I wouldn't mind if it happened again.

But that's not what I'm here for. I'm not here to hook up with my brother's best friend. I'm here to…to…to what?

Make her feel better?

Help her through a difficult time?

Work on my own bullshit that I carry around in my head?

Let's not go there.

I take a few deep breaths, and after what feels like an eternity, everything returns to normal. I pee quickly, and then I head back to the tent, where I find Scottie outside brushing her teeth. When her eyes meet mine, they softly smile.

Fuck, she's pretty. I told her only the facts last night. She's absolutely gorgeous. But I didn't tell her that it's made me wonder if she thinks the same about me. That I've wondered if she likes me despite my lack of future ambition. That I've wondered if she'd ever consider dating me for real, even though I'm confused as all hell if *I* really want that. She's slowly turning me inside out and upside down, and it's been a long time since I've felt that way. If ever.

"I've never seen someone exit a tent so fast before."

Because you were about to find my dick thrusting in your palm, and I wasn't about to have that.

"Yeah, guess the open air makes me really need to pee," I say as I pull on the back of my neck.

She chuckles, rinses her mouth, and then says, "Do you think they're going to come get us this morning?"

"Unsure," I answer as I pick up my toothbrush as well as a bottle of water and start brushing too.

"Was there breakfast food in the bin?"

I shake my head and then spit my toothpaste out. "Not that I saw."

"Which means they're probably going to get us this morning." She glances at the tent. "Do you think we should take that thing down?"

I finish up with my teeth and then rinse my mouth before answering. "It would be my pleasure to take it down. I'd enjoy nothing more."

Then together, we start pulling it out of the ground and unsnapping the poles.

"How did you sleep?" I ask her after a few seconds of us silently working together.

She looks over at me, the sun hitting her in this way that makes her look almost...angelic. For a moment, I get lost in the way she can be so effortlessly beautiful in the morning. Her hair rumpled, her cheeks pink, her eyes sleepy but also alert. Christ. Imagine if she woke up like that, but I was looking down at her still wrapped up in my arms?

I can tell you one thing for sure—we would not be taking the tent down.

"I slept pretty good, actually," she says as she breaks down the poles and gathers them together. "You're good at snuggling."

"Now there's a compliment. Besides my strong chin, I'm a good snuggler—something to keep in mind."

"Maybe something to put on the dating profile."

"If I ever joined one of those apps, I would."

"You haven't been on them?" she asks, sounding surprised as the tent falls all the way to the ground.

"No," I answer. "Just...I don't know, haven't really thought about being with anyone, and I feel like people who go to those apps, at least the right people, are looking for a relationship, you know? And I don't want to do them a disservice by not wanting to be in a relationship."

"Ever?" she asks.

"No, not ever. Just, I guess, when I'm ready."

"Not to pry, but you know, we've talked a lot about me. So it's your turn. When do you think you'll be ready?"

"I don't know," I answer honestly as I start rolling up the sleeping bag that was pulled from the tent before we started taking it down. "I think when everything just seems...right. If that makes sense."

"Can I ask what that means?"

I can see her tiptoeing, clearly after an answer that I'm uncomfortable talking about. Then again, she's talked about a lot of uncomfortable things, so maybe it's time for me to share.

"Uh, well, with Mika. I want him to be comfortable, mentally healthy. I feel like I have some baggage where my mom is concerned and with my dad's death and his accident. There are some things to unpack there."

"I thought you said baggage wasn't a bad thing."

"It's not," I say, looking her in the eyes. "It's really not. But I haven't really dealt with my own baggage, so how can I inflict that on someone who wants to be in a relationship with me, you know?"

"I understand that," she says. She sticks the poles in the tent bag. "Mika said that your mom cheated on your dad." When she looks up at me, she winces. "I'm sorry, I don't know why I said that. It was a dark moment for him when he told me."

I pause, my limbs going still as the words float around us, just out there in the world. Words I try to ignore, to suppress, because it's such a fucked-up situation.

My dad was in a horrible car accident that left him quadriplegic. It was tough on everyone, especially my mom, who had to work extra hours to pay for his home care and then come home and take care of us. She… she was stressed, she didn't have my father the way she used to, and one night, after hearing Mom on the phone with someone clearly making a time to meet, Mika followed her to our dad's best friend's place. He saw them kiss in the front doorway, and from what looked like clothes coming off quickly, he surmised the rest. She owned up to it when she got home.

It was devastating to say the least. From there, it felt like everything fell apart.

And shortly after, my dad ended up passing. I went to college, Mika dropped out of college and became a full-time bartender, and we haven't really healed from the situation. Well, I've had conversations with my mom, come to peace with it, but Mika, not so much.

"I'm, uh, I'm surprised Mika told you that," I say as I stick the sleeping bag in the bin.

"He doesn't tell me much about your family, honestly, but it was during his rough time, and mine at that. It was a drunk night. He was raging about Matt and then mentioned that at least Matt didn't cheat on me like his mom cheated on your dad. He said it in passing, and I wasn't really sure if it was true or not, but I guess seeing the way you treat this marriage counseling thing and the way you look after Mika, I just put two and two together. I'm sorry if I'm overstepping."

I shake my head. "You're not. You're Mika's friend first, so I guess there are some things you know about my family that I might not have thought that you knew."

"That's about it."

I nod and then start rolling up the tent. "Yeah, well, I've come to peace with my mom and what she did. I don't agree with it, but I also understand it. My dad didn't even talk. He was…he was not the man that he was before the accident. It was hard on her, and I sound like I'm making excuses."

"You're not," Scottie says. "That's…that's a tough situation. I honestly can't imagine. I know what it's like to feel loneliness. I've been there. Sure, Matt was able to walk and talk, but I also lived in a house with a man who didn't care to acknowledge or appreciate me. I know what that could do to a person."

I look up at her, the understanding in her eyes breaking down a wall inside me that I didn't even know existed. Because…she gets it. It's so hard talking to people about my mom, especially Mika. I don't agree with or condone what my mom did. It's terrible actually, but then again, if I step back and I put myself in her shoes, how could I possibly observe as a bystander and judge her? She lost her husband in that car accident. She was taking care of two kids. Being a caretaker for her husband who couldn't even acknowledge her. Working overtime. She was stressed and…and needed that comfort. Was it wrong? Yes. Do I understand it? I sort of do.

And anyone I've mentioned it to has judged my mom, chastised her, said what a horrible person she is, but I know she's not. I know she's not that woman.

But Scottie…she gets it. She fucking gets it.

"Thank you," I say to her.

She shrugs shyly. "You're welcome."

I move toward her and pull her into a hug. Her arms wrap around me instinctively, and she holds on to me tightly as I place my chin against the top of her head.

We stand like that for a few minutes, just holding each other, allowing understanding to wash over the both of us. And when we finally pull away, it's only a few inches. Our eyes meet, a palpable connection beating between us. It's more than just a friendship that we've formed. There's genuine honesty. There's an appreciation.

Her eyes fall to my mouth for a brief second and then travel back up to my eyes. Our arms are still wrapped around each other. It would be so easy to bend down right now and kiss her. To cup the back of her head and show her just how much I appreciate her. How much I've enjoyed these last few days with her, even when we were fighting.

And as I bite down on the inside of my cheek, I tell myself *don't.*

Don't cross that line.

Don't push any further than I already have, because I wasn't lying when I said that I wasn't sure about what I want. If I can handle a relationship.

But hell, she's making it fucking hard to keep myself away, especially when she looks at me with those expressive, nearly pleading eyes of hers.

"Thank you for last night," she says quietly.

"For what?" I ask.

"For reminding me about what it is that I want in life. I forgot how nice it is to have human touch, and you…you reminded me of that." She smiles. "I was kind of happy there was only one sleeping bag."

That makes me chuckle. "Jesus, is it bad that I was thinking the same thing this morning?"

"Really?" she asks.

"I mean…yeah. I forgot what it was like to snuggle with someone. It was nice. I enjoyed it. Not to mention I didn't mind the whole hand up the shirt thing. It was a nice touch."

"Of course you'd say that."

I wet my lips. "Can't blame a guy. But it should probably be just a one-time thing though, right? I mean, imagine if we snuggled in the sex cabin. Think about how the cabin would take it wrong."

"The walls would whisper," she cutely says.

I chuckle. "They'd torment us. Tell us to go further. Tease us relentlessly. The vibrators would vibrate. The cock rings would jingle."

"The lube would bubble. The condoms would crinkle."

I lift a brow. "Did you just rhyme?"

"I did." She winces. "And I said lube would bubble. I don't think it does that. Honestly, I wouldn't even know. I've never used it."

"Never used it?" I ask with a shake of my head. "Pips, we need to get you out of this hole you've been living in."

She's about to respond when we hear a motor approaching in the distance. We both look to the side just in time to see Sanders drive up toward us in his four-wheeler. Wearing a turkey-shaped hat on his head, he parks the four-wheeler and then sticks his head out the side, taking in our position.

"Well...that's more like it," he says as he hops out, revealing his Thanksgiving dinner shirt and matching pants. It's summer, and he's wearing mashed potatoes and pumpkin pie on his body, but at least he matches. He's got that going for him. "How was your night?"

I slip out of Scottie's embrace but keep my arm wrapped around her shoulders as I face Sanders. "It was good. Right, Pips?"

She looks up at me and then at Sanders. "Yes, it was good."

"Did we work out our issues like adults?"

I nod. "We communicated, aired out the issues, and both apologized with sincerity."

"Good." He folds his arms. "Because I have food in the back of the four-wheeler if I need to keep you out here another night."

"I think we're good." I grip my back and stretch. "Could use an actual mattress tonight."

"Then let's finish cleaning up, and then we can head back to camp. I have quite the activity planned for today."

I can only imagine what that is going to be.

Together, we gather up the rest of the tent items, stuff them all away, and then pile the bin on the back of the four-wheeler. I slide in next to Scottie in the second row and drape my arm behind her.

"So," I say. "Uh, the other couples mentioned the other night that there's some tent experience that they hoped they'd take part in. Was this that?"

"They said that?" Sanders asks on a laugh. "Yes, this would be it, but I'm not sure why they'd want to take part in it. To me, sleeping on the rock-hard ground over a fluffy mattress is way more of a punishment than anything. Then again, they're a different bunch."

You can say that again.

What is it with them? They were jealous about this outing in the woods with a tent? Christ, I wouldn't be frothing at the mouth to make that happen. Unless one of them heard about a different experience and then told the others.

"Tell me something you learned about each other while out here," Sanders says, continuing his therapy sessions whenever he gets a chance.

"I learned that Scottie likes it when my hand is up her shirt."

"Wilder," she scoffs while both Sanders and I laugh.

"You know, Ellison likes the same thing," Sanders says. "She also doesn't mind sharing a sleeping bag."

"Scottie didn't mind that either. She actually enjoyed it quite a bit. She got real handsy."

"Me, handsy?" she says, looking over at me. "You were the one who grazed my boob."

"If only it was the nipple."

Her mouth falls open while Sanders continues to chuckle.

"Yeah…well…Wilder had a boner this morning and pretended he had to pee when in reality, he was trying to hide it from me."

I gasp. "You saw that?"

"The woodland creatures from a mile away saw it," she deadpans.

I press my hand to my chest. "Babe, are you saying I have a prominent penis? Thank you."

"Jesus," she mutters under her breath.

"Okay," Sanders says. "So if you were aroused this morning, why didn't you want your wife to see it?"

Oh shit, that's right, we're married. Kind of forgot that detail for a second.

I clear my throat and say, "We took a vow of celibacy while we're trying to work out these issues. Didn't want to make sex a thing, since we're both so good. You know, as Sabrina Carpenter would say, we have really good bed chem."

"Ahh, I see. And if she saw your arousal, that would be…"

"Pressuring," I answer. "I never want her to feel pressured about taking care of me like that."

"So you took care of yourself?"

"Not so much," I say, not caring that I'm talking about this in the slightest. "I stood behind a tree, taking deep breaths as I tried not to think about Scottie's slumbering yet wandering hand that caressed my dick."

"What?" she asks, pulling back. "I didn't caress you."

"Oh babe, you most certainly did," I say with a smirk.

"No, I didn't."

"Uh, yeah, you did. You flipped over while I was on my back, moved your hand around my chest and stomach—she's always loved my abs, man—"

"You are a very fit man," Sanders says.

"Thank you. And then from there, her hand went right over the old dong. Made me nearly jump out of my shorts. That's when I scrambled out of the sleeping bag and the tent, claiming I had to go to the bathroom."

"And what would have happened if you didn't flee? What if you just let her touch you while she was sleeping?" Sanders asks as he avoids a rock in the path.

"Uh, well...I would have been panting and begging for more as she wandered her hand around. I probably would have slipped up on our pact, pushed her shirt up, and while she had her way with me, I'd have had my way with her."

I catch her gulp out of the corner of my eye as she looks straight ahead, avoiding me at all costs.

"Well then, maybe tonight will call for a redo. If you're in a comfortable place with your communication, then maybe it's time to reestablish that intimate relationship as well."

"You know," I say, gripping Scottie's shoulder. "I truly think we might be ready."

"I feel so much better," Scottie says as she comes out of the bathroom, fully dressed and her hair wet from the shower. "There's something about sleeping outside that just makes you feel gross."

"Well, you didn't look gross to me," I say as I lean back on the bed.

"Thank you." She scrunches her hair with her towel and says, "Can I ask you something?"

"Always," I answer.

"Were you telling the truth in the four-wheeler? Did I really touch you?"

My eyes meet hers. "Yeah, Pips, you did. That's why it seemed like I had fire in my goddamn pants, because if I didn't get out of there quick enough, you would have been touching a lot more if I had my way."

"Oh." Her teeth drag over her lower lip. "I'm sorry. I didn't mean to."

"Hey, it's fine. I'd be lying if I said I didn't like it, because I did. Sure, it was surprising, but also, can't deny a beautiful woman caressing me the way you did."

"Well, I had no idea. I wouldn't intentionally do that."

"Seriously, Scottie, it's fine. Nothing you need to worry about. Okay?"

"Okay," she says and then hangs up her towel. She takes a seat on the bed next to me and asks, "What do you think he's going to have us do today?"

"No idea," I answer. "But are we on the path to good now? Like, no more fighting? We're supposed to be showing that our marriage has a shot now, right?"

"Right," she says. "I think the tent was the perfect turning point for us. Now that we've had that moment and we've aired out our differences, we can move on with the rest of camp and show Sanders that he really is a magician when it comes to saving marriages. He can feel great about himself, he can tell Ellison that we're the miracle couple, Ellison will like me more, which in return will be great for when I want to move on to another job, and then all will be right in the world."

"Exactly, and I can always look back at the time that I went to a marriage summer camp with a woman I didn't know."

"Put it in your experience journal."

"Don't have one, but I might make one now."

"Good." She smiles at me. "Okay, shall we head on over to the main building?"

"I think we shall." I stand and then hold out my hand to her. "Happy couples hold hands."

"You're right. They do." She takes my hand, and together, we head out of the cabin and down the path toward the main building.

It's a beautiful summer day with a light breeze, making the humidity not that horrible. And the wind kicking off the lake is always an added bonus; it's like nature's air-conditioning.

We head into the covered area where all the furniture has been moved, and there are single chairs in various parts of the space.

"What is this?" Scottie asks. "Musical chairs?"

"Imagine that," I say just as Chad and his wife walk up.

"Heard you got the tent," he says through clenched teeth.

This guy. Jesus.

"Yeah, we did," I say with a smile. "And fuck, was it amazing. Shame you didn't get to experience it."

He rolls his eyes. "Well, I'm not here putting on a show like you." Then he directs his wife to the other side of the building, far away from us.

When I feel Scottie grow tense next to me, I say, "Don't worry about him."

"He knows," she whispers. "He has to."

"He doesn't. He probably has erectile dysfunction and is taking it out on us."

But she doesn't laugh, instead she worries her lip.

"I don't know," Scottie says. "He's the one who initially tried to catch me in a lie, and I think he might have gotten in trouble with HR from it. I feel like he's trying to sniff something out because I know he's not a fan of mine, and I'm not a fan of his."

"I can see why." And then I whisper, "Seriously, just keep cool, we have nothing to worry about."

Now Brad walks by us, looking semiguilty. "Umm, thanks for the handcuffs," he mutters. "I, uh, I was the one who got tied up."

"And…?" I ask.

He just nods, a light smirk playing on his lips as he heads toward Chad.

Ah, I see that he's pledging his allegiance, but there was a slight desperation behind his eyes that made me think he wants to switch teams. I'll just have to let him know that we'll welcome him and his wife with open arms.

Next, Duncan and his husband walk by. Duncan stops in front of us and places his hand on my shoulder. He gives it a few pats but then keeps walking. He doesn't need to say much more than that. I get it.

Everyone besides Chad seems well rested, happy...like they're ready to move on to the newest task and forget about the night around the fire.

The newest task seems like it's about to start as Sanders shows up still wearing that godforsaken turkey hat; how the man is not roasting under it, I will never understand.

"Welcome, everyone. We're starting a new practice that we haven't done here yet at Camp Haven. This is a play on musical chairs."

"Ha, you called it," I whisper to Scottie.

"But instead of musical chairs, this is called sensual chairs."

Uh-oh.

That doesn't sound like a game for two people pretending to be married.

"I'm going to start you off by having everyone pick a chair. Any open chair." When no one moves, he says, "Go ahead. Pick one."

I lead Scottie to a chair far off in the corner where no one else is so we can discuss whatever this activity is going to be.

"I'll be playing music in one-minute increments. There will be a card on the bottom of your chair. You are to read the card and complete the task on the card. I'll have staff roaming around, making sure everyone is participating and participating correctly. When the music stops, you move to a different chair to take care of another task. The game will be over once every couple checks off every chair and task. Understood?"

Everyone seems to nod their head, and then Brad raises his hand. "Question about the chair. Is this something we're both supposed to sit on?"

"Yes," Sanders answers. "Both of you, at the same time. You position how you feel necessary, but you need to be facing each other."

Which means Scottie is straddling my lap again. Just what I fucking need after the groping from this morning.

I turn to her and say, "Want me to sit on you?"

She cutely raises her brow, making me laugh.

"Yeah, didn't think so." It was worth a try.

So I take a seat on the chair, and Scottie slowly straddles my lap, facing me.

Fuck, she smells amazing. I think it's the shampoo she uses that she brought with her. It has this flowery scent that kicks me in the damn crotch every time I get a whiff of it.

And she fits so perfectly on my lap, like I'm her own personal seat.

I place my hands on her hips and ask, "Are you comfortable?"

She rests her hands on my chest, her fingers splaying across my pecs. "Yeah. Are you? I'm not hurting you, am I?"

Mentally, this is straining; physically, it's so fucking comfortable.

"Is that really a question you're asking me?"

"I guess not," she says as I playfully squeeze her hips.

"Now that everyone is in position, we're going to start the music, and that's when you need to read the card that's under your chair and follow the instructions," Sanders says.

"I hope they don't do this at regular summer camps," I say.

"Talk about a lawsuit," she mutters just as the music starts, and it's shockingly loud.

"Is that...'Wicked Game' by Chris Isaak?" I ask.

"I think it is," she answers as I reach to the side for the card that's Velcroed to the chair. "What does it say?"

I flip it open and read out loud. "Look your partner in the eyes, and tell them one quality that you admire about them." I look up at her. "Oh shit, I thought this was going to be harder."

She lets out a sigh of relief. "Me too. When he said sensual chairs, I was expecting...I don't know...dry humping or something."

I let out a laugh while she chuckles.

"Well, thank God we don't have to dry hump in public."

"Really saving some dignity this morning."

"We are," I say, unable to hide my smile, because she's just so damn adorable.

"Okay, we can do this," she says on a sigh.

"Want me to go first?" I ask.

"Sure," she answers.

I look her in the eyes, and I say, "Scottie, I admire your vulnerability. I know you put yourself in a weird and awkward situation, and you had the chance to just give up and move on, but instead, you decided to see this thing through. You decided to open yourself up to these conversations and to sift through the weight of your divorce with courage. And I don't think you see that sort of tenacity enough. I don't think you see people open up their hearts and expose themselves the way you have. So I'm truly impressed by you, and you continue to impress me each and every day."

Her eyes grow watery, and her hand gradually moves to my neck. "Thank you," she says softly. "That was...that was really nice of you."

"I mean it."

She nods. "I know you do, Wilder. I know you do."

And that right there, that makes me smile, because that's change. That's her coming out of this repressed shell that she's been living in and recognizing the fact that she's so much more than how her ex treated her. Sure, he might not have done anything physically bad to her, but ignoring someone, not showing their importance in your life, that is just as bad. Because that wears on you. It's manipulative and mental abuse. And she deserves so much more than that.

"Okay, my turn," she says on a deep breath. Her beautiful eyes match up with mine. "I admire your positivity, and I know you were probably hoping for something else—"

"Do not second-guess your answer," I tell her. "Be brave and tell me why you like my positivity."

"You're right. Okay." She clears her throat and continues, "I admire your positivity because as someone who spent the last few years living in a household where everything was negative, where nothing was done right, where complaining was the number one role of communication, you bring such a light to a dark, dim world. You're able to see things for their beauty rather than their flaws. You're able to find growth rather than encourage the regression. You're able to take an uncomfortable situation and put a fun twist on it. You don't let people hold you down, nor do you hold them down yourself. You lift them up. And you stand up for those who need it. I've never met anyone like you before." Her thumb strokes against my neck. "And I'm really happy that I did."

I rub my hands up her sides. "Thank you, Scottie. That was incredibly nice of you."

"I mean it," she says with a smirk.

"I know you do."

Then the music ends, and Sanders calls out. "Okay, rotate seats."

Scottie gets off my lap and takes my hand in hers as we move over to the next chair. I take a seat first, and once again, she climbs onto my lap, but this time, there's no hesitation; she almost seems at home as she sits on top of me. And I like that.

I like that a lot.

The music starts, and I pull the card from the side of the chair and, once again, read it out loud.

"Cup your partner's cheek, bring your foreheads together, and whisper what you like most about their body." I look up at Scottie. "Huh, this is a bit more intense."

"It'll be fine," she says with a wave of her hand.

So we both grip each other's cheeks, my palm to her soft skin. Then together, we touch our foreheads, the position oddly comforting given how close we are. I stare into her eyes, our noses nearly connecting.

She wets her lips, and then I do the same as a spark of electricity seems to bounce between us.

Yeah…way more intense.

She goes first and surprises me as she says, "You have the nicest stack of abs I think I've ever seen on a man. Like, incredible. Defined. Sexy. Just hard not to stare at."

I can't hold back my smile. I know this is hard for her, offering compliments. A part of me thinks it comes from years of little communication with her ex, but I love that she was able to jump right in and offer me a compliment. And a fucking good one at that.

"Thanks, Pips." I wet my lips again, wanting to pull her in just a little bit closer. "I've said it before and I'll say it again—I fucking love your legs. They're so sexy, and I bet…" I pause. *Do I say the rest? Do I tell her what I'm really thinking?* Why the fuck not? "I bet they'd look good wrapped around me."

Her mouth slightly parts as her grip on my cheek shifts. I wait for her to pull away, to almost be surprised by my answer, but instead, she replies, "I love your arms. It's obvious that you spend time in the gym, and I love that they're not super bulky but rather thick and carved, and they wrap around me perfectly."

I tug on my lip ring and say, "Pips, that ass of yours in those pajama shorts that you wear? Deathly. I can't tell you how many times I've snuck glances at you while you wear those."

I can feel her cheek heat from the compliment.

"You have a nice…um…bulge."

That makes me chuckle.

"Just…thick-looking."

"Checked it out?"

"Hard not to in the shorts you wear."

Satisfaction rushes through me. "You have great tits. I stared at them a few times while you were in your bathing suit. Also, amazing nipples, and you have no problem with them being hard, which I love. I hate when women hide their hard nipples. You don't. You just let them be hard, and it's sexy as fuck."

She wets her lips again, and I catch her chest rising and falling just a little bit harder. "I really like how big—"

"Time's up," Sanders says as the music stops, and we're forced to get out of our chair.

She takes my hand, and I lean down and whisper, "You really like how big what?"

She shakes her head. "That activity is over. On to the next."

"Tease," I say, tugging on her hand as we find the next seat.

Once we are situated, the music starts, and I pull the card.

"Take this time to freely touch your partner in any way you want." I lift a brow and smirk at her. "Any way I want, huh? Where should I start?"

"You seem far too excited about this."

"Damn right I am. After you fondled me this morning, it's my turn to have some fun." I wiggle my eyebrows, and she rolls her eyes dramatically.

Fuck, I'm loving this playful, lighter side of her.

"Well, I know where I want to start," she says.

"Yeah? Where's that? Where you left off this morning?"

"No," she answers and then lifts her thumb to my lip ring. "This fascinates me. I feel feral when you tug on it with your teeth."

"Feral, huh?"

"It's just one of those things that you don't expect to be sexy, but then it is. Just like your tattoo." Her finger drags over the ink. "It's really simple, understated, yet it looks incredibly hot on you."

"Is that all you want to touch?" I ask her, loving that she's taking free rein.

"No." Her eyes meet mine.

"What else do you want to touch?" I nearly whisper.

"Your stomach," she says.

"Have at it, babe." I scoot down a little on the chair and lift up my shirt between us, showing off my abs.

She immediately sighs and then moves her fingers over my stomach with zero hesitation but instead ready to own me with her touch. "This can't be real." Divot by divot, she lets her fingers explore, and I watch her eyes intently as they grow with hunger.

"It's real," I say.

And then to my surprise, she moves her hand up my stomach to my chest and over my left pec. Her palm connects with my nipple as she coyly smirks.

"You're feeling me up, Pips. Nipple and all."

Her cheeks blush. "Matt was never fit, and that's fine, but being near you, getting a chance to feel muscles like this, I don't know, it's kind of addicting. I like all your contours and sinew. Is that weird of me to say?"

"No," I say as I allow my shirt to fall down, but she keeps her hand in place, letting her fingers run over my stomach until they reach the waistband of my shorts. "Watch it there, Pips. You don't want to get too close."

"Yeah, wouldn't want that," she says and then pulls away, leaving my skin on fire. "Okay, your turn."

"To touch you?" I shake my head. "Anything I want to touch would be incredibly inappropriate in public."

"And what would that be?"

I give her a "get real" look. "Scottie. Minutes ago, I went off about how hot your tits and ass are. You really think I'm about to feel you up?"

"I just felt you up."

"That's different."

"How so?" she asks.

"I don't know, but it feels different."

She rolls her eyes, picks up my hand, and places it on her breast.

Our eyes meet, and I say, "Wow, this is really sexy."

She chuckles and says, "Give me a squeeze."

"Scottie."

"I'm serious, Wilder. Feel me."

I'm tempted. I'm so fucking tempted, but also, I know one squeeze won't be enough. "Scottie." I swallow. "I don't want to make you uncomfortable."

"I'm making you touch my breast. Do you think I'm uncomfortable?" she shifts on my lap. "Just feel me, Wilder."

The way she says it, with a pleading tone, it almost breaks me.

Almost…

"Babe, I'm not going to—"

"Time's up," Sanders says. "Move on to the next chair."

I drop my hand from her breast, and we stare at each other for a few seconds, disappointment washing through her eyes right before she stands. This time, she straightens out her clothes and then turns away from me, not taking my hand in hers as we move to the next chair.

Fuck.

It's immediate.

I can feel the cold coming from her. The distance she's putting between us.

Her body language changed.

Her demeanor is no longer easygoing.

And I wonder if denying her what she wanted was something her ex used to do?

But did she seriously want me to feel her up right here?

I was trying to be respectful.

Waging a war of uncertainty in my head, I take a seat on the chair, and she drops down on my lap as Sanders calls out, "Now remember, we need to be doing this correctly. Read the cards, and perform the tasks to the best of your ability. This is a learning exercise. If we don't follow through, we will do it again."

"Did you hear that, Wilder?" she whispers. "Perform your task to the best of your ability."

"I heard him," I say as I take the card off the side of the chair and read it out loud. "Kiss your partner, no tongue allowed." My eyes immediately shoot up to Scottie.

Kiss?

We have to kiss each other?

Well...fuck.

And here I thought this was going to be an easy activity with just questions. It started off so innocent but turned to fondling and now this?

"Um, are you okay with me kissing you?" I ask her.

"Doesn't look like we have a choice. Question is are you okay with it? You couldn't even touch me at the last chair."

"Don't," I say as I put the card back. "Don't start a fight. And don't start thinking things in that head of yours. I was being respectful."

"We're not supposed to be respectful right now, Wilder. We're supposed to be following directions."

"You want to follow directions? Okay," I say and then cup her cheek and bring her in close to me.

I let my lips barely drag over her cheek and then to her ear, where I kiss her lobe, then the spot below her ear and across her jaw. Her breathing picks up as I move over to her chin and then to the other side of her jaw.

"I wasn't not touching you because I didn't want to touch you," I say as I tilt her chin up with my thumb and then work my lips down her neck. "I wasn't touching you because if I did...I probably wouldn't have stopped."

My lips move up to her cheek, to the spot below her ear again, and then back to her cheek, where I reach her nose.

"If you haven't realized, Scottie, I'm really fucking attracted to you, and I'm trying to give you space. Trying to let you heal." I kiss the corner of her mouth, causing her to take in a deep breath. "I'm trying to be a goddamn gentleman, but apparently"—I kiss the other corner of her mouth—"you don't want that." And then I press my lips to hers, shattering the calm that's been building between us and twisting our situationship into chaos, because holy fuck, her lips are so soft.

Fucking softest lips I've ever kissed in my life.

And this is exactly why I was trying to stay away, keep a healthy distance, because I knew this was going to happen. One taste was all it would take to wake me up and start craving.

I slide my hand behind her head, cupping the nape of her neck, and cup her ass with my other hand, pulling her in even tighter. Her arms lock around my neck as she kisses me back.

She kisses me back softly, with no urgency, just enjoying the feel of our mouths entwining.

She's slow, thoughtful, not taking, just receiving.

Which makes me feel even more crazed, even more dazed. Because I'm thrumming inside.

Burning.

It's as if one touch of her lips to mine was like a bolt of lightning zapping through me, waking me up from a slumber I've been in for years.

"Okay, switch," Sanders calls out as Scottie pulls away.

Jesus.

Slowly, my eyes open as I take in her expression. Her tongue peeks out and wets her lips, making me feel absolutely fucking unhinged.

She gets up from my lap, and before she can walk away, I snag her hand in mine and move over to the next chair. Once we're settled, Sanders starts the music, and I try to gather myself as my heart hammers in my chest. I pull the card from the side and read it out loud.

"Make out."

My chest goes heavy as I set the card to the side. Her hand smooths up my chest to the back of my neck, and then she moves her body in close, her breasts scraping against my chest before her mouth connects with mine, but this time, she's in control.

And this time, she parts my lips, slipping her tongue against mine.

I sigh into the kiss and allow her to control it as I bring my hands to her shirt and slide them under the fabric and right up her back, my palms to her heated skin.

She scoots in closer and tangles her tongue with mine, taking the card incredibly seriously, which creates an inferno between us. And even though we're in a room where other couples are making out around us, I can only feel her. *I am only interested in her.*

Heat builds and builds inside me, lighting me up and making me so goddamn desperate for the next taste, for the next lick, for so much more than just making out.

I want to unsnap her bra and play with her breasts, feel her up like she wanted me to, like she felt me up this morning. I'd drop her down to the ground, bring her shirt over her head, and allow my tongue to wander. To taste her skin, to wait desperately to see what kind of sounds she makes. I'd find myself between her legs, licking, sucking. I want to explore her gorgeous body. Fuck, I want to feel those legs of hers wrapped tightly around me.

With every pass of her tongue across mine, that need grows stronger and stronger as a moan falls out of my throat.

Her grip on me grows tighter.

Her mouth opens wider.

And I take that moment to slip my hand past the waistband of her jeans, where I grip her ass just as Sanders calls out, "Time's up."

"Fuck," I mutter as she pulls away, leaving me in a goddamn daze.

Lazily, I watch as her tongue drags over her lips, keeping her eyes on me the entire time.

Fuck me.

Fuck fucking me.

I'm turned on.

I'm hard.

I'm now desperate for more.

I feel unhinged, and at any point, I might just snap from the need pulsing through me for this woman.

"Next and last chair," Sanders says.

Clearing my throat, I stand from the chair, adjust myself quickly, and then walk over to the last chair, wondering if this where we end up dry humping. I mean, we've built up to that point. I wouldn't be surprised, and frankly, I'm kind of hoping for it.

"Okay, read your cards," Sanders calls out.

I reach to the side, grab the card, and then read it out loud as my body buzzes from the kiss we just shared.

"Tell each other your favorite drink." My brows knit together. "That's the task? Tell each other our favorite drink?" I look at the back of the card, wondering if this is a trick. Where is the dry humping? Where's the kissing and fondling? Where's the "Get naked with your partner and have a good time"? "He's going to make us go from making out to telling each other our favorite drink? Why?"

"Maybe because you're parched after making out," she says.

"Are you parched?"

She just shrugs her shoulders, acting so fucking nonchalant that it actually doesn't settle well. Because we just made out, tongue and all, and she's acting like it's another day in the office. Like our kiss had zero effect on her.

That can't possibly be true.

Isn't she buzzing like I am?

Isn't she ready to move this to the next step?

Doesn't she want more?

"Well, I guess I'll lead the conversation since you seem a little stumped." She taps her chin with her finger and says, "Hmm, you know, I think I'll have to go with an Arnold Palmer. There's something about the iced tea, lemonade combination that gets me every time. But it has to be a good ratio, you know? It can't be too sweet with the lemonade, and the iced tea has to be unsweetened."

So she's just going to act like everything is normal and talk about iced tea to lemonade ratios? How?

How is she not inwardly panting?

How does she not look dazed and confused?

How is she not on the verge of licking me all over like I want to lick her? Claim her.

"What about you?" she asks.

I scratch the back of my head and say, "Uh, I don't know...Dr Pepper."

"Really? Kind of thought you would say Coke because of your soda app."

Shit, she's right. I can't even think of my favorite drink, that's how out of sorts I am.

"Are we talking your main love? Like that's what you need in order to live? I mean, I guess I don't need an Arnold Palmer to live, but that wasn't the question either. Just our favorite drink, so I think I'll stick with my answer. You sticking with Dr Pepper?"

I stare at her.

Blink.

Grow annoyed with her easygoing attitude.

"Yeah. Sticking with Dr Pepper," I answer, even though inwardly, I'm screaming Coke. I love Coke!

"Great."

"Time's up," Sanders says.

"Well, this was fun," Scottie says as she gets off my lap.

"Yeah," I say, still confused by her change of attitude.

"I actually think I have to go to the bathroom. Excuse me." She pats my chest and then takes off as if everything in the world is fine.

Meanwhile, I'm over here reeling.

Fucking reeling.

Because I just made out with Scottie, and I more than liked it. I loved it.

I want to do it again.

And again.

But this time, with her shirt off.

This time, with her bra off.

This time...in fucking private. *With every article of clothing off our bodies.*

CHAPTER TWENTY
SCOTTIE

OH MY GOD.

Oh my God.

Oh my *fucking* God!

I slip into the main building of Camp Haven and right up to the front desk, where I speak to one of the camp counselors...or whatever they're called.

"I need to make a phone call. It's urgent. Like, really urgent. Could you please give me a quarter so I can make said phone call?" When the girl doesn't answer the second I'm done talking, I slam my hand on the counter and say, "Please. I need to make this phone call. Like right now. Right this very instant."

"Okay," she says, looking terrified.

I don't blame her; I'm giving off irrational energy, because that's exactly how I feel.

Irrational.

Terrified.

Confused.

She hands me a quarter, and I run over to the godforsaken red phone booth, slam the door behind me, and dial Denise's number. If she doesn't answer, I'm going to scream, because I need someone to talk to...stat.

The phone rings.

And rings.

And rings...

My stomach bottoms out, and then, "Hello?"

"Oh my God, Denise, I have to talk to you, or I might burst into nothing. Thank God you answered, because if you didn't, I would have one hundred percent turned into dust, and I don't want to be dust, because holy shit, oh my God, and what the fuck!"

"Umm...Scottie?"

"Yes, it's Scottie. My God, who else would it be?"

"Okay, you just caught me off guard—"

"There's no time for pleasantries. I'm on a freaking pay phone, and I'm unsure of how much time I have here. So I'm just going to tell it to you straight. I just made out with Wilder. Like tongue action and all, and not because we wanted to but because it was part of an exercise we had to do, but Jesus, was I into it. I mean, I got lost in the feel of his mouth, the way his tongue pressed against mine, his light moans. It was visceral. I felt that kiss all the way to my freaking loins, Denise. My loins!"

"Dear God," she whispers. "Not the loins."

"The loins!" I shout, and then realize the receptionist is looking at me. I turn away from her and lower my voice. "And he was kissing me back. Like desperately. I tried to play it cool, like 'Oh, ain't no big thing, I kiss people all the time,' but I throbbed, Denise. I throbbed in places I don't think I've throbbed in a long time. If I were to be honest, the last time I throbbed like that, I stumbled across *True Lies* with Jamie Lee Curtis, when she's trying to seduce Arnold in the bedroom."

"Why is that the example you gave me?"

"It's not an example. It's the truth! There was throbbing."

"Okay, enough with the throbbing. There are things I don't need to hear."

"I need to tell you about the throbbing so you can understand where I'm coming from. And I mean, I've throbbed a little. I had to share a tent with him, but this was like...things are moving around down there."

"Please, for the love of God, stop describing your parts."

"It's true!"

"That's great. Keep the truth to yourself. So why are you calling?"

"Because I shouldn't be throbbing and making out with Mika's little brother. What am I thinking? God, he's so hot. Have you ever seen him? He's so muscular and handsome, and his eyes are unlike anything I've ever seen, and Jesus, the lip ring. My God, Denise, he has this black lip ring in the corner of his mouth that drives me absolutely insane. He tugs on it with his teeth in this innocent way that makes me believe he's not so innocent. And he says such nice things about me, and he really likes my legs and my boobs, but he doesn't say boobs, he says tits, and that is so much hotter."

"Okay, hold up. You're rambling."

"I know, because I have limited time, and I need to tell you everything."

"I think what you need to tell me is that you're crushing on Wilder, and you don't know what to do about it."

"Crushing?"

"Yeah, you're crushing on him."

"No, I don't think that's a thing."

She laughs. "It is one hundred percent a thing. You are clearly crushing on him, and that's okay. You're allowed to crush on your fake husband. You've been single for a while now. You're allowed to look and mingle and see what else is out there."

"But…"

"But what? Girl, if I were you and I was sleeping in a cabin with a hot guy, I'd have fun. I mean, why not? What's holding you back?"

"I don't know. I didn't…I didn't come here to make out with a guy and have fun touching him."

"Yeah, you went there to show your boss that you weren't lying even though you were lying, and then you started making out with your fake husband, so I don't think you actually went there for anything other than a bunch of fuckery. So why not fuck around?"

I mean…she's sort of right. I did come here for a bunch of fuckery. There was no rhyme or reason, just to make it through the eight days. But do I really want to fuck around?

"I don't know if that's a good idea," I say.

"Why? Are you worried about Mika? Because he was telling me the other day that he'd be shocked if you two don't end up hooking up. He said his brother would be stupid if he didn't at least make a move."

"Mika said that?" I ask.

"Yup. He doesn't care. He actually likes the idea of the two of you."

"I…I can't think about that. And honestly, I'm not worried about Mika. I'm worried about me."

"Worried about you why?"

"Because," I say softly. "He's…he's too nice, Denise."

"Um, why is that a bad thing?"

"It's not. It's a good thing, but what if, I don't know, I fuck around and get attached? I could see that happening. He's really kind and sweet and thoughtful and has a way with his words that makes me feel special. He's told me time and time again that he means everything he says, but I still have this thought in the back of my mind, this doubt that maybe he feels bad for me and he's saying all these nice things and kissing me the way he kissed me because he wants me to see what it's like to be treated well. And then what? I get attached, and he walks away, unscathed, while I'm left to lick my wounds again?"

"Do you really think he'd do that?"

"I…I don't—"

The line goes dead, and I'm tempted to scream, but instead, I take a deep breath and hang up the phone. I take a few seconds to gather myself, put on a smile, and make it seem like my emotions are not completely out of control, even though they are.

"Everything okay?" Wilder asks as I sit down next to him on a bench that overlooks the lake.

"Yup, everything is great," I answer. "Did I miss anything after I left?"

"No," he says. "Just that Sanders was very proud of everyone."

"Good," I say with a head nod. I watch a duck fly down to the lake and dip its head underwater. "Well, that was a fun experiment, wasn't it?"

"Very fun. Almost so much fun that it seemed like you had to run away to get your energy out."

"What?" I say on an awkward laugh. "Run away? Why would I do that?"

"I don't know," he responds. "Just seemed odd, because I was over there feeling a certain way, and then all of a sudden, you were gone."

"You were feeling a certain way?" I ask. "What do you mean by that?"

He drags his hand over his face. "I don't know, Scottie, I—"

"Scottie, Wilder, come join us," Sanders calls out.

We look over our shoulders to where he's waving us down.

"It's cocktail time."

Cocktail time?

As in alcohol?

I distinctly remember him saying there were some nights we'd be allowed to have alcohol. Well, if there was ever a night when I truly needed it—this would be it.

I stand from the bench, but Wilder takes my hand. "Hey, we were in the middle of a conversation."

"I know, but he's calling us over."

He frowns, clearly not happy with my retreat, but I can tell you right now, I'm not mature enough to have this conversation with him, even though I know he is. How ironic, given he's younger than me.

Standing, he keeps my hand in his, and we walk over to the dining hall, where Sanders has a bar set up along with a bunch of finger foods and some games.

"There they are, the hottest couple of the day," Sanders says with a wink.

"Hottest?" I ask.

"Oh yes." He starts making us each a cocktail...with copious amounts of rum. "I talked with all the counselors, and they agreed your make-out session was the most intense. Seemed like you guys couldn't get enough of each other. The night in the tent must have really done its job."

I chuckle nervously. "Well, you know what they say. Holding out has its charms."

"I might need to put that into my practice. Seems like it has really worked for you two. But don't get complacent. You still need to work at this and practice your communication."

"I could not agree more," Wilder says. "Communication is key."

Could he be any more obvious?

"That's right. Now, take your drinks, fill up a plate of food, and head on over to table number twelve, where you'll be playing a game. We have certain games picked out for each couple, so I hope you enjoy."

"Thank you," we both say and then head on over to the food, where we stack our plates full, and find table twelve, which is in the back.

There's nothing on the table other than a stack of cards. The other tables have games like Connect Four, Battleship, even Pictionary, but we just have a stack of cards.

Makes me nervous...

We both take a seat, and Wilder holds his drink out to me. "Cheers," he says. "On a successful make-out session."

My smile wobbles as I say, "Cheers."

He takes a large gulp of his drink and then hisses while setting the glass down. "Fuck, that's a lot of rum."

Thank God.

I take a large sip as well and feel the alcohol burn all the way down my throat. Yup, that feels nice. Let's keep them coming.

"Hello, you two," Sanders says, startling the both of us. "Thought I'd let you know that I chose a particularly special game for the both of you. One that I hope you have fun playing. It's just a question-and-answer game. And once you answer, you must take a drink of your drink."

"Wow, are you trying to get us drunk?" Wilder asks.

Sanders winks. "That's the plan." Then he walks away, leaving us to our game, drinks, and food.

Not wanting to get sick with too much drinking, I pick up one of the beef crostini and take a large bite while Wilder picks up a card.

He reads it over, smirks, and then looks me in the eyes.

Uh-oh, I don't like that look.

It smells like trouble.

"Scottie," he clears his throat, "what is your favorite sexual fantasy?"

I nearly choke on my bread when I say, "It says that?"

He turns the card toward me and says, "Yup."

So I see where this evening will be taking us.

I should have known given the activity we just had.

And I know there is going to be no escaping it. Wilder won't let me, so I might as well just live in it.

"Favorite sexual fantasy? Umm...I don't know, coming while he's inside me."

Wilder has his drink halfway to his mouth when he pauses and then lowers his glass back down before leaning forward and saying, "Wait, that's your fantasy?"

I shrug. "I know it's not wild, but it would be nice to know what that feels like. I want myself coming over his cock, you know?"

Wilder's eyes go wide as I sip my drink. "Jesus," he mutters and shakes his head, sipping his drink as well.

"Are you judging me?"

"No," he says. "I'm judging Matt."

"Good answer." I pick up a card and ask, "What's your favorite type of porn to watch?" I set the card down and wait for his answer as I pick up a piece of cheese and eat it.

He smooths his hand over his jaw, thinking about it. "Uh, you know, I flock toward more of the sensual kind of porn. I don't like anything fake, and I prefer when it seems like the couple actually knows and likes each other. Nothing too over-the-top."

"Huh, didn't think you'd answer that."

"Why not?" he asks before drinking.

"I don't know. You seem irritated with me."

"I am irritated with you, but it doesn't mean I'm not going to answer the question."

"And why are you irritated with me?"

He leans in close and says, "Because we made out, and you acted like it meant nothing."

"Did it mean something to you?"

He drags his tongue over his teeth and then says, "Scottie, I felt that fucking kiss through my entire fucking body."

"Oh," I say, unsure how to really reply to that, other than…same.

And I'm about to when he grabs a card and reads it out loud. "What do you think about when you masturbate?"

Oh, God, these questions are not what I was expecting.

"And don't tell me you don't masturbate. That's a lie," he says.

"I wouldn't say that." I give it some thought. "Umm, I don't think I think about anything. I kind of just go for it and let my body feel the pleasure. That's pretty much it."

"And how do you masturbate?"

"You can't ask two questions."

He flashes the card to me. "It's on the card."

Damn it.

"Um, I mean, with my fingers."

"That's it?" he asks. "You don't watch anything?"

I shake my head. "No, I like playing with my nipples first, teasing myself. And then I work my hand down between my legs where I'm ready, and then I just...circle around, you know?"

He slowly nods, wetting his lips. "Yup, I do fucking know."

The way he's looking at me—it's dangerous. Very dangerous. So dangerous that I fear what it might be like when we get back to the cabin.

I pick up a card and read him the next question. "Would you prefer to be loud when having sex or quiet, as if you're pretending that no one can hear you?"

"Loud," he answers and then drinks. "I want everyone around me knowing that I'm fucking my girl, that she's having a good time...and that she's coming on my cock, because that's how my girls come."

Well...there you have it. He's fulfilling my sexual fantasy with other people. Then again, I would have easily guessed that Wilder is the kind of guy who can make that happen. Just from the way he pulls on that lip ring, I can tell that he has the moves, the swagger that makes a woman lose all control when he's inside her.

And yup...there I go, throbbing again.

I clear my throat. "That's, uh, that's really good to know. Happy for you."

"Thanks," he says and picks up another card just as a second round of drinks is dropped off at our table. "Is spanking something you'd like to try with me?"

My eyes widen from the thought.

Try with...*me.*

Why does that feel like an invitation?

"Uh, I don't know. Remember, standards are low. I'd just like to orgasm at this point."

He sets the card down, looking incredibly disgruntled.

Not wanting to dive into those feelings, I pick up a card and read it out loud. "What color underwear would you like to see me in?"

"None," he answers without skipping a beat. "Absolutely none."

"Oh—"

He leans in and says, "And I'd want you to tease me about it. I'd want you to be wearing a short skirt with no underwear and then come up to me in my office or while I was on the phone and bend over right in front of me. I'd want to see everything, Scottie. Fucking everything. I'd want you to torture me with the knowledge that you're not wearing underwear, to the point that I could not do anything about it until many hours later."

Wow.

That humid summer air is pumping.

"Um—"

"And when I did get a chance to take care of it, I'd keep you bent over, spank that fine ass of yours, and then bury myself between your legs until you're coming...on...my...thick...long...pierced cock."

Dear God in heaven. Is it...is it hot in here?

Because I'm hot. Is anyone else hot?

I need a fan.

Did he just say pierced?

I think he said pierced.

He downs the rest of his drink and then says, "Your turn."

My turn?

He expects me to just answer a question after he announced to the table that he's pierced down below? Does he really think I can just function? As if everything is okay?

Because it's not.

Everything is not okay.

I have questions.

Serious questions.

Like...where exactly is he pierced? Does he like it? Does it feel good for him? Would it feel good for...other people? Why did he decide to share that private information?

Why is he looking at me right now as if he could put me on this table and…eat me?

"How's it going over here?" Sanders asks, startling me.

"Fine," I yelp. "Fine. Everything is fine."

"Really? You seem a little jumpy."

"No, not jumpy." I push my hair behind my ears.

Just turned on and questioning every choice I've made leading up to this point.

"She does seem a little jumpy, doesn't she?" Wilder asks. "I think it's the questions that are making her jumpy."

"Ah, yes, I can imagine. Which one did you just answer?"

"What color underwear I like her best in," Wilder answers, clearly not caring at all about privacy. "Of course, it's a clear-cut answer. None. Then I went into detail about a scenario I've thought about when she's not wearing any underwear."

Sanders chuckles. "Hence the jumpiness."

"I'm not jumpy," I defend.

"Seems like you're jumpy," Wilder presses. "Not sure she could handle my suggestion of what she'd do with no underwear."

"Uh, I could handle it," I say, even though I don't believe it for a second.

"You know, there's only one way to find out," Sanders says with a wiggle of his brow before he takes off.

I cross my arms at my chest and huff. "I could handle it."

"I don't know if you could. Have you ever gone without underwear?"

"Uh, yeah, every night. I don't sleep with underwear on, so…eat that."

"I'd love to fucking eat you," he says and pops a piece of cheese in his mouth.

"I didn't say 'eat me.' I said 'eat that.'"

"I know. I heard you."

And then, as if he knows…he tugs on that godforsaken lip ring, and I feel my nipples go hard as I watch in slow motion the most nonsexual

sexual thing to ever happen. A black lip ring. Who knew? Who knew that would be my kryptonite? Who knew that it would make me weak in the knees? Who knew that a freaking piece of jewelry the radius of my pinkie finger would turn me on to the point that I'd want to howl for attention?

"You ready for another question?" he asks, knowing damn well he has me in a position of horniness.

I clear my throat. "Yes."

"Good. Where would you like to be kissed other than your mouth?"

"Umm…" I look away, because his stare is far too intense. "Cheek is great. Thanks."

"Cheek?" he says, skeptical. "You can't tell me you like being kissed on the cheek more than somewhere else."

"What are you implying?" I ask, dabbing my mouth with my napkin.

"I'm implying that you would prefer to have your pussy kissed."

"Dear God," I hiss-whisper as I look around to see if anyone heard that. "What on earth has gotten into you?"

"What are you talking about?" he asks.

"I'm talking about this…this seductress you're turning into."

"I'm not turning into a seductress."

"Then why are you so cranky and acting very sexual?"

"Because," he says, leaning forward. "I'm trying to get a reaction out of you, since you refused to react after we kissed."

"I reacted. And, uh, before you start pointing fingers, you refused to squeeze my breast."

"So this is payback?"

"How am I paying you back?" I ask, confused.

"By having zero reaction to our kiss. Not even an ounce of a reaction. You acted like it was nothing."

"Because maybe it was nothing," I say, regretting the words the moment they come out of my mouth.

He leans back in his chair, hurt, pain, frustration all crossing his features. "I see. So you felt nothing back there?"

God, don't do this, Scottie.

Don't make it worse.

I feel so out of sorts, because I don't think I've felt that kind of passion in years, if ever.

"Wilder, that's not what I meant. I think we're just, you know, trying to figure everything out."

"No, I don't know." He shakes his head and then pushes his chair away from the table. "I have to go to the bathroom."

And then with that, he takes off, heading toward the main building.

He wanted a reaction? Well, I should have told him about the throbbing, because that was one hell of a reaction I wasn't expecting.

CHAPTER TWENTY-ONE
WILDER

"HEY, UM, I NEED TO make a phone call," I say while tapping my fingers on the reception desk. "I need to check on my brother."

"Wilder, right?" the receptionist says.

"Yes, that would be me."

"Okay, hold on one second." She reaches into her desk drawer, and I wait impatiently as she locates a quarter and then hands it to me.

"Thanks," I say, taking the quarter from her and walking over to the booth. I have no idea if Mika is going to answer, but I'm hoping he will.

I dial his phone number and then wait for him to pick up.

Thankfully, he answers on the second ring. "Hello?"

"Mika, it's Wilder."

"Hey, brother," he says, sounding like he's in a jovial mood. "Glad to hear from you."

"You are?" I ask.

"Very."

Okay, something's going on, because this is not the usual Mika.

So because I have very little time, I ask, "What's going on? Why do you sound happy?"

"Oh, just got done talking to my good friend Denise. She went and told me that you and Scottie are having a good time at camp."

"Did Scottie call Denise?"

"Oh yes, she did."

"What did she say?" I ask so quickly that it sounds like one giant word all smushed together.

"Oh, just that you two made out."

Well, news travels fast, that's for damn sure. That's what she was doing instead of going to the bathroom like she said she was—she called Denise, just like I called Mika. I'd be amused if I wasn't so irritated.

My voice comes out stern as I say, "Tell me everything she said."

"No 'How are you? How are you doing? Everything okay over there?'"

"Mika, you know I don't have a lot of time on these phone calls. You good?"

"I'm good."

"Okay, then tell me everything."

He chuckles and says, "Just that she was freaking out that you guys kissed and that she really liked it and that she thinks you're really hot, and Denise called her out on having a crush on you."

I feel like a crazy man, because what?

"Wait, so she was freaking out about the kiss?"

"She was. Big time. Why? Is she acting differently?"

"Uh, yeah. Really fucking differently, as if the kiss didn't even affect her in the slightest."

"Oh, it affected her. Pretty sure she used the word 'throbbing' when talking to Denise."

Throbbing?

That liar!

"You've got to be fucking kidding me," I say as I shake my head. "Jesus, here I was thinking that she couldn't care less about it, but in reality, she was throbbing."

"I heard there was a lot of throbbing."

A lot?

I mean...that does make me feel better.

"Well...fuck."

I drag my hand over my face.

"What are you going to do about it?" Mika asks.

"I don't know. What do you want me to do about it?"

"You want my honest opinion?"

"Yeah, I really do," I say, feeling lost, confused, on edge.

Mika chuckles again. "Brother, listen carefully, okay? I want you to show my best friend a good fucking time. The best fucking time you can give her. She needs it."

"Really? You think I should?"

"I know you should."

"And you're okay with that?"

"Uh, the moment I found out you two were headed to a camp together where you have to share a cabin, there was no doubt in my mind what you two would end up doing. I'm just shocked it took this long. But the question is, do you want to do anything with her? Are you attracted to her?"

"Dude, she's gorgeous. Has the prettiest fucking eyes I've ever seen, and her lips are fucking incredible. Soft, dude. So fucking soft. And she kissed with confidence. I was almost waiting for her to be shy about it, but she wasn't. She was so goddamn confident. I want...I want another taste. I'm desperate for it."

"Okay, I don't need the details."

"You asked."

"I know, but seriously, keep the lip stuff to yourself."

"It's true."

"I'm sure it is. I'll trust you on this. But if that's how you feel, then maybe test it out, have some fun."

"And what happens when we get back home and camp is over and we're no longer pretending?" I ask. "I'm not...I'm not one to be in a relationship or anything like that. I don't want to hurt her."

"And why don't you want to be in a relationship again? Because of Mom? Because of me? That's no fucking excuse, and you know that."

"I'm not looking for an excuse, I'm just looking to be ready is all."

"I get that. My love life is all kinds of fucked up, so I have no room to judge, but I will say this. Scottie is a once-in-a-lifetime girl. She's loyal, she's smart, she keeps her friends close to her heart, and she deserves the world, something I believe you could give her."

He really believes that about me? I haven't really thought of any of the girls I've dated as long-term material. I haven't even wanted a relationship, if I'm honest. He's not wrong about Scottie though. Scottie *is* a once-in-a-lifetime girl, and she deserves the moon. At the very least, she deserves to have her world rocked sexually, and it sounds like that has never happened. *Fucking Matt. What a tool.* I'm honestly still surprised that she's only been with one guy.

But if Mika thought we were such a good fit, why hasn't he said anything about her before?

"If that's the case, why didn't you introduce us sooner?"

"I was planning on it," he says. I can hear the smile in his voice. "But I was just waiting for her to be ready. She beat me to it with this marriage farce. So now you have to ask yourself: now that you know her and have been around her, what are you going to do about it?"

Great fucking question.

"Let's go for a walk," I say as I step up to the table, startling Scottie and causing her to spill her drink on her hand right before she looks up at me.

"You, uh, you startled me."

I pick up her napkin, take the drink from her, and then dab the liquid off her skin gently. When I'm done, I slip her hand into mine and pull her from her seat.

"Are we allowed to leave?" she asks, looking around for permission.

"We can do whatever we want," I say into her ear, causing her to shiver. And then I pull her toward the exit just as I make eye contact with

Sanders. I nod toward our cabin, and he smiles brightly. That's all the permission I need.

Hand in hand, we make our way outside into the humid night air, where I guide her down the pathway that runs parallel with the lake.

"What, uh, what are we doing? Are we not going back to the cabin?"

"Not quite yet."

"Okay," she says, glancing around. "Umm, nighttime stroll then?"

Ignoring her, I ask, "Are you drunk?"

"No," she says. "I mean, I can feel some of the alcohol, but I wouldn't say drunk. Comfortable."

"Good," I say and then pull her toward the forest, where I gently press her against a tree.

"Oh my." Her eyes meet mine. "Wh-what is going on?"

Slowing down and taking my time, I gently run my finger over her forehead, only to tuck a stray piece of hair behind her ear. Her eyes shine under the setting sun, and I know in this moment exactly what I'm going to do.

I don't want her pretending like that kiss meant nothing.

I don't want her acting like everything is normal.

Because it's not.

There is nothing normal about the connection I feel with her.

About the energy bouncing between us.

About the sparks that flew when her lips met mine.

Nothing normal at all.

So I lean into my decision and softly say, "Kiss me."

"Huh?" Her nose cutely scrunches up.

"Kiss me, Scottie. Without people watching, without the pressure of the camp, just...kiss me."

"Why would I do that?"

I move in closer, pressing my hand to her hip. "Because you want to. Because you need to. Because the kiss we shared back there wasn't just for pretend."

And then to remind her about the palpable connection between us, I slip my thumbs under her shirt and drag them over her hipbones, trying to get her to drop the obvious shield she has up and admit to her feelings.

"What if…what if I don't want to?"

Still holding back. I'm going to break her though.

"Then don't kiss me," I say simply. "But…" I lean in close, my lips brushing against her cheek, causing her chest to lift with an intake of breath. "I don't think that's the case. I think you do want to kiss me. I think you want to touch me, get lost in me, but you're not allowing yourself to."

Then I kiss the spot below her ear, causing her to suck in a sharp breath. *That's it, Scottie. Let yourself feel.*

I press my lips down her neck, then across her jaw while my hand climbs up her sides.

Her breath grows heavier, her lips lightly parting. As I move across her mouth, she inhales sharply before I move back to her jaw, then to her ear.

I can feel her shaking ever so slightly under my touch. I can feel her breath hold still. I can feel the vibration of want coming off her, but instead of giving in, she holds out.

She doesn't make the move.

And because I want her to be the one to make the move, because I want her to be the one who loses control, I pull away. Her eyes lift to mine, and I can see it, right there in her dilated pupils. She wants me. She just doesn't know how to claim me.

Time to show her how.

"Come on," I say as I slip my hands from her shirt and take her hand again. This time, I lead her toward our cabin. It's a fast-paced walk, not stopping for anything or anyone. When I reach the cabin, I unlock the door for the both of us and then hold it open for her to walk in first. Then I follow in behind her and lock up.

When she turns to face me, I reach behind my head and pull my shirt off, dropping it on the floor. Her eyes immediately eat me up, which is exactly what I was hoping for. I want her to be tempted. I want to push her to a limit of no return, because I know she wants this. She just needs to learn to be more assertive.

She needs to learn that it's okay to give in to her feelings.

To take what she wants.

That I'm not going to shame her.

Or block her from finding satisfaction.

Or play games with her emotions.

I move over to the bed, where I kick off my shoes and socks, and then sit up against the headboard.

"Scottie."

Her body turns to face me again.

"Huh?"

I take my time, giving her a long once-over, allowing my gaze to roam every inch of her body before I reach her eyes and say, "Strip for me."

"Wh-what?" she asks, shocked, but with a hint of intrigue.

"You heard me. Strip for me."

"I...I don't...um, that's not something—"

"I know it's not something we do. But that kiss just now, that changed everything. The relationship is different now. The intensity between us just became heavier...hotter. So...strip for me. Get fucking naked."

She bites down on the corner of her lip, and I can actually see her contemplating whether she will or not. So I decide to give her courage. I reach down to my jeans and unbutton and unzip them, letting them flap open.

"I'm halfway there. Join me, Scottie."

She waits, tugging on her shirt, looking nervous but also intrigued.

So I say, "Don't make me beg, Pips."

She still doesn't move, which makes me feel insane. I know she fucking wants this.

So I slowly walk up to her. I grip her jaw and tilt her head back so she has to look at me. "If you won't strip and show me how fucking beautiful you are, then strip me down. Take off my pants. I know you want to. You want to know what kind of piercing I have. Admit it."

She wets her lips.

"Admit it," I say again with a little more gruffness behind it.

"I...I do," she finally says, allowing her wall to lower.

And I take full advantage of it.

"Then find out," I say as I place her hands on my waist, but I don't force her. I let her decide whether she's going to do it or not.

There's a momentary pause, but after a few agonizing seconds, she slides her hands around my waist, and her fingers dip past the waistband of my jeans.

That's it, babe.

"Push them down. Push them all the way down."

Her eyes meet mine again as time seems to tick by so slowly, the energy in the room building, the tension between us sucking all the air away.

Her fingers slide an inch lower so now they're touching my ass.

And I can't fucking take this torture, so I grip her cheek, tilt her head up, and bring my mouth down to hers, where I kiss her. I kiss her fucking hard.

She sucks in a sharp breath, caught off guard, but then to my fucking pleasure, she quickly kisses me back with all the force I initially wanted from her. With all the intensity, matching mine. She pulls me in close and runs one hand up my bare back, the other one pushing my pants down lower.

"Fuck," I whisper against her mouth, getting lost in her taste. "Your mouth."

Her lips part, and her tongue darts out, causing me to groan as I deepen the kiss, sliding my hand to the back of her head, my fingers tangling in her hair.

She pushes my pants down a touch farther—they're barely hanging on now—to take control of my mouth, to make me feel fucking wild inside. Like I'm losing all control, like whatever happens next, I won't be able to contain myself.

Her palm slides to the front of my body, to my hip, right next to my growing erection. I groan into her mouth as she inches closer and closer, making needles break out over my skin, my heart pounding wildly in my chest, and causing a sweat to break out on the back of my neck.

Because please, fucking please, just make the move. Make the goddamn move, Scottie. Touch me. Play with me.

Watch me.

I don't care what it is. But make the move.

Her tongue slashes against mine, and her hand moves another inch until she slides her palm right over my erection.

"Fuck," I breathe out as I pull away for just a moment to catch her widened eyes. She gently squeezes me, and I feel everything in me fall apart—I'm hers to control. She could do whatever she wanted at this point, and I'd say yes.

She wets her lips and then slowly lowers to her knees, where she takes the waistband of my jeans and then pulls it all the way down, along with my boxer briefs. She helps me out of my clothes, and then she presses her hands to my legs and crawls up them until they reach my cock, and that's when she looks up.

Her eyes widen and her mouth slightly parts as she takes me in.

I'm stretching up my stomach now, showing off my magic cross piercing—four piercings, all on the head, forming a cross.

Before she can touch me, I take a step back and then another until I'm backing up on the bed. I take a seat, lean against the headboard, and then as I grip my cock, I say, "Strip for me."

This time, there isn't much hesitation on her end.

She lifts her shirt up and over her head, revealing a purple bra with pink embroidered flowers. And then she pushes her shorts down, revealing a matching pair of underwear.

Jesus, she's so fucking hot.

I let my eyes wander as I look over her breasts, firmly cupped into her bra with a sizable amount of cleavage that's making my mouth water. Her hourglass curves are what she keeps hidden under her looser-fitting clothes. Such a goddamn shame.

I slowly move my hand over my cock, and in a husky voice, I say, "Crawl to me, Pips."

Standing in her lingerie, she wets her gorgeous lips and then moves to the end of the bed, gets on her hands and knees, and then, to my fucking delight, crawls to my legs, where she sits up and straddles them.

"Good girl," I say and then smoothly let my eyes roam one more time before saying, "Take your bra off."

Nervously, she reaches behind her and undoes her bra. The straps loosen, but she doesn't let it fall down quite yet. Instead, she tortures me as she slowly lowers the straps but keeps the cups in place.

"Stop hiding from me," I say. "I want to see you, all of you."

She bites down on her lip and looks off to the side—a flash of insecurity—so I grip her chin and bring her attention back to me.

"Don't," I say. "Don't get lost in that head of yours. Stay present with me." I tip her chin up. "Stay here…with me."

She nods and then lowers the bra, revealing her perfect tits.

"Jesus Christ," I mutter as I reach out and cup them. "Fuck, you're so hot."

Her nipples are small, pink, and hard as fuck. They're sexy, and I can easily see myself becoming addicted.

I let my thumbs run over her nipples, playing with them, stroking them, making her feel just as wild as I do. Her chest puffs out, and she tilts her head back as I squeeze her breasts, lightly pinch and roll her nipples, and then lean forward and pull one into my mouth.

She gasps, but her hand falls to the back of my neck, holding me in place.

"Yes," she says quietly, so fucking quietly that I almost missed it.

"Don't hide from me," I say as I switch to her other breast. "Let me hear you. You know I like it loud."

But she doesn't say anything, just remains quiet, so I decide to take matters into my own hands. I release her from my mouth and then push her back on the bed, laying her down. I reach for the waistband of her underwear, and I pull it down until it's completely off, leaving her bare.

"You're such a good girl," I say as I spread her legs, pushing them wide, only for her to close them back up. "What are you doing?"

"Wh-what are *you* doing?" she asks.

"Fucking taking a taste. Spread them."

"I…I don't…I feel like maybe skip that."

"Skip that?" I nearly feel my eyes pop out of my sockets. "You're going to deny me from taking a taste of you?"

"Just…you won't like it. Matt never—"

"Let's get one thing fucking straight," I say as I move over her. "I'm not Matt, and I love eating pussy, so spread your goddamn legs."

Hesitantly, she spreads them, but I help her spread them even more and then bend her knees up, all the way to her chest, exposing her just the way I want.

"Oh God," she whispers.

"Louder," I say. "I want you louder, Scottie. Don't make me repeat myself."

Then I move down to her bare pussy and glide my finger over her slit.

"Shit," she says, this time a touch louder.

"You're so fucking wet." I swipe at her slit again and then bring my fingers to her eyes. "See that? You're wet and ready for me." Then I suck on them. My eyes nearly roll to the back of my head from the first taste. "Motherfucker," I say right before I swipe at her pussy, lapping up her sweet taste. "Fuck, you taste amazing. Jesus, Scottie."

I part her with my fingers and lose all semblance of control as the sweetness of her arousal overtakes me. Like goddamn honey. Matt never liked this? He had lost his goddamn mind, because I would live here. It's obvious from the way I go feral as I try to lap up as much of her taste as I can. Soft, wet, fucking delicious, easily the best pussy I've ever eaten.

She tenses below me and tries to close her legs, but I keep them apart with a push while I drive long strokes over her clit.

"Fuck," she moans.

"Louder, Scottie."

I glance up to see her eyes squeeze shut as she shudders out a long breath. "Fuck," she says louder. "Oh…fuck." Her hand falls to my hair, where she pulls on the strands. "God, right…right there."

"That's it, baby. Talk to me. Tell me what you want."

"Sl-slower. Drag it out."

I listen and slow down my tongue, applying pressure as I drag over her clit.

"Oh my fucking God," she breathes out as she tenses. "Oh fuck, yes, Wilder. Oh my God, like that."

I continue to stroke and stroke and stroke until her breathing becomes incredibly labored and her legs fall open, no longer trying to hide from me. That's when I pull my mouth away and let her just feel.

Her eyes fall open, and she's about to ask what I'm doing when I bring my mouth back to her clit, but instead of long, flat strokes, I press the tip of my tongue against her and flick.

"Jesus." She shifts beneath me, and her hands fall to the sheets under us. "Oh God, what…oh fuck, what is…oh my God, Wilder."

I flick harder.

Faster.

Her head falls back. Her nipples point straight to the ceiling. Her hands curl into fists as they grip the sheets.

"Oh my God. Oh fuck. Wilder, I'm…I'm…" She doesn't get to finish her sentence, because her orgasm tips her right over the edge.

I push my fingers inside her and continue to ride out her orgasm, letting her walls contract around my fingers.

I envision that feeling around my cock.

I salivate over the thought of fucking her.

Of driving deep inside her.

Of pleasuring her with my piercings.

Giving her a new experience she'll never forget.

I continue to lick her until she has fully settled and relaxed. Her eyes flash open, and the smallest of smiles passes over her lips before she covers her mouth.

"Are you about to fucking laugh?" I ask, sitting up.

She shakes her head, but she's lying.

"You are. You're about to laugh." I grip her side and give her a tiny shake, which of course causes her to let out that laugh of hers. "Why the fuck are you laughing?"

"I'm sorry," she says in a cutely shy way. "I just...I've never spoken like that before."

I lift a brow. "You mean when you come?"

"Yeah," she says. "I just shocked myself is all."

"Good," I say and then smooth my hand up her stomach and between her breasts, where I rest my palm, right at the base of her neck. Her smile falters, and her breathing picks up again. "I like that you shocked yourself. It was incredibly hot, Scottie."

She swallows and then lifts up and pulls me in close so her lips press against mine.

And I fucking love that.

I love that she has no problem kissing me after I've gone down on her. I love that she wants more. I love that she feels confident enough to even seek out more.

"I...I want to touch you," she says.

"Touch me all you want, babe," I say as I play with her left breast, rubbing her nipple in between my fingers.

"I want you to lie down so I can touch you."

Seeing a bit of confidence in her, I take that moment to kiss her one more time and then lie back on the bed, my cock still hard as a rock.

She gets in a position where she nearly hovers over me, then her hand trails over my pecs, around my nipples, which makes my cock twitch, and then down my stomach, bypassing my cock altogether and teasing me.

"Is your plan to torture me?" I ask.

"No, just gaining some more courage."

"Courage for what? Pips, you touch me any way you want, and I'm going to fucking love it."

"You're just…intimidating." She glances down at my dick, and it takes everything in me not to chuckle.

"It's just a dick, Scottie."

"An intimidating one." Her finger lightly grazes the side, and I twitch again.

"Is it the piercings?" I ask.

"I mean…yeah. Do they hurt?"

"No," I answer. "They're really fucking sensitive and make the entire experience so much fucking better."

"Oh," she says and then moves her finger around the piercings, causing me to stiffen from the gentle touch.

"Jesus," I hiss as she starts doing figure eights around the four piercings. I didn't think I could grow harder, but here I am, aching for more, throbbing for more.

Reaching for more.

"You're so big," she says. "Thick. I…I don't know how you would fit."

"Easily, babe," I say as precum comes to the tip. She rubs it with her finger, continuing the circling, driving me absolutely nuts. "You have to give me more, Scottie. You're…you're going to make me lose it."

She glances over at me, looking surprised.

"Please, babe," I nearly beg. "Give me that mouth, that hand. Something. Anything."

Her tongue peeks out and wets her lips right before she lowers her mouth down to my cock and takes me past her lips.

Heaven.

Fucking heaven.

"Fuck," I moan and ease my body into the mattress as she starts sucking. I move her hair out of the way and watch as her cheeks hollow, her tongue swirling over the head of my cock. "Shit, Scottie. So good, you're so fucking good."

She pulls her mouth off my cock and then drags her tongue down my length until she reaches my balls. She gently cups them and then brings them to her mouth, where she runs her tongue along the seam.

I spread my legs for her, and she moves in closer, pulling my balls all the way into her mouth and gently sucking.

"Motherfucker," I call out as more precum slides onto my stomach. "Scottie, babe."

She sucks just a touch harder, and I lift up to look down at her as my cock strains up toward me, ready to fucking burst. I always liked ball play, but this, this is new. This is different. This has me questioning everything I fucking knew.

"I'm...I'm getting there."

She pauses and looks up at me. "Really?"

"Yeah, fucking really."

Is she insane? She's sucking my goddamn balls. Of course I'm getting there.

She smirks and then positions herself between my legs, drags her tongue up the underside of my length, and then opens her mouth again and takes me to the back of her throat.

"Fuck," I cry out when she swallows, causing my balls to tighten.

She pulls off and then sucks me back in, applying just enough pressure to curl my goddamn feet. It's so damn good.

So fucking good.

"Scottie, more. I need more. I want…I want your cunt."

She pauses and looks up at me.

I caress her cheek with my thumb and say, "I want that cunt. Fuck me with it."

She sits up and straddles my lap, making my mouth water. She lines herself up with my length and then lowers herself down, letting her wet center glide over my length, never inserting me but just letting me feel her clit rub against me.

"Jesus, you're wet again."

I grip her hips and help her rub against me.

"Because you turn me on," she says as her hands land on my pecs, and she moves her hips faster. "I'm so attracted to you, Wilder. Really attracted. More than I probably should be." Her fingers dig into my pecs. "And the moment we kissed, I knew it wouldn't be the last." Her eyes meet mine. "I knew I was going to need more."

Then she stops, lifts up, and positions my cock at her entrance. On a deep breath, she sinks down, and her eyes widen as she takes me all the way in.

"Oh my God!" she says as her chest heaves.

"Fuck," I cry out from how goddamn tight she is.

"Oh God, Wilder." She takes deep breaths. "I…oh my God, I'm so…I'm so full."

I need to fuck her.

Badly.

I need to pump into her. Drive my cock so far inside that I want her tasting me. I'm desperate. She's so goddamn tight that I need to feel this. I need to feel her.

But also…I need to go at her pace.

"You're fucking perfect," I say, my voice clearly in pain.

"I need to move."

For the love of God, please do.

"Move, Pips. I'm yours. Fuck me how you want."

Her head drops down, and she starts moving her hips over me, and it's the best fucking feeling I've ever felt.

Having her on top of me like this, watching her tits sway with her movement, feeling her tight cunt suck me in. Fuck, I want this to last forever.

"Oh my God, I can't, the sensation. It's...it's too much."

"No, babe, it's perfect. Now ride me, use me, fuck me, make yourself come."

Her fingers curl on my chest, and she picks up her pace even more, making my mouth go dry.

"God, yes, Wilder." She sits up and grips her breasts, continuing to ride me. "Fuck, it's so good."

"Squeeze those tits, Pips. Make me jealous you're touching them."

She runs her fingers over her pebbled nipples, squeezing, playing, making me mad with desire. I'm dripping with need, feeling far too possessive, and before I can tell myself no, I flip her to her back, spread her legs, and start driving into her, bottoming out with every pulse.

"Fuck," she calls out. "Oh fuck, Wilder."

"Take these piercings, Pips. Fucking take them." I slide my hand up to the base of her neck and gently claim her, not wanting to apply too much pressure but just enough for her to know who is fucking her...owning her.

Her chest heaves. Her breath is labored. Her perfect legs wrap around my back, and that's when I lose it.

I pump like a madman, sweat breaking out over my skin, fucking her into the mattress as she cries out in ecstasy, her walls tightening and tightening until she gasps and lets out an uncontrolled moan that seems to take over her body as her torso arches and she comes...on my cock.

"Oh my fuck!" she yells, her pussy squeezing me so goddamn tight that my legs go numb. All my pleasure pools at the base of my spine, and with one final thrust against her squeezing me, I come, spilling inside her.

"Fuck," I shout and then still, letting my cock spasm inside her. It takes a few seconds for us to both come back to reality, but when we do, I lift up to look her in the eyes and say, "That was fucking phenomenal. Jesus, Scottie."

Her eyes are heady, and swollen lips smile up at me before she reaches up and kisses me once more.

I sigh into her kiss and make out with her, because I can tell you right now, this woman, with one night together, has me wrapped around her goddamn finger. I want her world to be rocked. *I want her insane with pleasure.*

So that's what I'll do…ensure she's sated beyond her wildest dreams but also instilled with all the confidence she deserves.

CHAPTER TWENTY-TWO
SCOTTIE

"YOU OKAY?" WILDER ASKS AS he slips under the sheets and moves in right behind me, pulling my back into his chest.

"Perfect," I answer. Because I am, I feel…perfect. I feel like I'm on top of the world. I feel like this black cloud that has been hovering over my head for God knows how long has been lifted and I can finally see the light.

I've never felt so beautiful before.

I've never felt so wanted.

I've never felt so needed.

And within one night, Wilder changed all that.

Sex with him is so incredibly different from anything I ever experienced with Matt. Not that I need to compare the two, because there's a giant difference between the two men—and I mean giant—but it's the way Wilder handled me that truly has set them apart.

"You know, you didn't have to slip a shirt on. You could have slept naked," he mumbles into my ear.

"I'm wearing your shirt."

"I know. It's the only reason why I'm not pitching a fit."

I chuckle, the lightness in my chest a direct reflection of him. "I also didn't want to assume anything by sleeping naked."

"What do you mean by that?" he asks, his hand sliding under my shirt and right to my stomach.

My stomach hollows for a moment, because I'm so not used to this. I'm not used to this sort of attention. His touch. His constant need to hold me.

"Well, you know, we had sex—"

"Wait, we did?" he asks jokingly.

Faintly exasperated, I answer, "Yes, Wilder." He chuckles, and I continue, "But I wasn't sure if that was just a one-time thing—"

He laughs. "Scottie, I can tell you right now, that was not a one-time thing. Being inside you...that most certainly was not a one-time thing." His thumb skims the underside of my breast. "There is no way I could handle only fucking you once." His lips find the back of my neck.

Goose bumps break out over my skin as I shift my head to give him better access.

"Are you sure?" I ask.

He chuckles against my skin. "Positive, Pips." His lips trail up my neck and to my cheek while his hand tugs me down to lie on my back. When our eyes meet, he smiles. "There you are."

I sigh into his touch and can feel myself getting emotional over the way he treats me. And I don't want to be that person. I don't want to be the one who cries after sex, but I can feel the sting of my tears starting to form because he's so gentle. So sweet...

"Hey." His brow creases as he notices my impending emotions. "What's going on?"

I try to suck them down, hold them back, but it's no use. I've been so fucking unhappy. The last few years of pain, disappointment, and hurt come tumbling down like a boulder, destroying my feeling of joy. Because it was never like this with Matt. He never sought my pleasure. He never delighted in me, in my taste, in my body. And I can see how that damaged me now that I'm not living in it anymore.

I stayed with someone who didn't treat me the way I deserved for so long. I stayed faithful to a man who cherished his gaming console more than he cherished me. I don't believe he had a physical affair, but in some sense, he had an emotional affair with the gamers he chose to spend time with rather than his wife. *And I stayed.* It's breaking my heart all over again, simply because this stunning man holding me *showed* me what it was like to feel adored. Revered.

"Scottie, talk to me," he says as my tears brim, ready to fall over.

"I'm sorry," I say, sucking in a breath. "I'm just...my mind is reeling right now."

"Good or bad?"

"It's not about you." I caress his cheek. "You were...you were perfect. You did nothing wrong. You actually did everything right, and I'm starting to realize that I spent so much time in a relationship with someone I shouldn't have been with. I'm seeing that there is more out there in the world. There are people who'd appreciate me the way that I want to be appreciated."

"Damn right, Scottie. You deserve so much more than that fuckhead was ever able to give you. And you can't let him leave his mark on you. You can't let him live rent-free inside your head, because he doesn't deserve your time. You're so much better than that. Better than him."

"I'm really starting to realize that." A tear falls down my cheek, and he swipes it away.

"Then why are you crying?"

"I think it's a combination of a bunch of emotions. Sorrow for the woman who spent so much time with him. Joy for the woman who's no longer with him. Excitement for the woman who just had the absolute best time of her life with a man between her legs."

That draws a smirk from him. "Good answer. And for what it's worth, easily the best experience I've ever had being between a woman's legs."

I'm about to tell him he doesn't have to say that, but I stop myself, because I know I can trust him. I know he's telling the truth. I know he wouldn't say something just to say it. He's not that man.

"Thank you." I drag my finger over the scruff on his jaw. "Your piercings were unlike anything I've ever felt before."

"You liked it?"

"More than I probably should."

He chuckles. "Well, make sure you take full advantage of it. Hop on whenever you want."

"Better watch what you say. I might just take you up on that."

"Pips, if you don't, I'm going to be pissed."

———

"Why are you wearing a towel?" Wilder asks as he lies on the bed... freshly showered and naked.

"Because I just got out of the shower."

He shakes his head. "Not an excuse. Drop the towel, Pips."

"We have a therapy session to get to," I say, even though I start walking toward him.

"Well aware of the schedule. That's why you need to drop the towel."

"Wilder—"

"Drop...the...towel."

He scoots off the bed and then crooks his finger at me, beckoning me over.

I slowly walk toward him, only for him to tug on my hand, forcing the towel to drop, and bring me up against his chest, where he wraps his arm around me and then uses his other hand to grip my jaw and tilt my mouth up to his.

In seconds, he's consuming me.

His lips owning mine.

His hands claiming me.

Scooping me up.

And plopping me on the bed only for him to hover over me, where his tongue dances across mine, over my jaw, down my neck, and to my breasts, where he plays, lapping at them.

Squeezing.

Nibbling.

"God," I moan, shifting beneath him and widening my legs, giving him more room.

He leans in more, pressing his body to mine, letting me feel just how hard he's grown in the matter of seconds.

"We have…we have to be quick," I mutter right before his lips find mine again, silencing me. He parts my mouth and then dives his tongue against mine, tangling them together and lighting me up in a way that I've only felt with him.

He makes me feel desired.

Needed.

Like I'm important.

He brings his hand down between my legs and runs his finger over my slit, gliding right against my clit with ease.

"Fuck, you're ready," he whispers, and then to my surprise, he lifts up and then turns me around so I'm on my stomach. He tugs on my hips, bringing me to the edge of the bed and then says, "Stick your ass up for me, Pips."

I tilt my ass up in the air, he parts my legs, and then he slips his cock into me with one solid thrust.

His piercings run along my inner walls until he bottoms out, making me cry in pleasure, because nothing has ever felt this good.

Nothing.

"Take my cock. Take all of it," he says as his hand wraps around my wet hair and tugs my head back just slightly as he pumps into me.

My back arches, my nipples rub against the comforter, and with every thrust he makes, he bottoms out, filling me up to the point that I lose my breath.

"Fuck," I whisper, just before his hand connects with my ass. "Oh God," I yell, surprised and turned on at the same time.

From my response, he does it again.

And again.

And again, setting my skin on fire.

"Christ." I tighten around him as he continues to thrust. "I'm...I'm close."

"I can fucking...tell," he grits out and then leans forward, letting go of my hair, but pressing down on my head and neck. "You make me so goddamn hard. Fuck," he growls, pulsing harder.

"First...first thing I thought about..." I take a deep breath, his cock so stiff, so powerful that he steals my breath. "Was...how you...fuck me."

"How do I fuck you?" he asks, his hand tightening around the back of my neck now.

"Like you own me."

He grunts. "Because I fucking do."

Then he lifts up and spanks me, the sensation of the snap against my skin and the warmth spreading through me making me squeeze around him.

So he does it again.

One more time.

And on the third, when I'm breathless, unable to stop the building of my orgasm, he grips my hips on both sides and thrusts in deeper, sending me into a tailspin of pleasure.

"Fuck, Wilder. Oh God...oh fuck."

"Come on my cock, baby. Drench me."

His words.

His grip.

His piercings rubbing against my G-spot.

It's all too much and before I can stop myself, I'm calling out his name and falling over the edge.

He pounds into me a few more times, letting me run out my orgasm until he flips me over and pulls out of me.

Surprised because he hasn't come yet, I'm about to protest until he swipes his fingers up my slit.

"Taste yourself," he says before bringing his fingers to my mouth and sliding them past my lips.

Eyes wide, I suck on his fingers, watching him the entire time as he leans in closer and starts pumping his cock.

"See what I get to fucking taste? So goddamn good."

Then he brings his hand back between my legs, swipes again, but this time, he sticks his fingers in his mouth, doing the tasting this time.

He licks, sucks, and then groans right before leaning forward and coming all over my chest.

Pump after pump, his warm semen coats me and I love every goddamn second of watching him come undone.

"Fuck," he shouts as he finishes, and then takes a deep breath, his eyes finding mine.

They're feral.

They're almost unhinged.

And then with one finger, he scoops up some of his cum and then brings it to my lips.

I part and he watches me suck him dry.

The headiness in his expression, it speaks promises for so much more.

Clearing his throat, he says, "Stay there, I'll clean you up."

Then he leans forward, places a kiss on my lips, and takes off toward the bathroom.

In disbelief, I drape my arm over my eyes.

God…and that's…that's what sex is supposed to be.

Don't look at him.

Do not look at him.

I glance over at Wilder, who's leaning back on the couch, his arms draped casually across the back of it, one ankle crossed over his leg, looking like a freaking king. I can't help the smile that passes over my lips, because oh my God, he's so sexy.

This morning, after he played with me, it felt so raw, it felt so freaking good, and the only reason I'm not back in the cabin with him, exploring some more, is because we were beckoned to our therapy session.

When Wilder glances in my direction as well, he smirks and then pulls on that lip ring of his while his eyes scan down to my breasts, which are currently on display thanks to my low-cut shirt.

Sanders clears his throat, drawing both of our attention to where he's sitting, perched up on his chair with a baseball glove and a baseball.

"Uh, care to tell me what's going on?"

"Nothing's going on," I say with a shake of my head. How I wish I was sitting so much closer to Wilder.

"Nothing's going on?" Sanders asks. "Why don't I believe that?"

"Because it's not the truth," Wilder says. "We fucked last night."

Of course he'd just come out and say it. That's Wilder. Never holds anything back. And even though I can feel a hint of embarrassment creep up my back, I kind of really like that about him.

"You did." Sanders smiles widely. "Would you like to tell me how it went? I mean, from the way you two are smiling at each other, I'm going to assume it went really well."

Wilder adjusts the bracelet I made for him that has my name on it, a bracelet that he's kept on his wrist the entire time. "She's fucking phenomenal in bed." Then he looks at me and says, "No one compares. Pretty sure I blacked out last night...and this morning."

Okay, now my cheeks are really flaming.

"And what about you?" Sanders asks as I fidget in my seat. "How do you feel?"

I glance over at Wilder, and not able to hold back my smile, I answer, "Amazing."

"Well, this is exactly what I wanted to hear." Sanders tosses the ball in the air and catches it. "I truly felt like you guys needed a moment to clear your minds, and you did that on your own. You found each other again, talked out some issues, and now you've started being intimate once more. Do you feel like you're communicating well again?"

"For the most part," Wilder says, eyeing me. "I think there was some holding out on communication last night, but once I pressed, she let me in."

Sanders turns his attention to me. "Why were you holding out on talking to Wilder?"

"Um, because I just wasn't sure if he was in the same frame of mind as I was," I answer honestly. "And I didn't want to feel embarrassed if he wasn't."

Sanders nods his head. "Holding information out of fear is the biggest form of miscommunication, but it's also the most common. Every relationship, no matter how excellent you are at talking to your partner, experiences a form of miscommunication. It's human nature. We become guarded, we don't want to get hurt, we're unsure of how the other person is going to respond, so we hold our cards close to our chest. We don't tell the entire truth, which always hurts the relationship in the long run. It's so incredibly common, so much so that Ellison and I suffer from the same thing at times. It's one of the biggest issues among all my couples."

"That makes sense," Wilder says. "In a world where we live in our phones, it's easy to hold out, to not practice simple conversational techniques."

"Exactly. It's why we confiscate phones while you're here, because we want you hearing your partners. We want you seeing them. We want you at your rawest form."

"Well, we were pretty raw last night."

"Wilder," I chastise.

"What?" he says on a laugh. "The condoms are fifteen dollars a pack. I wasn't paying that much to cover up when you're on birth control."

The only reason I know he knows that is because he's seen me take the pill at night before I climb into bed.

He then looks Sanders in the eyes and says, "Fifteen dollars? Really, man?"

Sanders doesn't even balk at the number as he says, "Capitalism at its finest."

"How do you sleep at night?" Wilder asks.

"With my wife next to me."

Wilder nods. "Smooth answer."

"Thank you." Sanders sets the ball and glove down and then folds his hands together. "You have three more full days left here. I want you spending them together, working out any other issues that might be plaguing you, and coming up with a plan for how to deal with them in everyday life, because when you return to society, I don't want you to fall back into your old habits. I want this marriage to work. To thrive. So spend the next few days coming up with that plan, and at the end of camp, I want to hear that plan. Understood?"

We both nod together.

"Good. Now, for today, I want you to go on a date. I want you to plan it together and then see it through. It could be whatever you want. We have a booklet in the main building, where you can decide what that will be. But I want it to be fun. Think you can handle that?"

"I think we can," Wilder says.

"Perfect." Sanders stands, so we do as well. "I look forward to seeing what you picked. And remember, we're moving forward, not backward."

"Right," I say. "Forward."

Wilder takes my hand, and together, we walk out of the cabin and down the path toward the main building.

"I can't believe you told him we had sex last night and this morning," I say.

"Why? He's our therapist. He needs to know that."

"He's our pretend therapist."

"Feels pretty real to me. Also, just be happy I didn't write on everyone's cabin window this morning that we fucked, okay? Because if I had it my way, I'd let everyone know. I would have called in a marching band, some skywriters, maybe even a magician who would make me magically appear out of a box only so I could shout into a megaphone that we fucked."

"That seems a bit over the top."

"You're right. Maybe a touch too much. How about this? Should I just say it in greeting to everything I see? 'Good morning. How are you? Scottie rocked my world last night with her pussy. How was your night?'"

"Oh my God, stop it," I say, pushing at him, causing him to laugh.

"It's true."

I stay silent, shaking my head, because I really don't know what to say to that.

After a few seconds of silence, he says, "You don't believe me, do you?"

"Yes, I do."

He stops and turns me toward him. "Look me in the eyes, and say you believe me."

I sigh heavily and look him in the eyes. "I'm...I'm trying to believe you. And it doesn't have anything to do with you but instead everything to do with me. Just one of those roadblocks I have to get over."

"I understand," he says softly while tilting my chin up with his finger. "But just know, I'd never lie about that. You...Scottie...created a monster, because after last night, I'm addicted. And I'm counting down the fucking minutes until I can have more of you."

I move into him and place my hand on his chest. "Me too."

"Here's an idea. Why don't we plan our date in the cabin? We can just—"

"You cannot plan your date in the cabin," Sanders says, scaring the both of us.

"Jesus," I say, gripping my chest. "Where did you come from?"

He eyes the both of us. "You're to pick a date from the date book in the main building. Understood?"

"But don't you always say you want your couples to be intimate?"

"I do," Sanders says. "But the point of these dates is to build that anticipation, to learn to flirt with each other again. You can't do that if you're hiding out in your cabin, screwing each other."

"I don't know. I'm pretty good at flirting," Wilder says while scratching his jaw. "I might not need to practice."

Sanders points his finger at Wilder. "Stay out of your cabin until nighttime."

"What if...we want to go in the lake and need our bathing suits?" Wilder asks, clearly trying to find a loophole.

Sanders thinks about it for a second and then says, "I'll allow it. Just for swimsuits. I want you building that anticipation."

"Trust me, with my Pips wearing that shirt today, the anticipation is already there."

My Pips.

Did he really just say "my Pips"?

I think he did.

And why do I love it so much?

Maybe because my ex never claimed me the way Wilder so easily does.

"Come on." Wilder loops his arm over me. "We have a day to plan."

"Babe, we have to do the tandem bike."

"Have you ever ridden a tandem bike?" I ask as I stare down at the pamphlet.

"No, but how hard can it be?"

"Uh, hard."

I turn to the receptionist and ask, "Is it hard?"

"No. Once you get the hang of it, it's quite enjoyable. You just need to communicate well."

"Oh, we have excellent communication," Wilder says.

There's a snort from the corner, and that's when I see Chad, sitting in a chair with a Diet Coke in hand, looking none too pleased.

"Do you have something you want to say?" Wilder asks.

"Nope, just enjoying my drink," he answers. "Going to rate it in my Soda Tracker when I'm done. Camp Haven, flat Cokes, lukewarm at best."

Did he just say Soda Tracker?

From the way Wilder just stilled next to me, I'm going to say he did.

Does Chad know?

Is he going to expose us?

"Then I'd keep your derisive snorts to yourself," Wilder says.

Not wanting to have this break into a fight, because Wilder really doesn't like Chad—like actually hates him—I say, "You know, the tandem bike into town with the picnic and floats later sounds great."

"Great. Since you already signed waivers when you came here, you can fit yourself with a helmet out back and then take the bike when you're ready."

"Okay, thanks," I say and then tug on Wilder's hand as he stares Chad down for a few more seconds. "Come on."

We head out of the main building toward a green-and-white shed.

"That fuck is testing me," Wilder mutters under his breath. "I'm a chill guy, but don't fuck with me, and don't fuck with the people in my life."

I smooth my hand over his chest. "Just like you tell me not to let Matt live in my head, don't let Chad live in your head."

"Yeah, but he's disrespecting you, and I don't fucking like that. You deserve better."

I smile and stand on my toes to press a kiss to his chin. "Thank you."

That seems to ease some of the tension as he wraps his arms around me and brings me in close. "You're welcome."

"So should we tandem?"

"I think we shall," he says and then kisses the tip of my nose.

CHAPTER TWENTY-THREE
WILDER

"THIS IS HUMILIATING," SCOTTIE SAYS.

"For all these people driving by us know, we have a flat tire," I say as we turn into a Stewart's gas station.

"I really thought we would be better at this."

"I think the problem is you have no balance," I say while we push the tandem bike up against the gas station's wall. I unclip my helmet and fluff out my hair as I turn toward her.

"I had plenty of balance," she grumbles.

My brow quirks up. "Pips, it's insulting that you think you can blatantly lie to me."

She huffs. "It was just different. I didn't think you were going to be so...large."

"Come on now. You've seen me with my clothes off. You know how large I really am."

Her expression falls flat. "Really, Wilder?"

"Uh, we were told to flirt. I am flirting."

"That is not flirting."

"Would it have helped if I wiggled my brows while saying it?"

"No," she answers like the grump she knows how to be. "Are we going to push the bike back to camp?"

"I mean, it's not that far away, so we can try biking again."

"Yeah, we can, I guess."

"But first, I think we need some ice cream," I say and then take her hand, pulling her toward the gas station. "Have you ever been into a Stewart's before?"

"Uh, I don't think so," she says while I open the door for her.

"Pips, they have the best ice cream."

Her face contorts in confusion when we get to the ice cream counter. "This gas station has hand-scooped ice cream?"

"Yup, one of the great things about Stewart's. And you can even buy cartons of it if there is a flavor you really like. My dad, before his accident, would come home from work on Fridays during the summer, and he'd bring home a carton of ice cream."

"Really? That's sweet. What was his favorite flavor?"

"Crumbs Along the Mohawk," I answer. "It was everyone's favorite."

"What's in that one?"

"It's graham cracker–flavored ice cream, caramel swirl, and graham cracker pieces."

"Ooo, that sounds good. I think I want to get that."

I smile. "Cup or cone?"

"Cone."

"Good girl." I wink and then pull out my wallet and walk up to the counter, where I put in our order and pay. I hand her the first cone, grab some napkins, and head out toward where we parked the bike.

We both take a seat on a bench, and I loop my arm around her while she takes her first lick.

From the sight of her tongue running against the ice cream, I feel my mouth go dry, envisioning what her tongue did to me last night.

Then she moans, her eyes closing. "Mmmm."

That moan immediately sends me into a tailspin of desire.

"So good," she whispers and then licks again, but this time, she moves her tongue over the top, like she's rimming it.

"What the hell are you doing?" I ask as I shift in my seat.

A grin spreads over those delicious lips as she says, "I thought we were supposed to flirt."

"That is not flirting," I say seriously. "That is taunting."

"Are you saying you can't handle a little ice cream licking?"

"I'm saying I can't handle you rimming your ice cream like you're running your tongue over my goddamn piercings."

She chuckles. "Quite the imagination on you."

"Oh, you know what you were doing. Should I flick my ice cream like I flicked your clit last night?"

"Have at it. Show me what you've got."

I purse my lips, studying her. "You know what? No, I'm not about to give you a free show."

"That's your choice, and I respect it." She smirks and then starts rimming her ice cream again…while moaning.

"Stop that."

She laughs and leans deeper into my chest.

"In all seriousness, this is really good."

"I know," I say as I take a bite, the flavor bringing me back to summer Fridays when we'd eat ice cream out on the porch and bird-watch with my dad. "God, I haven't had this in a while. It's reminding me of my dad."

"Do you want to talk about him?" she asks. "What kind of guy was he?"

"He was a great guy," I say, thinking back to when he was around… and mentally present. "He was a jokester, always teasing me and Mika. He was infatuated with our mom, treated her like she was a queen. He would stand up for what was right and never partook in what was wrong. He made sure that Mika and I had the same morals. He loved being outdoors and bird-watching. That's where I found a love for it."

"He sounds very familiar," she says as she leans back and kisses my neck.

I squeeze her tighter. "Yeah, I look like him too. Same eyes. Same hair. Same bone structure. Almost a copy-and-paste situation. But he spent a lot of time with me and Mika. He loved being a dad. Every weekend, we could count on him doing something with us, whether it was hiking, playing in the backyard, or taking us to a movie. There was always something."

"I love that. You must have the best memories with him."

"I do," I say softly. "I think his later days sometimes outweigh those earlier memories, because when he was in a wheelchair, it was really hard. We were all sort of caregivers for him, especially when Mom wasn't home. Those days were difficult. I remember this one time though, maybe a month or so before he passed, it was a cool summer day, Mom was at work, and Mika was with friends. I took my dad outside and set up a blanket in the backyard with pillows. I took him out of his wheelchair and propped him up so he could see the trees, and then I held binoculars up to his eyes, and we bird-watched. I told him all the birds we were seeing and recited everything he told me growing up. He had vocal cord paralysis as well, so he couldn't talk with us, but that day, he looked me in the eyes, and he cried." I shake my head, remembering that moment. "I knew he was telling me he was proud in that moment."

Scottie lifts up and turns toward me. "God, Wilder." She presses her hand to her heart. "That...that makes me so sad."

"Nah, there is no need to be sad. It was a good moment, a moment I needed from him, because there were times when my frustration for the situation sometimes outweighed my patience. But that day, I was able to slow down. I was able to have a moment with him. A moment like we had when I was younger. And I always cherished it. I actually carry a picture of that day in my wallet."

I pull out my wallet, and with my ice cream in one hand and my wallet in the other, I remove the picture and show it to her. She takes it and stares at the picture for a few seconds before she says, "Wow, you really do look like him. Just missing the lip ring."

I chuckle. "Yeah, my dad would have hated that."

"Really?" she asks, handing me the picture back so I can stick it in my wallet again.

"Yeah. He didn't like piercings or tattoos or anything that could alter your appearance."

"So why did you get a tattoo and piercings?"

"I think it was a way of dealing with my pain. If I marked myself up somewhere else, maybe I wouldn't hurt as much inside."

"Did it help?" she asks.

"No. Shocking revelation, you actually have to talk about your pain in order to heal. Can't keep it all bottled inside."

"So I'm assuming you went to therapy, then?"

"Yeah," I answer. "After piercing my dick, I thought, maybe this self-mutilation thing isn't working. So I went to therapy, and that's where I learned to forgive my mom—for the most part—there's still some animosity that I'm working through. I learned to grieve my father's death, and I learned some coping techniques for how to help Mika. He actually sees my therapist as well."

"Were you the one who got him to go into therapy?"

"I did," I say, thinking back to that horrible day when he told me he wasn't doing well. It was one of the worst days of my life.

"Wil, I don't think I can do life anymore. I'm sorry. My heart is just too broken, and I've just got no fucks to give…"

And when he started asking for my forgiveness for not being able to stay around, I knew I had to get to him.

It was the most terrifying twenty-four hours of my life, traveling without knowing if he'd still be there when I made it to his home.

"I stayed with him for a while, living in the same apartment. I think you were in Ohio at that point."

"Yeah, I remember when he told me that you were staying with him. I didn't know you, but I was grateful. He needed someone watching over him."

"I babysat him for a while, didn't let him go anywhere without me. It wasn't until I started to see a shift in his demeanor that I started to believe that he was going to be okay. I wasn't going to lose my father and my brother. Thankfully, I had the ability to be by his side at all times."

"I can't imagine what that must have been like. I'm glad you were there for him."

"That's how Dad raised us. He said no matter what happens in life, we're supposed to have each other. Because there would be a day when he and Mom were no longer around, and we had to take care of each other. Well, that time came sooner than we expected. I would never let anything happen to Mika at this point. He's my number one in this world."

"You're such a good man, Wilder."

"I try to be," I answer. "I really try."

———

"Pedal," I say to Scottie.

"I am. I think there's something wrong with this bike."

"No, babe, I think there's something wrong with you." I stop the bike and set my legs on the ground, straddling the bike. I look over my shoulder, where Scottie is looking all kinds of disgruntled.

"It is not me. It's the bike."

Chuckling, I step off the bike. "Look, there's a path that leads to the lake. Let's take a break for a moment, gather ourselves, and then we can get back on."

"Or we can walk it back, because that is the devil's form of transportation, and I'd rather not take part in his form of torture again."

"Whatever you want."

We move the bike off the road and up against a tree before unsnapping our helmets. We hang them on the bike handles, and then I take her hand and help her down the narrow, rocky trail to a clearing that overlooks the lake.

I clear a spot on the ground, and then I take a seat and pull her down in front of me, allowing her to lean her back against my chest.

"Is it kind of weird that we only have a few days left here?" she asks as I loop my hand around her stomach.

"Yeah. Feels like we were just checking in the other day and marking up a golf ball with a Sharpie about our nonexistent relationship. And then opening our prize to be shocked by dildos and cock rings. Kind of wish I didn't go on a tirade and toss those to all your coworkers now."

"As if you would have used them," she scoffs.

"Uh, Pips, you're damn right I would have used them. If I had known that we'd be hooking up in the sex cabin, I would have kept every single thing, even the nipple picture."

She laughs. "You know, I kind of miss the nipple picture."

"So do I. Also, what the hell happened to the porn videos? Weren't we supposed to get those every night?"

She pauses to think about it. "Were we?"

"I don't know. I thought we were."

"Maybe they didn't send because we were fighting, and they saw the room all cleared out. I bet you they checked on our room every day to ask the walls if we were doing it. You know how Sanders is. He probably told everyone to hold with the sex until we were actually ready for the sex."

"So does that mean there could be a video tonight?" I ask.

"I don't know. Do you want a video?"

"I want to watch one with you," I say honestly. "I think it would be hot as hell, seeing you get turned on, letting me play with you while you watch."

"You'd like that?"

"Fuck yes, Pips. I'd love to fuck you with my tongue while you were turned on by someone else getting off. You don't think that sounds hot?"

"I mean... I never thought of things like that before. My sex life was very bland with Matt. There wasn't much that we did other than the regular things because he felt comfortable doing that. So watching someone else get off while I was getting off, I don't know…maybe that does sound thrilling."

I move my hand under her shirt and say, "Well, if they don't send us a video, then we can do it when we get back to the city."

I feel her stiffen. "Back to the city?" she asks.

"Uh, yeah. Do you think this is over when camp is over?"

"I don't know." She turns to look at me. "I thought that maybe this was just a here thing."

I lift my brows. "Do you want it to just be a here thing?" She wets her lips, and I can see she's about to say "I don't know," so I cut her off. "Tell me the truth. Don't tell me that you don't know. Don't beat around the bush because you're scared of what I might say or do. Tell me what you want."

She looks down and takes a few seconds but then says, "I don't want to get hurt. Matt hurt me…badly. And being here with you, that's helped me so much with dissecting those feelings and finding closure. But I know where you stand when it comes to relationships, so…I don't want to grow too attached, you know? I think fooling around here, having some fun, I think that's fine. But I don't know what that means for after camp."

I get it.

I really do.

She's strong but she's also incredibly fragile. I understand that feeling of not wanting to get hurt, and it's not like I've given her any indication that I'd be ready and willing to be in a relationship. Hell, I don't even know where I stand with all that.

I do know that I like Scottie. A lot. She's unlike anyone I've ever met. She intrigues me. She keeps my attention. She challenges me. She makes me laugh. She's fucking fun to be around, and if that wasn't enough, she drives me fucking wild with need, and I've never felt that before. I've never felt this unfiltered urge to claim someone, to make them mine.

But the second her lips met mine, there was something inside me that snapped, popped, that woke me the fuck up and told me to pay attention. And now that I am paying attention, I know one thing for certain: I don't think I want this to end in a few days. I want to keep seeing her, but given the doubt she carries in her chest thanks to her ex, I don't think me coming out and saying I want to try things out with her will go over well. I know that doubt would creep in, especially after I told her I wasn't ready for a relationship. So maybe I need to handle this a little differently.

"I respect that," I say. "But I need you to know something, Scottie." I smooth my palm over her stomach. "I have no intention of hurting you. Ever."

"I know that. I've found that out quickly while being here with you."

"And I like you...a lot. Okay. And I don't need you to respond or really say anything about what life is going to look like after we leave camp, but I do need you to sit on those two facts. I would never hurt you. And I like you. Can you do that for me?"

She nods her head. "Yes, I can do that."

"Good," I answer and then bring my hand down to the waistband of her shorts. "Now, spread your legs."

"What?" she asks.

I lean in close to her ear and whisper, "Spread your legs." I undo the button and zipper on her jean shorts and then pull her shirt up and over her head, leaving her in just her bra.

"Wilder," she says in shock.

"Tell me to stop and I will," I say. "You have all the control, Pips." I kiss the side of her cheek. "Tell me no." I drag my hand up to her breasts, where I wait for her to stop me, for her to ask for her shirt back, but when she doesn't, I pull on the cup of her bra and release one of her breasts. I stare down at her over her shoulder and marvel at her hardened nipple. "These fucking tits. I'm addicted."

I pass my thumb over the hard nub a few times while my other hand runs along the waistline of her underwear. Her body sinks into mine, and I love the comfort she finds in being with me. The trust she has that I was able to win because of my care, because of my patience.

With my index finger and my thumb, I roll her nipple, pinching ever so slightly and causing her to lift her chest and moan.

"Yes, Wilder."

"Fuck, I love how responsive you are." I bring my lips to her neck, and I suck on the spot below her ear while I continue to play with her nipple, circling around it, flicking it, and then pinching it. She brings her hand to the back of my neck, and she holds on as she raises her chest and then lets it fall, her breath taking control.

"More," she says.

"You wet?"

"Yes," she groans.

"Prove it."

She pauses and then on a whisper asks, "How?"

"Touch yourself, Pips, and bring your fingers to my mouth."

She's hesitant at first, but then she carefully slides her hand between her legs.

"Don't pull out right away. Play with your clit. Rub it for me."

Her teeth pull on her lip before I watch her hand start to work between her legs, the jean fabric shielding me from viewing her touch herself.

"That's it, Pips. Rub that clit. Play with yourself. Pretend it's me playing with you."

"I wish it was," she groans. "You're so much better."

Smiling, I say, "Then bring your fingers to my mouth and prove that you're ready for me."

She pulls her hand from between her legs and lifts her hand to my mouth. I suck her fingers past my lips and taste her, the first hit of the day, and she tastes just as good as she did last night. Fuck, why didn't I fuck her with my tongue this morning? Big mistake.

"That's a good girl." I then push down on her shorts, because I know my hand won't fit properly under them, and she sheds them to the side, leaving her in a pair of green bikini briefs. They rise high on her hip but cover her entire ass, and I have never found anything so sexy in my life. She's not dressing in a thong every day. No, she wears comfortable yet sexy underwear, and I'm so goddamn obsessed. "Spread your legs and bring them up."

She listens so well and drapes her legs over mine, keeping them wide and in place.

I take out her other breast, and then with both hands, I start playing with her. I drag my fingers around and around her nipples, making circles and watching as they grow impossibly hard.

"Please, Wilder," she begs, the sound so euphoric. "Please touch me."

"Patience," I whisper and lightly dance my right hand across the elastic of her underwear, teasing her, then moving my fingers back to her breasts with a featherlight touch, barely caressing her skin.

When I catch a wave of goose bumps breaking out over her body, I do it again, passing my fingers over her skin with such light pressure that she attempts to lift her body for a deeper sensation.

"Patience," I whisper again and bring my fingers to her taut nipples, where I lightly roll them.

"Fuck," she drags out, her head pressing into my shoulder. "Harder."

God, she could get her nipples pierced, the way she reacts to my touch. I bet she'd fucking love it. I pinch her nipples harder, and she lets out a long moan.

"Uhnnnn, yes."

From that one sound, my dick presses into her back, aching for relief, wanting to play, but this is about her. So I drag my fingers back down her stomach, floating them over her underwear, teasing, playing, never going near where she wants me.

"God, please," she says, her legs spreading. "I'm so wet."

"Mm," I growl into her ear. "That's what I wanted to hear."

I keep one hand on her breast while slipping the other beneath her underwear, sliding my fingers over her slit. I love how aroused she is.

"Motherfucker," I say as I nibble her neck, only to kiss the spot. "You're so fucking wet, Pips."

I slide my fingers over her hard clit and marvel at how her legs fall open even farther, how she relaxes into me, and how she tilts her head to the side, granting me more access to her neck.

I take advantage and start nibbling up the column and back down while I circle her clit and her nipple at the same time. I get lost in the feel of her, in the way I can so easily bring her to a point of arousal that has her begging, pleading for me to bring her relief.

I love it.

I fucking need it.

I bite down on her shoulder, and she yelps as I slide my fingers farther and inside her.

"Yes, Wilder. Right there," she says as I move my fingers in and out of her while my thumb plays with her clit.

Her breathing grows heavier, nearly erratic. Her hand clamps over mine, keeping me in place, and her body tenses as her orgasm climbs.

"Fuck, yes, right there. Please don't stop."

"Never, baby," I whisper as I bite down on her again, causing her walls to contract around my fingers.

"God, yes. Please. Again."

I bite one more time and follow it with a lick of my tongue. She cries out my name and encourages me to move faster with my thumb. So I circle her clit, over and over and over again until her legs start to clamp around me, her hand tightens over mine, and her mouth falls open.

"Fuck," she yells just before she tilts over the edge and starts calling out my name while her orgasm takes her over. "Oh God, Wilder. Oh, fuck. Oh, fuck."

I relentlessly play with her, loving how she closes around my fingers, pulsing. I envision it being my dick inside her and how great it would feel. How great it felt last night and this morning. Seriously, her mouth is a sin, but that cunt of hers, what I wouldn't fucking give to be deep inside her right now.

When she finally catches her breath, I lick my fingers clean.

"You taste so fucking sweet," I whisper.

She lifts up and turns around to face me. Her face is flushed, her hair is ragged from thrashing against me, and her tits are still out of her bra as she kneels between my legs and starts undoing my pants.

I stop her and say, "Scottie, you don't have to—"

"Don't tell me what I don't have to do. I need your cock in my mouth."

Well, I'm not going to stop her when she says shit like that. So I allow her to undo my pants, and then I lift up so she can drag them down along with my briefs. My cock stretches upward, and a satisfied smile spreads across her lips before she grips the base of my length and starts slowly squeezing. Short pumps of her hand, just squeezing while her mouth hovers over the head. And the anticipation, it's fucking killing me. Because I know what that mouth feels like. I know how that tongue can dance over my piercings. I know what that throat can do.

"Babe," I whisper. "Keep doing that, and I'll come."

"Good."

"No, I want you to swallow me."

She looks up at me, grins, and says, "I want it more than you." Then she peeks out her tongue and starts dancing the tip over my piercings, and I swear to fuck, she knows how much it drives me crazy.

One of the reasons I got the piercings was because I thought it would distract me. I got the ones that I did because the sensation of playing with them and fucking with them is so much stronger.

"Jesus," I breathe out as I push her hair out of her face and cup her cheek softly. "Keep...keep doing that."

Precum wets the tip of my dick, and without even a second thought, she licks it right up.

Then she looks up at me and says, "I want more."

"Then let me fuck your mouth."

Grinning, she moves to the side and lies down. Seeing what she wants, I sit up and straddle her before bringing my cock to her mouth and running the piercings over her lips. Her tongue peeks out, playing, teasing, and I let it happen even though I need to be inside her mouth. I'm waiting for her to take charge.

And she fucking does because as she's playing with my piercings, her hand moves between my legs and grips my balls.

My body falls forward from the light squeeze, and I prop myself up with my hands.

"Fuck," I breathe out, realizing that this has to be some of the greatest pleasure I've ever experienced. No one has ever played with my balls as much as she has, and I'm realizing that this is a necessity in my life.

Her thumb drags between them, tugging just hard enough for me to enjoy it.

And as I start to get comfortable with the feel of her hand and the pressure of her tongue, she brings her finger to the spot just behind my balls, and she presses down.

My fist punches the ground in surprise as I buck my hips and yell, "Fuck me!" as a shock wave of pleasure flies up my spine. "Holy fuck."

I have no time to adjust as she opens her mouth wide and takes me inside her warmth. And that about does it. I lose control and start thrusting into her mouth. Her tongue slides against the underside of my cock, her throat gags when I hit the back of it, and she continues to play with my balls, rolling them and lightly squeezing, firing me off in all aspects.

"Fuck me…fuck…uhhhhh," I groan as she handles me like she's been doing it for years. "Fuck, baby, you're so good. So fucking good."

I thrust over and over, and she starts to swallow when I hit the back of her throat, causing my eyes to roll in the back of my head.

It's too much.

Too fucking much.

My balls start to tighten, my muscles bunch at the base of my spine, and my cock swells just as she swallows one more time.

I pull out of her mouth, grip my cock, and say, "Open."

She keeps her mouth open, and I finish all over her tongue, watching drop after drop hit her until my orgasm wears off.

"Shit," I mutter as I try to catch my breath.

I watch with hungry eyes as she swallows me. Then I bend down, and I bring my lips to hers to kiss her softly and whisper, "You're too perfect. Everything about you. Too fucking perfect."

CHAPTER TWENTY-FOUR
SCOTTIE

"WILDER, YOU HAVE TO STOP looking at me like that."

"Like what?" he asks, still grinning. He hasn't stopped grinning since we left the lake.

"Like you're going to take me back to that spot at the lake and do... things."

"Yeah, well, don't fucking tempt me. You made me a man back there."

I let out a laugh. "You were already a man."

"I thought I was until you started pressing things on my body, places I didn't even know existed." He leans in close as we lie on a blanket at camp, under a large oak tree. "How did you even know about that...spot?"

I smirk and take a bite of a pepperoni. "I read it in a book. I tried doing it to Matt once, and he swatted my hand away."

"That man is a fucking fool. Hell, I'm tempted to bend over and pull my pants down right now so you can play with me some more." He wiggles his eyebrows, and I push at his forehead.

"You're so horny."

"You made me this way. I was fine living a life of celibacy, the occasional hookup here and there just to feed the beast, until you came along and awoke something I don't think is ever going to go away. Seriously, if I bend over, will you do it again?"

"Oh my God, Wilder." I shake my head in mirth, causing him to laugh.

"I'm going to take that as a maybe."

"What you need to do is keep your voice down, because you and I both know if Sanders gets wind of the fact that we"—I look around and whisper—"fornicated, then he very well might separate us for the rest of the camp."

"First of all, way to use the word 'fornicate.' I approve. Second, he can try to keep me away, but I'd sniff you out so fast, I'd undo you from whatever chains he has you tied up in." He pauses for a moment and then says, "And then maybe take the chains back to our sex cabin so I could use them on you properly."

"You're ridiculous."

He grins. "You like it."

"I kind of do." I wince. "What does that say about me?"

"It's all right. You can have mixed feelings about it. It takes a second to get used to the idea that you could possibly like someone like me after being with such a bore for several years."

"He was a bore, that's for sure."

"Sad, especially when he had someone like you he could play with." I roll my eyes, but he places his hand on my thigh and says, "I'm not just speaking sex. I mean in general. One of the reasons you're in a marriage is to have a partner in life that you can do things with, that you can experience things with, you know? And if you don't take the time to have those experiences, then what's the goddamn point?"

I nod, thinking back to all the things that I wish Matt had done with me.

"I can see you thinking of those things. You know what? We should make a bucket list of things you want to do now that you're no longer with an actual ball and chain." He reaches into the bag of activities that we were given for our picnic, and he pulls out a pad of paper and a pen.

"Was that really in there?"

"Yup," he says and then flips open to a blank page and writes *Scottie's Ball and Chain–Free Bucket List* at the top.

"Quite the title," I say.

"A necessary one." He poises the pen. "Okay, what are we putting on here?"

I glance at his hand, the bracelet I made him still fastened around his wrist. "Um, I mean, I don't know."

"Yes, you do," he encourages. "Don't be shy about it. Tell me what's on that list."

I lean back on my hand and look up toward the sky. "Umm, well, he never wanted to do anything outside the house, said it was a waste of money. There was a cooking class I wanted to go to, and he would never go."

"Great. Cooking class." He writes it on the paper.

"And he never took me to the movies because he said we should just wait until it was on a streaming service, but I always thought that seeing a movie in the theaters was so much better."

"I could not agree more. See a movie in the theaters." He jots it down.

"With popcorn and the movie theater candy. Like go all out. No sneaking anything in."

"Spend fifty dollars at concessions, noted."

I think about it some more. "You know, we were once on a kiss cam, and he drank his beer rather than kiss me. So I want to be on a kiss cam and kiss someone, even if it's myself."

"He drank his beer?" Wilder shakes his head. "What a douche."

"Yes, that would be an accurate description."

Wilder jots down the note, but I can see the irritation in his expression.

"Go skinny-dipping," I say, thinking about the time we were at his parents' house, alone with a pool, and he didn't want to go skinny-dipping with me. "I've always wanted to do that."

"Easy. Okay, keep going."

A smirk crosses over my lips. "Watch porn."

Wilder's lips turn up as he directs his attention at me. "That's an easy one, Pips. We can hammer that out tonight."

"He always made it like...a bad thing."

"He only said that because he was watching it like crazy, probably."

"You think?"

Wilder nods his head. "Oh yeah, babe. There is not a guy on this earth who's not watching. And if they're telling you they're not, they're liars. Probably had a ton of subscriptions."

"Well then, I want to watch. I want to see what all the fuss is about."

"You got it, babe. It's on the list. Anything else?"

"Hmmm." I tap my chin.

"There has to be more. From what you've told me, Matt is a wet blanket. Were there things you wanted to do that he thought were stupid? Was he ever romantic with you?"

That makes me snort. "Never. Well, I mean, maybe when we first started dating, but that romance quickly wore off, especially after we got married. He didn't know romance."

"So then maybe there's something romantic you want to do that he never did with you."

I give it some thought, and then when it hits me, I slowly start to smile. "Okay, this is going to sound maybe a touch childish and possibly cheesy, but there is this thing I always wanted to do when living in New York, something I know Matt would never do."

"What is it?"

"He would totally scoff at this, but I think it would be fun to take a paddleboat through Central Park."

A genuine smile passes over his mouth. "Nothing cheesy about that. It's really sweet actually," he says, writing it on the paper. Then he takes a look at the list. "This is pretty solid, Pips."

"Let me see." He hands me the list, and I look it over. "I think it's a pretty good start."

"I think so too. And I know one we can check off tonight." He wiggles his brows. "Not to mention what I did to you only moments ago, which I'm sure Matt the Douche never would have done."

"Fingered me in a public place?" I ask.

He slyly nods.

"Yeah, never, nor would he have let me blow him in a public place either."

"Well, frankly, I'm glad you divorced him and that I earned that experience over him." He lies back on the blanket and stares up at the sky. "Now come over here and try to find dirty-shaped clouds with me."

Chuckling, I slide in next to him, rest my head on his shoulder, and stare up at the sky, feeling carefree, like nothing could change my mood. Never have I felt so valued—*so seen*—as I do in this moment.

———

"I can't show you." I shake my head, humiliated by my lack of creative skills.

"The deal was you paint me, and I paint you, then we show each other." Wilder gestures around to the other couples near us. "They're doing it."

"But theirs are nowhere near as bad as mine."

He leans in and whispers. "Pips, did you take a look at Finky's? I can't tell if his wife has three eyes or if that thing in the middle of her face is supposed to be a nose." I snort and cover my mouth. "Trust me, it's not going to be as bad as that."

"Oh, it's bad. Plus, you're good at drawing. This isn't fair."

"I'm not good at using paint. This isn't my medium, so I struggled quite a bit."

That eases my worry. "You promise?"

"Yeah, I mean frankly, when I show you this, I'm going to ask for forgiveness, because I don't want you thinking that this is how I truly see you. You're so much prettier than what I have on this canvas."

"Really?"

"Yeah, Pips." He tugs on his hair. "Actually, maybe we should try again."

"No," I say, holding out my arm. "We said we would show each other. So we have to show each other."

"Okay. You go first."

I stare down at the ten-by-ten canvas in front of me and then back up at Wilder. His eyes are too far apart and way too wide, his nostrils are way too prominent, and I used black paint to outline each individual tooth, which was a bad mistake. But his lip ring, that looks pretty good. And I think I did a decent job on his hair.

Maybe it's not too bad.

I lift the canvas and turn it toward him. I watch his expression as he takes it all in, his eyes curious, his lip quivering.

"Are you about to laugh?" I ask.

"What? No…" His lip tilts up.

"Wilder," I admonish.

"What? I'm not laughing. I'm…I'm observing."

"You're going to laugh."

"No, I'm just…" He sits back and folds his arms. "I'm trying to decide if you took creative freedom with my nostrils or not."

I place the canvas back on my mini easel and fold my arms. "If you think you're that much better, show me what you have."

He looks at his picture, winces, and then picks it up. Ready to bust out in laughter at what he painted, I steel myself, only for him to turn the canvas around, revealing a very real caricature painting of me.

And sure, it's a cartoon, but it very much resembles every piece of me…even hard nipples.

My mouth falls open as he says, "I know, could be better. I don't think I captured just how soft your lips are, and I probably should have added more volume to your hair, but that ass and those tits, I think I nailed them."

I stare at the picture, mesmerized by his talent. He actually did that. Drew that. It looks just like me.

"Wilder, you lied to me."

"What?" His brow genuinely creases. "No, I didn't. I told you you're more beautiful than this, and you are. I haven't done caricature art in a long time, so I struggled a bit with it. I think I could have done a much better job if I was using charcoal or even a pencil. This paint, it was hard to work with."

"Hard to work with. You added shading. You mixed colors so you could do shading."

"I had to make sure people knew I included your hard nipples. That's a very important feature of yours."

I shake my head. "You tricked me."

"What? No. Babe, yours is way better."

"Wilder, if you ever want to be inside me again, I suggest you don't lie."

He winces and then runs his teeth over his lip ring. "Shit, when you say it like that." He leans in close and whispers. "Pips, I can't be certain if you put a nose on my face or a mini golf course with two holes."

I gasp, but he keeps going.

"The eyebrows look like leeches. The eyes have zero dimension. And the hair looks like a dead raccoon."

"Hey, I thought I did a good job on the hair."

He shakes his head. "Terrible, Pips. Real bad. The only redeeming quality about the entire thing is my lip ring."

I sit taller, because I thought the same thing. I smirk and say, "I did do a good job on the lip ring, didn't I?"

"Very. Honestly, brings the whole thing together."

"Yikes, who is that supposed to be?" Chad asks from behind me.

I look over my shoulder and stare up at him. "Your mother. Did I not capture her correctly?"

His face falls flat, and Wilder lets out a bark of a laugh while I sit there stunned, because where the hell did that come from? I don't think I've ever been that quick on my feet.

Ever.

Yet I oddly feel really proud.

"Cute," Chad says, moving away from me.

"Let me know her address so I can send it to her."

He ignores me and walks over to where his wife is sitting while Wilder still laughs, trying to catch his breath.

"Oh fuck, that was good. Did you see the look on his smarmy face? Shit." He wipes under his eyes. "I think you're finally coming into your own, Scottie."

I smile. Yeah, I think I am.

CHAPTER TWENTY-FIVE
WILDER

"WELCOME TO OUR EVENING ACTIVITIES," Sanders says as he struts around in a pair of basketball shorts and a construction vest with nothing underneath.

It's a look, that's for sure.

Scottie's standing next to me, a smile on her face, looking happier than I've ever seen her. And it makes me fucking happy.

Ecstatic.

I remember the day I met her—she was worried, unsure, desperate to just make an impression and then get the hell out of the therapy session. Even when we first arrived at the camp, you could see there was something hanging over her. Something that was tamping down her joy, her energy.

But now...now she's smiling. She exudes joy. She has an essence about her that's addicting. And today has been no exception.

To be honest, I can't remember the last time I had this much fun. From the complicated tandem bike ride to the ice cream to the lakeside blow job to the picnic and cloud watching, it's been a day that I know I will never forget. And it's not the activities that made this day special, it's her reaction to the activities. It's the innocence and the amusement in her expression that I will remember, because she's come out of her shell.

Not to sound like a corny fuck, but she's blossomed right in front of my eyes, and it's one of the sexiest things I've ever seen.

"Tonight we will be mixing drinks, but not just any kind of drink. I want it to be a drink that represents you as a couple. I want you to think long and hard about your relationship, your journey, and morph that into a cocktail. Then we'll be handing out the drinks to our judges, and they'll pick a winner based on taste and creativity. As always, our winners will get a prize, and trust me, you're really going to want to win this one."

I lean into Scottie and say, "Hear that? A prize. A really good prize. Want to go three for three?"

"I don't think we even have an option. We need to know what's going to be in that basket."

"That's my girl," I say, pulling her into my side.

"Please review the ingredients on the menu in front of you, pull your ideas together, and when you're done, bring your tumbler up to the bar, tell our bartender the ingredients, mix them, and then set your drinks in front of the judges' table. It will be a blind taste test, so the judges are hiding at the moment. Don't forget to name your drink. Good luck."

Okay, this could be fun.

I pick up the menu in front of us and say, "Any ideas?"

"Well, we have to pick something that represents us, but we also want to make it good. So we can't be pulling in a lager and Fireball together."

"I mean, if you want to grow hair on the judges' chests, we could do that."

"I don't think it's recommended," she says on a laugh.

"Yeah, probably not. Okay, well, let's pick an alcohol base and work around that."

Chad and his wife already head up to the bar, clearly ready to win as they lean over, hiding whatever the bartender is pouring in their tumbler. Seems premature—they didn't want to think it over at all? Just heading right on up there?

"Look at those overachievers. Bet they're doing something unimaginative like…Sex on the Beach," I say.

"Or Bloody Nipples."

I pause and turn toward Scottie. "What the fuck is Bloody Nipples?"

"Uh, is that what it's called?"

"I sure as fuck hope not."

She laughs and then says, "Wait, it's a Slippery Nipple."

"Oh, okay, yes. Jesus. Not Bloody Nipples, Scottie."

"Yeah, that didn't sound right. Bloody Nipples is definitely not something I would want to put in my mouth."

"Slippery nipples though…" I nudge her shoulder.

"You know what, that's something we should add to the bucket list."

"Slippery nipples?" I ask.

"A naked massage, where my nipples get all slippery."

My brows raise. "And who do you plan on checking that bucket list item off with?"

She smirks up at me. "Was hoping with my fake husband."

"Damn right."

"We have about five minutes left," Sanders calls out.

"Shit, this has a time limit? He didn't say that in the beginning, did he?" I say.

"I don't think so. Okay, we need to focus. Umm, let's go with tequila."

"Why tequila?"

"Umm…I don't know. This is where you need to lean on your improv."

"Okay, how about…we got drunk off margaritas on our first date and ended up riding the subway all the way to Coney Island and back, chatting the whole time."

"Aww, that's kind of cute."

"It is."

"Okay, and then maybe…some prickly pear, because our relationship has been prickly," she says.

"Ooo, good one."

"Then we add some triple sec and lime juice. I think Mika always puts that in margaritas."

"He does. And some sweet-and-sour mix because we are sweet and sour."

"Love it." We circle the items on our menu. "Should we add strawberries," she asks, "like a few crushed on the bottom?"

"I'm not opposed to it."

"Then let's do it."

Together we walk up to the bar, hand one of the bartenders our drink, and he gets to work while we crush up some strawberries and put them at the bottom of three glasses.

"We need a name," I say.

"How about the Prickly Pair, but we spell it p-a-i-r?"

"Nice play on words, babe."

"Thank you." She kisses my cheek, and I smirk.

"Fuck, we're cute."

"I could not agree more."

The bartender pours our drink into the glasses, and it comes out a light pink color that's actually pretty cool. Then we set our drinks on the judges' table, fill out a name card, and go back to our table.

We both take a seat, and I loop my arm over Scottie's shoulder. "What do you think? Do we have a chance?"

She looks around at the competition. "I don't know. Brad's using a smoker with his wife, and Duncan rimmed his glass with something. Looks like...crushed-up graham cracker. Should we have done that?"

"I have no idea."

"Margaritas are usually lined with something."

"Yeah, but I hate that, don't you?"

"Despise it actually. I don't want a mouthful of salt as I drink my drink."

I turn to her. "Scottie, are we...are we meant to be?"

She chuckles and says, "I think we might be."

That makes me smile. I press a soft kiss to her lips just as the judges come out and Sanders introduces them as if we don't already know them.

It's Ellison and the keeper of the quarters at the front desk. Sanders takes a seat as well but lets us know he's just trying them in case there's a tie.

We all wait patiently and quietly as the judges go through each drink, taking sips and making notes on a notepad. Their faces reveal nothing. They remain stone-faced the entire time, indicating zero favoritism.

So when Sanders stands with the results, we truly have no idea who the winner will be.

I glance over at Chad, who's rubbing his hands together like the tool that he is. Brad is rocking back and forth. Duncan has his fingers crossed in front of him. And Finky's holding hands with his wife and covering his eyes at the same time.

Clearing his throat, Sanders addresses the room. "Thank you for all your entries. There was quite the variety up there tonight and some real innovation, but there was a clear-cut winner." He looks over his shoulder and says, "Drumroll please."

Ellison and Quarters both drum their hands on the table in front of them, and then Sanders holds up his hand to stop them.

"The winner of tonight's mixology competition is…"

I hold my breath, hoping we can go three for three.

"The Prickly Pair."

I leap up into the air, toss Scottie over my shoulder like a sack of potatoes, and start spinning her around while I whoop it up. She laughs the entire time, and I bring her up to the front, where we address the room.

I set her down and keep her close as I say, "I'd like to thank my brother, who couldn't be here tonight, for being the best bartender I know. Without him, we would have forgotten about the sweet-and-sour mixture, which would have destroyed the overall flavor." I press my hand to my chest. "I would also like to thank my beautiful wife for being the prickly pear in this relationship. Like I always say to her, she's prickly, but sweet like a pear. Babe, do you have any words?" I gesture to her to take the floor, and for a second, I think she's going to back down, but to my surprise, she steps up.

"Huge shout-out to our first date, where we got drunk off margaritas and rode the subway all the way to Coney Island and back. I knew that night that if this man would ride on a subway with me for thirty-one stops while street performers did the Macarena in front of us, then he was a keeper."

I lean in and say, "Our first dance was the Macarena."

Scottie waves her hand. "Thank you and good night."

Duncan, the good man that he is out of all of them, claps while we walk back to our seats.

"Well, that ends the competition portion of our night. You're free to go back to your cabins or test out the drinks," Sanders says. "As for Scottie and Wilder, you come with me."

Time to collect the prize.

Hand in hand, we follow Sanders out of the dining hall area.

"Easily, that was the best drink out of all of them," Sanders says. "The smoke one I think is going to sit with me for a while. I think it killed some of my taste buds."

Yikes.

"Thank you," Scottie says. "We wanted to keep it simple but also reflect our relationship. We might have been prickly when we got here, but I think we're finding the sweet now."

"I think you are too," Sanders says, leading us out by the lake and into the forest, where there is a blanket set up, some wine, and chocolates. "This is your prize. An evening by the lake." He winks at us. "Have fun."

He takes off, leaving us alone in a partially secluded area.

"Well, would you look at this," I say, taking in the spread. "And look, a present as well."

"What do you think is in it?"

"Only one way to find out," I say as I take her down to the blanket that's plusher than I thought it was going to be. I hand her the gift, and she opens it.

We both look in the box at the same time, and I smirk while she gasps.

I reach in and pull out a curved orange dildo. One side is clearly for hitting the G-spot, and the other is a clit simulator, with a little flap that must simulate licking. And then right next to it, a matching cock ring and perineum stimulator.

I look up at Scottie and smile. "I know what we're doing tonight."

"What, uh…" She points at the orange dildo. "What is that little flap thing there."

"That, Pips, is a clit stimulator. It flicks at your clit."

She wets her lips and nods. "Um, interesting."

"That's all you have to say? Interesting?"

"I don't know what else to say. I've never seen something like that before."

"Does it intimidate you?"

"I mean…a little. And what's the other thing? Is that for you?"

"Yeah, it's a cock ring, and I think this is supposed to play with my perineum."

She studies it. "Is that going to fit around your penis? It looks small."

"I appreciate the compliment, and yes, they stretch. See." I show her and watch her eyes widen as she takes it all in.

"And you want to use those…tonight?"

"Yeah. Doesn't that turn you on?"

"I mean…it's scary."

"Scary?" I shake my head. "Not scary when you're with the right person who knows what he's doing."

"And you know what you're doing?"

"Yeah, Pips."

She wets her lips again and then shyly asks, "What, uh, what would you do?"

Smirking, I lean in closer and gently push a piece of hair behind her ear as I say, "I would first make sure you were naked. I would strip you myself, but slowly. With every article of clothing I took off, I would make sure I spent time dragging my tongue and lips over every inch of your exposed skin, spending a luxurious amount of time on your perfect tits, then moving down between your legs, where I would lick you everywhere besides where you really want me."

Her breath hitches in her chest, and her cheeks flush, which I find too fucking hot.

"Then I would move my fingers up your inner thigh to your cunt, where I would test to see if you were turned on. Tell me, would you be turned on?"

She nods her head slowly, and I reward her with kisses along her jaw.

I move over to her ear, where I continue, "With you ready, I would slowly slide the dildo inside you, letting you get used to the feel of it, but I wouldn't turn it on just yet. Instead, I would slip my cock ring on and turn it on, letting you watch me unravel. Letting you experience the kind of pleasure these toys could bring. Precum would fall past the tip of my cock, and I would swipe it and let you lick it off my fingers. That desperate mouth of yours would lick me clean. Wouldn't it, Pips?"

She nods again, and when I pull away, her eyes are heady, dazed, so I lay her back down on the blanket.

"I would let you watch me grow, let you see how goddamn stiff I am, how much I want release, and then I would turn it off. I would lie there and let my dick twitch, looking for relief. Searching for it."

I bring my hand to her shirt, and I lift it up just enough to press my palm to her heated skin.

"I would be so goddamn out of my mind with need that I would immediately turn on your dildo, because I would want you to feel the same thing. I would need you to be in the same position as me, begging for release, barely able to hang on. And at first, you would be surprised. You wouldn't know how to react to the new sensation, not until I lowered my mouth to yours and started helping you relax, letting our tongues do the work."

I lift up her shirt some more, exposing her bra. I pull one cup down and play with her nipple, rolling it between my fingers.

"And while we made out, I would play with your nipples like this. Just enough to turn you on even more but not so much that it takes away from the sensation you're feeling down below."

Her teeth pull over her bottom lip.

"And when I saw that your orgasm was starting to climb, I would turn my cock ring back on, and I would ask you to pump me. To let me fuck your hand. I would be so goddamn desperate for it that I would barely be able to hold back as your fingers wrapped around my girth. And as we climbed together, you getting all the goddamn pleasure you deserved while you were helping me come, I would stare into your beautiful goddamn eyes and think how lucky I am, how infatuated I am, how much I would want this moment to last forever. And when I'm on the verge, ready to come, you arching your back as your orgasm took over, rocketing through your body and making you clench around your dildo, I would lift my dick to your mouth, beg you to swallow me, and then bust all over your lips and tongue." I finish with pinching her nipple just enough to make her moan, then I remove my hand and say, "Does that seem scary?"

She wets her lips, and then in the sweetest fucking voice I've ever heard, she says, "With you...no."

The lights go out in the dining hall when Finky and his wife are the last to retreat to their cabin. We're the only ones left out in the open, and it's what I've been waiting for ever since Sanders showed us our spot out here in the trees.

"What kind of wine is that?" Scottie asks as she sucks down the last drop from her glass. "I think there is something special in there. I'm buzzing."

Laughing, I nod. "I know. Me too." I smirk at her and then tug on her arm. "I like you."

"No." She shakes her head. "I like you."

"Babe," I grow serious. "I like...*you*."

"Wilder...how many times do I have to tell you this: I like you!"

"How about we both agree that we like each other?"

"Yeah, I can get on board with that. Because I think you're great."

"And I think you're great."

Her fingers drag over my chest. "And I think you're sexy." She leans in and whispers, "The first night we slept in the same bed, I thought about you possibly touching me." Then she brings her finger to her lips and shooshes me.

Fucking adorable.

"The first night we slept together, I had a dream about you," I admit.

She clamps her hand over her mouth. "Was it a sex dream?"

"I don't think so. But a few nights later, I definitely had a sex dream about you. It was after you wore your bathing suit. Your ass is so fine."

"Your ass is fine." She pushes at my chest.

"No, babe, your ass is fine. The finest of all asses to ever ass."

"Is that a thing?"

I nod. "It's a thing. An award that is only handed out to the best ass to ever walk, and, Pips, that's your ass." I blow out a heavy breath and then pout. "But I'm sad."

"Oh no, why?" She cups my cheek.

"Because I want to see your ass again, and it's all covered up."

"Gosh, that is sad."

"I wish that it wasn't covered up."

"For your sake, I wish it wasn't as well."

"Well then, maybe...maybe you can take your shorts off."

She glances down at her shorts and then back at me. "Want me to take them off and bend over in front of you?"

"Please."

She nods. "I mean, I can't have you sad." She shimmies out of her shorts and then stands from the blanket, only to back up in front of me and bend over, where she touches her toes.

"Christ," I mutter as I run my hands up her hamstrings and straight to her ass, pushing the bikini briefs to her center and gripping her ass tightly.

"Oh God," she moans and then stands. Staring down at me, she asks, "What about my boobs? Do you miss those too?"

"So much I might start crying."

"Please don't cry," she says as she reaches into her white shirt and undoes her bra. She tosses it to the side but leaves her shirt on.

"That's not good enough."

"I'm not done."

Then to my surprise, she walks to the lake, steps into the water, and dips herself all the way down until the water reaches her neck. When she stands back up, the water weighs down her shirt, making it see-through as the fabric clings to her body.

Mother of God.

"Holy fuck," I whisper as I stare at her perfectly hard nipples poking through the fabric.

She straddles my lap and pushes me onto my back. My hands fall to her thighs as she starts to slowly undulate on top of me.

"Christ, Pips," I say while my hands run up her wet torso, my mouth desperate to touch her, to feel her, to suck on her.

Her hands move to her breasts, and she starts squeezing them while on top of me, giving me one hell of a show. I grow stiff underneath her, letting her take the reins, enjoying this newfound freedom she's gained.

"Matt never let me dry hump him."

"He's a fucking moron," I say as she leans her hands against my chest now, anchoring herself.

"I need your shorts off. I want to feel more of you."

I undo my shorts and pull them off as she helps me, leaving my boxer briefs on. She starts working my cock once she's seated again.

"That's it, baby," I say. "Take what you want, what you need."

Her teeth pull on her lip as she continues to move over me. "You're so big, I love it. I love the way you fill me up. I've never felt anything like it."

Her fingers claw at my shirt, which is growing wetter and wetter from her, so I tear it off my body and toss it to the side right before she bends down and takes my nipple in her mouth.

"Fuck," I shout, not caring if someone hears us. "Yes, play with me. Use me."

Her tongue flattens out and drags over my nipple, over and over again, while her hand pinches my other nipple, making it hard and sending a wave of pleasure straight to my cock, which causes me to jolt upward.

I move her off my lap, and she looks up at me, confused, but I say, "Stand up." Like the good girl that she is, she stands up, and I pull her shirt over her head, then push her underwear down her legs, leaving her completely naked. I strip out of my boxer briefs as well and take her hand. "Let's check off something from your list."

With that, I carry her to the water.

"Are we skinny-dipping?"

"We are."

The water is decently warm, thank God, and when we reach the deeper part, she wraps her arms and legs around me.

She presses her forehead against mine, and I can hear the smile in her voice when she says, "Can we fuck in here?"

"We can do whatever you want."

She reaches between us, and she takes my dick in her hand, lines me up at her entrance, and then sits down, impaling herself.

Her head falls back, and her grip on me grows tighter as she adjusts to my size.

"God, you're huge." She takes a few deep breaths and then brings her head back to mine, where she looks me in the eyes for a few seconds and then kisses me.

She keeps me in place with her hands in my hair while her tongue darts into my mouth, opening me wide to her. I slide my hands around her and am filling her up with my cock while we float in the water, making out.

It's so fucking intimate.

Unlike anything I've ever done with a woman, yet it feels so right.

It feels right being inside her.

It feels like I belong here.

Like this is who should be around me, with me...filling up this hole I've had inside me for so goddamn long.

Our tongues tangle, dancing over each other. Fuck, she tastes so good. So goddamn good. It makes me need so much more, so I find my footing on the bottom of the lake, grip her ass, and start moving her up and down on my cock.

She presses her forehead to mine. "Oh my God," she whispers as her hands slide to my cheeks. "Fuck, Wilder, keep doing that."

Water sloshes around us as I continue to pump her up and down, the water helping me maintain a good rhythm, creating an immense amount of friction.

"Your piercings," she says. "They...they feel so good. God." She starts tightening around me. "I'm sorry, fuck, I'm...I'm close. I'm sorry."

The way she tightens around me makes me go feral. This feeling is what I crave—*need*—when she's about to contract on my cock over and over again.

"Come for me, Pips. Come on my cock like a good girl."

Her fingers dig into my shoulders, and she moves faster over me, controlling the pace as she lifts up and down.

And it's so fucking good. The best goddamn feeling.

"Wilder." She sucks in a sharp breath. Then she starts throbbing around me, pulsing. A moan falls past her lips right before she bites down on my shoulder to keep herself quiet.

It's all I need, the pain and the pleasure; my orgasm shoots right down my spine, and I spill into her, both of us coming at the same time.

I cup the back of her head as I dip down into the water and let it slosh over us as we both catch our breath. After a few seconds, she pulls away and smiles up at me before pressing a soft kiss to my lips.

Then she chuckles...again.

"You know, this laughing thing after sex, not sure I'm a fan."

She chuckles some more and then says, "I'm sorry. It's just...I don't know, this is crazy. I just had sex in a lake with a man who has four piercings on his penis. Like...if you had told me a year ago this is what I would be doing, I would have told you you were crazy."

"Yeah, well, if you had told me a year ago I was going to pretend to be someone's husband at a marriage summer camp, I would have said, where do I sign up?"

She laughs. "Have you always been like this? Up for anything?"

"Not always," I say as I stay inside her, loving this connection as I still live off the high of our orgasm. "When my dad passed, I kind of made a promise to him to do as much as I could, to always say yes. That's why I got into improv, not just because I needed more to do but because the rule is 'yes, and'... I wanted to build that into my brain, that I'm a yes-man, that I will live life to its fullest, because you never know when it's going to end."

"I love that," she says, cupping my cheek. "I think I need to do more of that."

This woman is courageous, beautiful, sexy as fuck. Brave.

"I think you already are."

CHAPTER TWENTY-SIX
SCOTTIE

"MORNING," WILDER SAYS AS HE kisses my shoulder, stirring me awake.

I peep my eyes open and look around, taking in our cabin and the lovemaking minibar on the counter.

"How did we get here?" I ask as I turn over, feeling Wilder's hand cross over my stomach.

"I carried you back to the cabin," he says, his thumb caressing my skin.

"You did?" I ask, surprised. "Wait…did I pass out last night?"

He chuckles. "Yeah, Pips. You did. I had other plans when we got out of the water, but you changed those plans the moment you closed your eyes and started sleeping on my shoulder. I didn't have it in me to wake you up, so I brought you back here."

"Ugh, I'm sorry. Wine does that to me."

"It's fine." He leans down and kisses my forehead. "Breakfast was delivered to us this morning."

I lift up and spot a tray on the table near the window. "What time is it?"

"Nine."

"What?" My eyes shoot open. "Seriously?"

"Yes." He chuckles. "That wine really conked you out. I made a note to never give you wine ever again."

"Are we missing anything?"

Wilder shakes his head. "Sanders left us a note that said to take our time this morning and reemerge when we're ready. Which means we won't be ready until dinner." He wiggles his brows, and I push at his forehead, laughing.

I roll away from him, surprised he doesn't grab me and pull me back into bed. I find his shirt on the ground, so I put it over my head. When I turn around to look at him, he has a disgruntled look on his face.

"Uh, was kind of hoping for a naked breakfast this morning."

"You can be naked," I say. "But I can't possibly sit there naked and eat a meal. Having my boobs out in the open like that while having a casual conversation is not ideal."

"Really? Because it's ideal for me."

I roll my eyes and take a seat at the table. Wilder grumbles and slips on a pair of shorts before joining me.

Today, it's a make-your-own yogurt parfait, so I start by scooping some yogurt into my bowl, adding berries, granola, some chia seeds, and then a drizzle of honey on top. I cross one leg over the other and then pick up a spoon and start eating as I look over at Wilder, who hasn't moved. He's just staring at me.

"What?" I ask.

He slightly tilts his head to the side and says, "You're beautiful, Scottie."

I can't hold back my smile as I look down at my yogurt. "Um, thank you."

"I'm serious."

This time, I look him in the eyes and say, "I know you are."

He nods and then still leaves his bowl untouched as he says, "Can I see you after this?"

"Huh?"

"Can I take you out on a date after this, when we get back to the city?"

"Oh." I shift in my seat. "I mean…is that what you want?"

"I wouldn't ask if that wasn't what I wanted."

"I know, but you said you weren't ready for anything like that. Dating. Relationships."

"Well aware what I said," he replies. "And I'm also well aware of what I'm asking now."

I set my bowl down on the table as things grow serious very quickly. "I'd like to see you again," I say, not holding back the truth. "But I just...I want to make sure you're in the right headspace. You know? Sure, this all feels great now, and there is some clouding of the brain from the fun we've been having, but when reality strikes and we're back in the city, I'm back at my job, and you're volunteering, I think there are a lot of factors that we need to consider. And I don't...I don't think I can risk the idea of being with someone who doesn't know completely what he wants."

"Scottie, I know I want to see you again."

"And I really appreciate that," I say, the scars on my heart feeling like they're being tugged on. "But I've been hurt badly, and I can see myself becoming very attached to you—a part of me already has—and even though we're having fun, I can't risk that attachment out of fear that you're not going to be ready to take that step forward."

"But I am."

I shake my head. "It's so easy to say that when you're here at camp, with nothing else going on in your life. I just think...maybe we need to have this conversation later, you know?"

He slowly nods his head. "Yeah, I understand." He picks up a bowl, and I can see the defeat in his shoulders, which makes me feel awful.

"Please don't be mad at me," I say.

His eyes meet mine. "I could never be mad at you, Pips," he says softly in that deep timbre. "My number one priority when it comes to you is making sure you're comfortable. I want to make sure you're taken care of. And if this is how you feel, then that's that. This journey, it's about you. It's not about me."

"That makes me seem selfish."

"It doesn't. But even if it did, don't you think it's time for you to be a little selfish?"

"I don't think there is ever a good time to be selfish," I reply.

"When it comes to your mental health, yeah, there's always a good time to be selfish. And you've worked hard while being here, Scottie. I'm really proud of you, so I don't want you to lose that momentum."

And when he says things like that, it makes me want him that much more, because he's so understanding, supportive, the kind of guy that I want in my life. And that's why I worry, because I'm already attached. What happens when we get back to the city, he takes me out, I grow even more attached, and then he decides he's still not ready?

He said it to my face; he doesn't do dating. He doesn't do relationships because he's not ready, because there are things hanging over his head that are preventing him from committing. I can't risk the possible heartache of falling for someone who, in the end, figures out that they're not ready.

He might be feeling a certain way now, but how do I know he won't change his mind when we're back in reality?

"I can see your mind working over there," he says.

"Just trying to figure out what's going on in my head."

"It's fine, babe," he says casually. "I understand the assignment."

"What assignment?" I ask.

His eyes meet mine as he pauses, scooping some yogurt into his bowl. "That I'm going to have to prove to you just how serious I am about this."

"Wilder—"

"Don't worry. There'll be no pressure, and this'll be entirely your decision, but don't think I'm not going to make it damn hard on you." He smirks and then plops more yogurt in his bowl. "Get ready to be wooed, Pips."

"Tomorrow is our last day," Sanders says as he sits in his chair in a cutoff T-shirt with a green tie and jeans. "You're free to go home, and I always take this day to go over what your plans are for when you return to regular life."

Wilder has his arm around me as we sit side by side on the couch. After breakfast, he pulled me up by my hand and took me to the shower, where he teased me with the flesh sword. I swatted it away multiple times. There are things I will do, but backing up to a suction-cup penis on the shower wall is not one of those things. Instead, I sat on top of Wilder and rode him, which was so much better than any other device in the cabin.

"Keeping the communication open," Wilder says. "We were just talking about what we're going to do when we go home."

Oh God, what is he going to say?

"And what was that conversation like?" Sanders asks.

"She's hesitant," Wilder says. "I think even though we had a good time here and made some great strides toward a better marriage, there's still the concern that if we aren't here at the camp, being challenged, we might fall back into old habits."

"That's a very valid concern," Sanders says as he picks up a hockey stick. He starts balancing a puck on the blade as he walks around. It's so distracting, something I will never get over. "And it's the main concern I get from all my couples. So how do you think you'll combat it?"

"I think we just need to keep having honest conversations and putting in the effort to be better," Wilder says. "I know I have plans of my own to show her how committed I am to her."

"Care to share those plans?" Sanders asks.

Wilder shakes his head. "Nah, they're not for her ears."

"Keeping a little mystery in the relationship. That's always good. As long as it's not hindering your communication." Sanders pops up the puck and catches it on the blade again. "What about you, Scottie? What are your plans for when you get back?"

"Umm…" I look up at Wilder and then back at Sanders. "I don't…I don't really know."

Sanders pauses, and his brows shoot up. "You don't know?"

Feeling the pressure, I shake my head. "I'm, uh, I'm just, you know, trying to figure things out."

He now takes a seat on the arm of the chair. "Can I ask what there is to figure out? Is there doubt about your relationship with Wilder?"

Tongue-tied, I try to figure out how to answer, but before I can, Wilder says, "I think she's been hurt." Wilder squeezes my shoulder. "And I think it's easy to spend eight days in the woods, where you can forget about real life, but when you go back to your normal life, when you go back to your home, where you've experienced that hurt firsthand, it reminds you of the bad. And I think that's something we are going to have to overcome together. I don't blame her for having these feelings," Wilder continues, making tears well up in my eyes. Why is he so understanding? Why is he so great? "I'm glad she has these feelings, because that means she's processing, which means she's trying to figure out exactly what she wants in her life. This time at Camp Haven has given us the chance to explore our wounds in neutral territory. Now the hard work is ahead of us, healing those wounds."

I swipe at my eyes as tears fall down my cheeks.

"Why are you crying?" Sanders asks.

I suck in a deep breath and say, "Wilder just...he has shown me what I deserve while I'm here, and I guess I'm trying to accept that."

It's a confusing statement for someone who thinks we're married, but it's also a true statement for the relationship that Wilder and I really have.

Sanders looks over at Wilder for confirmation, and of course, Wilder, being the honorable man he is, says, "She deserves the world, and I'm ready to give her that."

My eyes well up again while my emotions get the best of me.

Because I want what he has to give me. I do.

But I also know he has reservations.

I know he might not be fully ready.

And I know that I'm already growing attached.

Not wanting to have this moment in front of Sanders, I stand from the couch and say, "Excuse me."

The water laps against the dock poles below me as I dangle my feet, my hands resting on the edge of the dock. Ducks float across the water in front of me, and the distant sound of the camp winding down is behind me.

There are some couples playing volleyball off to the left, another couple out on the lake in a rowboat, and a few couples are over at the dining hall doing arts and crafts.

I've been sitting on the dock for probably a solid twenty minutes, quietly crying to myself, when I hear footsteps along the wooden planks. I know exactly who it is.

I wipe at my eyes, ready to be enveloped in Wilder's strong embrace, when someone clears their throat behind me. I look back, and instead of seeing Wilder standing there with his handsome face, it's Chad.

God, not what I want to deal with right now.

I turn back around, not wanting to give him the time of day, but he says, "Can I join you?"

"If you need to," I say in an annoyed tone. I swipe at my eyes again, trying to clear out the tears.

Chad doesn't get the hint and instead takes a seat next to me, causing me to scoot over so we're not sitting shoulder to shoulder.

"I'm really not in the mood to spar, Chad."

"I'm not either," he says in a subdued tone, any antagonization completely gone. That's when I look over at him and see just how defeated he seems. He lets out a shaky breath and says, "Uh, things aren't looking good for me and my wife."

"What?" I ask, turning toward him.

This is not what I was expecting at all. They seemed fine. Happy.

He slowly nods, staring down at his hands. "We're having a really hard time getting pregnant, and it's taking its toll on us. She's been taking hormones, and we've been having sex like clockwork, taking all the romance out of it because now we're pinned to a calendar of ovulation." He pulls his hand over his face. "And I thought that maybe being here, getting a chance to reconnect, would help but, uh, it doesn't seem like it's working."

Stunned that he's even divulging this to me, I say, "I don't want to sound rude, Chad, but given our history, are you being serious? Is this a real confession?"

"I can see where the skepticism comes in, since we haven't had the best camaraderie since being here or in the office for that matter, but yeah, I'm being serious. She told me last night that she's no longer happy, and I honestly don't know where to go from here."

"Once again, not to be rude, but why are you telling me this? Aren't you closer with Brad or Finky? Or even Duncan?"

"I am," he says. "But you're the one who I admire. You're the one that seems to have turned it around with your husband. You seem like someone who could give me some good advice."

And just like that, guilt consumes me. So he didn't think we were faking it? He really believed me and Wilder?

How?

He made it seem like he was on to something.

And now he wants advice?

How can I sit here and give this man advice when I'm the one with a failed marriage?

I'm the one who couldn't turn it around.

I'm the one who couldn't muster up enough interest from her husband to even try.

"I know that we haven't really gotten along, and I know it's because I've been frustrated, and I took that frustration out on you unjustly. I was jealous. I was out of my mind, trying to hold it together, and unfortunately, you were the one I decided to take my anger out on. I'm really sorry, Scottie. I've been...hell, I've been incredibly shitty to you."

More tears well up in my eyes, and I let them fall, hitting my shorts, because I know that feeling. I know what he's going through, those thoughts of helplessness, yet he's coming to me for advice.

"Shit, I'm sorry, Scottie. I didn't mean to make you cry."

I shake my head. "It's not you. It's me."

This is all on me.

"Are...are things with you and Wilder not going well?"

"No, they are," I say as the truth bubbles up inside me. It's the guilt. It's the uncertainty. It's Chad thinking that I'm some sort of perfect person who can revive a dying marriage, when in reality, I'm just a fraud. And before I can stop myself, I say, "Things with Wilder are just...they're not real."

He pauses for a second and then asks, "Wait...really?"

I nod.

"So all of this...it was...it was a farce?"

I cover my face and let out a small sob, shaking my head. "God, I'm so stupid."

Gingerly, he pats my back, and I take that as his uncomfortable way of trying to comfort me. But he shouldn't have to be comforting me, because this is all a lie. My entire relationship with Wilder, it's been a lie, and I didn't think it was that big of a deal, but now that Chad is coming to me for advice on how to fix his marriage, I can see it's very much a big deal. Because I don't want people getting the wrong impression about me and Wilder, thinking that maybe some communication can solve things, because that's not true at all.

I tried communicating with Matt.

And look where I am now...at a marriage camp with a fake husband, learning that there are actually good men out there. *I had just married a dud.*

Despite a slight concern this could backfire on me, I decide honesty is better for Chad. It's time to be honest all around. That's probably the best way to step forward.

"Wilder is not my husband," I say. "He's my best friend's brother. He came with me here to pretend to be my husband. The fighting, the arguing, it was all a farce." I turn to look at Chad through watery eyes. "I was trying to fit in at work, and when you called me out in the conference room, I. . . I just felt like I needed to save face, so I went along with the lie. I'm so sorry, Chad. It was stupid, and I shouldn't have made you think that my marriage could be so easily fixed when that's not the case at all. Because the reality is I was married to a man named Matt, and we couldn't work it out. I carry that guilt with me every day, something I didn't realize until I came here. So yeah, don't come to me for marriage advice, because my marriage failed."

Silence falls between us, and I don't blame him. What can he really say to that?

"Wow," he says, and I brace myself for the snide comments, for the victory parade that he's in the right and I'm in the wrong, but instead, he turns toward the lake and says, "I'm sorry, Scottie."

"What?" I say, wiping at my eyes.

"I'm sorry. I know what it feels like to have your marriage slip through your fingers, watching it slowly float away, and no matter what you do, you can't do anything about it. I'm really fucking sorry."

Umm, wow. Was not expecting that. Chad taking the high road. I'm. . . I'm shocked.

"Thank you," I answer softly. "I'm sorry about you and your wife. Matt and I never tried to get pregnant, and I think it's because when we were ready, we both kind of knew that it wasn't something that would help the marriage, only hinder it, so I can't imagine what you're going through."

"Yeah, it's not easy." He blows out a heavy breath and then lightly chuckles. "You know, at first, I thought that maybe something was up, something was fishy, but then the more I watched you, the more I pushed that thought away. And to be honest, you had me fooled. I could have sworn you and Wilder were married. The way you two interact together, how he looks at you…it seems real, at least from the outside."

I press my lips together, more tears coming to my eyes. "It, uh, it turned into something when we were here. I wasn't expecting it, but yeah, there are feelings between us."

"Then why are you crying?" he asks.

"Because I'm scared," I answer honestly. "I put my whole heart into my marriage, but I was ignored. My needs were ignored. He wasn't interested in me, and it did a number on my confidence. When I moved to New York, I was trying to start a new journey, a new chapter, but I realized that it was pretty hard with all the baggage I was carrying. Wilder, he opened my eyes to that baggage and had me face it head-on with him by my side. He made me see my worth and made me stand up for myself. He's been so different from Matt, and that…that scares me, because I can see myself growing attached—"

"But you don't want to get hurt again," Chad finishes for me.

"I can't get hurt again," I say softly. "I'm still so raw, and Wilder previously told me he's not in a position to know what he wants when it comes to relationships and dating, but he wants to try."

"But you're too scared to try when you know you already have an attachment."

"Correct," I say, surprised that Chad gets it so well.

"It's hope," he says. "It's debilitating, because when it doesn't work out, you have to be the one that sits in that crushed hope and figure out how to swim your way out. I get it. I'm there right now. Coming here, to a place we loved before, I had all the hope in the world that we would make things work, but I just don't think that's going to happen." He sighs. "I'm really sorry."

"I'm sorry too," I say and then put my arm around him and rub his back. "And I'm sorry I lied. I'll come clean to everyone."

"No, don't," he says. "This can stay between you and me. I get why you did it. We haven't made it easy for you to fit in at the office."

"Yeah, but I can't keep up this farce. People will ask."

"So are you saying you're not going to at least give it a shot with Wilder? Because there has to be something there, right?"

"There is," I say. "I've never been treated the way he treats me, and I know he's genuine, because he's not the kind of man who would blow smoke up my ass, but he's also two years younger and doesn't quite know what he wants, and I can't be his guinea pig, you know?"

"I get that."

I pull my legs in close. "It feels so weird talking to you about this, but I just think...I think I need to come clean. As I'm hearing you talk about you and your wife, it makes me think I shouldn't give out false hope. And I know everyone is different, and I truly hope that you and Danielle work things out, but Wilder and I shouldn't be the ones that people look up to."

"I understand," he says.

And then we sit there in silence for a moment, both of us staring out at the lake.

"If you ever want to chat about this some more, Chad, you can always come into my office."

"Same, Scottie. Same."

"Is everything okay?" Sanders asks as I take a deep breath.

I asked Sanders, Ellison, and Wilder to meet with me in the therapy cabin. I haven't seen Wilder since I left our session, so when he came up to me, looking concerned, I felt incredibly guilty. But this needs to be done.

"Um, no, not really." I twist my hands on my lap, feeling really nervous and hoping this doesn't affect me and my job. "I need to come clean about something." I feel Wilder stiffen next to me, but I keep pushing forward. "When I told the office that I was married and that my husband and I were going through some rough times, I lied."

Ellison sits up straight, looking confused.

"Wilder is my best friend's brother, who is into improv and volunteered to act as my husband."

"What?" Sanders says, looking confused.

"What are you doing?" Wilder asks me under his breath.

"I can't do this anymore," I say and then address Ellison. "I'm sorry I lied. I wanted to feel like I was a part of the company and the marriage clique. I tried to fit in like an idiot, and well, you see how that went. The truth is I was married to a man named Matt, and we couldn't make it work. All the things I told you in our sessions, Sanders, those were things about Matt. All the struggles I faced, the lack of confidence, they all derived from my first marriage. Wilder was just kind enough to go along for the ride and take the brunt of all my complaints."

"I see," Sanders says as he leans back in his chair and studies us.

"I'm really sorry, Ellison, and I know if you want to hold this against me, I understand. Lying does not belong in the workplace. I want you both to know that this was all on me and not on Wilder."

"No," Wilder says. "I played an equal part."

"Why are you telling me this now?" Sanders asks.

"Because I just had a conversation with another camper, asking me for advice on how I was able to make things right with Wilder, and I realized that being deceitful is helping no one. And in the long run, I don't want to keep up with the charade." I look Sanders in the eyes. "I'm really sorry I wasted your time. That I made a mockery of this camp by lying. You deserve so much more respect than what I've given you." Then I look at Wilder. "And I'm sorry I wasted your time and that I put you through a week of carrying my baggage."

"You didn't," he says quickly, but I keep moving forward.

"I called my friend. She's coming to pick me up. I really don't want to stay much longer. I hope that's okay. And again, I'm really sorry."

I go to stand, but Sanders holds out his hand. "One moment." He crosses his arms across his chest and studies me and Wilder. "So you're telling me you two are not in a relationship?"

"No." I shake my head.

"But you pretended to be?"

"That's correct," I answer. "And like I said, I'm really—"

"I know you're sorry," he says. "I'm just trying to understand what the hell I see between you two though. Because what I've noticed the last few days, that is not made up. The way you look at each other, touch each other, work so well together—that's not improv."

"It's not for me," Wilder says.

I wet my lips. "It wasn't for me either."

"So then you two have feelings for each other." Sanders motions between the two of us.

"Um, I mean—"

"Yes," Wilder says. "I have feelings for her."

I look in his direction and he nods.

"I do, Pips. I have feelings for you."

"I do too," I say shakily. "You know I do."

"Then why are you having Denise, I'm assuming, come to pick you up?"

"Because I'm scared," I answer honestly. "Really scared. I shouldn't have feelings for someone I just met, and here I am…thinking about you all the time, loving being next to you, wanting to see your handsome face whenever I get a chance. I don't…I don't want to get hurt, and everything I'm feeling right now is setting me up for that."

"Are you going to hurt her?" Sanders asks Wilder.

He pauses for a moment, his eyes moving between me and Sanders. Then, in an uncertain tone, he answers, "I don't want to."

And that right there…that's the problem.

That single answer pushes a wave of insecurity through me.

He's an honest man, I know this about him. Yet he doesn't seem to give a definitive answer when asked about relationships. It's an "I don't want to" or "I think I want that."

I can't work with "I think." I need to know exactly what he wants.

"But you think you might?" Sanders asks.

Wilder looks me in the eyes and then glances down at his hands. "I don't want to."

And that's the answer I was looking for.

That's the answer I needed.

I like him a lot.

I do.

But until he can figure out what he wants...I can't risk it. Which means I'm also extremely thankful for what we've had. I wouldn't have learned as much about myself had I not spent this time with Wilder. I wouldn't have learned that it's okay to say no to uncertainty. I wouldn't be able to walk away even if it hurts.

CHAPTER TWENTY-SEVEN
WILDER

WHAT THE HELL IS WRONG with me?

The minute I said it, I knew it was the wrong answer. It was almost as if I could feel Sanders's internal groan, telling me, "Wrong answer, you fool."

Trust me, I get it.

"I'm going to go," Scottie says as she stands. "I need to pack."

"Scottie," Ellison says, standing as well.

Scottie turns to her, and I can see tears forming in her eyes.

"Don't worry about this. I understand the pressure you were under to fit in, and it takes a lot of character to recognize when you were wrong. Take the next few days off, and I'll see you in the office on Monday."

"Really?" Scottie asks.

"Really."

"Thank you." She smiles softly. "For what it's worth, Sanders, you did help me close a chapter on a marriage that I struggled with."

He nods. "But if you're still scared, did I really help you close a chapter?"

She worries her lips and then sadly smiles. "Thank you for everything." She starts to leave, so I get up as well, but Sanders stops me.

"Wilder, a word."

I glance toward Scottie and then back at him. "Um, sure. Scottie, I'll meet you in the cabin."

She takes off, and I sit back down and wait for whatever is to come my way.

He turns to Ellison and says, "Could you give us a moment, darling?"

"Of course."

She places a kiss on his cheek and then takes off, leaving me alone once again with the man who has the most interesting wardrobe I've ever seen.

When the door closes, he picks up a football and tosses it to me. I catch it, and he asks, "What's the holdup?"

"What do you mean?" I toss it back to him.

"That answer. What's the holdup on reassuring her that you're not going to hurt her?"

"I don't know," I say. "It was...it was the wrong thing to say, I know that. But what if I do end up hurting her? I don't want to be that guy."

"I understand that," he says, "But let me ask you this." He tosses me the ball, and I catch it. "If she were to end things right now with you and say that she just wants to be friends, how would that make you feel?"

"Ill," I say. "Actually fucking ill." I grip the ball tightly. "I wasn't expecting to come into this marriage camp thing and grow feelings for someone I'd never met, but every day I spent with her, I started to see how fucking cool she is. How strong she is. How independent and determined. She's funny, and she challenges me, and I like all that about her."

"Yeah, I can see that."

"And I want to prove to her that I can be the man that she needs, but I also want to be careful, because I know that she's cautious. I just don't know what the fine line is."

"The fine line is you're either in or you're out," Sanders says. "With a woman like Scottie, you can't casually pursue her. You're either all in, or you don't do it at all. And I can see it in you. I can see that you can be that man who goes all in. But you have to commit to it. What were your parents like?"

"They had the greatest marriage until they didn't," I say. "My dad was in a car accident, became a quadriplegic. It was hard. My mom carried a lot of stress and ended up cheating on my dad. It was really shitty, and I've worked through a lot of it in therapy. My brother is still working on it. My relationship with her is decent. My dad passed, and my main concern is taking care of my brother and making sure he's okay. I don't want to lose him as well."

Sanders nods. "Ever think that you're possibly committing to your brother and that's why you can't quite commit to Scottie, because you're afraid it might stretch you too thin?"

"I…" I pause and think about it. Shit. Is that the holdup?

"I can see by the surprise in your expression that I might have just hit the nail on the head." He claps his hands for the ball, and I toss it to him. "You need to speak with your brother, because if you want a shot with Scottie, *that* relationship needs to be resolved. Chances are he doesn't want the emotional commitment you've enveloped him with."

"True. I hadn't thought about it like that. He was bullied as a kid, and I guess I just wanted him to feel secure in himself. He…he wanted to cut out of life early after Dad died, if you get what I'm saying." I grimace, hating that I've just shared something so personal about Mika.

"That would have been extremely traumatic to walk through for the both of you. And now? Where do you think he is emotionally? Does he still need you as his crutch?"

"Well, he's my brother, so I'll always prioritize his emotional health."

He tosses me the ball, and I catch it. "Commendable, but maybe a conversation needs to be had there."

"Yeah, probably," I say.

"And then what will you do if there is no need for you to be his emotional guard dog?"

"I, uh…" I drag my hand over my jaw. "I need to think some more."

"Well, do that. Decide if you're all in. And if you are, be as honest as you have been while at camp, because your honesty helped Scottie find hers."

Huh. That's a good thought to take away.

"You're right."

"I know I am." He smirks, lightening the tension.

I stare at him for a second and then ask, "Why all the sports stuff? Do you really think marriage is like a team sport?"

He chuckles. "Sure, you can look at it that way. You can also see it as something that eases anxiety for some people who might be against a traditional therapy session. It also takes people's minds off speaking the truth and relaxes them more. Also keeps me busy and entertained. There are many reasons for it, and they all seem to work. They don't call me the best for no reason. Hell, I was able to bring two people who didn't even know each other together."

I laugh. "Yeah, you're right about that."

"I'm right about a lot of things," Sanders says with some cockiness.

"And the clothes?" I ask nodding to his attire.

He glances down at his outfit and then back up at me. "What's wrong with my clothes?"

"Dude." I eye him.

"Your point?"

I shake my head. "Never mind."

At this point, heading to the cabin to talk to Scottie and tell her to come home with me is not going to happen. She has her mind set on leaving, and if that's what she wants to do, then I'm going to let her do that. What I need to do right now is reassure her.

I open up the cabin door and find her suitcase on the bed, and the sight of it makes my stomach turn. God, Sanders is right. How would I feel if she just ended things right here and now? I know I wouldn't like it, not one bit, which means I need to have some conversations.

Scottie walks out of the bathroom with her toiletries but doesn't look at me as she sticks them in her bag. She's avoiding, and I can understand why. She's been through a lot the last few hours. I'm sure she just wants to get the hell out of here.

"Can I help you?" I ask.

"Um, I think I got everything," she says as she closes her suitcase and zips it up. She pulls the suitcase to the floor and then reaches for her purse. She stuffs a few things in there and then sets it on top of her suitcase.

"When is Denise going to be here?"

"Soon-ish, I think. She started driving when I called her, and she was actually up in New Rochelle for a job, so it worked out."

"Good." I stick my hands in my pockets. "Uh, can I talk to you for a second?"

"Yeah, of course," she answers.

I move over to the bed and take her hand, pulling her down to sit with me. I keep her hand in mine and rub my thumbs over her knuckles for a few seconds before I look her in the eyes. "I think you're really brave," I tell her, causing her to look down. I place my fingers under her chin and lift her gaze up so she has to look at me. "What you did back there, telling the truth and apologizing, that takes a lot of guts, and it's something not a lot of adults can do. I'm really proud of you."

"Thank you," she says quietly.

"Which means I need to do the same." I continue to stroke her hand. "I'm sorry for not answering the question back there properly. I don't want to hurt you, and I don't want to be in a position where I might hurt you, because you deserve to find the right person to make you happy, not bring you tears. Do I think I can be that person? I do," I say with a nod. "But there is something I need to take care of first, and before I commit to you, I need to deal with that."

"I understand completely."

"But I need you to know something before you leave this cabin, okay?" She nods.

"I need you to know that this is not goodbye. That when you get back to the city, I will most likely be at your doorstep, wanting to see you. Wanting to hang out. Just wanting to talk. I've grown accustomed to having you around, and I can't just go without talking. How do you feel about that?"

"I feel the same."

"You do?" I ask, surprised.

"Yes. I do."

"Okay…good. That's—"

"But I'm also hesitant," she adds.

"And I get that, and I know that earning your trust is something I'll have to work on."

"I trust you, Wilder."

"Trust in what I can provide," I say, wanting to clarify. "I know you've been through a lot. If there's one thing I don't want you to ever experience again, it's that feeling of insignificance. I'm in awe of you, and I know with certainty that I want to be a better man… *for you*. You deserve to be worshipped, so I'm going to prove that I can be the man who can do that. I'm going to prove that and more to you."

"Wilder, you don't have to prove—"

"I do," I say, feeling that answer all the way down to my toes. "I do." I bring her hand up to my lips and kiss her knuckles. "Okay?"

She nods. "Okay."

"Good." I stand up. "Now, there's one thing I need to give you before you leave." I pull out the Nerds Clusters from one of the baskets on the dresser that we didn't finish. When I pass them to her, it makes her chuckle. "When you eat these…think of me."

"You're really giving me the Nerds Clusters?"

"Babe, that's how much I like you."

"Busy?" I say as Mika opens the door to his apartment.

"Holy shit," he says, pulling me into a hug. "I didn't think you were coming home this early."

I hug him back and then release him. "Yeah, neither did I. Think we can talk?"

His expression falls. "Uh-oh, did you hurt her?"

I shake my head. "Nah, man, trying not to hurt her."

"I don't like the sound of this."

"Can you just let me in?"

He scans me with his eyes, debating in his head, but then he lets me in his apartment and leads me into the living room. As I take a seat on the couch, he says, "I have water and Coke Zero from the corner store."

"The good corner store?"

"According to your app, the best corner store."

"Then I'll take one."

He grabs two Coke Zeros, opens them effortlessly like the skilled bartender that he is, and then hands me one before taking a seat. "What happened?"

"To make a long story short, I have feelings for her. She got scared because of her past, and when asked if I would hurt her, I said I didn't want to."

He pauses mid-drink and then lowers his can of soda. "You said you didn't want to instead of saying I won't hurt you?"

"Yeah." I pull on the back of my neck. "Not my best showing, that's for damn sure. But it's why I'm here, because I need to talk something through with you."

"Okay," he says, seeming nervous.

"I need to talk about Mom."

His expression falls. "Dude, I'm going to need something stronger than a Coke Zero to have this conversation."

"I know I'm springing this on you, but it's important, okay?"

He lets out a huge sigh and then turns to me. "Okay, what's going on?"

"I need to know something, given all the hard work you're doing in therapy and the strides you've taken to better your mental health. Do you think there will be a time when you might be okay with being in the same room as her again?"

He lets his tongue run over his teeth as he looks off to the side. "I want to," he says. "I really fucking do. There are times that I miss her. Times that I wish that we could do things together as a family, like Thanksgiving or Christmas, but every time I see her, I just, I think back to that day, and I get so angry."

"I know," I say. "I get the same feeling."

"Then how are you able to be around her?"

"Because I know that Dad would not want us to be split apart like we are. I think about him, and I think about what he would have thought about the division."

"Cheating on him with his best friend? You think he would have been okay with that?"

"No, but also…Dad wouldn't have wanted us pausing our lives to take care of him. You and I both know that. He probably would have asked us to move on, to put him in a care facility if he had a chance to express himself."

Mika shakes his head. "No, he would have wanted to be with his family, his wife."

"Mika," I say softly while setting my drink down. "Do you remember Dad before he got in the accident?"

"Of course I remember him," Mika says, sounding insulted.

"Do you remember how he told us over and over how much he wanted us to live our lives when we were older? How he wanted us to explore? To love. To live…"

Mika nods his head.

"He wouldn't have wanted us hanging around, waiting on him. You've got to know that, Mika."

He glances down at his hands. It takes him a second, but then he slowly nods. "Yeah, I know you're right, but it's hard to look at it that way when you love someone so much."

"It is. It's really fucking hard, Mika. This entire situation is hard. Losing our dad when we were in high school and college. Our mom having to raise us, keep a smile on her face like everything was okay while her husband was slowly dying. The entire situation was fucking awful. But I think we need to find some forgiveness. And I know that's something you're working on, and I'm proud of you for it."

"Yeah." He tugs on his hair. "It's been harder than I expected."

"And that's okay—everyone goes at their own pace—but I need to know that you're working your way in that direction."

"Why?" he asks, seeming confused. "Why do you need to know?"

I let out a breath and prepare myself, because this is going to be the hardest part of this conversation. "Because I need to know that you're going to be okay. I can't...I can't lose you, Mika. I've lost a piece of Mom. I've lost Dad. You're all I have left, and I can't fathom the thought of losing you as well."

"Wilder, I'm fine—"

"No, don't do that," I say with a stern voice. "Don't bullshit me. Don't tell me you're fine just to say it. Look at me, and tell me how you're really fucking doing."

He blows out a heavy breath and stares out past my shoulder for a few seconds before he brings his gaze to mine. "I'm doing better. I am. It's been small steps, but I'm doing better."

A hint of relief washes through me.

"I think when I was in that dark time of my life, I didn't find much hope in anything, but now that I'm in therapy, now that I'm working on myself, I'm finding joy in simpler things."

"Really?" I ask. "Don't lie to me just to appease me."

"I mean it. Really." He sits up. "I've been making changes in my life, changes to adjust my trajectory."

"Like what?" I ask, surprised by this.

"Well, I started taking some mixology classes, because I was talking to a friend about becoming a bartender at an exclusive club. I would be paid way more, plus I would have benefits. And the work would be more challenging, more precise. There would be more opportunities to be creative. Not to mention mixing drinks would be more about the quality at an exclusive club rather than the quantity."

"Wow, when did this happen?"

"While you were at marriage camp." He smirks.

"Ah, yeah, that makes sense. Well, this is great. I'm happy for you, man."

"Thanks." He fully turns toward me. And I can see it, right there, the lightness in his expression, the joy in his demeanor. He really is doing better. "So how does this have anything to do with my friend?"

"Right." I move my hand over my jaw. "I don't want you to get upset when I tell you this, but I've sort of put things on hold in my life as I've tried to navigate the family drama and make sure that you're okay. And what it comes down to is I don't think I can move on or give Scottie my everything if I'm not sure that you're going to be okay."

His expression morphs into surprise. "Wait, really?"

"Yeah, man. You matter the most to me."

"And I appreciate that, but, Wilder, you need to live your life. Is that why...is that why you haven't gone anywhere? Why I keep telling you to go on a trip, but you won't; you just stay here in the city? Because you're worried about me?"

"Yeah, Mika. Listen, what happened that day—"

"Was a mistake," he says.

"But it scared the fuck out of me." I point to my chest. "And I never want that to happen again."

"It won't," he says seriously. "I promise, it won't. I'm better. I'm in a better place. I promise you. You won't ever have to worry about that again."

"Really?" I ask.

He nods. "I fucking promise."

"Okay," I say, feeling myself relax for the first time in a really long time.

I stare out the window, but he pulls my attention back by saying, "So what about Scottie?"

"I like her," I say simply. "And now I need to show her how she deserves to be treated."

"Because you messed up?"

I shake my head. "No, because she needs to know that she's worth another human's time. She needs to realize that she's not forgettable."

Mika nods his head. "And you think you can do that?"

"I know I can."

I just need to visit someone to help me out.

CHAPTER TWENTY-EIGHT
SCOTTIE

Denise: You seriously not coming out tonight?

I STARE DOWN AT THE text from my friend and sigh as I stand in front of the window AC unit of my apartment, trying to get over the city's summer heat.

> **Scottie:** No. It's hot, muggy, and I just want to stay home.
> **Denise:** You can't hide forever, Scottie. I know I told you we didn't have to talk about it in the car yesterday, but I feel like going out to the bar, having a few drinks, and just discussing things to get them off your chest would be a really good idea.
> **Scottie:** Really, I'm fine.
> **Denise:** You didn't seem fine in the car.
> **Scottie:** Trust me, I am. No need to worry about me.
> **Denise:** I'm worried.

I shake my head and set my phone down, because I'm not in the mood. I spent all day cleaning my apartment from top to bottom, making sure I scrubbed every last inch. I did this to keep my mind off things, off the camp, off my last conversation with Wilder. And it worked up until I had nothing else to clean. So then I cleaned myself.

And once again, I scrubbed every inch, even took an old toothbrush filled with soap between my toes. That was a new experience.

So now I rival the cleanliness of a bleach-scrubbed wall, which feels great, but because it's so muggy in the city today, it's ruining the vibes.

Knock. Knock.

I glance behind me at my door and roll my eyes.

Denise.

God. I love her as a friend, but seriously, when she has her mind set on something, she does not let it go. Should have known she was going to come over.

I peel myself away from the AC unit, head over to the door, unlock it, and open it.

"Denise, I—"

I stop midsentence as a pair of steely gray eyes meet mine.

"Wilder," I say, feeling incredibly surprised. For one, I didn't expect to see him this soon, and two, I didn't know he knew where I lived. Also… he didn't buzz into the building. "What are you doing here?"

"It's fucking hot out today, isn't it?" he asks as a greeting.

"Uh, yeah. It is." I grip the door tightly. "Um, again, what are you doing here?"

"Good to see you too, Pips." He folds his arms and leans against the doorframe. "I was coming to see if you want to go to the movies with me. It's hot as hell, and I have the perfect place that has salty popcorn and sweet Icees."

"You want to go to the movies?" I ask, feeling all sorts of confused.

"Yeah, your pick. There are quite a few showings in the next half hour that you can choose from. Some old and some new. Plus, it's air-conditioned, and I'm pretty sure it's one of the things on your bucket list that you want to check off, right?"

Uh…

What's happening here?

I cross my arms as well and say, "I don't understand."

He steps in close and then presses two fingers under my chin, lifting my gaze to his. In a deep, rumbly voice, he says, "I promise, I won't hurt you, but I know actions speak louder than words, so I'm here to prove it." He cups my cheek now and whispers, "Come to the movies with me. Give this a chance."

I stare into his eyes, and all I can see is sincerity. This man is genuine. He's serious. He...he came to me when he said he would.

"I told you, you don't have to."

"And I'm telling you, I need to," he says. "So please, come to the movies with me."

Nerves pulse through me, insecurity runs rampant, and before I can answer, I need to talk this out.

"Um, can you give me a second?"

"Sure," he says. "Want me to wait out here?"

"No." I shake my head. "You can wait in my living room."

I let him in, but he stops right next to me, wraps his arm around my waist, and cups my cheek. He pushes my chin up with his thumb and then lightly kisses my lips. The press of his familiar mouth and the grip of his comforting hold reinforce why I have feelings for him. Because he's everything Matt was not.

When he pulls away, he whispers, "Missed those lips." Then he walks into the living room, and I shut the door behind him. He takes a seat on the couch, and I grab my phone off the coffee table.

"Just one second." I hold up my finger.

"Do what you need to do, Pips." He drapes his arms over the back of the couch. "I'm just going to get comfortable."

"Okay," I say and then move to the back of my apartment and into my tiny closet that is stifling hot, but I don't care, because I need privacy. I click on my group FaceTime with Denise and Mika and wait impatiently for them to pick up.

Denise is the first one to answer. She's eating a peach and cleaning her makeup brushes. "Where are you?" she asks.

"In my closet," I answer as Mika picks up as well. He's wearing his earbuds, and he's walking down the street, probably on his way to work.

"What's going on? Why is it so dark where you are?"

"Listen," I whisper in my closet. "I don't have much time, so I need to be quick about this. Wilder is in my living room."

"Then why the hell are you in your closet?" Denise asks.

"Is that where you are? What is that paisley fabric next to your face? Ma'am, that's a no from me."

"Please, can we not do this right now? I need some advice."

"If it's if you should go out with my brother, the answer is yes," Mika says.

"I agree," Denise says. "Is that it? Did we solve the problem?"

I mean...sort of...

"There's more to it than that," I say.

"Okay, then what's the problem?" Mika asks. "Because as far as I know, he's the greatest guy you will ever meet."

"I can vouch for that. Derek has had him over a few times, and he's a really stand-up guy. Super respectful and always helpful."

"I know that," I say.

"Okay, so once again, what's the problem?"

"Yeah, because I don't really see one. The guy is hot, he's rich, he has an upstanding personality, and we know if he's there, his intentions are pure, because he's not going to do anything that hurts his brother's best friend. We all know how much he cherishes his brother. Therefore, he would never do anything to hurt him."

"Very poignant, Denise," Mika says as a car honks in the background.

"Thank you."

"So...this call really isn't necessary," Mika says.

"I'm...I'm scared," I'm able to squeeze out.

They go silent for a second, and then Denise says, "You can't live in fear, Scottie. Don't let what Matt did to you control your future. You have to put yourself out there again, physically and mentally. I know it's scary, and I know you don't want to get hurt again, but I wouldn't encourage you if I thought this was going to hurt you in the long run."

"He won't hurt you," Mika says. "He won't. Let him show you how you're supposed to be treated."

"Give him a chance," Denise adds.

I squeeze my eyes shut for a moment, letting their words sink in. They're right, I know they are. Wilder has shown me nothing but patience, understanding, and kindness. He's been a shoulder to lean on, a sturdy rock when times are tough, and he's helped me have more confidence in myself. He's helped me see my worth.

There should be no question.

This should be an easy answer.

I let out a deep breath and nod my head even though they can barely see me. "You're right. You're both right."

"We know," Denise says in a lighter tone, making me chuckle.

"Give him a shot. You won't regret it," Mika says. "We love you, and we know you can do brave things."

"Thank you," I say. "Love you guys too."

Then we say our goodbyes, and I let myself out of the closet and take a second to steady my breathing and calm my nerves. Denise is right. I can't let what Matt did dictate my future. I need to rise above that, not be scared to give someone else a chance and let people into my life.

And if I can trust anyone, I think I can trust Wilder, especially after what he said to me yesterday—words I can't ignore.

"If there's one thing I don't want you to ever experience again, it's that feeling of insignificance. I'm in awe of you, and I know with certainty that I want to be a better man...for you. You deserve to be worshipped, so I'm going to prove that I can be the man who can do that."

He heard me. He wasn't deterred by my resistance to dating him. Because he heard me. My fears. My desires. My hopes. He's such a good, good man.

So with courage, I walk back into my living room, where Wilder is waiting for me and I say, "What movie should we see?"

"Okay, what do you want?" Wilder says as he holds my hand in front of the concessions.

"Popcorn," I say, feeling oddly giddy.

This seems so stupid, so mundane, but then again, when you spend years of your life wanting to do something so simple like this and your partner in life doesn't want to, the experience is heightened.

"That's a guarantee. What else? I'm going to get an Icee. There's Coke-flavored over there, so I think you know where I'm headed. Do you want one too?"

"Yeah, I think I do want one," I say.

"Awesome. And we need some candy too. But the important question is do we go with a chocolate base or a gummy base?"

"Umm…"

"Wrong choice," he says with a wink. "We get both."

He pulls me up to the register, asks for a bucket of popcorn and two large Icees, and then has me pick out the candy. I go with Peanut M&Ms and Red Vines. He praises my choice, and then we head on over to fill up our Icees and popcorn.

"What if I mixed the cherry Icee with the Coke-flavored one?" I ask.

He pauses and slowly turns toward me. "Pips, I don't think I've ever heard of a better idea. We must."

Chuckling, we take turns mixing our drinks, passing the cups back and forth as we layer up the flavors. Then we cap off our drinks, grab our napkins, and head to the theater with all our goodies. Of course we're about twenty minutes early, so when we find our seats, the theater is pretty empty.

"Okay, let me see the popcorn," Wilder says.

I hand him the popcorn, and he starts pouring it into the nacho trays he asked for—which confused me at first, but now I see why he wanted them. He opens the M&Ms and sprinkles them over the popcorn, then places some Red Vines on the side.

When he's done, he hands me a tray and says, "When you need a refill, let me know. Also, try eating an M&M along with some popcorn. Pure magic in your mouth."

"Okay, let me test this out." I pop a piece of popcorn and an M&M in my mouth and let the salty and sweet combination mix on my tongue. After I swallow, I look Wilder in the eyes and I say, "Umm, that's really good."

He smirks. "I know." Then he pops some in his mouth as well. "Follow it up with some Icee—that's the real treat."

"You act like you do this all the time."

"Well, for a guy who doesn't really do much, I'm not shy about attending a matinee."

"I can see that." I turn toward him as ads play on the screen. "Not to bring down the mood, but I feel like we need to talk about what happened at camp."

"Sure," he says. "What do you want to talk about?"

"Can I ask what made you change your answer?"

"I had a conversation with Mika," he says, growing serious. "We talked about our mom and his mental health. I explained to him the roadblock I've had with moving on with my life. He told me that he was going to be okay and promised he wouldn't go to that dark place again, and if he felt like he was going to, he would tell me. So"—his Adam's apple bobs—"with that behind me, I felt confident that I could move forward in my life too. Sanders actually helped me comprehend that I'd possibly inserted myself into Mika's life as a crutch and that Mika might not need his brother in that capacity anymore. So we talked that through, and here I am."

"But do you really think you're ready for it?" I ask. "Because I don't want you jumping into something that you're not fully ready for."

His lips turn up. "I knew you were going to say that. And I have a response for you. Yes, I am ready, and I'm going to have a lot of fun proving that to you."

"What do you mean?" I ask.

He boops me on the nose. "Let me figure that out, and you just sit back and enjoy the ride."

"What does that mean?"

"That means"—he leans forward, cupping my chin—"you relax and enjoy." He kisses my lips softly and then leans back and tosses more popcorn in his mouth.

"I really wasn't expecting that twist at the end," Wilder says as he walks me up to my door.

I pause and turn to him. "Seriously?"

"Seriously. Wait, were you expecting it?"

"Wilder, the entire time, they alluded to it."

"No, they didn't," he says playfully.

"Uh, yes, they did. It was so obvious. Honestly, one of the worst twists ever executed."

His eyes widen. "You're kidding. Please tell me you're kidding."

"No, I'm not kidding," I say. "Seriously, one of the worst."

He shakes his head and grips my hips, the playful man that I knew at Camp Haven taking over. "Wow, I'm going to need to remember this. She's hard to impress, folks."

I chuckle and then say, "Do you want to come in?"

He winces. "God, yes, but I'm not going to."

"You're not?" I ask, feeling sad from his answer.

"Nope, I'm not. Because if I go in there, I can't promise you that I won't somehow find my hand up your shirt. And then if my hand goes up your shirt, that will lead to me playing with your seriously sexy tits, which then of course would lead to so much more, which would be amazing, trust me, but I have a process here. A process that I'm trying to work through."

"Okay," I say, my brows pulling together in confusion.

"Don't worry. It's a good process," he says and takes a step forward. He kisses my forehead gently, then continues, "I do have a question for you though. One that I would love for you to answer."

"Okay. What is it?"

He squeezes me tight and says, "When you were with Matt, what was one thing that made you sad when you were together?"

"Why are you asking that?"

He tugs on me. "Trust the process, babe."

Unsure of where he's going with this, I say, "Okay, um, one thing that made me sad when I was with Matt was... I guess he never complimented me, even when I dressed up."

He nods and softly says, "You deserve better." Then he leans down and kisses me. He pulls away, takes his phone from his pocket, and hands it to me.

"What's this?" I ask.

"Going to need a selfie with you for my wallpaper." He winks, and for some reason, when I take his phone, it's the first time I notice he's still wearing the bracelet I made him.

"You're still wearing your bracelet."

He glances down at it, playing with the elastic string. "Yeah, of course I am." He looks up at me. "This bracelet says you're mine. Why would I take it off?"

CHAPTER TWENTY-NINE
WILDER

Scottie: Just got off the subway, be there soon.

I POCKET MY PHONE AND stand outside the building, waiting for Scottie. I thought about picking her up at work but then decided to let her meet me. All weekend, I sent her text messages. Making sure to say good morning and good night. Telling her about my day, asking about hers. Engaging in thoughtful conversation. She even sent me a picture of her yesterday, sitting on her couch, looking fucking adorable in her tank top as she fanned her face from the heat.

I told her that I was going to buy her another AC unit, but she told me not to.

I considered disobeying, but I figured she probably got enough of that from Matt, so I practiced restraint and listened.

But fuck, it was hard, because I don't like her being so uncomfortable.

I look to the left just in time to see her approaching in a black flair dress with her hair tied back and cute loafers. Smiling, I meet her halfway and pull her into a hug, kissing the top of her head.

"Hey, you," I say and then pull back. "Jesus, you look good."

"Oh, this is just—"

I grip her chin softly and say, "Pips, you look good, really good. Do not tell me differently."

She slowly nods her head, a smile peeking out on her lips. "Thank you."

"You're welcome."

She playfully tugs on my beanie. "You know it's the summer, right?"

"Nothing stops me from representing my emotional side."

She rolls her eyes but then sweetly kisses my chin and, to my surprise, hugs me. Knowing this girl needs all the affection, I wrap my arms around her and hold on to her tight, kissing the top of her head once again.

After a few seconds, she pulls away and smiles. "Where are we?"

"Glad you asked," I say as I take her hand in mine. "Come with me."

We head up some steps to a brownstone, and I open the door for her, only to press my hand to her lower back to guide her up another set of stairs. "Are you ready to partake in a cooking class?"

She pauses. "Wait, really?" Her eyes grow big as pure joy crosses her expression.

"Yeah, really. I was looking up different classes, and this one is six weeks. I hope you have time to spare, because I signed us up for all six."

"Oh my God, that's...that's so exciting."

"Yeah, you want to cook with me?"

"I really do." She stands on her toes and kisses me, and the feel of her mouth, her excitement, her gratitude, it hits me differently.

I like this.

A lot.

———

"Don't stop stirring," I say. "We can't screw this up like the other couples."

Decked out in black cat aprons—for no reason other than Scottie said the tied strings in the back resemble a tail—we're in the back of the class, and we're the only couple who has not burnt something yet or that the teacher—Miss Mary—didn't have to help.

But this stage, making the cheese sauce, this is crucial.

"Oh, we're not screwing this up," she whispers as she continues to stir the cheese sauce while I sprinkle cheese inside the pot to melt. "Steady, not too much all at once. We don't want a clumpy cheese."

"Fuck no," I whisper. "Our cheese will be the smoothest in all the land."

"Kings and queens will bow down to it."

"Pictures will be taken."

"Autographs will be asked for."

"And before you know it, there will be billboards around the world with our mac and cheese on full display. Written underneath, it will say... they brought the cheese to the table."

She lets out a laugh and shakes her head. "That's a horrible slogan."

"What do you mean?" I ask, insulted. "That's what people like most about mac and cheese: the cheese. So if we state we're bringing the cheese to the table, that implies that we are." I finish sprinkling the rest of the cheese as she continues to stir. Thankfully, we're so good that we can talk and work at the same time.

"Sure, I guess."

"And," I continue, "what does the man with the deep voice in the Arby's commercial say? 'We bring the meat.' People know, they go there and they're going to get a mouthful of meat, just like I give you a mouthful of meat."

She snorts so loud that it gathers attention from other couples. I casually wave at them as they turn around, hovering over their hot plates.

"Hey, watch it. We might bring the cheese to the table, but I don't want to bring boogers with it too."

She glances up at me, mirth in her eyes. "You bring the meat... with piercings."

"Proud of it, babe." I kiss the tip of her nose and move behind her back, where I place my hand over hers and begin stirring. "Should I start humming 'Unchained Melody'? Have a *Ghost* moment with you?"

"How do you even know that movie?"

"I'm cultured, Pips. So what do you think?"

"I think the other couples would hate us."

"Jealousy looks ugly on them."

"It sure does," she says and starts me off with a hum.

"That was so much fun. Thank you."

"You're welcome. Don't forget, it's a standing date. Mark it in your calendar," I say.

"Consider it done." Her hand tugs me closer to her door. "Want to come in?"

"Dying to," I say, "but I'm not."

She pouts, which I think is the cutest thing ever.

"I do have a question for you though."

She leans against her door and says, "Okay."

"What is one thing you wish you had spoken up about when it came to Matt?"

Her lips purse to the side as she thinks about it. "Umm, there were a lot of things, but I guess one of them would be that I wish I asked him to be more affectionate, more loving, to treat me as his wife, not his roommate."

"I can understand that. I'm sorry he wasn't more affectionate," I say as I move in close, pinning her against her door. I press my hand to her hip and use my other hand to cup the back of her head. "His loss, my gain."

Then I kiss her...passionately.

"Comfortable?" I ask as we both take a seat in the front-row seats of the suite that I bought out for the night.

She looks around, taking in the baseball field in front of us, the full stadium, the game that's already been playing for two and a half innings.

"Uh, yeah. I'm just a little confused."

"Why?" I ask as I open a box of Cracker Jack. If the prize is a ring, she's getting it.

"Because you never told me you liked baseball."

"Oh, it's okay. Can be boring at times but also thrilling when runners are on the field and there's a possible chance for a goal to be scored."

"I think it's called a run," she corrects me.

I chuckle. "Sure."

That makes her laugh as well. "Are you telling me that I might know more about sports than you?"

"Nah, I'm only kidding. I know all the sports. Go, balls."

She laughs again, and the sound is so sweet to my ears. And considering when I first met her, it's such a contrast. There was zero joy in her expression. Just worry, maybe a hint of depression. It was as if she was living under a dark cloud the entire time. But now—now it's different. There's joy in her eyes. There's playfulness. She has no problem laughing and no problem getting lost in the day, in the hours, in the minutes…in the seconds.

"Well, I'm excited to cheer for the balls."

"Because you like balls."

Her eyes roll. "Your maturity is really showing."

I press my hand to my chest. "Aw, thank you."

She snags my Cracker Jack from me and then pops some in her mouth.

"You know, if you didn't look so hot eating those, I'd steal them back. But I don't know. Kind of enjoying the view, especially in that skirt."

She glances down at her flirty white skirt and then back at me. "First time I'm wearing it."

"Trust me, won't be the last. Your legs look amazing in it."

"Thank you," she says as her cheeks stain. And I wonder if it will always be like that, if my compliments will always garner a cute, innocent reaction from her.

I sure as hell hope so.

My phone buzzes in my pocket, so I quickly take a look at it.

One minute and counting.

I slip my phone back in my pocket and then turn toward her. I take the Cracker Jack and offer her a drink.

Confused, she says, "Uh, thank you."

"You're welcome. Drink up, Pips."

She eyes me suspiciously. "What is going on with you?"

"Nothing."

"You're lying."

"Maybe."

She chuckles. "Okay, so tell me what's going on."

"Take five sips of your drink, and then I'll show you."

She eyes me for a few more seconds, probably trying to figure me out, but then she takes her sips and sets the drink down.

"Okay, tell me exactly what's going on."

Thankfully, it's perfect timing, as the jumbotron flashes over a couple. They're framed in a camera shot with *Kiss Cam* written at the bottom.

Smirking, I point to the jumbotron just as we both come on-screen.

When she takes in what's going on, I grip her cheek, pull her in, and kiss her…wildly. I kiss her like no other kiss cam has ever seen.

The crowd erupts in cheers. I pump my fist to the sky while I continue to kiss her—even with a little tongue—and the stadium laughs. When I pull away, I smirk at her and then lean back in my chair.

She blinks a few times and then says, "Did we just kiss on a jumbotron?"

"Yeah, Pips, we did. You can check that off your bucket list." I wink just as my phone buzzes in my pocket. I take it out, and sure enough, there's the picture I was hoping to get.

I flash it to her, a picture of us kissing on the big screen, my clenched fist up in the air.

"Did you…did you plan this entire thing?"

"Of course." *As I'm slowly learning, I will do anything that brings you*

KISS CAM

true joy. "We have to make sure we're checking things off that list, Pips. Because once we do, it means we can add more. Together."

"How did it go?"

I catch the football and toss it back to Sanders.

"Like clockwork," I say. "Thank you for helping me score that suite. It was perfect. After the whole kiss cam thing, we snuggled and watched the game, even though we couldn't care less what was going on."

"Not a problem. Glad it worked. How do you think she's feeling right now?"

"Good," I say. "Last night, when I was at her door, I asked her another question."

"What was it this time?"

"Asked her what's one thing she wished Matt did different in the bedroom?"

"Perfect. That's the question we were considering, right? To show our progress with her?"

"Yes."

"And what did she answer?"

"She said she wished he was more adventurous."

Sanders nods and tosses me the ball.

Ever since I got back from Camp Haven, I've had weekly meetings with him. We talk about me and my relationship with Mika and my mom— he doesn't just focus on marriages but all kinds of relationships, which I like—and of course, I've been heavily focused on educating myself on what Scottie experienced in her marriage. No man is perfect, so I know I won't ever care for her perfectly. But that man made vows to Scottie. He declared that he'd do everything in his ability to love her well, and he didn't take those vows seriously. It just pisses me off, as not only did she learn to devalue her needs, but her self-confidence suffered terribly.

I have also learned that even though she might seem happy on the outside, she's probably comparing every new moment I have with her to her ex. Sanders said it's a natural thing to do, especially when it comes to someone who was in a mentally absent relationship.

Which is exactly what Scottie endured.

Sanders explained to me that being mentally absent from a marriage can dismantle a person's confidence, because it makes it seem like they're not important, that they have no significance. And if treated like that for sufficient time, they start adapting those qualities, which is why when I first started complimenting her, she wouldn't accept the compliment.

It's why I ask her a question about Matt after our dates, because I don't want to repeat the same mistakes. I also want to ensure she feels significant. Valued. Listened to. *Happy.*

"More adventurous. Do you think you can make that happen?"

I catch the football and give him a look, making him laugh. "What do you think, Sanders? My damn dick is pierced."

He lets out a roar of a laugh. "Adventurous it is. So is that what you're going to do next as one of the big dates?"

"I think so," I say, thinking back to all the little things we've been doing during the week.

Dinners, walks in the park, riding the ferry just to fucking ride it and spend time together. There are moments that I've been capturing with her the last few weeks, and when we're not together, we're constantly texting or talking on the phone. But the big dates, or the dates that are centered around the bucket list that we wrote out at Camp Haven, those are the ones that I've been planning and putting effort into.

"You ready to get intimate with her?"

"We've already been intimate, Sanders."

"Well aware," he says. "We heard it at the camp."

That makes me smile.

"And I saw you two in the lake."

I chuckle. "That was hot."

"I'm surprised that water didn't make everything shrivel up."

"You know, I'm just that attracted to her that no cold water could make my dick disappear."

"Aww. To be young again."

I toss the football to him and answer his question. "But yes, I am ready to be intimate. I think it's time. We've been doing this for about three, four weeks now, and every time I answer no to her request to go into her apartment, I can see her get sadder and sadder. I think it's time."

"Good. You have everything you need?"

"Yup," I say. "I've got everything. Just have one question for you."

"What's that?" he asks.

I glance around his room, taking in the wreck of an office he maintains. "There's something that's been on my mind, ever since we signed up for the marriage camp."

"What's that?"

"Well, from a quick Google search, I was able to find that your grandparents owned Camp Haven before you. It was a sports camp, right?"

"That's correct."

"And then it was passed on directly to your mom, right?"

"Yes," he drags out, trying to see where I'm going with this.

"Of course, being the curious one that I am, I looked up who your mom is."

His smile grows wider.

"Fucking Whitney Martin is your mom."

He slowly nods. "Uh, she was a legend matchmaker in the seventies. Not that you need to know this, but Camp Haven was where the most infamous couples were matched. Olive and Rund, the cat burglars of Brooklyn. Nancy and Hank, the pyramid schemers. Georgina and Tom, the Assassins of 8th Avenue."

I blink a few times. "She matched up felons."

He chuckles and then rubs his hand over his cheek. "Yeah, she really knew how to join people together with common interests."

"Please tell me you didn't study at the same school she did. Because I really like Scottie and if you helped me figure out things with this girl and she ends up being a night killer..."

He smirks. "About that." He stands. "Didn't really go to school for any of this."

"What?" I nearly shout.

He shrugs. "Yeah, was kind of good at the matchmaking thing in college, where I was studying kinesiology. That's where I met Ellison. Found that I was pretty good at cooling down arguments after a night out at the bars and, well...went from there. Ellison hooks me up with couples she knows and, well...the rest is history."

"Wait, you're serious."

He tosses the football in the air. "You don't become the best by going to school and studying. You become the best by life experience." He taps the side of his head. "Think on that."

"Hold on, so you've been offering marriage counseling to couples without ever being certified."

"You know, Wilder, lawyers always tell you to read the fine print for a reason." He winks and then nods at me. "Go long."

No fucking way.

CHAPTER THIRTY
SCOTTIE

"WELL, WELL, WELL, LOOK WHO decided to show up," Mika says as he places a napkin in front of me.

"I know. I'm sorry."

"It's fine." He smirks.

I roll my eyes.

Apart from spending so much time with Wilder, I've been busy at work. Strangely, everyone has worked harder since the camp. So I can definitely see how taking couples away for marriage enrichment produces greater productivity in the office. Chad has been more subdued, and we haven't spoken about his marriage since coming back, but there's definitely a better work environment now.

"I know you've been busy." Mika winks. "With my brother." He sets some pretzels in front of me and starts making me a drink.

"It's not what you think."

"What do you mean?" he asks.

"We haven't been doing anything like that."

He pauses midpour of tequila and says, "What do you mean, you haven't been doing anything like that?"

"He's, uh, he's been holding out on me."

"Who's been holding out on you?" Denise asks as she takes a seat next to me at the bar and pulls me into a hug.

"My brother, apparently," Mika says.

"What?" Denise asks. "He's holding out on you? My God, I thought the reason you weren't around all that much is because you'd been bopping up and down on Mika's brother."

"I wish," I grumble as Mika hands me my drink. "That is not the case. He has only kissed me.

I feel like I went back in time to when you're celibate until your wedding night."

"That's depressing," Denise says as I take a sip of my drink.

"What's depressing?" a very familiar, deep voice says.

I nearly spit up my drink as Wilder takes a seat next to me.

"Hey, Pips," he says and places a peck of a kiss on my cheek.

Pips. It's taken me a while, but I now love the nickname. It's said with such genuine affection.

"Speak of the devil," Mika says with a smirk. Almost a knowing smirk.

"You guys talking about me?"

"No," I say, just as Denise says, "Yes."

Wilder picks up my drink and takes a sip, his eyes going wide. "Jesus, Mika, put enough tequila in this?"

"I should have put more given how horny our girl is because you won't put out."

"Oh my God, Mika," I nearly shout as Wilder chuckles next to me.

He wraps his arm around my waist, and he whispers in my ear, sending chills up and down my arms and legs. "You hard up, babe?"

"What? No." I nervously laugh. "No, I don't know what he's talking about."

"Why aren't you boning our friend?" Denise asks, leaning over the bar to look at him. "Because she wants it."

His smile grows wider. "I know she does." And his hand grips me tighter.

Dear God in heaven, why is this happening to me?

"So then what's the holdup?"

He casually sips my drink again. "I'm trying to demonstrate her worth to her first."

Denise leans back and brings her hand to her heart. "Can you teach Derek to talk to me like that?"

"I'll work on it." He pops a pretzel in his mouth and nods at Mika. "You good, brother?"

"Good," Mika says. "Want me to get you a drink?"

"Nah, I'm leaving soon."

"You are?" I ask, feeling sad, because he just got here, and I thought he would at least stay for a little while.

"Yeah, and you're going with me."

"I am?"

"Yup." Wilder holds my drink out to me. "So drink up."

Denise leans forward and whispers in my ear, "He has that look in his eyes. A look that says you're about to get fucked."

"So, um, we're back at my apartment," I say as I stare through the windshield of his Jeep.

"We are." He reaches behind us and pulls up a duffel bag.

"Is that, uh, is that an overnight bag?"

"It is." He moves around to my side, where he opens the door for me and holds out his hand.

I take it, and he helps me out of the car and then guides us into the apartment building.

When we reach my door, he nods toward it. "You going to invite me in?"

"Are you going to turn me down?"

"What do you think?" he asks, his voice seductive.

"Can't be sure."

He chuckles and cups my cheek. "Let me in, Pips."

A thrill of excitement shoots through my spine as I unlock the door and let us both in.

Keeping my hand in his, he pulls me toward the bedroom after shutting and locking the door. Recently, due to heat exhaustion, I put in an AC window unit in my bedroom. I found one that would fit the window, and right about now, I'm very grateful for it.

He takes a seat on my bed and then places his hands behind him and looks up at me. "Strip, Pips."

"Wh-what?" I ask. He's just going to jump into it like that? After not being intimate for weeks?

"You heard me: strip."

"Right now?" I ask.

"You think you can wear that fucking skirt and act like I'm not going to ask you to strip?" He shakes his head. "Nope. Time to strip."

Nervously, I shift as I tug on my bottom lip. It's been a few weeks since I've been naked in front of him, and all of a sudden, I'm feeling shy.

"Do you need help?" he asks.

"Just…nervous."

His expression stays neutral, but he beckons me with his finger. I move in between his legs, and he sits taller, placing his hands on my hips.

"Why are you nervous in front of me?"

I shrug. "I don't know. I kind of like you and don't want to look stupid."

"You *kind of* like me?" he asks with a cute raise to his brow. "Because I'm going to tell you right now, Pips, I *really* like you."

I chuckle. "That's what I meant. I really like you."

"Uh-huh, and what does that have to do with stripping in front of me? Because last I remember, we fucked in a lake."

I feel my cheeks heat up. "That was different. We're sort of like a couple now."

"Sort of?" He shakes his head. "No, babe. We are a couple."

"Exactly, and what if, I don't know, you're like, 'Whoops, not like I remembered'?"

The corner of his lips tilts up as he shakes his head. "Trust me, not going to happen." He drags his palms up and over my ass. "Every night, I think about you, Scottie. Every morning, when I'm hard as a fucking rock, I think about you. I think about you in the shower. I think about you fucking midday. My mind is always on you, and it's been fucking torture not being intimate with you."

"It's been torture for me too," I say as his hands slip under the waistline of my underwear and he slowly pulls them down. I step out of them and slide them to the side.

"Then why nervous?"

"Because it feels like the first time again."

He shakes his head. "It's not." Then he untucks my shirt and tugs on it, so I pull it up and over my head. His eyes feast on my chest while his hands tug on my ass and force me to take a seat on his lap.

He unzips the back of my skirt and lets it fall open while he brings his hands up my sides and to the clasp of my bra, which he undoes. The straps go loose, but he doesn't take it off right away.

Instead, he trails his fingers over the cups, slightly past the swell of my breasts, and then up my neck to the back of my head, where he brings my mouth down to his. I sink into his touch, and all the nerves, all the worry, melt away as his lip ring caresses my lips and his tongue swipes across mine.

"Fuck," he whispers as his large palm splays against my back. "I've missed this."

"Why did you wait so long?"

"Because you needed to be loved in a different way."

My heart thumps madly.

My yearning for this man is growing wild.

And everything I was feeling a few seconds ago drifts away as I shed my bra and capture his mouth in mine.

He moans against my lips but then gets lost with me as I push him back on the bed. His hands move under my skirt and grip my ass as I cup his face to make out with him.

My tongue dances with his.

My fingers thread through his hair.

And my pelvis starts rocking over his hardening length.

He moves me to my back and hovers over me, letting his hand glide up my stomach to my breast, where he gently squeezes it. Then he lowers his head and takes my nipple into his mouth.

He licks.

He sucks.

He nibbles.

He's sending bolts of pleasure through my body with every move he makes with his mouth.

"Yes," I whisper as I shift underneath him, looking for more.

But he doesn't get the hint. Instead he moves to my other breast, giving it the same treatment, so I bring my hands to his jeans and undo them, then push them down with my feet, freeing him. I find his length in my palm, and I grip him tightly, lightly pumping.

"Fuck," he gasps as his back arches, and he stares down at what I'm doing. When his eyes find mine again, they become feral.

He moves off me, sheds the rest of his clothes, and then grabs his bag.

Confused, I lean up on my elbows and watch him pull out an iPad. "Sit back," he says, his cock straining between his legs.

Still in my skirt, I sit back on the bed, and he brings his bag with him as he hands me the iPad. On the screen is a paused video of two people, naked.

I glance at him in shock, and he smiles before tapping Play.

Seductive music starts playing as the man lays the woman back on the bed and starts kissing her all over her body.

"Oh my God," I say, my eyes fixed on the screen.

"Spread your legs, babe."

I do as he says while I continue to watch the screen, the man spreading her legs and starting to press his tongue against her clit. I'm so fucking consumed by what's going on that I don't even realize Wilder is in the same position until his tongue swipes against my slit.

"Oh, God," I sigh as I spread myself even wider.

And in unison, Wilder licks me, kisses me, swipes at me just like the man on the screen. The woman writhes under him, playing with her tits, biting her lower lip, moaning ever so slightly.

It turns me on so much that I'm throbbing. I'm ready. I could tip over at any freaking point.

"Fuck, Wilder," I say, shifting down more. "Oh my God, I'm so close."

"Not yet, baby," he whispers and pulls his mouth away.

I continue to watch the video, my center pulling and tugging inward, making me feel a deep sense of pleasure that I've never felt before.

This is so…naughty.

So erotic.

So positively everything I've ever wanted when it came to—

"Oh my God," I say as I sit up and watch Wilder finish slipping a vibrator inside me.

But not just any vibrator. The one we won at Camp Haven.

He turns it on, and I immediately fall into the mattress as my entire body tenses. Inside, the head of the vibrator swirls against my walls, vibrating at the same time, while the little tongue flicks across my clit, quick strokes that have my pleasure driving fast up my spine.

"Jesus, Wilder. Oh my God."

"Watch the video, Pips. I want you coming while watching."

I suck in a sharp breath, my body tingling, my inner core tensing.

"Wilder, I can't…"

"Keep watching, baby."

I glance at him, and he's sliding the orange cock ring over his erection.

His chest tenses, his teeth pull on his lip ring, and the muscles in his stomach contract as he lets out a long, deep moan.

Forget the people in front of me.

Forget the iPad at all. The real view is in front of me as Wilder starts stroking himself, precum already forming at the tip.

When his gaze falls on me, he lets out a deep breath and says, "Babe, watch the video."

I wet my lips and shake my head. "You're what I want to watch."

His eyes turn darker, and he takes the iPad from me, sets it to the side, and then straddles my chest, where he strokes himself, faster, harder.

Between watching him and the way he loses control to the feeling of the vibrator moving inside me, my orgasm climbs and builds to the point that I'm not sure I can hold on any longer.

"Fuck," he huffs as his hand lands against the headboard while he continues to pump himself, the muscles in his forearm popping off, his abs defined.

The little flicks against my clit, the vibration, the feeling of my feet going numb…my entire body tenses, and I bring my hands to my breasts as my chest lifts up and a moan slips past my lips right before I fall over the edge.

"Wilder," I yell as I come over the vibrator, shock wave after shock wave hitting me, causing me to thrash side to side until… "What are you doing?"

He removes the vibrator, and then in a second, he's sliding inside me while I'm still contracting.

"Motherfucker," he yells as he starts pumping inside me.

Between the size of him, the vibration of the cock ring, and how he thrusts so deep inside, I feel my body tense again. Sensations of an orgasm shoot through my limbs, continuing the most delicious feeling I've ever felt as he stiffens and his cock swells just before he spills inside me.

"Fuck…me," he groans, lightly pumping until he collapses on top of me, letting me feel his entire weight until he pushes up on his forearms and connects his gaze with mine. His smirk nearly breaks me in half as he kisses the tip of my nose. "Christ, Scottie."

Still catching my breath, I say, "You're the one who did this to us."

"Yeah, but you're the one that makes it so fucking good."

"What did I tell you about wearing clothes to bed?" Wilder says as he walks into my bedroom after going to the bathroom and brushing his teeth. He's completely naked, making it incredibly difficult to keep my eyes on anything but his body. "You know, my eyes are up here," he teases me.

"I know, but you're so hot."

He chuckles and loops his arm around my waist, pulling me in close. "Why do you think I want you naked? I feel the same exact way about you." He presses his lips to mine, and I loop my arms around his neck, making out with him, loving the feeling of being…loved.

Cared for.

Worshipped.

He makes me feel important.

Needed. *Significant.*

Like there couldn't possibly be anything else in this world that could distract him from me.

When I pull away, he grabs the hem of his shirt that I put on and pulls it up and over, depositing it on the floor. His hands move up to my breasts, across my nipples, and down to my ass.

"Fuck, you're so warm. This is what I want. You, naked…all the time."

"Even when I go to work?"

He tilts his head to the side. "No, this body is for me and me alone."

"You claiming me?" I ask.

"Damn right. Why do you think I still wear this bracelet? Mine. You're mine."

God, I could hear him say that over and over and never get tired of it.

He kisses me again, but this time, it's a chaste kiss. "Now, I have a question for you."

"Okay," I say. "What is it?"

"After you had sex with Matt, was there something you craved? Something *you* might have wanted?"

An orgasm?

I think back to the times when Matt and I would have sex and how he would roll out of bed after, clean up, and then go off to his office. It was so cold. Made me feel used.

I nod. "There is something."

"What is it?"

I look into his eyes and say, "I wanted desperately to be cuddled."

His brows shoot up in surprise, but then understanding sets in. He takes my hand in his and slips us into my bed. With my back to his chest, he pulls me into him and drapes his arm over my stomach.

"You're telling me he never did this?"

"No," I answer.

"What a fucking fool." He kisses the back of my neck. "Once again: his loss, my gain."

I sigh into him, realizing just how much I've been missing out on.

How much I was sitting in the dark, thinking the way Matt treated our marriage was normal. But if I truly think about it, he was never as attentive as Wilder, even in our early days.

And that's the big difference. That's what Wilder has taught me. That I deserve better.

That maybe...just maybe...this is where I was supposed to end up all along.

"You know, there's only one thing left to check off on your bucket list," he whispers. "Because we've done a cooking class, a movie in a theater, the kiss cam, skinny-dipping, watched some porn...and now, just one more thing."

"What is it?" I ask, not able to remember.

"Paddleboat."

I chuckle. "Oh right, because Matt never wanted to do anything fun."

"Exactly."

I turn in his embrace to face him. "You really went out of your way to do all those things for me."

"Pips, I never went out of my way. It's all things I wanted to do."

I bring my hand to his cheek. "I want to say you're too good for me, but I don't think that's the case, Wilder. You're…you're just perfect."

He smiles. "That's what I like to hear." Then he leans forward and kisses me.

CHAPTER THIRTY-ONE
WILDER

"IS TODAY THE DAY?" SANDERS asks as he putts a golf ball across his office toward a cup we set up.

"Today is the day," I say.

"Nervous?"

I shake my head. "No. Not in the slightest."

"You think she's ready?"

"Yeah," I answer. His ball goes off to the right, so I step up to the tee and get in position.

"What have the last two weeks been like?"

"Well, still reeling over the scandal of you not being a real therapist."

He rolls his eyes. "Grow up."

"Grow up?" I chuckle. "Dude, you're selling a scam."

"And yet, you're still here."

I let out a heavy huff. "Yeah, I know, something might be wrong with me."

"Nah, you've just been swooped up by the Sanders Effect, trademark."

"You really have issues."

"Am I the one with the issues, or are you?" He lifts his brow, causing me to laugh.

I think I'm the one with the issues.

"So once again, how have the last two weeks been?"

Moving on with the change of subject, I glance up at him, a smirk on my face.

"Ah." He nods. "No need to say more. I can see from the look on your face that it's been good."

"Really fucking good," I say. "I've stayed at her place almost every night. I've taken her to mine a few, made her dinners. We joined a pinochle league, and we are fucking terrible."

Sanders chuckles.

"But we're learning, and that's all that matters. We're still doing our cooking class and killing it. I've brought her flowers at work, and honestly, I've had the best fucking time. I don't think I've ever been this happy. At least not for a really long time."

I felt immense pride when my app sold. It was an incredible experience. But this feeling? Feeling so connected to a woman that dreams are made of? Nothing could ever surpass that. She's simply it for me, and there's both joy and relief in feeling that.

I putt the ball and miss terribly, pushing it to the left.

Sanders retrieves our balls as he says, "How is Mika?"

"Doing well. We, uh, we had brunch with our mom the other day. It was at a restaurant, and I gave Mika an escape route if things got too heavy. He wound up staying through the entire thing, which I was proud of, but fuck was it awkward at first."

Sanders chuckles. "That's how it usually goes. How did it end?"

"Good. I gave Mom a hug, and Mika stood his distance and waved. But we promised to do it again in a few weeks."

"That's progress," Sanders says.

"Little progress, but I was happy about it."

"When do you think you'll introduce your mom to Scottie?" He sets down his golf ball and gets into position.

"Uh, probably not for a little while and not before Mika and Mom have a better understanding of each other. I don't want to make Mika feel pressured to make amends because Mom met Scottie."

"That's really considerate," Sanders says, hitting his ball off the lip of the cup. He snaps his finger in disappointment. "Does Scottie know that?"

"Yes," I say. "I'm very open and honest with her about everything."

"Good. I'm sure she appreciates it."

"She does," I answer and set my ball down.

"And how are you feeling in general? Everything with Mika, your mom? Are you finding peace?"

"I am," I answer. And that's almost a strange realization, as I hadn't realized my life was lacking peace. I'd thought I lacked nothing. How wrong I was. I line up my putt and shove the ball into his desk. Shit, I'm terrible at this. "I like how feeling internally at peace is allowing me to focus on what Scottie needs and deserves in her life." It reminds me of how my dad loved our family. *I miss him.* And I wish he'd gotten a chance to meet Scottie. They'd get along very well.

"Has she found peace?"

I set my putter to the side and take a seat on the couch. "Honestly, I think she has. I've seen a change in her. No longer is she second-guessing herself or turning down compliments. She accepts them wholeheartedly. She has more confidence, she's feeling herself, and she's made great progress with her coworkers too, which I think is a big deal."

"Why do you think that's a big deal?" Sanders asks, lining up another putt.

"Because at first, she just kept to herself, and I think that was from a lack of confidence and not wanting to engage with men since the last one she was with ignored her. But now she goes out to lunch with them and has truly made some more friendships, which I think is great."

"Interesting observation." He putts the ball, and I watch it sail over the carpet and right into the cup. Sanders does a subtle fist pump and then takes a seat across from me. "Maybe I should hire you as my assistant."

"I don't have a degree in the matter, so I would fit right in."

"Hence why I asked."

———————

"When are we going to start jogging?" Scottie asks as we walk hand in hand through Central Park.

It's a perfect summer day in New York City. Not too hot, a light breeze, and partially cloudy with the sun peeking out every once in a while. Everyone is out of their apartment buildings having picnics, tossing Frisbees, and going for walks.

The laughter of kids chirps in the background, the promise of ice cream in the air. I couldn't have picked a more perfect day.

And oddly, I had to con Scottie into coming out with me today. Her idea of a perfect Saturday was to lie around her apartment naked and order food in. And I agree. That is the perfect Saturday. But I have one thing I need to do with her, and once we do that, then we can go back to the apartment and do what she wants to do.

To get her out here, I told her I wanted to go on a jog through Central Park. It's lame and I'm sure not what she wants to do on a Saturday, but I was telling her I was cramping a bit, and I thought it would help limber me up.

She asked if we could take a shower together when we got back to her place, and that was an automatic yes for me.

What are we really doing though?

Well, finishing out the bucket list of course.

We turn the corner toward the Central Park Boathouse, and I tug her toward the rentals.

"Wait." She stops and turns toward me. "Are we really going for a jog?"

I smirk and nod toward the paddleboats. "What do you think?"

"Eep!" She pulls me into a hug and kisses me on the jaw. "Thank you."

"Anything for you, Pips."

We walk over to the boathouse rental and rent out a paddleboat, Scottie beaming the entire time. She's so fucking adorable. The way she accepts and displays her joy for the world to see, it's so goddamn cute.

I pay for the rental, and we are escorted to the boat, where we carefully get in, me first and then Scottie. We're given a bit of a push, and then together, we start peddling.

"This is so…ridiculous," she says on a laugh as we move around the lake.

"Ridiculous?" I ask. "I thought it was supposed to be romantic."

"You're not holding my hand. How is that romantic?"

"Ahh, you're right." I pick up her hand and entwine our fingers. "That better?"

"Much."

We move toward the center of the lake just as the sun is covered up by a cloud and a light breeze picks up. "That feels so nice." She tips her head back, soaking it all in. "Thank you for this, for bringing me and checking off the last thing on my bucket list."

"You're welcome," I say and then clear my throat. "I, uh, I didn't necessarily bring you out here just for this."

She turns toward me now, the boat just floating. "You didn't?" she asks, looking confused.

"No, I had a selfish reason too."

"What is it?"

Here goes nothing.

With her hand still in mine, I look her in the eyes and say, "You know, I didn't realize how monotonous my life was until Mika told me his friend needed a fake husband. Ever since you stepped into my life, you've opened my eyes, you've helped me face my fears and my insecurities, and you've made me really fucking happy, Scottie. And I just…I can't keep it in anymore, so I brought you here because I wanted to tell you that I'm in love with you."

Her eyes well up with tears.

"I love you, Pips, more than anything. And I needed you to know that…in the middle of this lake in the middle of Central Park."

She chuckles and wipes at her eyes. "Had to be here?"

I nod. "Because we're closing out the bucket list, so it had to be here."

She scoots in a touch closer and says, "You think I'm the one who helped you?" She shakes her head. "No, Wilder. You're the one who helped me. You're the one who opened my eyes, who made me work hard to see the person I really am and not the person I thought I was. You were patient, you communicated, you taught me lessons I didn't even know that I needed, and I know I'm a confident woman now because of you." She kisses my knuckles and then says, "I love you. I'm in love with you, and I'm so grateful I have you in my life."

My smiles stretches across my lips, because hearing those words from her, fuck, it's the best fucking thing I've ever heard. I pull her in, gripping the back of her head. I press our foreheads together and say, "Thank you, Pips."

"How could I not love you, Wilder? You are everything I didn't know I deserved."

"You're everything I didn't know I needed," I reply, making her smile.

She gently moves her mouth over mine, and I follow her lead as we slowly make out on a paddleboat, drifting in the middle of Central Park.

After a few minutes, she pulls away and says, "Maybe we can make a new list, one that we want to cross off together."

"That's exactly what I was thinking." I kiss her forehead. "And here I thought we were going to be a whole 'till summer do us part' situation."

"What does that mean?" she asks on a laugh.

"You know, married for the summer, but after that, we were done."

She looks me dead in the eyes. "I mean, that probably was going to be the case, but I think I knew the minute I felt those piercings—there was going to be no parting whatsoever."

I let out a bark of a laugh and nod my head. "I'm oddly proud of myself."

She kisses me again and whispers, "I love you."

"I love you too, Pips."

EPILOGUE
WILDER

"PIPS, DO YOU WANT A drink?"

Scottie looks up from where she's painting a portrait of our relationship and shakes her head yes. "The Prickly Pair," she says with a wink.

"Coming right up." I head over to where Sanders is leaning against the bar in a three-piece suit, happily looking over all the couples. "You really stepped up the outfit this year for the welcome dinner."

Sanders smirks. "It's Velcroed in the back. Wait until you see what I have underneath here."

I chuckle. "Oh, I'm sure it's nothing short of amazing."

"You've got that right." Sanders nods toward Scottie. "That ring looks good on her."

I glance back at my girl, who is wearing a giant yet classy engagement ring that I gave her last weekend.

It was the perfect evening. I bought out Stockings and had Denise invite her out for drinks. When she arrived, the entire bar was lit up with candles, and I was up onstage, waiting for her on bended knee.

I knew the minute I told her I loved her that I was going to marry her, but I had to give her time to adjust to loving me, so I waited…and waited. I dated her, we moved in together, we started seeing Sanders for maintenance, and then when I thought the time was right, I started planning the proposal.

I roped in Mika and Denise, asked them for their thoughts. We considered coming to Camp Haven and having me propose here, but I thought it would be too much of a spectacle, and that was when Mika offered up Stockings. He no longer works there since he's working at a private club now, but he still has connections, and we still frequent the bar together every Friday where we all hang out, so it felt like the right thing to do.

And from the look on Scottie's face when she saw me up on the stage, I knew it was perfect. We spent the rest of the night with friends and family, drinking, dancing, and having the best time ever.

And now we are here, at Camp Haven, where it all started.

"It does look good on her, doesn't it?" I say before I ask the bartender for two Prickly Pairs. It's a surprise that we're able to drink on the first night at camp, but then again, Sanders said we are celebrating our engagement, so we are going to take full advantage of it...as well as the sex palace.

Yup, we asked for the same cabin, because this time, I want to make sure we use every last thing offered in the sex palace, suction-cup dildo included. I have plans. Lofty plans, but I have them.

"It does, and that smile on her face, it's grown and grown with every passing month I've seen you two." Sanders pats me on the shoulder. "You've done well, Wilder. You helped her find confidence, and you offered her understanding and patience. But most importantly, you've made her feel seen again."

I stare off at Scottie, who is lightly stroking the canvas with her paintbrush drenched in pink. "I can't unsee her. She...she captures my full attention. I can't imagine anyone else ever passing up on the opportunity to talk to her, to joke with her, to spend time with her. She's such a bright light that I never want to lose."

Sanders smirks. "I'm glad to hear it."

Our drinks are set on the bar, and I grab them and offer Sanders a nod of appreciation before walking back over to my girl and taking a seat next to her. I set her drink in front of her and then lean in and kiss her cheek.

"The canvas is looking great, Pips."

She scoffs as she turns toward me, her knees knocking against my thigh. "You're being nice. It looks like trash."

"Nah, everything you touch is gold, babe."

She snorts and then sips her drink. "You can butter me up all you want. I will not be using the suction-cup dildo in the shower."

I let out a roar of a laugh. "What little faith you have in my convincing skills. Trust me, by the end of these eight days, you're going to want to take it home."

"Keep dreaming."

"Hey," Chad says with a wave as he walks up to us with his arm around his wife, Danielle. "We miss you over at Butter Putter."

A few months ago, Scottie left Butter Putter and started editing freelance. It started when Sanders was telling her about an article he had to write about his practice and his "unusual" style of couple's therapy. The piece highlighted his office, his techniques, and his values. He asked Scottie if she would take a look at it, and she offered him some very valuable insight, so much so that he recommended her to a few other people, and it trickled down from there.

Now she's editing on her own time, giving us the flexibility to travel, something she's been pressing me to do.

And we finally did. We took a ten-day trip to Ireland where we toured the entire country, drank too much Guinness, and talked to some sheep while lying in the fields and staring up at the sky. It was a big step for me, being that far from Mika, but with his encouragement, along with Scottie, I made the leap, and I'm so glad I did, because we had an amazing time. I was able to see and experience things I've never seen or done before, and I was able to put my mind at ease, knowing that Mika—who has made leaps and bounds in his life—was going to be okay.

We are planning another trip, this one to Edinburgh, Scotland. I know it's not much farther, but baby steps.

"You know, I kind of miss you guys too," Scottie says with a sly grin. "I miss the distinct sound of chino shorts, rubbing together as you all moved about the office."

Chad laughs. "I can record it for you if you want."

Scottie holds up her hand. "Really, I don't want to trouble you." She then turns her attention to Danielle. "How are you feeling, Danielle? Is the morning sickness gone?"

She nods and rubs her stomach. "Yes, thankfully."

"Now she's in the fun phase of pregnancy," Chad says, wiggling his eyebrows, causing Danielle to elbow him in the side.

It was a long year for them, Scottie being at the forefront of helping Chad by being a close confidant to talk to. They would often go to lunch during the week and talk, Chad airing out his fears about losing his wife while Scottie told him about her fears of falling in love. She was very open and honest with me about it all, which I appreciate about our relationship.

Thankfully, Chad and Danielle were able to work things out and then went on a trip up to the Finger Lakes and, well, that's apparently where they got pregnant. Chad joked around about naming their baby after one of the lakes. I don't know. Skaneateles, Cayuga, and Owasco just don't have a good ring to them.

"And hey, congratulations are in order," Chad says, nodding to my ring on Scottie's finger. "When Scottie sent me a picture, I was elated for you two."

"Thanks, man," I say, finding it odd that just a year ago, I was ready to drive this man's head through a tree trunk. "We're really happy."

Chad places his hand on Danielle's stomach. "Well, if you need a ring bearer or a flower girl, you know where to find us." Then with a wink, he takes off.

"You know, that's not that bad of an idea," I say. "Think of the little chino pants and embroidered vest the baby could wear."

Scottie laughs. "It could be one of those *27 Dresses* type things, but instead of bridesmaid dresses, all the guys I worked with have to wear their chino shorts and company vests."

"Babe, I don't think you've ever had a better idea."

"Wow, the bar is pretty low then."

"Yeah, that's okay. We have the rest of our lives for you to raise it."

She rolls her eyes and turns away, but I wrap my arm around her and pull her into my chest while kissing the top of her head.

"Love you, Pips."

She chuckles. "Love you too, Wilder."

When I release her, I lean in and whisper, "I spoke to Sanders last week. He said we could have the tent again this year, but maybe this time, we sleep naked."

"Why? So I can accidentally zip your dick up into the sleeping bag?"

I gasp jokingly. "No, not the return of the Serial Zipper."

"Threaten me with the suction-cup dildo, and yeah, she might come screeching in, looking to do some damage."

"Babe," I say levelly. "Just give it a try." I bat my eyelashes at her. "For me."

She palms my face and pushes me away. "Not going to happen."

THREE HOURS LATER

"So...do I need to tell you I told you so?" I ask as I try to catch my breath.

Scottie turns off the shower and pushes at my chest with her finger. "Mutter those words, and consider this your last shower with that flesh sword."

I hold my hands up. "Noted." Smirking, I add, "But Pips, that shit was good, wasn't it?"

She smirks and wraps her towel around her torso. "No, Wilder, it was great."

DISCOVER MORE FROM
MEGHAN QUINN WITH
A SNEAK PEEK AT

PROLOGUE
MAGGIE

"YOU'RE BREATHING DOWN MY NECK."

"No, I'm not."

"Yes, you are." I gesture to my neck where he's hovering while we peer out toward the restaurant from the bar. "There is breath on my neck that's forming a dewy condensation, and frankly, it's giving me the ick." I turn toward the worst human I've ever met and look him dead in the eyes. "You're giving me the ick."

He glares at me for a moment, those dark brown eyes like spotlights, examining every inch of me. "The spinach that's been stuck between your teeth for the last hour and a half has been giving me the ick."

I let out a horrified gasp before I rub my finger over my teeth frantically. "Where? Did I get it?"

I bare my teeth at him, and he throws his head back and laughs before shaking his head. "Jesus, you're too easy."

And this is why I can't stand this man.

I smooth my tongue over my teeth just for good measure before I say, "I hate you so much."

He grins the most annoying grin ever presented to another human. "Not as much as I hate you."

And that in a nutshell sums up my relationship with Brody McFadden.

The bane of my existence.

My current nightmare.

And my brother's best friend.

I would like to say it wasn't always like this, the disgust between us, but honestly, I don't know. My brother, who is seven years older than me, met Brody in college. They were in a fraternity together.

Sigma Phi Delta! Let's go! ← said in annoying bro voice.

Yeah, I'm gagging too.

I met Brody when they graduated, and he'd simply been "my brother's best friend." Nothing more.

My brother, Gary, was best known in his bro-hood college days for jumping off the frat house roof and into the pool, breaking his leg in three places. A vastly unintelligent move, but hey, he got high fives from everyone, so clearly a winning decision.

And then there's Brody. He's best known for making out with two hundred and thirty-two women throughout his college career. He kept count. I know this because he's told me…twice. Can we say…douche?

The pair of idiot bro-hards formed a bond over the Chicago Rebels, a baseball team they love so much that to this day they will cry like itty-bitty babies if their cherished team loses in the playoffs.

I've seen it.

It's unflattering and uncomfortable to witness.

Gary's face will turn a dangerous shade of red while Brody will sniffle over and over…and over. Just blow your nose! We all know you're crying.

And of course, because they're not responsible in the slightest, instead of applying for jobs right out of college, they spent the summer visiting every ballpark in America and putting together a detailed list of which one serves the best hot dog. They created a website for the entire endeavor and last I checked, they've only had a little over one thousand visitors, so…time well spent. Really went viral with that idea.

So, why do I hate him?

Great question.

Because the night Gary and his now wife, Patricia—bless her soul for putting up with my brother—got married, I became woman two hundred and thirty-three. Ehhh...well, probably more than that, but you get the idea.

I fell victim to a Brody McFadden make out session.

And it wasn't just some kissing.

Ohhhh no, there was groping.

Huffing.

Grunting.

Smacking lips.

He felt my boob.

I touched his erection.

Cupped it, actually.

Sometimes I can still feel him in the palm of my hand. *There was girth, damn it.*

It's infuriating. But what's more infuriating than the imprint of Brody McFadden's large wiener on my hand is the fact that he gave me the best and most passionate kiss I'd ever experienced in my twenty-three years of life.

All the practice he had in college turned him into the Master of Mouths.

The Conqueror of Caresses.

The Sultan of Salacious Tongues!

I felt that kiss all the way to my champagne-painted toes that night.

He owned me with his mouth, dragging me into a vortex of his carnal hotbed.

I was useless.

Played like a fiddle by his large hands and his masterful lip-locking.

Pressed up against a wall, living out every romantic heart's fantasy as the most attractive, tuxedo-clad man in the room devoured me with one simple slip of his lips over mine. It was a dream.

A fantasy turned reality.

And right as he cupped my breast over the burgundy chiffon of my dress, he lightly pinched my nipple, releasing the most feral sound I've ever produced.

The moan sounded like angels above to me, but to him...but to him...it apparently acted like a wet blanket, suffocating his monstrous erection and turning it into a shriveled-up bean pod.

He pulled away so fast that a string of saliva dangled between us before hitting me in the chin.

And then I'll never...ever...forget this part. It was utterly humiliating.

Degrading.

Flat-out freaking rude.

Looking me square in the eyes, my hazel to his deep brown, he wiped the back of his hand over his mouth, *uh yeah*...wiped it off in front of me—as if disposing of the layer of lust we created to avoid catching infection. *What did he expect? Cholera?*

Then without a word, just a snarl on his lips, he turned away and bolted, leaving me aroused, confused, and sexually annoyed...at my brother's wedding.

Yup, let's hear it. Go ahead, let in the boos.

Send your curses in his direction.

Any hate mail can be addressed to Brody McFadden, 233 Locked-Lipped Loser Lane.

You're allowed to hate him. I actually hope that you do. I plead that you do.

So, after hearing all of that, you must be wondering, why am I letting this Henry Cavill look-alike—chin dimple and all—breathe heavily on my neck after he teased me with his tongue and then left me unsatisfied?

Well, sometimes desperate times call for desperate measures.

Sometimes we're dealt cards in our life that are harder to shuffle through than expected.

And sometimes you're stuck on a small Polynesian island with no other option than to pretend the person you hate most in the entire world is actually your boyfriend...

ABOUT THE AUTHOR

New York Times, #1 Amazon, and *USA Today* bestselling author, wife, adoptive mother, and peanut butter lover. Author of romantic comedies and contemporary romance, Meghan Quinn brings readers the perfect combination of heart, humor, and heat in every book.

Website: authormeghanquinn.com
Facebook: meghanquinnauthor
Instagram: @meghanquinnbooks